# Table of Contents
## (Continued)



*Hope is the foundation of progress. Hope has led to every innovation, every advancement, and every idea that humankind has ever created. Hope for survival. Hope for change. Hope for a better future.*

Commander Leonard Braylon

Second Edition
ISBN 978-1-7349585-7-7

Editing by Geetha Krishnan
Cover Art by Gabriel De Leon
Interior Illustration by Fictive Designs
Icon Illustration by Gabriel De Leon
Map Illustration by Joshua Morley-Smith

# Table of Contents



---

*As knowledge and technology sufficiently advances, science fiction will always become science reality.*

Sovereign Joaquin Bastion

---

# PROLOGUE

Humanity stood on the precipice of undying legacy, ready to leap. Their history's greatest undertaking was set to begin. Humankind would finally expand its reach across the galaxy, conquering the great unknown. Centuries old dreams would finally come to fruition. Nothing could ruin this day.

Across the solar system, all was still. The Sun burnt brighter than it had since before the Earth formed. Light flashed and dimmed, rippling across its surface. Dozens of dark spots littered the outside of the star. The lifeblood of human civilization grew unusually active.

Five freshly minted UPC colony ships pulled out of dock around the Ivanako Lunar Space Station. They parked in orbit above the Moon as their images were televised across the system. Humankind collectively held their breath as they waited for their historic departure. Launch was only minutes away.

Orange gave way to yellow. Light flashes grew in intensity. Blue flares intermixed with the orange and yellow corona of the Sun. Orbiting solar panels cracked and shattered. Captured energy was released into space as the sun reclaimed what was hers.

Within the confines of Earth's pull, the Moon continued its orbit, a natural shield to those living in its own orbit. People scurried about, rushing to secure a viewing spot as humanity's next great step was taken. The broadcast began with the Sovereign's signet appearing on all monitors and displays across the sector.

A blaze of blinding white light expanded from the core of the system. Satellites vaporized in a blink. The solar system froze in an unending moment. One by one planets and moons were extinguished in a fury of all-consuming whiteness. Mercury. Venus. Soon, Earth.

Ship emergency lights strobed red. Sirens blared out, desperately warning doomed passengers. The ILSS and Moon were soon to follow from the far side of Earth.  Alarms echoed verbal warnings: CRITICAL DAMAGE IMMINENT.  CLOSE PROXIMITY SUPERNOVA DETECTED.  No one moved.  No one understood.  This should not be possible.

Elemental particles and stardust erupted from the dying star in a wave, radiating out just behind the light.  Colors with greater variety than any rainbow filled the system, expanding ever outward.  The lightshow vaporized oceans.  Melted rock.  Unforged metal.  The wall of matter smashed through the rest, shattering worlds.

Among the trillion watching, one man did not panic.  One man acted through the Sun's terrifying grip on all its dependents.  One man spoke to those who could still listen.  Those that could still act.  His words echoed among the increasing chatter in the radio waves.  They sounded across five Command Decks.

"Ripple drives, now!  Everyone must evacuate, immediately!  It's too late to save anyone else!  Don't be a hero!  Greshinski out!"

In those few minutes, the legacy humankind, millions of years in the making, was wiped away.  The sun betrayed those who held her most dear.  Her death leaving a wave of annihilation, ripping through the system like a nuclear blast shredding a straw cabin.  Destruction at the atomic level.  Light, matter, radiation.  All necessary for life.  All brought death.

In the chaos, five ships blinked out of danger.  Five ships, among millions, escaped.  Alone in the space beyond, quietly drifting.  Five ships, desperate to save the remnants of humanity.  Earth's last ships.

Only an hour before the five ships escaped the supernova, Joaquin Bastion, stood admiring the engineering marvels before him.  The Sovereign looked out of his office viewscreen over the five Salvation-Class starships docked outside the enormous space station.  UPC stood proudly emblazoned along their hulls.  United People's Commonwealth.  The body for which he was the head.

Bastion heard giggling behind him.  He turned to see his four-year-old grandson behind him, crawling on his cabinet.

"Excuse me, young sir.  What are you doing?"

The boy squealed and dropped to the ground, dropping something reflective and bolting out his office door.  Bastion smiled at the kid's antics.

"You better be heading to the conference room, Jason!" he called after his grandson.

He checked his watch. Only an hour until his speech. It was time to get going. He wanted to be the first person in the conference room. He would mentally review his speech on the way down. His state of the union speech was as ready as it would ever be. His final one. And it would be one for the history books.

He would enter his final year with this undertaking. It would be his legacy. Then he could finally spend time in retirement, exploring with his son. He would bring his grandson as well. Though Jason was not his by blood, the boy had been the light of his life.

He looked around his office one last time. Medals and plaques lined his walls. To some, it may have been a little ostentatious, but each commendation was a memento. A memory of where he had come from. A reminder of where humanity had come from. His eyes settled on the Silver Star lying on the ground. His grandson had dropped it. He picked it up to hang back on the wall.

Screams echoed in his head as his fingers wrapped around the reminder. He slammed his eyes shut and covered his ears with his hands. Those nightmarish screams. His friends still called to him for help. Even awake, they bothered him. It was worse at night, like a phantom plaguing him. He wife could no longer even stand to sleep in the same room with him anymore.

He was still haunted by the memories of the final war. The colonial rebellions had been waged while Sovereign Bastion was still a young man, decades ago. The brutality of it was unmatched by anything previous in human history. Many civilians had been caught in the crosshairs of that war. Tens of millions had died.

He could still remember the fear he had felt as he charged across the rocky surface of Io in a space suit. He had prayed that he not only managed to keep from getting shot, but that the environment would not tear a hole in his suit. They had charged headfirst into overwhelming numbers. His heart jumped into his throat even now, so far removed from these events.

His friends had died all around him. He fired his blaster, watching the white streaks of light strike enemy combatants. Air support had saved him, but he still wondered if his friends had been the lucky ones.

They tell you that you cannot hear somebody scream in space, but that was a lie. They had been on the exposed surface of the moon between domed colonies, sure, but their comms had been open mic'd so that they could communicate faster. He had heard every scream from every friend, even the ones too far away for him to see.

He sometimes lost himself in his waking nightmares from that event. He straightened himself, heart still in his throat. His spine shivered as he drew himself back. He brushed off his suit jacket as he regained his composure.

No side had truly won that war, but they had brokered a peace that had resulted in the creation of the United People's Commonwealth. As part of the new government, he could never allow humanity to devolve into war among itself again. Once peace had been found, it was time humans turned their eyes outward.

He shook his head, clearing his mind of the tough memories. He placed the medal back on its hook and reminded himself to always look forward. Working together to explore the galaxy would bring humanity together, he had reasoned. His plans would prevent further wars. Further loss. He would honor his fallen friends. Unity would erase his nightmares.

He took a deep breath, finally steadying his heart. He stepped out of his office and moved down the brightly lit hall. He alone had the plan to save humanity. He alone, had the drive and dedication to push these people to be their best selves. As he walked, he went over his speech in his head.

*As knowledge and technology sufficiently advances, science fiction will always become science reality.* That would be his opening line. It was his own take on another famous quote from nearly a millennium before by Arthur C Clarke. That man had been ahead of his time. He wondered what that legend would think if he were around to see how things were these days. To see his thoughts and laws come to life.

Bastion continued his way down the hall, nearing the museum. The space station had a lot of amenities on it, but he had insisted on this one. He had requested it placed near his office and spent most of his free time here, thinking about the past and how to move into the future. It was his sanctum. His Fortress of Solitude. He spent nearly all his free time here and brought Jason as often as he could.

As he neared it, he thought back on all the events throughout the years that culminated with today. A lot had changed in his lifetime. He had grown up experiencing man's ever-expanding reach across the stars. He had witnessed incredible technologies rise and fall as everything new was quickly rendered obsolete by an even newer thing.

*As knowledge and technology sufficiently advances, science fiction will always become science reality.* Bastion knew his opening line to be a fact of life, though, not just a fancy theory. He had seen it with his very own eyes. Technology had advanced by leaps and bounds in the last millennium. What was commonplace now would most certainly have appeared as magic then. Magic did not exist though; everything that had once been considered magic in the past was now understood through science.

He reached the first museum display. It was a miniature model of the Wright Brothers' first aircraft. It had carved the way for humanity's journey to the stars. *Apollo 11* was his favorite display, proudly erected a few pedestals away. Many had said it ended the space race, but in reality, it had only kicked it off.

Humans had advanced from barely taking flight on Earth all the way to light speed travel around nearby star systems. Each display showed the next step in flight's evolution over the past thousand years. It even included the tragedies that shaped safety and procedures: The *Challenger*, the *Columbia*, and the *Enterprise*.

The private space exploration really changed things. He paused next to the *Falcon 9* and *Crew Dragon*. He still admired the ingenuity that humanity displayed sending people into space on giant, explosive missiles. Every time he left his office, it reminded him of what he was working toward. Of where humankind had come from. The last display was the *Conquistador.* It had been decades since its discoveries.

A new display was set up just past it, empty. The first addition to the history books since he had become Sovereign. The Salvation-Class colony ship would be unveiled after his speech today. Jason would get to yank off the sheet to reveal his brainchild.

The interior of the museum held many other wonders and displays of what was. No longer were people driving cars on the ground, they were flying them among the hovering cities of Earth. They had colonized nearly every planet and moon in their star system. They had even spread as far as their neighboring star systems for research and resource gathering. The museum even had live plants, the only place on the station with such a rarity.

Many of the advancements inside the museum had been driven by war, but many of the greatest achievements had come more recently. Peace had finally been established. Old governments had been disbanded along with their militaries. He continued past the museum down the stairs to the lower level. His mind was no longer on his speech as he walked. It had wandered off into his past.

Bastion had taken the opportunity to transition into the civilian side of the new government. He wanted a better life for his sons. He had joined the newly formed security council as other military personnel were moved into new positions as peacekeepers. The peacekeepers were used as law enforcement and security across all human territories and their missions into space. Bastion hoped there would never be war again among their own kind. No one should ever have to endure that type of loss.

The peacekeepers still had a militaristic professionalism about them; Bastion had insisted on this while wearing his freshly pressed suit. Being prior military had engrained a deep desire to travel within him and the peacekeepers could ensure the safety of all explorers. His new career had put him in the perfect position to make that happen. Without war keeping him close to home, he could finally pursue his dreams, but it took work. Bastion focused far more on grander ideals than his co-Councilors. He was a visionary for his people.

Despite harnessing light speed technology, humans had not managed to travel very far across the galaxy. Bastion had been exceedingly disappointed by this. The Milky Way itself, was much larger than anyone had grasped. Space exploration had stalled out decades ago; the gears of war had continued to turn, preventing humanity's reach from extending as far as they had dreamed. In his new role, Bastion diverted resources into researching advanced technologies. It was a shot in the dark.

Researchers had looked to reach higher speeds for starships, shortening the time to travel to other star systems. Naturally, it would not be that simple. Traveling at faster than light speed created a time dilation on the ship, resulting in time moving slower for the passengers than it moved out in normal space. They had jokingly blamed Albert Einstein for this dilemma, due to his theory of relativity.

It would still take months to reach the nearest star systems. That would require sleep chambers, so the crews did not use too many resources during travel. Cryogenic sleep would allow the crew to skip the experience of the long trip. Bastion shuddered at the thought of being trapped in a tube for years on end. This would never be an efficient way to travel across the galaxy. He would never allow Jason to suffer this.

He reached the conference room where he would give his momentous speech. It was still empty but would begin filling soon. Jason must be playing around somewhere, no doubt shadowed by peacekeepers. Only thirty minutes left until his broadcast began. He walked to the viewscreen behind the podium, taking another look out at the five ships, his mind continuing its thought pattern.

Bastion had led the security council toward funneling increased resources into other technologies. He had sold it as a way to increase their security and stability across the colonies; pirates were becoming a problem. They could improve trade and resource management as well as deploy peacekeepers faster if needed. Winning this vote had paid off.

The Temporaneous Ripple Effluence Xenoastria Drive was engineered. In simplest terms, it was supposed to mean temporary ripple emission for foreign travel to the stars, taken from Ancient Greek roots. There was speculation that the scientists who created the drive established the acronym prior to officially naming it. Regardless, the TREX Drive opened the door for humankind to spread further across the stars.

The drive created a bubble around the starship that rippled space to bring the destination closer. The physics behind it were named the Interstellar Ripple Effect. It was as if space were a stretched accordion and when the TREX Drive created the ripple, it collapsed the accordion, bringing points closer together; not to be confused with bending a stick to bring two points together. Then the ship simply traveled across the ripples at light speed. The ripple drive effectively shortened the distance required to travel by an incredible factor.

Unfortunately, this required colossal amounts of energy. Current fuel technology could not sustain the requirements for long. The TREX Drive allowed ships to reach their destinations far faster than previous technologies ever could, but they were unable to sustain it long enough to reach further destinations, due to inadequate fuel storage. Bastion's hopes for seeing the galaxy had gone down the drain.

The hope for first contact with intelligent alien life had gone with it, too. Humans had long desired to meet other intelligent life and he had been no stranger to this. Despite the passage of time and advancements of technology, sentient life had still not been found elsewhere.

Bastion hoped that advanced alien life existed, but the reach of humans had not made it far enough to discover it. It was widely believed among humans that intelligent life existed elsewhere and that it had even visited Earth. With an infinite number of galaxies across the never-ending expanse of space, it was a mathematical certainty to exist, but where it could be, was anybody's guess.

Though, to Bastion's disgust, the alternative theory was that humans were the first advanced species to exist, and others would rise as time allowed. This theory was less probable, but the only one with empirical data to support it. They had discovered other life, but it was much earlier in its development, barely more than bacteria.

The only comfort Bastion found in this theory, was that there were no hostile aliens out there, though he had a nagging feeling that was not accurate. Still, the likelihood of encountering anything was miniscule. Still, research was conducted to find other alien life through signaling, telescopes, and deep space exploration missions; many of those were established in nearby star systems with unobstructed views.

It had been on one such research mission, at the very edge of human territory, that a different, incredible discovery had been made. The *Conquistador* had been exploring the edge of a star system just one hundred light-years away from Earth, when it had come across an intriguing, unidentifiable substance. Once it had gotten near enough, the ship had sent a small science team to examine the substance and determine if it was safe enough to bring back for study. Upon contact, the substance had detonated, destroying the science party and nearly wiping out the *Conquistador*. Anti-matter had just been discovered in nature.

Bastion had used this discovery to leverage his position into one on the UPC Senate. It was his push for expanded research and exploration that had led to this newest development. It led to quite a hike in his popularity. A politician who cared about advancing humanity rather than profiting from it. He then pushed more resources into developing the ships of the future.

Extensive research had to be conducted on the new material to ensure it could be transported and used safely. Despite its liquid-like appearance, they could not simply store it in a fuel tank, then pour it through a fuel line into a reactor. Any contact with normal matter resulted in a cataclysmic explosion. Anti-matter had to be suspended by electromagnetic fields inside small vacuum-sealed cells.

Bastion encouraged his loyal researchers to reuse previously abandoned data from the twenty-first century regarding antimatter. The European Organization for Nuclear Research (CERN) had done experiments and created minuscule amounts of antimatter. The production had been too expensive to further the research at the time, so it had been discontinued. However, their data had survived and assisted in this new wave of discovery.

He was so lost in thoughts of his past that he had not noticed people beginning to trickle into the conference room. He could hear someone's alarm going off in a nearby room. He shook his head and focused on himself, keeping himself psyched up for his speech, now just minutes away.

This newest research was where Sovereign Bastion's legacy had come into play. Once he had been elected as Sovereign, he commissioned the creation of the five Salvation-Class starships before him now. He had come out strong on exploration, right at the beginning of his term.

The idea for using massive starships with room for expanded fuel storage to travel further had been brought to him by his panel of scientists. The decision to make them colony ships had come from his desire to leave his mark in the history books, as most politicians attempted. All he had wanted in life was to travel amongst the stars. This project would give him and Jason that opportunity, once his term was over.

That was only a little over a year away. He would join the second wave of colony ships venturing out into the unknown. His ship's path would bring him close enough to see his son again. He had a suite reserved at the top of the central spire of the 'Haven.' Just one of a million civilians living in the ship's central city in the midst of an expansive high-rise skyline.

He could envision himself sitting out on the balcony of his room staring out at the stars as the whisked by beyond the transparent steel bubble surrounding the city. Jason would get to laugh and play under the wobbling streaks of light. Retirement would serve him well. He had earned that. He could hardly wait for his turn and envied those on the first wave.

Bastion had recommissioned a few orbital stations that had not been used previously to build the Havens and help with budget issues. Those darn budgets had prevented him from incorporating every technology that he had deemed critical. He had been forced to pick and choose, leaving him to wonder if he had made any mistakes. He wished he could have given these adventurers every piece of advanced technology available. They deserved it.

He was no fool though. Despite the lack of evidence, he could not shake the feeling that there would be danger out in the Milky Way. He had ensured the safety of each mission with a contingency of peacekeepers and heavy firepower. Fifteen thousand peacekeepers would have battle cruisers, fighters, lasers, plasma torpedoes, rail guns, and even the newest prototypes: IGAMMs.

Should the humans encounter hostile alien life, they would not fall without a fight. They had to be ready for this probability as they delved deeper and deeper into the unknown. That preparation had been costly though.

These colony ships had a purpose beyond just their fancy designs though. With these marvels, they could colonize distant solar systems and spread the human species throughout the galaxy. Their size increased their capabilities exponentially, as well as the cost.

Compared to early colony ships, their size allowed them to efficiently store anti-matter and the necessary supplies for extended missions. They had terraforming equipment allowing them to establish new homes on nearly any planet in just one year. They had cellular storage and frozen embryos of Earth's native plants and animals to create new life for their colonies while still managing to carry some live animals like pets and livestock.

Humans would finally be the dominant species throughout the galaxy as they had always dreamed. These missions also had a secondary purpose; they greatly increased their chances of discovering sentient life. From these new homes, they could research any other life found and explore the outlying areas. These were to be the first five of many human colonies located outside the local sector of the galaxy.

Bastion stood there, marveling at the manifestations of his dreams. He laughed internally for a moment as he examined them. Everything had been so exciting as it had happened. He remembered the rush he had felt as each new discovery was made. Yet he suspected these things would not be remembered adequately. They would be relegated to the history books, only experienced by those readers who were bored out of their minds combing through the monotony. He knew it would all be worth it to make it through his story.

He had ensured his tale and vision would leave a lasting memory among humanity. Nostalgia mixed with cutting edge technology would do that. Each massive ship was shaped and designed to represent old twenty-first century naval aircraft carriers. He had a flair for history and wanted to do their ancestors justice.

His son would be on board his ship by now and settled into his own suite with his family. He had been given the finest accommodations. Ones that Bastion had never experienced during space travel.

During his own travels, among military frigates, he had lived with the bare necessities. Once at his destination, his son would get to ride from the comfort of his room as his building was dropped from orbit. These buildings had a special function. Each was a Haven-Class dropship, designed to be jettisoned at their destination to become the first structures of their new colony. Another of his brain children. They would serve as the basis for humanity's new homes. *I really have thought of everything.*

He took one last looks at the ships. Bastion struggled to see the rear end of the ship five kilometers away. While he had wanted them to be representative of the old water-based ships, they were so enormous their length was roughly the equivalent of lining up fifteen of their aircraft carrier forefathers.

The year was now 2816 CE, and the Sovereign was entering his final year as the leader of humankind. He looked out at the vessels in front of him, knowing that he would be joining them in the coming years. A self-assured smile spilled across his face. This was all the result of his hard work. *No one would ever forget my name.*

He turned away from the viewscreen and examined his surroundings. The crowd had gathered in the conference room with media outlets lining the walls, all trying to record his momentous speech. The plan was for him to give his speech, then the five ships would depart the space station on a symbolic maiden voyage around Jupiter, before returning. After the ceremony was over, they would top off their fuel supplies and load the last bits of crew and supplies.

He glanced back outside and watched as the ships pulled out of their docks before turning to face the people in the conference room. His eyes caught a glimpse of his grandson darting through the crowds. A peacekeeper desperately tried to keep up with him.

Sovereign Bastion took a deep breath to steady his heart before he spoke. His heart always raced before a speech, but he was ready. Everything was ready. Everything was perfect. Except that alarm was still sounding nearby.

"As knowledge and technology sufficiently advances, science fiction will *always* become science reality—"

The lights flashed red. Sirens wailed in warning. Bastion scanned the people in front of him, desperately searching for answers. His heart quickened as he witnessed the crowd beginning to panic and flee the room. *What is happening to my ships?* He turned around, looking for the cause of the alarm. He watched as the ships jumped away prematurely, gone in a heartbeat.

Jason appeared at his side, clutching his leg. "Papa, I'm scared. Where's Daddy?"

"Don't worry, Jason. He's okay. We'll all be okay," he lied as he picked up his grandson for the last time and tucked his head against his chest, shielding him from the blinding light growing outside.

It was a supernova. The alarms spouted the information. He watched, shielding his eyes, as the sun's light approached. Its corona would follow quickly after.  Even if he survived the blinding hot wall of light, he would never survive the following shockwave.

The sensors had not detected the danger quickly enough to give anyone else time to escape. *This cannot be happening.* He refused to accept this was how his term would end.  His legacy was over.  He closed his eyes, hugging his grandchild, trying to clear his racing thoughts.  He would never get to see his son again.  He could feel a pain cutting through his heart like a knife to the chest.  One trillion humans were about to die.  At least his son had survived…

*Dedicated to those who wish to rebuild their lives
from the ashes of their past.*

UNDAALAN
BLACK PEAKS
ENIKEA
LENAKAI FOREST
REVOLUTION CLIFFS
CHRONDI DESERT
ELDRA
ENITALI
ERMYTA
LANKIN
ENNIKA
ELKASK
ENTALE RIVER
ABERASH
MANTERIAN PLAINS
UNDAARI VILLAGE
YAXKIN STRONGHOLD
NOXXON STRONGHOLD
UNDAALERIA

# BOOKS BY RYAN RODRIGUEZ

**Earth's Last Ships**
The Jericho
The Phoenix
The Minotaur

# Earth's Last Ships:

## The Jericho Legendary Edition

### By: Ryan Rodriguez

Book One

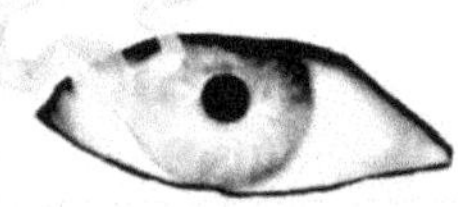
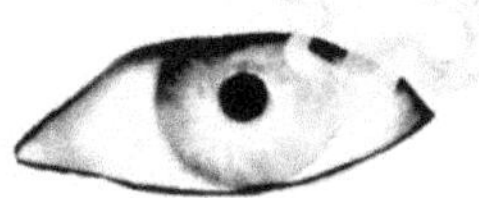

**Rising Phoenix Books**

# Chapter 1

## Escape

*What did you do the day the Sun betrayed you? Panic? Die?* Everything around him was true and utter chaos. Commander Braylon had never before felt true fear. But in this instance, he experienced a debilitating terror. He watched the sun die in a supernova and its corona rapidly expand toward his new ship. He could not bring himself to move. He had no answers.

He heard yelling, but not from his crew. Braylon realized it was an emergency broadcast from another Commander. The transmission answered his previous question. The day the Sun betrayed you, all you could do was survive.

"Ripple drives, now! Everyone must evacuate, immediately! It's too late to save anyone else! Don't be a hero! Greshinski out!"

The Commander repeated the orders to his crew as he quickly found his seat. The coordinates had been pre-programmed into the ship's navigational computers, so no time was wasted. The words were barely out of his mouth before he felt the acceleration of the *Jericho* as it jumped out of the solar system, just in the nick of time. The alarms stopped wailing, but his heart continued to race. They would be safe from the supernova.

He could not say the same for a trillion other people. For every crew member, peacekeeper, scientist, and passenger on this ship, one million other people had just died. His stomach churned as the realization struck him in the face like a baseball bat. Handling death had never been his strong suit. He was a thinker and a strategist, not a fighter.

The Commander barked orders to his pilot and navigator, "Lieutenant Jaspar, pull us out of ripple! Captain Neckrel, figure out exactly where we are. We need to send a ship back to look for survivors."

Lieutenant Jaspar shut down the TREX Drive and fired the reverse thrusters bringing the ship out of the ripple.

"General Titus," Braylon called, eyes scanning for the commander of the *Jericho's* peacekeeper force.

General Titus was never far from the action, already standing on the Command Deck.

Braylon spoke, his Academy formalities showing, "General, I need you to organize a search party to send back to our solar system. Give them the *Ark.* Keep them on standby until the chaos in our system has calmed. They will need to determine the extent of the damage and search for survivors. Be sure they drop out of ripple early to avoid debris. We cannot be sure what things will be like there."

"Yes, sir," the First Officer grunted with a salute.

General Titus turned and departed without another word. Braylon knew the seasoned veteran could be trusted to execute his orders effectively, no matter the situation. The Commander was thankful he could safely leave this in the General's capable hands.

Once Titus was gone, Braylon decided to broadcast a warning signal and rendezvous coordinates out into space. The five colony ships could not be the only survivors. There had been several small colonies established, as well as people on exploratory ships. People who would be baffled as to the sudden loss of contact with Earth.

These survivors may even try to jump back to investigate, leading to their demise on some piece of asteroid debris from what was once Earth. The *Jericho* would not be too far away, still local in comparison to the galaxy. They had only traveled a fraction of the distance to their destination. He stood and walked to the navigation station, directing Neckrel and Jaspar to bring them to the nearest viable planet while he recorded his message; that would be their established rendezvous point.

"To all human vessels: This is Commander Braylon of the *Jericho.* There has been a catastrophe beyond humanity's ability to prevent, divert, or even survive from. Our Sun has gone supernova and vaporized our solar system. Earth is gone. Nearly one trillion people have perished.

"Five colony ships were lucky enough to escape. These five ships carry a million survivors each en route to five separate destinations with the mission to colonize the furthest reaches of the galaxy. We will attempt to establish new homes for humanity.

"To all other survivors, I have set up a rendezvous here at the origin of this broadcast. We must all do our part to ensure the future of humankind. Together, we can assist survivors and guarantee our colonization mission is successful.  We will set up medical facilities and shelters on this planet.  Commander Braylon out."

The Commander had a communications buoy launched into orbit around the planet.  It would carry this message forever, transmitting for all to hear.  The Chief Engineering Officer, Colonel McNeil, came on deck.  She kept her head down and eyes low as she slowly approached him.

"Commander Braylon, sir, I know there's a lot going on right now, but we have another problem," she said softly.

"What is it, Colonel?" The Commander asked, standing tall.

"Sir, with Earth gone, there will be no resupply.  Ever.  Which means no anti-matter, weaponry, rations, or anything. We only have enough to last us a couple years at best.  After that, we're done for.  We *need* to find new resources or we're dead in the water."

"Once we have a new home, we can cultivate new crops. We do not *need* any of that other stuff," he replied.

"Our primary mission may be to terraform this new planet, but continued exploration and expansion is part of that.  And we're going to need that.  Without a home to fall back to, it's up to us to continue life as we know it.  We don't know what we might encounter and will have no way to defend ourselves.  We'll need these things if we hope to survive for any extended period of time.  If we hope to save humanity.  This is so much more than just a colonization mission anymore."  The Colonel's voice grew firmer as she spoke.

*Why hadn't I thought of that?*

His shoulders slouched as he replied, "Thank you for the information, Colonel.  We shall address your concerns once we make it to ZX-746.  Once we reach our destination, you will oversee finding and harnessing new resources to supply us."

Colonel McNeil held her head up high. "Yes, sir.  Thank you, sir," she said with a new energy. "But food for thought, we need to make sure ZX-746 isn't our only option.  We can't put all our eggs in that single basket."

She turned away from him and sped off.  He looked back to the crew on the Command Deck.  There was so much going on. His crew bustled about, following his orders.  Braylon could barely think anymore and struggled to keep standing tall.  All he wanted to do was curl up in a ball on the floor and cry.  No one was trained for this kind of thing.  But *he* was in command. *He* had three Commander stars on his collar.  It was up to him to save these million souls.

*I must do my best.*  He had been given command for a reason. *If I weren't capable of saving these few remaining people, then I wouldn't have advanced this far in my career.* He set his resolve, straightened his back, quickly brushed the wrinkles out of his navy-blue uniform, and blocked out any negative thoughts. They would only hinder him now.

He was going to set up this rendezvous for survivors. He was going to set up a medical facility on the planet below. He was going to save the people on this ship. He was going to continue their mission as if Earth were still there.

He walked back over to the command console, reinserted his ID crystal, and pressed the intercom button for the medical bay.

"Colonel Hanley, this is Commander Braylon."

"Go ahead, Commander."

"I need you to organize a small medical detail to go to the planet below and set up a medical facility. Unfortunately, you're too important to stay on the planet, so keep yourself on the ship and continue the mission. I have a feeling our solar system will be devoid of survivors, but others may come from elsewhere, searching for help. Make sure the detail has everything they need to survive independently, understood?"

"Yes, sir," she replied over the intercom.

"Thank you."

Braylon was on the verge of calling for General Titus when the man returned to the bridge.

"Commander," the General started in a low, gravelly tone.

"General! Just the man I was looking for. How is your task proceeding?"

"I have a detail organized under Major Nazario. According to our readings, the conditions back in our solar system are far too unstable for them to return. I left orders for them to continuously monitor the situation, and once it appears safe enough to travel, they'll depart. Is there anything else?"

"Just one more thing. I need a one hundred peacekeeper detail to remain with the medical facility below and help however required. They should be young peacekeepers, as they may be doing grunt work the entire time. Place a lower ranking officer in charge of the detail. Someone who can make decisions. Understood?"

"Understood. I'll report back once it's complete," Titus said, his thick white mustache wiggling as he spoke.

"Thank you," the Commander said with a nod.

Braylon walked over to the Navigator, "Captain Neckrel. Any

updates on the planet below?”

"Actually, sir, yes I do.  Luckily for us, if anything can be considered lucky, the planet below had been previously colonized.  There was a mining colony that failed due to financial reasons, not efficiency.  There's still some equipment and supplies that might be usable.  Apparently, it had been cheaper to leave the equipment and infrastructure rather than transport it elsewhere."

"Now that is a positive turn of events.  Good work, Captain."

The extra supplies would help the medical facility get set up faster and be more self-sufficient.  While the planet itself was not habitable, the colony was built under several large domes that were still structurally sound.  There had been a large operation at this site, so there was room for plenty of people.

The Commander turned back to stare aimlessly out of the viewport while he planned their next move.  He tried to look back toward their old home, looking for the explosion rocking their solar system.  He remembered that this system was sixteen light years away.  *The medical facility will have a heck of a light show in sixteen years.*

Braylon felt like he could finally take a breath.  His heart had been racing.  He realized that with everything happening, he had been too focused on Earth.  This ship required his focus now and he had been neglecting his greatest responsibilities as a leader.  He rushed back to the command chair.

He needed to gain accountability of those on board.  He called for his leadership to meet him on the Command Deck.  There were several department chiefs and peacekeepers who oversaw the civilians' safety.

"We need to know exactly how many people survived the events of today.  Get head counts of everyone on board.  Make sure no one got hurt during our abrupt jump," he ordered, not bothering to get up from his chair.

He sat erect in his seat, reviewing data of the cataclysm, and scanning through all the standards and procedures saved on his computer. He needed to find answers.  His mind still scrambled about.

Half an hour later, the report came in.  Lieutenant Daniels, his Second Officer, had gathered the information and compiled it into a single report.  Eight-hundred-sixty thousand civilians were on board out of the nine-hundred-eighty-five thousand assigned.  He slumped back in his chair.

The weight on his chest grew heavier.  He had trouble accepting this information.  A lot more civilians had stayed behind to hear the Sovereign's speech and witness the maiden voyage than he had realized. Thankfully, all fifteen thousand peacekeepers were on board.  General Titus had insisted they would all be present at the start.

He scrolled through the files on his console, desperately trying to distract himself. Answers continued to evade him. Finally, he stood and departed the Command Deck. He needed to lie down for a few. There was nothing left to do except wait for all the tasks to be completed.

Over the course of the next month, a lot changed. The survivors had managed to get the old mining colony up and running again and had even set up facilities inside. They had only taken volunteers to operate the medical facility, as they might be stranded there indefinitely. Unfortunately, no new survivors had arrived seeking refuge.

Commander Braylon's broadcast had yielded no response. He was confused as to why no one would reach out. He assumed that, like him, they had been devastated by the loss and were still struggling to find a clear path. *It's possible no one has received my message yet.* He tried to revert to his training and follow standard procedure, but this was no standard event.

His first night after they had reached this planet had been a rough one for him. He had broken down crying with his family and struggled to even communicate. He had felt so lost and could not understand what had happened. He had found little comfort from his loved ones that night.

When he had returned to work, he began tasking some of the scientists to figure out what had happened. He wanted answers, as did all the survivors on the *Jericho.* They had limited data from the ship leading up to the event, and it all led to one conclusion: they had no idea what could have triggered a healthy star of that small size to explode in such a way.

No other star like it had ever been recorded dying in supernova. The smallest stars observed to supernova were at least eight times the mass of the sun. Nothing smaller had enough power to explode so fiercely. That theoretical limit had been smashed at the expense of a trillion lives.

He often spent time checking on the people throughout the Haven using the camera system. He had been joyful to see the people standing strong and supporting each other at first. He even tried to support them with announcements and keeping them informed of progress.

The people only stayed united in solemn support for a few weeks, though. They began to panic as their resolve eroded. Word had gotten out about their limited resources. He tried to increase security across the city, but that just made things worse. Rationing only exacerbated the problem. Vandalism and looting spread through the city like wildfire as the people feared certain death.

He was losing what little control he had of the situation. He isolated from his family in shame, while trying to solve every problem that kept arising on his own. He learned quickly that one person could not solve everything. He needed help.

He was thankful he could turn to General Titus to think outside the box. The General was an invaluable help in their unique situation. Without Titus, he was sure he would have already failed the mission.

He had heard the stories of what Titus had achieved during the Colonial Rebellions. The man had single-handedly led the Europa Federation's forces in a counterattack against the colonial rebels on Io. That mission had actually saved Sovereign Bastion's life.

Titus had been against far superior numbers and fought with such savagery that he effectively ended the Colonial Rebellions. It was no wonder he'd advanced so high. Braylon did not know how he had gotten this position over Titus but was even luckier to gain such a distinguished war hero under his command.

He could not imagine having to go through that. The veteran was unmatched by anyone in the UPC. He was a man of conviction who would do anything to accomplish his goals.

Unfortunately, Titus had recently voiced his opinion that they needed to continue their mission, not worry about the few survivors that might be searching for help. Braylon felt that was inhumane, but Titus was the one person he did not want to butt heads with. Braylon felt the need to save every last human.

With everything going on, Braylon was thankful for the day the reports came in that Nazario could depart. That mission would buy him time before they had to depart and give up on survivors. Titus stood at his side as he sent Nazario on his way.

# Chapter 2
## Reunited

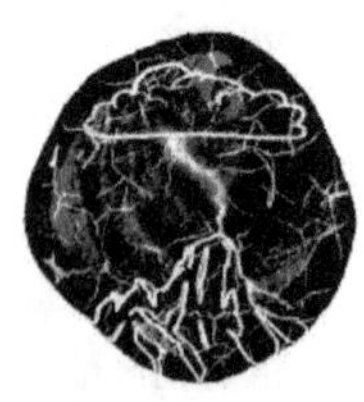

"*J*arreck! Go now! Hide!" his father hissed at him.

He raced to his hiding spot behind their fireplace, knowing better than to question his father. His heart threatened to break out of his chest. He had never seen his parents act that way. *Why were they so scared?*

He cradled himself in a tight ball inside his safe place. The familiar hiding spot comforted him while he listened through the cold, stony masonry. Yelling echoed throughout the cabin. It was his father's heated voice. *What was going on?*

They had been spending a cozy evening together in their family cabin, isolated deep in the Lenakai Forest. His mother had spent the day picking fruits from their garden and had just served them a fresh pie made from them. It was Jarreck's favorite dessert. She was far from a homebody, but she loved to take care of her family.

Jarreck's father, Jace, had been telling him wondrous stories about magic and good triumphing over evil. Jarreck always loved the stories his father told him. Jace had told him the stories were what had forged the world as it was. He would often tell Jarreck about meeting his strong, fierce mother in battle.

Jarreck was blessed to have such parents. He knew how much his parents loved each other and him. Though he was still young in years, he knew he had the best family in the entirety of the Three Kingdoms. *But what had he done to cause their anger this evening?*

He continued replaying the evening in his head, searching for answers. Jace's pointy ears had perked up. Jarreck could tell something had bothered his dad. Jace had looked over to his wife. Her face was stiff, and her ears had perked up as well.  In unison, they had both turned to look at the door.  That was when Jace had told Jarreck to hide.  Jace had moved quickly to the window as Jarreck hid himself.

Someone must have come to their home.  *What else could it be?* Their day had seemed normal, better than normal even.  The yelling outside the safe room quickly turned into metal clanging.  He recognized that sound; he'd been around his parents' sparring enough.  There were people fighting with blades.  Jarreck's body shook as he considered the situation.

He knew he was not supposed to, but he cracked open the door to see what was happening.  He saw a red glow filling the cabin.  He caught a glimpse of his mother swinging her blade, locked in battle with three large, armored, Noxxon brutes at once.

She was holding her own against all odds, until a fourth appeared behind her.  It stabbed her through the back with its sword bursting out of her chest.  Jarreck jumped and gasped.  Crimson blood sprayed the wall as his mother let out a blood curdling scream that drowned out all other noises.  Another heavily armored Noxxon crushed her head with a mace, flinging bone and brain matter across the cottage.

He quickly shut the door again and curled up into a ball as small as he could.  Jarreck rocked back and forth on the ground, his heart racing.  His body shook as tears poured down his cheeks.  Every muscle in his body was tense as he tried to wipe the picture of his dying mother from his memory.  Sweat poured over him while he gasped for air, unable to catch his breath.

As he sat there, ears listening intently for approaching monsters, he began to hear crackling.  It was the same crackling he had heard a hundred times from their hearth; their cabin was on fire.  His hideout was fireproof, since it was hidden so close to the fireplace, but the temperature still inched upward during the blaze.

His breathing quickened as each pull of oxygen was shallower and shallower.  He looked around the hiding spot and felt as though the walls were closing in on him.  The temperature continued to creep up as the fires encircled the room.  His eyes darted back and forth.  His breaths barely took in oxygen anymore.  His head grew light.  Jarreck collapsed on the ground, losing consciousness as he hyperventilated.

When he awoke later, there was nothing but silence.  He felt groggy and confused by his sudden nap.  Memories flooded his mind.  He cracked open the door and looked around.  There was no one else moving inside the cabin.  He emerged from his hideout and inspected the area more thoroughly.

He could see the burnt body of his mother, as well as several other blackened bodies of Noxxon raiders. The smell of burnt flesh terrorized his nasal passages. The cabin was mostly stone, so its bones still stood, scorched from the fire. The furniture and framing were reduced to ash.

He left the remains of the cabin and saw a few unburnt Noxxon bodies lying around in the snow. *When had it snowed?* His eyes settled on his father, lying still in the center of the barbarians. Their obsidian, rocklike skin had been no match for his father's blade.

Jarreck spotted a large slit in his father's throat. His dark red blood pooled in the snow around him, staining it and melting through to the grass below. His parents had taken dozens of the vile creatures with them. Jarreck fell to his knees on the ground, tears streaming out of his blue eyes. He tried to stand tall for them, but the sight of their mangled bodies was too much. He let it all out.

Minutes later, he finally wiped the tears from his eyes. He managed to look up and noticed a hooded man standing in front of him. He never heard the stranger approach. And though he did not know the man, Jarreck did not feel in danger.

The tall, greying man had the same symbol on the clasp of his bright cerulean cape that his father had hanging in his bedroom. That meant he was a friend. During his quick assessment of the man, Jarreck began to feel his surroundings. It was cold out; the coldest he ever remembered. He could see his breath in the air. Snow started falling again.

He ran to his parent's bedroom and found the secret compartment under the bad that Jarreck was not supposed to know about. Inside, he recovered his father's old cape, burnt, but with a clasp that was still pristine and undamaged. It was a relic of his father's past. He took the clasp from the debris, a memento to his family, and tucked it into his pocket to keep to himself.

He did not know what else he could do. He was all alone now. He stepped outside and eyed the old man. Without another option, he joined the man. His gut said he could trust the man. The man had come too late to help his parents, but he could still help Jarreck. The newcomer even allowed Jarreck to wear his cape for warmth.

*Ssshhhthuuuuccckkkk!*
An arrow embedded in the tree right by his head. Jarreck came

back from his childhood memories. He did not flinch though a raised eyebrow slipped his control. No one should have been able to get so close to him without his knowledge. Silently, he disappeared into the darkness before another arrow could be released in his direction. While not truly invisible, it would be nearly impossible for anyone to spot him.

There had been no one else in the woods for quite some distance as he made his way to the clearing that opened to his childhood cabin. This section of forest was uninhabited. On top of that, he only knew of a handful of others in the world who could sneak up on him, no matter how distracted he was. *How long have I been standing here?* The day had grown old, he noted as he saw the sun setting through the tree canopy.

He shook the memory of his worst day from his mind as he scanned the woods around him. Jarreck calmed his mind and allowed his senses to feel for the presence of another in the area. This had been completely unnecessary. His adversary was standing in plain sight, looking his way. A small smile started at the corner of his mouth before he made his way toward the woman.

The lingering memory still taunted him as he walked. Jarreck had not been back here since his parents had died. This place had become an unnecessary distraction to his mission. He shook his head at himself and his mistake as he reached the woman.

"You're getting old, Jarreck. Just two years ago, I never could've gotten within arrow range of you," his assailant jested.

Jarreck nodded as he approached his former apprentice, knowing she was right. His greying hair betrayed him, but he admitted to nothing.

"You only got that close because I knew you were coming. It's been too long since I've seen you, old friend. What brings you out this way?"

She faced him with her eyes on the ground and her arms wrapped around herself.

After a moment's hesitation, she answered, "Just some rumors. I need help and didn't know where else I could turn. I heard you were in the area."

Jarreck cocked an eyebrow and asked, "How'd you learn of my whereabouts? And why do you continue to question your abilities, Kiva? What's going on?"

Kiva responded hesitantly, "Rumor has it that they've infiltrated our Society and gained access to our teachings. Those are the only advantages we have in the war. If they've discovered our secrets, we won't be able to stop them. I don't know who else to trust in the Society. They don't even know I'm looking into this. It's just a rumor, but it has me shaken. I heard it from my most reliable source out on the border of our kingdom."

Jarreck looked at his old apprentice with a frown.

"This is likely nothing. Just fear being spread," he said, but decided against dismissing her fears and added, "but it's worth looking into. I have to complete my current mission first, though. Care to join?"

Kiva replied with a wide smile, "What are we doing?"

Jarreck looked at her for a moment before explaining, "The Council received report of a large Noxxon force moving throughout the Lenakai Forest. We need to find out if there's any validity to this claim and if so, how they got here."

"That's impossible," replied Kiva.

"Exactly, so it concerns me if they're capable enough to get this deep into our territory. Especially with all the protections we have in place. Truthfully, it adds to the validity of your rumors, so let's make this quick."

"How have I not heard about this? I know about *all* our missions!" Kiva said with visible surprise.

"This mission was extremely private. The Council doesn't want anyone knowing about it. Not even you. I'm the only person who was told about it and no records were kept. This mission is completely off the books. The slightest rumor could create panic."

Jarreck's wrinkled forehead furrowed even more.

"It'll be good having my apprentice back in case of heavy lifting. I really am getting too old for this."

He walked off without further conversation, knowing that she would follow closely and not speak another word. Their bond had grown deep during her apprenticeship. She was one Skovi he never had to worry about placing faith in.

He moved in silent contemplation. He had gotten lost in his past. The Noxxon threat had escalated. Now there were rumors that his Society had been infiltrated and betrayed from within. His entire body shuddered as he walked.

Jarreck subconsciously let his hand reach up and feel his father's old clasp under his shirt. He wore it as a necklace these days. No one knew it existed except for him. He never even told Kiva, his most trusted friend. He wished his father were here for this. Jace was the wisest man he had ever known. He would have known how to handle this situation. He had always known things that others did not.

They continued to walk through the peaceful green forest before they heard noises in the distance. His apprentice peeled off to cover his flank. She was well-trained to keep a large space between them while gaining a different perspective. As he approached the source of the sounds, he disappeared into the shadows again. He trusted Kiva to do the same and next to no one would be able to detect them.

He came to another clearing. He felt a pit in his stomach. The rumors were true. This clearing was not natural. It was full of heavily armored Noxxons moving about and operating digging equipment. There was a camp in Undaari territory full of Noxxons. By the looks of things, there were nearly eighty bulky Noxxons operating in the forest. *What in the world had brought them here? What were they after?*

He had gained a lot of experience in battle against the Noxxons since he had been a boy. Their broad shoulders and long, muscular arms gave them a greater reach than Undaari. Their short legs were like tree trunks, strong, but slow moving. They were not easy to kill, but the Undaari were faster and more agile. He had learned how to use these advantages, but that was not enough of an edge over such superior numbers.

Jarreck snuck around the perimeter of the clearing, attempting to gain a clearer view of the dig site. He moved quickly and quietly, avoiding sentries. He reached the far side of the clearing and spotted Kiva shimmering in the distance, mirroring his movement. The Noxxons would not be able to see either of them.

Once he reached his objective, Jarreck saw the prize that the Noxxons coveted. They were using a rope and pulley systems to lift a massive, engraved stone disc out of the ground. Whatever this thing was, it had captured their attention. This information was more valuable than the Council had realized. That meant its discovery was dangerous as well.

Jarreck continued to monitor the events going on, taking note of every detail of the operation for his report to the Council. The sun's last light shined down as the stone disc fully surfaced. As the ropes suspended the disc in the air, it began to rotate and twist.

Engravings came into clear view in the fading sunlight. Jarreck's jaw dropped at the sight. It was made from black stone with glowing cyan fractures spread across its surface. At its center, large and clear for all to see, was the symbol of their Society. *This must be an old artifact of the Society that had been hidden away and forgotten.*

"Oh no," he whispered, barely audible.

He cautiously made his way over to Kiva and stated, "We must hurry back to the Council; this is bad."

# Chapter 3

## Return

$\mathcal{M}$ajor Nazario had his mission, his crew, and his ship. He was ready, but not sure if he was up to it. This might be the toughest mission he had ever been tasked with. He had certainly been through more dangerous missions than this, including several so-called suicide missions with Special Operations, but this was its own monster. He had been at war and fought against vicious enemies. He had made it through the Colonial Rebellions. But nothing had measured up to the difficulty of this one.

Technically, it was one of the simplest missions he had ever been assigned, but it weighed heavier than any of the others. Which was the only reason the Commander of Special Operations was assigned this task. He just had to fly to his destination, look around, pick up anyone he saw, and return to 'base.' *Base, now that's a funny word to use in this context.* There was no longer a base.

It was hard to maintain focus on the present. His mind was constantly trying to wander off. Their base had been destroyed, along with his home, most of his family, and everything he knew. Not exactly what he wanted to deal with right then.

Thankfully, some of his family was on board the *Jericho.* They were distant relatives, though; he had no immediate family. His parents had died years before and he had never married. Still, his cousins had provided some comfort.

Like many others on the *Jericho*, he struggled to comprehend the massive loss and felt utterly alone without many supports on the ship. There had been a week-long period where he had not even left his quarters. He had lacked motivation to even keep his maroon uniform pressed and presentable. He envied some of his peers who had their close families with them.

It was common practice for most officials on the crew to bring their families along as civilians. This helped make the long mission more bearable. It also made it easier to choose who got selected to join and assist the mission, as their families were given priority positions. That left fewer positions requiring selection hearings.

Nazario pulled himself back from his trail of thoughts. He called to Lieutenant Franks, his pilot, to prepare for departure, then radioed the bridge of the *Jericho* to request permission to set out. Upon receiving the green light, he told his pilot to detach from the *Jericho* and set course.

The *Ark* was docked on the grey underbelly of the *Jericho*. He watched out of the viewscreen as they slid out from between two heavy battle cruisers. He wondered how well they would fare in a battle. Like everything else on the *Jericho*, they were prototypes and untested in real situations.

Nazario could see the dock they had just departed from. He smiled at the shape of the perch. The *Ark* was shaped like a horseshoe crab and fit snugly into the dock. This ship was highly maneuverable and armored but lacked weaponry. It had its antennae trailing out the back with its engines hanging below, completing the horseshoe crab look. This was the largest transport ship docked on the *Jericho*.

Nazario watched the stars wobble and speed by on the viewscreen as they traveled at ripple. The augmented reality overlay showed them rapidly approaching their old system. Suddenly, the view was hazed with red, and the ship rattled in ripple.

He braced himself through the turbulence and yelled at Franks, "What is that? What's happening?"

"We're passing through some debris."

"What debris?" Nazario questioned as the viewscreen shifted to blues and greens."

"Ionized gasses from the supernova. Stardust. We're almost there."

The color shifted through the spectrum to blue and green on the viewscreen before it faded back to black just as the *Ark* dropped out of ripple. They had reached the outer edge of Earth's system.

"I thought we were stopping further out to avoid such debris," Nazario stated.

"We are. That wasn't the debris we were worried about."

As if on cue, alarms blared.  Red lights flashed and filled the Command Deck.  Despite the inertial dampeners, Nazario felt the ship being jostled about.  He nearly fell over as the ship rocketed around.  After struggling to find his seat, he was able to determine what was happening.

"That is," the pilot said with a strained voice.

The alarms were collision warnings.  There was debris everywhere, even this far out.  The pilot's fast reaction times had been all that saved them from crashing.  Franks was pushing the transport ship to its limits dodging through the new asteroid belt.

Not all the red light was not coming from inside the ship.  Major Nazario's next thought was that the supernova was still raging, but he realized that the light was coming from multiple sources.  The pilot was too busy avoiding debris to pay close attention to the sources of the light.

When Major Nazario demanded Franks to direct closer to the nearest source, the pilot started to object.  A second look helped Nazario realize the debris was thickest near it.  But Franks bit his lip and followed the order.  He even tinted the viewscreen, so they would not be blinded.  As the ship approached the source of the light, Nazario finally understood what he was seeing.

Planets were reforming.  Giant glowing orbs of ruby magma floated in their path.  Readings indicated they were still rotating rapidly after all the energy that had slammed into them previously.  It was an awe-inspiring sight, and he ordered his executive officer on the bridge to record the sight via video and picture.

The recorder captured the images of the four oblong orbs of spinning molten rock, each roughly the size of old Mars.  In the distance, there was a tiny white neutron star.  It glowed white, relatively faintly, but had a strong enough gravitational pull to draw the four young planets into orbit around it.  Paled by the nearby sources of light, Nazario could just make up a faint blue or teal haze in the distance in all directions.  A shell of supercharged particles.

Major Nazario spoke to his navigator, "Start up the scanners, search for signs of life."

There was an audible blip showing signs of a ship near the center of the solar system, but it was only there for a second before disappearing. *Probably just a glitch from all the debris.* There could be a lot of glitches with all the radiation bouncing around the system still.  Safe enough levels for them, but that did not prevent it from wreaking havoc on their equipment.

Captain Braxton responded, "Sir, it'll be really difficult to pick up signs of life with all this debris and radiation. We're more likely to find survivors through a visual search."

"Then keep an eye out the window," Nazario responded sarcastically.

They swept through the solar system searching for any surviving life. They were nearing Mars' previous orbit when they picked up a small blip indicating life near the ship. It was too small to be human or even insect life, but it could be some highly resilient bacteria.

They pulled in the source of the blip. It turned out to just be a large chunk of rocky debris, roughly four meters in diameter. There were no visible forms of life on the asteroid, so they stored it in the cargo bay for later examination on the *Jericho*.

Nazario continued to monitor all the scanners but could see the obvious evidence of devastation out the viewscreen. The ship still dodged debris. The remnants of the old system were gone. One day, a new system may rise, but nothing could have survived this. He felt the ache in his heart as the reality finally sank in. He hung his head. There had been a slight glimmer of hope in his heart before, but it was gone now.

A large blip appeared on radar. Nazario's head shot back up. It was a ship.

He immediately hailed the newcomer, "This is Major Nazario of the United People's Commonwealth, commanding the *Ark*, from the colony ship *Jericho*. Please identify."

"This is Colonel Wainwright of the *Shepherd,* from the *Phoenix.* Glad to hear the *Jericho* made it out. We're on a rescue mission looking to aid any survivors from this disaster. How are you holding up?" the Colonel replied, voice coming through deep but broken over the intercom.

Nazario let out a sigh of relief and relaxed his tense shoulders.

"We're doing as well as can be hoped, sir. There's no way anyone could have survived the blast. Outside of a small asteroid, which showed signs of microscopic life, we haven't found anything. And I'm sure we won't find anything significant."

"Yeah, we haven't spotted anything either. Scanners are too sporadic in this mess anyway."

"Commander Braylon has set up a medical facility in an adjacent solar system, on the third planet, to handle any survivors. They're also there to help gather any explorers who were outside the solar system during the supernova. They can do more from there than we can here."

"That's a brilliant idea. We stopped the *Phoenix* at a colony named

Fringe. We're currently rendering aid there before we continue our mission. We need all of humankind working together to make a comeback from this disaster. I thought our sun had a few billion years left before it died."

"In all fairness, that was calculated nearly a *millennium* ago. It was always a trusted number and never questioned enough to reinvestigate. They were clearly wrong, so you're right, that was completely unexpected."

"Sir, I have another ship on scope, I'm hailing them now," said Captain Braxton.

Both the Major and the Colonel fell quiet while awaiting word from this new ship.

"It's Major Delinmir of the *Neptune* from the *Griffin*. He's also returned on a search and rescue mission."

"Excellent work. Put him on screen, make it a conference call with the *Shepherd*," said Nazario with even more energy.

He looked back to the viewscreen and continued the conference call.

"Major Delinmir, this is Colonel Wainwright on the *Shepherd* from the *Phoenix*," he said with a gesture to the viewscreen before placing his hand on his chest and continuing, "and I'm Major Nazario on the *Ark* from the *Jericho*. We've been sent back here for a search and rescue mission, as well. My Commander has set up a medical facility to assist any survivors, or people seeking refuge."

"Roger that Nazario. Sounds like all we need to do is an official search and rescue sweep, then we can pack up and get back to our ships. Have you found anything yet?" asked Major Delinmir.

"Nothing human. There's really nothing left here. We've only been here a little over two hours, but judging by the state of things, we could be here for weeks and not find anything. Has anyone heard from the *Chimaera* or the *Minotaur*?" asked Nazario.

"Nope," said Colonel Wainwright.

"Negative," replied Major Delinmir.

"That's a shame. I hope everything went okay with them. I'm sure the *Chimaera* got out okay. They were the first ship to jump, and they ultimately saved us all with their Commander's quick reaction," Major Nazario admitted flatly.

Another blip. Another ship.

"I'm hailing the new ship now, sir." Braxton informed him quickly.

Major Nazario anxiously awaited word with the other two ship Commanders.

"It's a civilian ship," Braxton informed them.

A frown crept across Nazario's face.

Braxton continued, "The *Beagle*.  They're a research ship that's been exploring nearby solar systems for life.  Their Commander is Mr. Harmund.  His son is supposed to be on the *Jericho*."

"Good news.  Conference Mr. Harmund in and forward the coordinates of the medical facility to all three ships as well, please.  He'll be most pleased to learn that his son is okay," Nazario turned back to the conference screen and addressed the other ship commanders, "Well, here's what I propose."

Major Garren paced around his grimy barracks room in the control tower.  He was one of the lucky few with a viewport, but he avoided staring out of it.  His last view had been of the Moon and the Ivanako Lunar Space Station they had been orbiting.  It was a memory he wanted to keep.  A memory of what could have been.  A memory of better times.

He could not bear letting it be overridden by their new view of the vast emptiness of space.  Though they orbited another world, he would not have a planetary view should he look. Seeing the blackness would erase his last view of his son in the ILSS.

The reports had devastated him.  Garren had not bothered to change or shower in weeks.  His face had overgrown with stubble, and he wore the same sweat stained undershirt and boxers every day.  His laundry pile was overflowing from his basket.

He was privy to a lot of information as the Recon Commander and had grown accustomed to bad news over the decades, but some things were too awful for even him.  He had delivered his fair share to families as well.  But the confirmation about home had nearly destroyed him.

Garren felt like little more than a husk of his former self.  Everything he had fought for since well before joining the peacekeepers had been for nothing.  He shook his head, still struggling to accept one fact: nothing he did had kept his son safe.

Worse, escaping the death of Earth had been no act of good fortune.  More an eternal punishment for failing his family.  He had tried so hard to protect them, but the more he tried, the more he was away when things went wrong.  And they could not have gone more terribly wrong.

A ring chimed at the door to his quarters.  It had happened at the same time each day this week, but not once had he answered it.  He could not face anyone. He could not bear to show his shame to anyone. He ignored the visitor once again.

The door slid open anyway. Taylor walked into the room. The last person he wanted to see.

"Hello, my friend," Taylor said.

Garren ignored him and turned his back to the door, instead of acknowledging his ex-best friend. That choice left him with only one other viewing option. He removed the man completely from his frame of vision and stared out the viewport. He could feel his grip on his son's memory slipping away as he saw nothing but distant stars twinkle back at him.

Taylor approached him from behind. Garren had been around people long enough to feel their presence when they got close. And Taylor got far too close for a man he was avoiding.

"You need to come out of your shell eventually. This hit everyone, not just you," Taylor pleaded.

*But it hit me the worst.* He continued to ignore Taylor. He heard the man take a deep breath and step even closer. Garren found it surprising that his stench could not repel the stubborn man. The weight of a hand rested on his shoulder.

"Don't touch me," he growled. "I trusted you and your father. Now my son is dead."

"Our actions were never meant to harm your son. You know that. You know you were a son to my father. Even more so than I was. And a brother to me. We both wished for your son's safety. I cannot even begin to express my sorrow for you. It strikes me just as deeply as losing my father the same day."

"Don't think you can draw sympathy just because your father died as well. His decisions were his own. My son didn't get a choice. I let your father convince me to leave him behind. Had I listened to my gut, Jason would be here with me."

"No one could have known about the supernova. Its cause still eludes us. A freak incident that cost a *trillion* lives. If we had known, many more lives would have been saved," Taylor reasoned in his soft voice.

Garren scoffed and turned around to face the man for the first time.

"You know, there's a rumor going about that your father *did* know. That it was the sole purpose for these missions. To try to save lives and sacrifice the rest that weren't important enough to waste resources on."

"You know darn well that my father would never do such a thing. You practically grew up in his house with me. How could you consider him so evil?  You know as well as I do that the decision was smart.  Your son needed you to make sure his new home was safe *before* he came on such a dangerous mission," Taylor countered. all but yelling at Garren.

Then the man had the audacity to look around the room, silently judging the mess.  Just because his uniform lay in a pile on the floor next to food scraps and his bed was unmade did not mean Garren needed to put up with his attitude.  He marched away from Taylor, creating as much space as he could.

"Get out.  I never want to see your face again," Garren roared through clenched teeth.

He did not bother to look back at his ex-friend.  Taylor sighed and turned, walking for the exit.  He paused before leaving entirely.

"You know, my father may have loved you more than he did me.  He cared more for your child's safety than his own grandchildren.  Your child was the one he kept behind to protect.  You were the favorite in the house.  He loved you until the end.  We both did."

# Chapter 4
## Crisis

**M**ajor Nazario disembarked the *Ark* in a hurry once they docked with the *Jericho*. He needed to speak with Commander Braylon about the events of the mission and the decisions he had made in his absence. He respected the Commander's rank but sometimes questioned his decision-making abilities. Nazario was a seasoned veteran whereas the Commander had never led soldiers on the front lines. Braylon was a likeable enough man, but he had spent most of his career behind his desk as a pencil pusher, occasionally issuing orders about things he had little experience on.

When Nazario reached the bridge, he was not even provided the opportunity to request permission to enter before being ushered in. Commander Braylon looked at him expectantly. Major Nazario snapped to attention and delivered his report with a salute.

"Sir, everything was completely destroyed. There was no reason to linger, so I ended our search early. We came across ships from the *Phoenix* and the *Griffin*, as well as a research vessel, the *Beagle*. The *Beagle's* Commander's son is on board the *Jericho*. His ship and crew are going to make their way to the medical facility here. I told him that he could join us on our mission. I extended that offer to his crew as well."

The Commander shook his head emphatically and answered, "We will not be continuing our mission. Our main focus, moving forward, should be to help any survivors, especially now that we *know* there are some out there. Our previous mission no longer matters. We must set up a new home for humankind here and reestablish our people."

"Actually, sir, with all due respect, the only thing that matters at this point *is* our mission. We can't abandon everything our people have sacrificed and achieved up to this point.  Besides, our entire mission was to set up a new colony on a new world.  The planet here would require far too many resources to make a viable new home.  It can barely support this medical facility."

Commander Braylon placed his fist under his chin, while pondering Nazario's words for a moment.

"So, what do you suggest?"

"That we continue to ZX-746.  It's our best chance at a real colony.  We can bring anyone else who wants to join from the *Beagle*.  They deserve a chance at a new home as well."

"I suppose you may be correct.  We need to do what our people asked us to do.  We can honor their memory by completing our mission.  Thank you for the reminder, Major.  We still need to do something for any other survivors that come back."

Surprised at how easy it was to get this decision out of the Commander, Nazario responded, "Yes, sir, we can leave any spare supplies we have with the medical facility here, setting them up to help anyone who returns.  Hopefully, we can give them enough resources to establish a self-sufficient colony here.  The ship Commanders, from the other ships I encountered, all hope to convince their Commanders to assist as well.  They're not too far away from here.  They'll have the *Beagle* for support as well."

Commander Braylon countered Major Nazario with a touch of arrogance, "Unfortunately, we already did a count of our supplies while waiting for your return.  There is not much to spare, and we are not even remotely close to being fully stocked.  We are limited on what we can do.  We will have to bank on finding something sustainable at our destination as it is."

"I'm sure whatever we can spare will be better than nothing, sir.  I appreciate you making this decision.  I know it's difficult right now."

The Commander turned to his Second Officer, little more than a glorified assistant, and said, "Lieutenant Daniels, please coordinate the supply mission to the medical facility.  Also, pass along a message to the Commander of the facility to come up with a new name for the colony.  If our mission fails, this colony might be our last hope to save humanity."

Two days later, all the supplies they could spare were on the planet. Their plan moving forward was set. They were prepared to depart the newly established medical facility, 'Bastion's Hope,' and continue their mission to ZX-746. Commander Braylon had meticulously gone over every detail to ensure this was the best course of action.

He called all his ranking officers to the Command Deck. He wanted to give one final statement about the medical facility to his team, as they looked out the viewscreen at the rocky planet. He stood straight, saluted the planet, and delivered a short speech.

"May their strength and determination give them more success than those before them. They may be our last hope, but they are a powerful hope. Now let us do our part."

He pointed his finger forward to signal his Navigator. The *Jericho* lurched forward as the pilot hit the TREX Drive. It would take over a month to reach their destination. Braylon sat at his command chair, regretting volunteering for the furthest planet from Earth.

Despite not being fully manned, the *Jericho* would have supply issues. They simply had not been prepared to depart when they had. Even with the greenhouses on board, without a new home, they would not live more than a couple years. The last of their supplies burned up with Ivanako.

The fuel level would be their most significant problem.

About halfway into their journey, the Navigator realized the issue. He called to Commander Braylon, who was in his seat overlooking Navigation.

"Sir, we have a serious problem. We don't have enough fuel to make it to our destination."

Commander Braylon looked up from his screen, "What do you mean? We left Earth at seventy percent capacity; it should have only required sixty percent to reach ZX-746."

"Correct, except that we consumed additional fuel stopping the ship and restarting our path. To make matters worse, this ship's systems were never tested outside of simulations. We're consuming fuel at a higher rate than theorized. I'm sorry I didn't notice this before," the Navigator stated.

Braylon asked solemnly, "What are you telling me? Is there no way to make it to our destination?"

"Unfortunately, not, sir. We'll stop less than a day short of the colony site.  The biggest fuel consumption occurs when starting and stopping the ship.  Maintaining the ripple requires a steady supply of anti-matter, but at a relatively low rate.  Unfortunately, we're burning through anti-matter faster than predicted.  Based on these readings, we may have passed through some strong gravitational fields, resulting in a higher burn rate than anticipated.  If we hadn't stopped, which was vital, we could have made it."

Commander Braylon's heart sank in his chest.  This was devastating information.  *My decision to stop and go back has doomed our mission.*  He had to figure out how to fix this.  This was so far out of the book that he had no idea what to do.  He was going to need help solving this newest dilemma.  He looked at his Second Officer standing near a console at the rear of the deck.

"Can you please call a leadership meeting?  I need you, Nazario, McNeil, Titus, Neckrel, Hanley, and Garren.  Conference room, one hour.  Can you invite Ambassador Anderson as well?  Thank you."

Lieutenant Daniels saluted and stepped off to complete his task.  Commander Braylon sat back in his command chair.  His central location on the bridge gave him a clear view of the five workstations surrounding him from an elevated floor.

His crew was diligently working away while he sat on his throne, useless.  On his left, communications, in front was the trifecta of navigation, piloting, and armament, and to his right, engineering.  Every station was a mess of blinking lights and rapid command inputs.  They would do their job to keep the *Jericho* moving.  He needed to actually do his.

He looked up at the viewscreen, which was now relaying all their sensor information and headings over a live view using augmented reality.  He scanned the gunmetal grey stations around him, internally pleading for answers.  The deck was bathed in true white light while all the consoles were brightly colored for easy monitoring of their systems.

He found the lighting to be oddly comforting.  There were no alerts flashing or sirens wailing.  It almost seemed normal.  There was a calmness to his surroundings that helped him relax and focus.  He considered moving to his office, which was accessible directly from the bridge, but felt he needed to present a more confident face to his crew.

The Ambassador's office was directly off the bridge as well.  Braylon shook his head while thinking about being near the Ambassador.  The Ambassador had no authority while they were on the ship, but he was the future leader of the colony.  *I would be smart to involve him in our long-*

*term planning.*

The Commander looked back over his console and pulled up information on his screen. Hopefully, his team would be able to come up with a plan. They had much more experience with improvising and using unique solutions to solve real world problems. He was internally berating himself for his lack of vision and forethought.

Braylon felt responsible for their current situation and desperately tried to find answers to their problem on his own. He found none. He made his way to the conference room located just aft of the Command Deck. The rest of the leadership team were already in their seats. They all had offices just one deck below, so it was a quick walk for them. *We need to get down to business.*

As the Commander walked in, everyone but the Ambassador shot up to attention. He looked around the conference room table. There were eight very intelligent already people in this room: Lieutenant Daniels, Major Nazario, Colonel McNeil, General Titus, Captain Neckrel, Chief Medical Officer, Colonel Hanley, and Major Garren.

Everyone on board the *Jericho* had been selected due to their skill, not their rank. These were his top peacekeeper leaders, and they were no exception. Together, they had to be able to solve this newest issue. They were the most talented minds among the peacekeepers.

Then there was Earth Ambassador Anderson. His ornate outfit stood out in stark contrast to the crisp, professional uniforms of Braylon's command team. His role during their journey was to be the *Jericho's* ambassador to any alien life that might be encountered, and this was how the man dressed? They had to assume there was a distinct possibility of this happening in their exploration, but Braylon did not like the idea of him representing humanity in such a loud, gaudy manner.

However, that would change once their colony was established. He was to transition into the first Governor of the colony and provide civilian oversight to the peacekeepers on the ground. Once that happened, Braylon would no longer care how the man presented himself. Until that time, he was not part of the leadership, but the Commander felt he ought to be involved in this meeting. *Might as well play nice and built rapport now.*

He waved the team to sit back down and addressed his Second Officer, "Lieutenant, have you briefed everyone on the current situation?"

"Yes, sir."

"Good. There is no time to waste. We need to develop a plan, so we are not stranded in the middle of nowhere. This is about survival. We cannot be left to die in the cold darkness of space."

Braylon pressed his finger into the table for emphasis.

He lowered his head before hesitantly continuing, "First though, I need to accept responsibility for the situation. Had I not stopped the *Jericho* to look back at Earth and wasted resources on a mission that had zero chance of success, we would not be in this predicament."

Major Nazario corrected him, "That was the right call, sir. Any of us would have made the same call, and without that, the *Beagle* might have been left stranded forever. Our people have a place to go now, near our old solar system, which can help other survivors. You saved lives with that call and haven't doomed us... yet," he added.

The Commander let out a half laugh and smiled. Nazario helped ease some of the tension he had been carrying in his shoulders. He felt them relax a fraction. He stretched and worked out some more of the stress. He was no Atlas; he could not carry the weight of the world on his shoulders alone. Though he was the one with three stars on his collar, he knew he had a lot to learn from Major Nazario.

He would never understand why Nazario had never gained more rank. Nazario had accomplished far more in his military career than Braylon ever had, or ever would. Yet Nazario had been stuck as a Major for over a decade. Still, Braylon was thankful he had been granted Nazario for this mission. Majors were typically not considered ranking enough for this large a role.

Braylon responded a moment later once his racing thoughts had fully cleared, "Thank you for the support, Major. However, we still have a predicament that requires our attention. How are we going to save the *Jericho* and make it to our destination? We still have a home to build."

No one spoke. Eyes bounced across the conference room. Each person seemed to be waiting for another to propose the first solution.

Colonel McNeil, in her black uniform, took the plunge and raised her hand first, "I just wanted to add in, without using the TREX Drive, it would take decades to finish the last leg of the journey. Most of our smaller ships aren't capable of reaching the planet from that distance, either. So, it wouldn't be possible to evacuate the *Jericho* in the smaller ships to make it the rest of the way. Sorry for the additional bad news, but from an engineering standpoint, conventional means are not the answer."

Major Nazario gingerly raised his hand and spoke once Braylon pointed to him, "I'm obviously no engineer or anything, but what would happen if we just shut the engines off while at ripple? Couldn't we just travel ballistically until we made our destination?"

Colonel McNeil shook her head vigorously, "Absolutely not. The TREX Drive maintains the ripple in a controlled manner. It *has* to be shut down in a specific process so that space doesn't recoil, unleashing a cataclysmic amount of energy. Think of it like a mini supernova. We can't just shut it off or let it run out of energy."

Her hands were moving wildly as she tried to break down her explanation, "The deceleration of our reverse thrusters blows off that excess energy in a safe, directed manner. If we don't follow procedures, the energy would build up within the ship and lead to an overload in our systems that would certainly destroy the ship and surrounding areas. There's a reason protocols are in place. We're not just traveling extremely fast, we're compressing space around us. Ballistically speaking, we're barely moving at light speed."

"I mean, a simple no would have sufficed. I'll just keep the dumb science questions to myself in the future..." Nazario said, trailing off.

She looked around the room at the other leadership, "The real question is how do we get going again?"

Colonel Hanley raised her green sleeved arm next, "Have we figured out where we're going to be stranded at? Is there any chance it's near a habitable planet we could use *instead* of our current destination?"

Captain Neckrel replied, "We've been scanning ahead of us, trying to get more accurate data than we could from Earth. Unfortunately, there's a reason we picked the five destinations we did. We're going to fall about two hundred lightyears short of ZX-746. There isn't anything in the habitable zone near where we're projected to shut down. We found very few possible planets in the galaxy that met our specifications. We would have to stop and change direction entirely and as has already been determined, we're too limited on fuel to do anything like that."

Ambassador Anderson took his turn next, speaking loudly and confidently, "Gentlemen, I don't feel like there will be any easy answer to this. We might have to leave the *Jericho* stranded along with most of our citizens and save what few we can. I must ensure that we establish a new home no matter what. Sacrifice, to save the species."

General Titus scoffed, "And I suppose *you* would be one of those few saved?"

"I would be a logical choice, yes. But it isn't for personal reasons. I was chosen to be our leader, so I need to be there to lead our people."

"And how do you expect us to choose the other survivors?" Titus continued laying into the Ambassador.

"By order of merit, of course. Don't worry, General, you would be on that list. There are minimum requirements to get a colony up and running, so the most important roles must be filled with the most qualified personnel," the Ambassador stated smugly.

General Titus' ears turned red as he stared down the Ambassador, "That is *unacceptable.* We cannot abandon all these lives when there are already so few left. We must find a way to save everyone, *no matter the cost.*"

"Then at least concede that if we can't save everyone, as a last resort, you'll follow my plan."

"Don't worry, we'll do everything we can to save your life."

Major Nazario interjected as things were getting heated, "Sirs, please, we could take the *Inquisitor* on a recon mission once we drop out of ripple. Major Garren and I could lead the effort. He looks like he could do with getting off the ship anyway."

Garren's head popped up revealing a face that said, 'he forgot he had even been here.'

"The *Inquisitor* is far more advanced than any other ship on the *Jericho,*" Nazario continued. "It can complete the trip and make it back. We can at least confirm if that planet is *actually* habitable. It could just be a massive rock without any potential. We need to know before we commit to abandoning ship for it."

Nazario looked around the room at everyone. When they locked eyes, Braylon gave a slight nod.

Nazario continued, more slowly this time, "We had contingency plans in place if our destination wasn't capable of sustaining life. Unfortunately, as Neckrel stated, those options no longer exist. Unless we can find new resources, we're dead in the water. Perhaps we can find something on the planet that will assist us. I'm sure there'll be other star systems nearby. We should investigate those as well. Anti-matter was original discovered in just as random of a place. We can't establish a final plan until we have completed this recon."

Across the room, the command team nodded their heads. Braylon did not feel good about the plan. They had not really decided anything significant, just pushed the decision back.

He reluctantly spoke, "Agreed. We need to go ahead and start consolidating our current supplies and rationing them. Who knows how long we will be stuck in space before we can find a new home. We will reconvene once we drop out of ripple. You are all dismissed."

As he left, Major Nazario whispered to Commander Braylon, "Why did you invite the Ambassador?  He's useless here.  He's only on this mission because of his political connections."

"If you remember, I am here due to similar reasons."

Major Nazario frowned at the Commander's reply.  Braylon was thankful for Nazario's support, even though he did not feel he deserved it.

The conference haunted Garren.  No matter what, they were in danger.  There were no safe decisions.  Nothing he did could have protected his son.  He could barely think straight, accusations running through his mind.  *If it wasn't Bastion's fault, and it wasn't his own fault, then whose fault was it?  Who had killed his son?*

His eyes watered as he raced back to his room.  He had only left it the one time since they had fled Earth, and it had only filled him with more worry.  More confusion.  Nazario had asked him to join him on the *Inquisitor*.  He was the Recon Commander after all, but he was not sure his head was in it.  He would need support.

There was only one person who could give it.  Only one person who had been with him as he struggled to be apart from his family.  Just down the hall from his own room, he reached his destination.  He tried to pat out the wrinkles in his uniform.  He checked his reflection in a glass viewport.

He was disgusting.  His maroon uniform needed a steam.  His insignia was crooked as well. And his face.  The stubble jutted out of his face in all directions.  He sniffed his armpit and nearly gagged.  He should not be meeting his friend now.  But he had no choice.  If he did not get help now, he never would admit he needed it.

# Chapter 5
## Stranded

*N*azario sat at the helm of the *Inquisitor* as the *Jericho* dropped out of ripple. He felt the blood rush to his face as the ship's oversized reverse thrusters slammed the great colony ship to a halt. His ship's moorings compensated for the deceleration where the inertial dampeners could not.

Navigational data popped up on the Inquisitor's viewscreen. They were just over two hundred light years away from their destination. Forty-nine thousand light years now separated them from Earth-that-was. In the forty-two days they had been at ripple, a lifetime had passed.

Events had unfolded quickly over that time on the ship. The Haven had fallen into chaos. There had been a streak of vandalism and rioting. People were upset about the loss of their home, and angry at the leadership for their handling of things, and fearful over the new rationing requirements. Nazario was thankful to be leaving all the hysteria behind.

Most peacekeepers were so busy trying to restore order, that they had not had time to process through the tragedy. Increased strain and stress among the security personnel caused Nazario to fear they would crack if something did not change. The *Jericho* was a ticking time bomb. The colonization endeavor might end before it ever began. He hoped their mission would yield favorable results quickly.

He settled into his seat. In spite of his previous mission on the *Ark*, this was his ship. It was customized to his exact specifications. The sleek black scout craft was technologically superior to any other ship on the *Jericho* and could travel further. *Special Operations has its advantages.* Unfortunately, it was no warship; weapons and ammo would limit its range and reconnaissance capabilities.

His team was ready to depart. He had a minimalistic eight-man crew, including himself. No need to risk anymore lives on such a venture. He had three security personnel —Sergeant James, Sergeant Piers, and Sergeant Reigns— as well as two recon specialists: Major Garren and his second in command, Captain Monkley.

Finally, there were two civilians despite Nazario's initial protest. They had joined at the request of the Ambassador. Braylon had hinted to him that the Ambassador might be trying to gain control during the emergency.

The civilian population on the *Jericho* had been kept in the dark about how dire the circumstances truly were. Once the Ambassador had gotten involved, the news broke, and he had since tried to influence the peacekeeper leadership.

These two civilians on the mission were his way of trying to control it. Nazario's reservations were quelled though, when he found they had specialties that could be highly useful on the mission. Regardless of his disdain for the Ambassador, he was not too upset about their presence.

Braylon had met Anderson in the middle by allowing the two. Doctor Brandon Jimenez was the lead environmental engineer and the most knowledgeable person on the ship regarding the science behind terraforming. He understood the environmental needs for their future home. No one else could confirm viability like him. He would be able to fine-tune the ship's terraforming equipment for maximum efficiency based on his readings of the planet.

Nazario was less agreeable to Doctor Jaina Svensson, Ambassador Anderson's most trusted assistant. Jaina was a result of the Ambassador sticking his nose where it did not belong. Commander Braylon valued diplomacy though and thought she could be helpful with decision-making since she could give a unique perspective on the mission that peacekeepers might not have. Nazario just could not trust the Ambassador and she was his representative.

So, with this less-than-desirable crew, he would save humanity. Special Operations had sent him on many dangerous missions in the past, but this one really had him on edge. The survival of humanity was riding on him to be successful. Usually, his missions could only affect a small population. This one affected the few remaining in their entirety. At least it was not as emotionally taxing as the last. He might find hope this time.

He spoke to his crew over the intercom, "I hope everyone is ready and strapped in, it's time to depart. We have a two-day journey ahead of us.

Get comfortable and get to know each other. This mission is reliant on us working closely together."

The *Inquisitor* unmoored and slid out of the side ship bay. Major Nazario punched the coordinates into their navigation system, and the ship jumped into ripple. He enjoyed piloting his small craft. It relaxed him as he focused on the passing stars and navigational information scrolling across his console.

This ship was not as fast or efficient as the *Jericho*, but it could still reach their destination. It was the smallest ship in the colony ship's fleet with a TREX Drive and it required much less fuel to travel. But smaller ships could not ripple space as tightly as a large ship, so their speed was significantly reduced.

Anti-matter storage on small ships had never been efficient, greatly reducing their range. As it was, the *Inquisitor* should theoretically be able to make the journey and back once without running out of fuel. It was one of the few ships that could make the journey both ways. Even so, it was a great risk.

During their travel, Nazario decided it would be a good idea to take the time to get to know everyone on his team. He was only familiar with Garren and Monkley, as he had worked with them on several missions leading up to this. He was mildly interested in these civilians he had been stuck with. He was not used to having civilians under his command and needed to ensure they would follow orders should anything happen. He moved over to the break area at the rear of the Command Deck, leaving the ship on autopilot.

He looked at the two civilians sitting in the far corner of the *Inquisitor's* Command Deck. Brandon was clearly uncomfortable being stuck with a bunch of peacekeepers; his eyes were glued to them. Jaina was trying to help him relax, but she seemed to be having little luck. Nazario called them over to join him in the break area. He gestured for them to sit at the padded booth while he stood.

"How are you two holding up?" he inquired once they reached him.

Brandon's face retracted in visible confusion.

"I... I'm surprised you care. I'm just nervous. There's a lot r-... riding on this mission... and life has been really t-... terrible lately. I had a lot of family back on Earth. I m-... miss them so much."

Nazario tried to be comforting, "At least it's really no different for you than it would have been. We wouldn't have been able to communicate with them for a long time after we left anyway."

Jaina shot him a dirty glance. Jaina and Brandon sat across from each other in the booth.

"Believe it or not, *Major*, that isn't actually a helpful thought. There was still a chance of future communications. And just the comfort of knowing we had a home. The likelihood of having blue skies over our heads again or smelling the fresh mown grass on a hoverhouse are abysmal now."

Nazario pursed his lips, chewing on the lower one. He had not had that experience in a long time. He had been on battlecruisers most of his life and for his entire adulthood lived in peacekeeper provided housing. He had always placed the peacekeepers first and had never settled down or bought a home of his own. He had forgotten what civilian life was like.

"I'm sorry. That wasn't my intent. I was just trying to distract from the reality of the situation, though I suppose it really was quite a lousy thing to say."

"It's fine. I-... I know you meant well. Thank you for trying," Brandon said, giving a half-hearted smile.

Jaina was not so forgiving, "You need to think about people before you speak. This isn't just some *military* mission. This isn't about the peacekeepers, or something you can *fight* your way through. It's about the lives of every remaining human on that ship, who are now not only responsible for establishing a new home for us but rebuilding humanity as well."

"I said I'm sorry. I just wanted to check in and make sure you were both doing okay. I know it's not always comfortable for civilians to work with peacekeepers. I just wanted to make sure that once we're on the planet, we're able to work together without issues," Nazario desperately tried to explain.

"You just want to make sure we follow your orders. You stand over us like you're above us up on your lofty throne. We're not your peacekeeper puppets. *We* actually think for ourselves," Jaina replied nastily.

He reflexively sat down in the booth next to Brandon. He was nicer. Jaina was intimidating as she defended the awkward man.

"I promise, I'm just trying to be helpful. We're all on the same team here. There's no need for hostility. I just wanted to try and get to know you two better, so we might be able to work more effectively."

Jaina continued to stare daggers at him as he sat there.

Nazario examined the two civilians in awkward silence before forcing himself to ask, "What brought you onto the *Jericho* for this mission?"

Jaina never relaxed her jaw as she hesitantly replied, "I applied for the Ambassador position. I thought I was qualified. It felt like it would be a great opportunity to explore the galaxy and have unique experiences. I couldn't pass up a chance to meet intelligent life if these missions finally brought us in contact. I have *dreamed* of the day I could meet them and broker a friendship."

*So maybe not Anderson's biggest supporter.*

Nazario nodded and continued the conversation, "I can appreciate that. General Titus requested me. We'd served together in the Colonial Rebellions. It was actually quite the surprise for me. He and I haven't gotten along in a while. I almost didn't accept. What about you, Brandon?"

Brandon did not make eye contact, but still responded, "I just wanted to make my family p-... proud. They pushed me to go on this 'once-in-a-lifetime' mission. I led the t-... team that developed the terraforming technology used on these colony ships. They said that if I d-... didn't go, then the mission would fail if anything went wrong."

Brandon shrank back in his seat with his head down. Nazario noticed the water dripping from his eyes, despite trying to hide it. For such an important person, Brandon seemed a little off.

Brandon's voiced cracked as he continued his tale, "Well, it's *definitely* gone wrong now. I j-... just wish I had them here to support me. N-... No one else in my family had been qualified to j-... join and to be honest, none of them wanted to. They were happy with the life they had," Brandon explained with his arms exaggeratedly emphasizing his words.

Nazario placed a hand on the man's shoulder, trying to comfort him.

"I know I haven't been good at this sort of thing," Nazario started, "but at least they died happy and proud of what you were doing for humanity. You can definitely prove them right on this mission."

Jaina was visibly surprised at the sincerity in his words. She eyed him with a cocked eyebrow for several seconds.

"Perhaps I misjudged you," she offered.

Brandon looked up at Nazario and smiled his appreciation. Nazario locked eyes with Brandon and could see the contemplation behind his eyes. Brandon leaned over and hugged Nazario, tears still streaming down his face. Nazario was caught off guard by the hug but embraced the man back. The importance of a hug to a person in pain outweighed his personal discomfort with the crying man.

"This is going to be a tough time on everyone, but together, we can find a way to survive. This mission can restore hope, if we're lucky. Who knows, maybe we'll find something really cool on our trip," Nazario stated optimistically.

"Yeah, m-… maybe," Brandon said with a weak smile, rising from the booth.

Jaina stood to join Brandon.

They moved to make their way back to the corner when Nazario asked Jaina, "Why didn't you get the Ambassador position?  I already like you a lot more than Anderson."

"Honestly, he had better connections.  I thought I'd earned it.  I brokered a bunch of peace treaties after the Colonial Rebellions.  I felt that I had better qualifications, but it comes down to who you know.  I'm just glad that I still got to be part of this journey."

Jaina smiled at him.

"Why did Titus request you if you two had conflicts before?"

For the first time in their conversation, Nazario could not make eye contact.  He did not have the answer himself and preferred not to think about his previous confrontations with the General.

"I'm not sure to be honest, but I'm glad he did."

"Well, what happened between you two?" Jaina asked.

"I should probably get back to work.  I've been away from the command chair too long.  Need to make sure the autopilot is still directing us properly.  Don't want to end up stranded like the *Jericho*," he said as he stood and stepped away from them quickly.

# Chapter 6
## Visitors

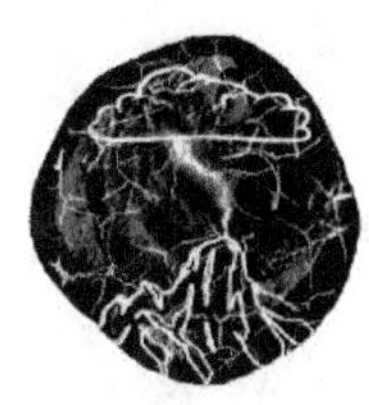

𝑦ntering the city gates, Jarreck noticed something was amiss. The activity lever in Ambrecia was higher than he had ever witnessed. People were bustling about, not attending to their usual duties. *Did something happen?* He peered under the hood of Kiva's cerulean cape and saw her scanning the crowds, just as confused.

It had been a tough two-day ride back to the capital city. Jarreck slowed his jentar as they approached the overcrowded streets; its long white hair stopped flapping in the wind. As quickly as they had returned, it might not have been fast enough. The entire population seemed on edge as they ignored their responsibilities to press toward the city's heart. *Have the Noxxons already attacked?*

Jarreck slowly steered them through the crowded streets. He had to be careful to avoid impaling anyone in the throngs of citizens with the long horn on the jentar's forehead. He dismounted and led them into the stables as their jentars' hooves click-clacked along the roadway. Jarreck patted his jentar on the side of its head near its large, sharp horn and handed it a piece of fruit as a thank you. With their mounts tended to, they could seek the Council.

Jarreck and Kiva wove their way through the packed streets. It looked like the people were massing around the large, towering palace. The central courtyard below the large overhanging convocation deck was densely populated as the townsfolk seemingly awaited word from the King. Whenever he chose to spoke, the buildings surrounding the courtyard would amplify his voice for all to hear, even with such a large ruckus below.

The convocation deck sat empty though. Jarreck assumed that

whatever the crowd was waiting for, it was not imminent. His curiosity grew as he noticed there was not fear, but excitement in the eyes of the people. They were wide eyed and smiling as they chattered away excitedly with each other.

He turned away from the courtyard and led the way to their Society's headquarters. They rounded a corner to an alley and quickly disappeared from sight. The Society of the Scar was hidden in the lower levels of the palace, but accessible only through an inconspicuous side building. They entered quickly, opening the magical lock. Kiva still trailed after him as he made his way to the Council Chambers. He sped through the cold dark tunnels, intent on delivering their report quickly.

As they neared the Council Chambers, one of the dark cobalt caped guards recognized Jarreck and immediately ushered him in with a cold greeting, "The Council has been waiting for you."

Jarreck raised an eyebrow as he entered the chambers with Kiva following close behind. He opened his mouth, but before he could begin his report, he was interrupted by the High Councilor.

"We've had some astounding events develop and we need your immediate assistance."

Jarreck was taken off guard but protested, "I'm sorry, High Councilor, but we have more pressing matters. The Noxxons have—"

High Councilor Vreeham interjected, "Jarreck, there is *nothing* more important than this. We have visitors from beyond the stars and I need you, and your old apprentice here, to report to the King's Council. You are to provide additional security and anything else the King requests."

"Yes, High Councilor, but can I please give my report first?"

"No, Jarreck, there isn't time for that. They needed you there earlier today, but you were off galivanting around. Please go immediately. No delays."

Jarreck held back the retort on the tip of his tongue and bowed before the High Councilor. His eyes slipped to Councilor Gierdahl before he departed, Kiva in tow. He had to pass along his report as soon as he possibly could. The Master of the Mountain would listen to him. After all, he was the Councilor who had assigned Jarreck to the mission. Even better, he may have answers to what they had witnessed the Noxxons excavating. He was the only living person who might.

As they left the Council Chambers, Jarreck pulled one of the guards aside and had him follow. He relayed his report to the guard as they walked and requested it be delivered directly to Councilor Gierdahl once they closed their session. Not exactly protocol, but he had to do something. It would take time to hear back from the Councilor on the matter. Despite what the High Councilor had said, Jarreck knew this was the top priority mission in the Three Kingdoms.

As they made their way up the back stairs into the palace, Kiva asked, "What do you suppose the Council meant when they said we have visitors from beyond the stars?"

Jarreck looked back at his old apprentice with a blank stare. It took a few seconds reviewing his memory of the meeting to recall what she was talking about. He had forgotten the Council had even mentioned that. He had been too caught up by his previous mission and trying to get his report out.

"I'm not sure, Kiva. I suppose we'll see shortly."

They entered the palace through an unornamented door and continued to the King's Court silently. The guards immediately opened the court doors when they arrived. The guards had been expecting them. Once they were inside, Jarreck noticed a rather full chamber.

Everyone seemed to be facing the sidewall rather than the King at the rear. Jarreck moved to get a clearer picture of the court. Standing against the sidewall were some very strange, shiny looking short people. Most of them seemed to be wearing some sort of metal suits on their bodies with odd glass masks over their eyes. There was a mesmerizing glow emanating from the center of their chests.

"Jarreck is going to be a problem," Vreeham said to the other Councilors. "I don't know what to do about his disobedience anymore. We must do something to quell his insurrections before more begin to act out and ignore the wisdom of the Council."

Three of the four other councilors nodded. Gierdahl did not. Instead, he countered the argument. *What else is new?*

"I disagree. We should encourage him to act on his instincts. The Alackai has led him down this path. Who are we to disagree with her?"

"The Alackai is wise and surely would not guide anyone to act in such a disrespectful and reckless way. He cannot be following her guidance if he acts out so openly against us. He will doom our Society if allowed to continue down this path unchecked."

"As you say, High Councilor. But he has a mission assigned. This could be good for him.  Perhaps when it is over, we may reconvene with him," Gierdahl offered.

*That won't come soon enough.*  Vreeham let out a deep sigh. Dealing with Jarreck had become a headache.  His defiance would doom everything he had worked so hard for.  He needed him either in line or expelled from the Society.  He could not do so without unanimous support, though.

Gierdahl always had a soft spot for him, ever since childhood.  It did not help that Gierdahl was friends with his father Jace, too.  And that Skovi got away with anything.  Being Master of Ancient Knowledge had granted Jace a lot of leeway and Jarreck acted as though he had inherited the lenience.  Vreeham could not afford to allow that freedom to last much longer.

He nodded to dismiss the other Councilors and left to gather his thoughts.  These visitors might be the blessing he had needed to reign Jarreck in.

As the *Inquisitor* approached the planet designated ZX-746, Nazario settled into orbit and began scanning.  The scanners could determine initial viability and assess any possible resources. Both Brandon and Jaina stood behind him, looking over his shoulders as data streamed to his console, interested in the scientific discovery.  It only took a few minutes to begin receiving significant readings.

"Well, this is interesting," said Nazario, surprised at how quickly the computer seemed to detect positive results.  "It appears there are three major landmasses on the planet.  It's about eighty percent the mass of Earth, with enormous oceans.  It rotates the opposite direction though, so the sun would rise in the west.  It has three moons, green plant life, a rich nitrogen/oxygen atmosphere, and... Well, this is unbelievable!  There are signs of civilization on one of the continents!"

Jaina nearly knocked him out of his seat as she jumped forward to examine his console more closely.

"Civilization?!" she exclaimed, grabbing his shoulder tightly.  "Like aliens?  That's fantastic!  The first good news we've had since we boarded the *Jericho*.  I can't believe we finally found intelligent alien life.  I can't wait to meet them!"

Brandon bore a goofy smile as he leaned in, crowding Nazario from the other side.

"Th-... That's amazing!  Does it show if the atmosphere is breathable?  Are the other landmasses occupied as well?  C-... Can we land people on one of the continents and begin a settlement?  What else do the scanners say?  We still need to g-... get geological surveys done."

"We will do all that, doctors.  The atmosphere appears breathable, so we can set down, but first, we need to send word back to the *Jericho*.  Then we need to find a safe place to land," he stated, then added, "Once the scans are complete of course."

They waited an additional half hour before the computer beeped to alert them the scans were done.  Detailed results displayed on the screen.  As they all viewed the results silently, Brandon looked up excitedly.

"I don't think we c-... could have gotten better news from this.  This may solve all our problems."

The other two looked up confused.  Brandon looked at them brightly for a moment before his smile faded.

"I f-... forgot.  You probably don't understand some of this data.  There are significant energy readings coming from the planet.  I d-... don't understand what is producing these energy levels, but they're off the charts and all coming from the smallest c-... continent.  The locals must be extremely advanced to have such large energy readings."

Nazario's eyes lit up.  *We're saved.*  He had done it.  Now all they needed to do was collect some of this new energy source and be on their way.

"W-... We need to perform further testing, but if this is something we can harness, we might have a way to power the ship's TREX Drive and get the *Jericho* the rest of the way here.  And it's a habitable p-... planet based on current readings.  I would venture to say there's enough room on the planet for us.  We might not even need to t-... terraform."

Upon hearing this news, Nazario nearly cheered.  This entire ordeal might finally be at its end.

Nazario told them, "We need to report this information back, then make contact with the locals so we can examine their energy source."

He sent a report back to the *Jericho*.  Despite how technologically advanced their communications were, it would still take almost a day for their report to reach the *Jericho,* and even longer before they heard back.

"Let's go ahead and land.  I don't want to wait for clearance.  The sooner we can conduct our research and communicate with the locals, the better," Nazario said.

They had just eclipsed the forty-eight-hour mark since their departure and conditions had already been strained on the colony ship. They could do with further scans and mapping, but that would take precious time.

He directed his ship down from orbit. He chose to land near the largest city, but far enough away to keep their ship hidden and protected. Good thing there was a dense forest nearby. It was dark on the planet as they descended toward their landing zone. He swung the ship over the city, using the darkness and clouds as cover.

Through the viewscreen, Nazario got a detailed look at the city below. The people seemed to be in some sort of iron age, similar to Earth's medieval days. There were no vehicles except carts. No apparent technology or electricity of any sort. Their city was made of stone.

Nazario leaned toward Brandon with a raised eyebrow as they made for the forest, "How is it these people have such powerful energy sources, but appear medieval in technology?"

Brandon shrugged as he replied, "Could have been a m-... mistake in our readings. Or the energy is coming from something else. We don't know anything about the geology of the planet, there could be a m-... mineral here that is producing these readings. That might even be preferred since it wouldn't require trade."

"I guess we'll see once we make contact," Nazario said as they touched down before turning to look at Jaina. "Will the suit translators work with the local language? I would imagine it's nowhere near what we speak on Earth."

Jaina nodded as she answered, "These translators aren't just databases of human languages. They actually examine context and body language to learn any oral language. Theoretically, it'll only take a few minutes. It might be awkward at first though since we won't be able to understand or reply while the computers are learning. But in the end, if they speak with their mouths, we'll be able to understand and communicate with them."

Reassured, he got back to his shutdown procedures for the ship. He did not have long to wait before colors appeared on the western horizon. Once day broke, they disembarked.

As everyone geared up in the small cargo hold, Nazario turned to one of the security personnel and gave orders, "Sergeant Reigns, please stay behind and maintain comms with the *Jericho*. Keep the ship safe until we return."

"Yes, sir," Reigns responded.

"Peace never dies," Nazario said.

"With keepers in the skies," Reigns responded with a salute before returning to the Command Deck.

Nazario and his peacekeepers equipped their Reliant Exosuits and secured provisions in the onboard compartments. Their civilian charges were not so well equipped. Comfort was a greater priority with simple clothing and backpacks full of their tools. The seven groupmates secured their Acumen augmented reality visors over their eyes and stepped off the ship into the green forest outside.

As they walked through the forest, Nazario noticed there was an energy about the area. It was electric. His senses jumped into overdrive. Despite the lush foliage surrounding them, he did not see any of the local animal life. What an odd place. Even the orbital forests of Earth had animal life. He scanned through the tall trees as he felt the presence of curious eyes on him.

Even more intriguing, the woods were completely silent. Nazario could only hear the rustle of their boots in the underbrush as they walked. No bird sung nor animal howled. He could not believe this forest was without creatures.

He continued to walk silently, unwilling to break the stillness around them. He breathed deeply, sucking down the highly oxygenated atmosphere. He had never smelt such fresh air in his life. The aromas were soothing. His shoulders relaxed as he walked at the front of the group.

The trees were different than the ones back on Earth, but not by much. They appeared to serve the same function, at least at first glance. They were still green leafed with bark, but closer in size to Redwoods. The difference was the sheer size difference; the leaves high above were the size of torsos. The plant life was more vibrant and colorful than on Earth as well. Intermixed among the green leaves were small flowers from a spectrum of different colors. Nazario moved slowly through the trees as he allowed Brandon to scan the plant life during their trek.

The temperature was cool and humid, but overall pleasant in the rising sun. Nazario wondered if this world had seasons and if so, what season it might be. It reminded him of late spring back on Earth during his childhood.

Nazario leaned over and whispered to Brandon, "What do you think? Can we settle here?"

Brandon thought for a second, his hand on his chin as they walked.

"At first glance, I would say we found a p-… paradise on this planet. It almost seems too good to be true.  Our scientists back home really knew what they were doing when they calculated our d-… destination.  As of now, I would say yes, we c-… can."

"And what else do we need to do to confirm?"

"There are a lot of samples I need to t-… take.  Have to make sure there's nothing poisonous or infectious that might ruin our stay here.  I'd hate for us to settle then get exposed to a new p-… plague or something." Brandon answered.  A moment later he added, "I cannot wait to examine the life here; it's so magnificent already.  I wonder what sort of evolutionary t-… traits life here has compared to back on Earth."

Nazario nodded his appreciation, though did not share the same curiosities.  The group continued in silence, weaving their way through the forest.  Nazario instinctively made to check his GPS on his forearm screen but remembered they had neglected to do the mapping before descending.  Those scans would have taken another several hours, so he was stuck doing his best to dead reckon their way toward the city.

An hour later, he finally caught sight of the edge of the forest. When they broke through to the grass plains beyond, he could see the city in the distance, only a few degrees off course.  Gazing out of the expansive fields before them, he could not help but feel the journey was too simple.  Only a few natives moved along a distant roadway.  Nazario could not be sure what to expect as they continued their trek.

As they neared the city in the bright sunlight, Nazario felt dwarfed by the white stone walls and structures towering over him.  The city was carved out in intricate detail leaving him awestruck by its innate beauty.  It was encircled entirely by a thick wall made of the same marblelike white stone.  Each surface was smoothed in elegant lines and with curvy runes carved along its breadth.

He made note of the massive wall around the city as they grew close.  *There must have been war here in the past.*  He passed his thoughts on to the others.  What buildings they could see poking out above the wall matched this same architecture.  Beautiful, yet resilient.  This city would stand for millennia, much in the same way as the ancient Greek and Roman cities had.

Nazario led the group to the road he had seen the natives using.  It was empty now as they completed the journey to the city gates.  Once they reached the city, guards, who presumably recognized them as foreign, moved forward to impede their progress.  Nazario looked to Jaina.  She answered his question without him needing to ask.

"It'll take time for the translators to learn the language. We need to ensure we appear non-threatening, so they don't attack us. I wouldn't imagine that'll be too difficult considering their size."

She was right of course. Nazario eyed the aliens standing before them. Like the city, these people towered over him, nearly half a meter taller. While slender in frame, they were muscular and intimidating as they stood there threateningly, giving commands in their language.

He continued to eye them as his team stood in awkward silence. Their leather armor was minimal, allowing a generous range of motion. It only covered their chest, groin, and extremities. It was clearly designed for speed, not serious protection. Then his eyes finally settled on the blades at their sides. The curved, serrated, black blades looked as though they could cleave his flesh like butter. There would be no need to worry about intimidating these people.

The guards shouted their orders this time, drawing Nazario's complete focus. He looked right up at their thin, angular faces into their narrow blue eyes. Then caught a glimpse of their long pointy ears sticking out of their hair. He hoped eye contact still conveyed respect in their culture.

As they continued to stand there awkwardly, Nazario decided these two were likely male, even with their smooth skin and soft features. With a quick movement of their tattooed arms, both guards drew their obsidian blades and menacingly pointed them at Nazario and his team. On the walls above, more guards drew bows and aimed arrows down at them.

Nazario instinctively raised his hands, as did his team. He was unable to understand what the guards were saying, but their gestures were clear. They wanted to be followed somewhere, likely to some form of leadership. *Hopefully, these translators work like they're supposed to. I don't want to have to fight our way out.*

As he fell in just behind the guards, he got a closer look at the tattoos extending down their arms. They were identical to each other and colored onyx with fine, curvy, flowing line work that interwove along their entire arm. There were interesting symbols embedded in the line work. *They must have some sort of meaning among their people.*

Once they entered the city, he was even more astounded by its grace and vibrance. The architecture was entirely made of the white stone. Some buildings resembled old cottages, while others had intricate decorations. The roads looked like cobblestone, but like everything else, were made of the beautiful, marble-like white stone.

There were plants everywhere. The roofs had grass growing over the tops and there were flowers and trees lining windows and roadways, respectively. There was life and energy teeming about the city, plants, animals, and people living in harmony. These people clearly loved nature and strived to be as closely intertwined with it as possible.

As they followed the guards, crowds of spectators formed around them and followed closely. Nazario looked at his travelling companions. He noticed Brandon was smiling ear to ear, excitedly observing everything about the people around them. The locals seemed even more curious about them, which was not entirely surprising. The people now lining the streets wore brightly colored gowns or robes. Nazario suspected most were not warriors.

Jaina proceeded through the city streets with the others until they came to a round courtyard, overlooked by a very large, ornately decorated building. Jaina had been taking in all the sights, but this building towered above all others, seeming to be the most important. There were other buildings tightly packed around the courtyard, but none bore the prestige of this one.

The guards led them into the important looking building, which she began to suspect was a palace or town hall. Before she knew it, they had been brought before what she could assume was their leader. They stood before what appeared to be an elderly man sitting on a great throne. He had lots of attendants and extravagantly dressed people surrounding him and doting on his every need.

Jaina was used to diplomacy and suspected he was a monarch, though he wore no crown. She noted there were a few white caped warriors standing watch over him armored in much the same way as the gate guards. Everyone in the hall was talking excitedly and clearly attempting to communicate with them.

It was time she earned her place on the *Jericho's* mission. *I never thought this day would truly come.* She took stock of the apparent structure in these peoples' society; that would help her determine how to proceed.

It only took a few more minutes of standing there, smiling and waving, listening to the locals speak, before the translators began to crackle to life and do their job. Jaina looked over to Major Nazario, silently requesting to proceed communicating with the locals. Nazario nodded and waved a hand forward, allowing her to take charge of their talks.

She spoke clearly and slowly into the mouthpiece that hung from her visor. The device translated for her and played said translation through built-in speakers. The effect was slightly off putting as her voice spoke, then a split second later, the speakers followed suit, interrupting her thought.

"I apologize for the delayed response." She looked around the room to make sure the locals were understanding. She continued, slowly and concisely, "We had to learn your language and could not reply until we knew how to do so effectively. We are human visitors from beyond the stars. We have traveled across the vastness of space to meet with you today. We are here searching for new friends."

The people in the chamber whispered rapidly with each other, quickly exchanging responses. The local man seated on the throne stood up and smiled. He seemed quite boisterous. She thought back on her past negotiations, trying to draw on similarities.

She assumed he had been a strong man, but his age was beginning to cover it up. It was evident that he used to be a warrior by the way he carried himself, but the years on the throne had hidden his muscle. He wore a gold cape and a matching gold blade on his hip. He appeared regal, despite the lack of crown.

He replied in his native tongue, which translated in their earpieces as, "We're honored to have you at our table. I'm Ambrecia'Cepheus, King of the Undaari. We've never met anyone who wasn't born in our lands. We too wish to meet new friends. We welcome you to Ambrecia and hope to learn more about you and where you're from."

They continued talking for nearly an hour, giving introductions and coordinating an exchange of knowledge. She could barely contain her excitement during their conversations. She wanted that excitement to show as well; it would bode well for peaceful alliances. She wanted them to appear to have the upper hand in any negotiations, rather than appear desperate. Jaina was careful not to divulge too many details about their situation. *Desperation would be unfavorable in our negotiations.*

Jaina focused on building rapport and a lasting relationship rather than any sort of trade. She took the approach of trying to learn about their new friends, rather than trying to get anything from them. She did not want them to think they were trying to use the Undaari people.

❩❩❩

Garren stared in awe of the people and architecture inside the hall they were now gathered within.  What a magnificent city they had discovered on an unbelievable world.  These people were certainly dangerous, but there was a familiarity to them as well. People, warriors, just looking to live their lives.  He could not have imagined this would lie at the end of their journey.  If Jason were here, he would have been absolutely giddy with excitement.

The pain of that realization tore him up.  He found it hard to breathe the air inside these cramped quarters.  His eyes darted around, seeking the exit.  He looked back at Jaina as she spoke to the Undaari leader, then to Nazario who watched with wide eyes.  This place did not feel right to him, he rushed the door, needing freedom.

He saw Monkley react to his sudden departure.  From the corner of his eye, he saw Monkley speak to Nazario before following him out of the hall.  Garren rushed to the courtyard but found himself surrounded by hundreds of Undaari.  He fled the crowds and ducked into an alleyway between the tightly packed buildings. He turned a corner, then another, and found himself in an empty alley.

He sat on the ground in the shadows of the buildings around him. Though he might be lost, this place provided him solitude and a chance to catch his breath.  His son would have loved to see this world, though he would be stranded in space should he have made the journey, still in danger.

"It's your son, isn't it?"

"What?" Garren asked, looking up to find Monkley standing over him.

"Your loss is still getting to you, isn't it?"

"I'm fine," Garren said, lying through his teeth.

"You don't need to lie to me, sir.  We've been through a lot together. I know when you're bothered.  And I know about your arrangement.  We have no secrets."

"You're right.  I just struggle to determine who's at fault.  Who got my son killed.  And why he isn't here to experience this place," he said, gesturing to the city around them.

"It's not anyone's fault.  Sometimes, bad things just happen.  If you'd have been there with him, you'd be just as dead, and I would be in charge of Recon.  Thinking about it, maybe you should have stayed with him."

Garren let out a half-hearted laugh.

"Then this mission would be doomed for sure.  I just keep asking myself why I didn't choose differently."

"Because it was the smart decision with the knowledge you had at the time. We could all be stranded on the *Jericho* right now dying slow deaths. Or we could have landed and been enslaved by these people or other aliens. I've known you for years. You did not make that decision lightly. You did the right thing. I know you did."

"Then why is he gone?"

"He's just in a new place. A place without pain or fear. He never doubted you, and neither do I. Now you just have a million other people depending on you. Your son wouldn't want you wallowing away in self-pity and failing them. He was a smart, loving boy. You've always done right by him."

With a weak smile, he just said, "Thank you, Monkley. I needed that. And I'm glad you joined me. I needed you around to be myself again."

"Oh, it's not over yet. We still have a lot of work to do," Monkley replied, stretching out a hand for Garren.

Garren took it, relying on Monkley to get himself on his feet again.

Before he let go, Monkley said, "Peace never dies."

Garren smiled and replied, "With keepers in the skies."

# Chapter 7
## Studies

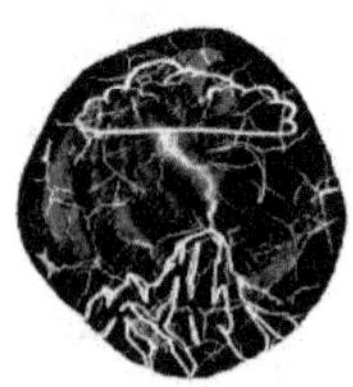

These apparent guests were such strange beings. Jarreck struggled to take his eyes off them as he examined all the odd details of their size and outfits. It was not until he realized the King had addressed him that he broke his eyes away and looked up at the King.

"I'm sorry, my Lord, I missed that question. What is it you wish of me?"

The King took a deep breath and asked again, "Would you, and my dear Kiva, be kind enough to escort our guests around the city and surrounding lands?  They wish to study our archives and the lands surrounding our city. We want to work with them and teach them about our culture so we can build good relationships.  We could do with some new friends."

Jarreck hid his frustration from the King.  They should be focused on the Noxxon problem, not these strangers.  Jarreck did not understand why these little people were being given such unrestricted access but kept his thoughts to himself and just smiled.

"Of course, my Lord.  It would be my honor."

He gathered these outsiders and led them from the palace. Outside, crowds packed in tighter to see the group. He continued eyeing the new people as he led them on a winding tour of the city. Jarreck watched as they marveled at Ambrecia's beauty.  He did his best to answer their questions, though they spoke his language poorly.

He could not understand their origin and worried that their arrival marked something disastrous.  People did not just come from the sky. Jarreck eyed the newcomers as he thought back to what Kiva had warned him of a couple days before. *This timing is suspicious. Why is the King going out of his way to help these strange people?  Cepheus didn't take the Noxxon threat seriously anymore.*

He observed the strangers closely.  *They don't seem too threatening, though.*  These strangers were diminutive in stature and physically frail.  But there was something about them that worried him.  There had to be more underneath the surface.  These people seemed smart for sure.  They had made it all the way to Ambrecia without challenge.  They had even learned their language extremely quickly, assuming they were not lying.

There was also something peculiar about their armor, the ones that wore it.  It did not fully cover their body.  It was more of a skeleton, or support system.  *Do they not have bones?*  He could not stop staring at the slowly rotating light on their chests.  He was utterly confused by these strange beings but had a mission to accomplish.  *Two missions,* he reminded himself.

Jarreck eventually brought the strangers to the Temple of the Mountain, back near the palace.  This was their religious center and inside its cellar were the primary Undaari archives.  These humans, as they called themselves, were to be granted full access to their entire history.

He was wary of allowing this, but it was the King's request.  He could not argue with him, no matter how naïve Jarreck felt King Cepheus was being.  He might have been able to convince the King to change his mind in private, but the opportunity never came.

He studied the humans as they pored over the archives.  Jarreck could not believe how fast they were going through the records.  They had asked for a few translations in the beginning but no longer seemed to need assistance.  He could not fathom how they were able to read so quickly, or speak their language, if they were truly from so far away.

*I just don't trust them.*  Things were not adding up.  None of this made any sense, and the timing could not have been worse.  Even more, his babysitting detail was taking away from the far more important mission of investigating the Noxxons.  All he could think about was the Noxxon threat.  He lost himself in his thoughts for what felt like hours while the humans examined the books.

One of the humans approached him as he stood there, ready to bash his head into the wall.  He looked up at her as she spoke.  It was weird listening to her.  She sounded unusual, like she had two voices.  One of them sounded odd, metallic, but spoke in his language.

She introduced herself as Jaina and asked, "Who are the Noxxons?"

Jarreck raised an eyebrow. How had she not heard of them when she seemed to know so much about the Undaari already? His eyes narrowed as he processed this information. If they had not heard of the Noxxons, then maybe they were exactly who they said. *Then again, they could be lying.*

"They're our greatest enemy. They're vile, ruthless barbarians. They lack both compassion and intelligence," Jarreck explained with a mouth full of venom.

"How long have you been fighting them?" Jaina asked further.

"For thousands of years. They won't go away. They've slaughtered our people on countless occasions. Every time we drive them away, they come back stronger. They must be destroyed once and for all." His voice rose as he got caught up in his emotions.

Jaina took note of Jarreck's attitude toward the Noxxons. This must be the enemy that Major Nazario had reckoned existed. His assessment seemed to be accurate about the Undaari defenses.

"Have the Noxxons been an issue lately?" she asked.

Jarreck looked up angrily, not bothering to hide his distaste.

"Yes. Yes, they have. I had just returned from a scouting mission before you showed up. The Council is ignoring my warnings because of you people!"

So that was why their escort had seemed distant and uninterested. He had priorities that did not include them and was frustrated with his leadership. She could not blame him. If an old enemy threatened her home and people, she would be trying to do everything in her power to keep them safe. *Maybe we can help.*

"Well, at least they're not attacking right now, right?"

Jarreck's tone was showing annoyance with her questions, "They're growing bold. They could attack at *any* moment. They've killed so many Undaari in the past. I can't allow them to kill anymore. I'm wasting my time here with you."

His voice had grown loud, attracting the attention of everyone in the archives. Jaina looked at Nazario who had been sitting back in the corner studying their escorts and noticed his posture was more erect as he watched the situation unfold.

Jaina walked over to him. He watched her as he nonchalantly flipped through the pages of some large book. She doubted he paid the book any attention as he monitored the Undaari in the archives.

She leaned in and whispered, "Major Nazario, I think there may be a situation brewing here with the locals. You were right about them having an enemy. They're called the Noxxons."

"Well, what do you want me to do about it? We're stuck in this archive doing *your* ambassador work. It's not like we're here to fight any wars for them."

"Well, Jarreck over here says he's some sort of scout and the Noxxons are becoming an issue. He's distracted because his leadership is ignoring it due to our presence. Maybe we can do something to help?" she pleaded.

Nazario gestured toward Jarreck and Kiva and countered, "Look at them. Do they look like they need *our* help? You can see how tall and muscular they are. They could easily end us in combat. Their blades seem particularly nasty as well."

She took the time to study the Undaari now, rather than the books. She noticed these two were dressed differently than anyone else they had encountered so far. They wore darker leather armor than the guards at the gate, but the style was consistent. Jarreck was clearly older with short greying hair and Kiva appeared young enough to be his daughter with her long flowing auburn hair done in large braids interlaced in the rear.

They were also draped in bright, electric blue hooded capes that matched their eyes. The capes wrapped their body from the left side of their chest around the back to their right shoulder, leaving their right arms exposed, as well as the large blades on their hips. They seemed even more dangerous than the gate guards had been.

Jaina looked at Nazario and admitted, "I suppose you're right. They do look like formidable warriors. I wouldn't want to be on the wrong end of that sword. But I still think we should try to help them. Jarreck doesn't seem to trust us, and it would go a long way to try and fix that."

"Should we even be involving ourselves in local politics? I worry that we could mess things up or ruin the natural order of things here."

Jaina was troubled that she had not thought of that already while some military muscle head had. She narrowed her eyes at him. He was not your average peacekeeper. He actually thought for himself.

She responded, "You are correct, but we also don't want our presence to hinder them either. If the Undaari are distracted by us being here and get attacked as a result, that could be catastrophic for our diplomatic relations. We're already involved, but we should work to minimize our impact by ensuring local efforts aren't impeded by us."

"I can agree with that. Anything to get out of this cramped library. What do you propose?"

Before Jaina answered, she looked over at Brandon to get his input. The man was sharp as a tack and may have invaluable input as well. Brandon did not seem very interested in the books either. He wore a smile from ear to ear. He was still admiring the locals, unable to contain his excitement at their discovery.

Major Nazario was looking at him as well and asked, "Are you doing okay? Why are you so darn happy at a time like this?"

Brandon looked at him, eyes snapping back to reality.

"Because they're freaking elves!"

Jaina looked at him, puzzled. Nazario wore a look of similar puzzlement on his face. That was such a strange thing to say.

Jaina asked, "What are you talking about? What are elves?"

"I realize you probably don't understand, but being the nerd I am, I read a lot of old fantasy b-... books and stories. I know that technology has all but rendered that genre extinct, but I still enjoy it. These people look just like elves from these stories."

Jaina could not help but let a tiny smile form on her face.

Nazario shook his head and kept his voice low as he said, "Now is not the time for fantasies. We're in reality, and the last time I checked, it's a reality in desperate need of help. Our people are stranded in space in case you forgot."

Brandon avoided eye contact with Nazario, instead eyeing the book in his hands.

"I'm s-... sorry. It's just that in the stories, they're often t-... tall and nearly always have pointy ears. They are very in t-... tune with nature. They often have c-... control of magic. The Undaari are obviously not elves, but I c-... can't help but compare them. It's like I'm living in an old fantasy st-... story."

Another worried looking Undaari entered the archives. He was even older in appearance than those they had encountered so far. Jaina's eyes followed the newcomer as he made his way straight to Jarreck.

He had the same sort of cape on that Jarreck and Kiva wore but lacked the armor. These were the only three Undaari she had witnessed wearing the cerulean capes. Jaina figured the capes must signify something special after seeing their blue ones, plus the white and gold she had seen in the King's Court.

Brandon leaned over and whispered so that only Jaina could hear, "I must s-... say, for a civilization that's so technologically inferior, they're very advanced socially.  In my readings, I have n-... noticed that they have an elected monarch with a council of advisors."

Jaina looked at Brandon as Nazario continued to monitor the three Undaari.

"That's rather unusual," she said.  "At least in Earth's history.  I still need to learn a lot more about their social system to help with diplomacy.  Is there anything that would point to them being the aggressors against the Noxxons?  Just want to make sure we're not helping the bad guys."

Brandon cocked an eyebrow before responding, "No.  Besides, the elves are rarely the bad guys.  What's m-... more interesting is that the monarch usually endorses their replacement before death and the people can choose to elect that person or vote for another.  They all work t-... together for the betterment of their people and planet.  They seem to want to be passive and only reluctantly enter c-... conflict against the Noxxons."

"Are you sure?  These people just seem too nice.  It's like they want us to believe that they're completely innocent.  I mean, they carry rather intimidating weapons."

Brandon laughed.  "Well, if the expression w-... wouldn't hurt a fly had a definition, it's these guys.  Despite their warrior appearance, they don't want anything to do with b-... battle.  We could actually learn a lot from them.  They're everything humans should have been.

"If you noticed, there is little wood used here.  If they have need of wood, they try to scavenge for it or only trim it off trees.  They even gr-... grow thick grass on the roofs of most of their buildings.  Even the books here in the library use more of a clothlike material for pages rather than paper.  Their c-... conservation techniques are far in advance of anything we've ever had.  Admittedly, these t-... texts are a little biased."

Jaina was very impressed by this information. *Hopefully, we can be good friends.*  Major Nazario shook his head at Brandon.  Garren and Monkley were at a table in the corner.  Each wore a smirk as they shook their heads as well.  James had fallen asleep at his desk and Piers was struggling next to him. *Freaking peacekeepers.*

Nazario nudged Jaina, drawing her attention back from Brandon.  He gestured for her to follow him. They walked over to Jarreck and the other Undaari, leaving Brandon to continue admiring from afar.

As they approached, Jarreck and the elder Undaari turned to face them.  Jarreck spoke quickly, preventing further conversation.

"This is Councilor Gierdahl.  He's an important person among my people.  We need to speak privately for a moment, please excuse us."

Jaina watched, slack jawed, as they walked away, then looked at Nazario.  She could see the disappointment on his face.  Jarreck had clearly not wanted them involved.  She suspected this meeting had to do with the Noxxons and Jarreck's frustrations.  Only Kiva was left in the room watching over them.

Jaina leaned over and whispered, "I told you they were suspicious of us.  Jarreck really doesn't want to deal with us, nor does he trust our intentions.  We need to do something to earn their trust.  Maybe the woman can help us out."

Nazario looked over at Kiva.  Jaina followed his eyes and began to study her as well.  There was an air of energy about her.  Jaina imagined she was a fierce warrior.  She had misleadingly soft features that Jaina thought many would underestimate.

Jaina looked back at Nazario and smiled.  He was ogling the Undaari woman.  *Does he find her attractive?  He's staring really intensely at her.*  She nudged Nazario and broke his concentration.  He looked back at her, blood rushing into his cheeks.  Before she could approach Kiva, Jarreck returned.

"If you don't mind my asking, what was that about?" Jaina questioned Jarreck.

Jarreck looked at her, surprise showing in his face before he snarled, "I don't believe you really need to know about it.  It's a private matter."

Jaina understood confidentiality well.  She knew that Nazario would, too.

Nazario replied, "If this has to do with the Noxxons, we'd love to be of assistance.  Maybe we can convince you that we're not a threat to your people."

Jarreck appeared surprised at the observation.  Jaina was impressed by Nazario's diplomacy and confidence.  Definitely not your typical peacekeeper.  Jarreck's eyes narrowed as he examined them both.

He hesitantly replied, "There's nothing that can be done from here.  I'm on the King's order to escort you around here.  Even Councilor Gierdahl didn't seem too interested in the Noxxons in light of your presence."

Without hesitation, Major Nazario responded, "Don't you have to escort us throughout your lands as well?  Maybe we could do some exploring?"

Jarreck smiled curiously but seemed to understand.

He stated, "I don't like the idea of taking you people anywhere else, but as long as you don't get in my way, at least I can do my job.  I suppose we could begin your outdoor research.  There are some interesting places further south where I'm sure you'll gain a lot of knowledge."

# Chapter 8

## Hunt

 They were packed up and on their way to the stables less than half an hour later.  When they arrived, Nazario was awestruck by the size of their mounts. They were called zakeri and had to be bigger than the elephants in the zoos back on Earth.  He kept his distance as he examined the great creatures.

Though feline in appearance, zakeri seemed far more ferocious than any cats back on Earth.  Like most other things throughout the city, they were vibrantly colored with turquoise feathers fringed in pink and purple covering them head to tail.  The pink and purple tips gave the zakeri a striped appearance.  The creatures reminded him of tigers with yellow noses and the same bright cyan eyes as the Undaari.

As a white cloaked Undaari brought them out of the stables, the zakeri stretched their wings, filling the street.  Nazario could see long feathery tails trailing behind them.  Standing near the great winged beasts, he realized he was barely the size of one of its legs.

Nazario looked over at his team.  They were all wide eyed as they shied away from the massive animals.  Brandon was barely containing his excitement as he bounced and smiled like a child.  Brandon was asking the Undaari lots of questions about the zakeri.  He noticed Garren had taken a peculiar interest as well, though was not as vocal about it.  Instead, Garren was the first to approach the zakeri and examined them closely without touching.

Nazario overheard some of the questions that Brandon was asking and learned that most Undaari rode the smaller jentar.  Their party was only allowed to take three zakeri out on this trip.  Since humans were smaller than their Undaari counterpart, they could squeeze an extra rider onto the backs of these animals. As it was, Sergeants James and Piers would not be able to join.

"James, Piers, get back to the Inquisitor and check in on Reigns. Also, please relay an update to the *Jericho* informing them we've made contact with the locals."

"Yes, sir," the Sergeants replied in unison.

"Peace never dies."

"With keepers in the skies," they replied with a salute then turned on their heels and were gone.

Those still continuing the mission would be joined by another Undaari named Ferani, to command the third zakeri. He was fierce looking man, with a white cape over his armor. He was a caretaker from the King's Guard and would ensure the animals were not misused. Apparently, the creatures were highly valued and kept close watch over.

They had only been granted permission to use these mounts because of the special circumstances. They did not discover aliens every day. Normally, only the King's advisors, the Councilors, and the White Guard got to use these fierce mounts. Nazario understood it was all for show and appreciated the diplomacy of it. *Sometimes negotiations can be fun.*

One by one, they mounted the zakeri on their lightweight saddles. Nazario sat behind Jarreck on the lead mount. They were followed by Brandon, Monkley and their Undaari escort, Ferani, squeezing on the second mount. Finally, Kiva commanded the rear mount with Jaina and Garren behind her.

With a whistle from Jarreck, the zakeri underneath Nazario bounded forward. Their mounts trotted through the city, weaving around foot traffic until they passed through the city gates. Once they were in the open grass plains outside, the zakeri accelerated to a full sprint. Nazario had to grasp Jarreck around the waist to keep from losing his seat. The zakeri showed off their speed and agility with a terrifying prowess.

Jarreck called back with a ready check, and then directed his mount to take flight with another whistle. Wide turquoise wings spread to the sides just in front of Nazario and the zakeri leapt three stories into the air before it even began flapping. The other two zakeri followed suit immediately, well trained to follow the commands of their lead.

Nazario nearly fell off the saddle as they soared into the sky, even with his death grip on Jarreck. *These things don't have inertial dampeners like our ships.* The acceleration sucked the air out of his lungs, leaving him unable to catch his breath until they slowed high in the air. The thin air at this high altitude did not help either.  His heart was pounding as the wind raced across his face.  It was a spectacular rush.  He could not hold back a smile this time.

The views were nearly as breathtaking as the acceleration had been.  Nazario saw the sun setting in front of them, painting the sky in majestic oranges and pinks, leaving him speechless.  Nazario was not sure that anyone on his team could find their breath well enough to speak, even if they wanted to.

The flight might not have been as comfortable as the ship, but it was far more exhilarating.  He could see the jungle extending a great distance to his right through the clear skies while there were mountains far to their left.  Then they turned south to follow the forest.

As the skies darkened, Nazario noticed there was something glowing blue in parts of the forest.  He was unable to discern the source of the glow when the zakeri began to descend toward their destination.  When they set down, Nazario realized he was not the only one to notice.

Brandon asked Jarreck, "W-... what's that blue glow in the forest?"

"It's the Alackai.  The source of our life and magic."

"Magic?  What do you mean by m-... magic?" Brandon asked, unable to hide his interest.

Jarreck answered with a question of his own, "Do you not have magic where you come from?"

"No, there's no such thing as m-... magic.  Humans used to believe in it, but we realize now that magic was just our explanation for things we didn't understand.  Very few p-... people even remember the stories of magic," Brandon replied before he looked sideways at Jaina and Nazario, a smug look on his face.

Jarreck cocked a thin eyebrow at Brandon before responding, "Well, maybe in your home you don't have it, but we have it here.  Only certain people are Graced by the Alackai and able to use its strength.  My Society is made up entirely of these people."

Brandon conceded, "I guess we just d-... don't understand how things in this world work.  We're new here and don't want to be ignorant. We would be most appreciative if you could t-... teach us more about your ways."

Jarreck smiled.  "Let me show you something small."

He took a deep breath and began tracing his hands through the air in a triangular pattern.  As he moved his hands, his cyan eyes started to glow brightly, his skin gained a blue tinge, and then bright blue flames encased his hands. He transitioned quickly from the pattern to thrusting his right hand forward. Cerulean fire erupted from his hand and blasted a large rock in the forest leaving black scorch marks across its surface.

Nazario jumped back. He was thankful to find he was not the only one. He did not understand what he had just seen. Everyone was staring at the rock. Nazario was certain he was the only one to notice a slight wince on Jarreck's face during the display.

He was also the first to speak. "Did you just create fire out of thin air?"

Jarreck nodded. "The air is not thin here. It is rich and full of life. The Alackai Graces us with the strength to protect our lands."

Brandon's eyes lit up again.

He leaned over to Major Nazario and privately whispered, "This Alackai m-… must be the energy readings we picked up. There has to be something in the ground producing the energy. Somehow, these people have evolved in a way to harness the energy with their body and mind. This is amazing. We n-… *need* to study this further. Maybe if we help them, they'll teach us more about it. If we can harness this energy, we can save the *Jericho*."

Major Nazario looked back to Jarreck.

"We clearly have a lot to learn about your people and the Alackai. Perhaps we can learn more once we figure out this Noxxon situation."

Jarreck squinted his eyes at the humans before correcting him, "*If* we can stop the Noxxons from whatever they're planning, I'll gladly teach you everything we know. Their camp was about an hour walk south from here. Let's hurry."

Brandon leaned over to Jaina and whispered quietly, "I c-… can't wait to start studying this. The scientific implications are as-… astounding. And I bet you're starting to take my love of fantasy seriously now. Elves were very often portrayed to be magic wielders. We're literally in the m-… middle of an epic fantasy book."

Jaina smiled and playfully rolled her eyes while shaking her head. Nazario watched their exchange. *How can they flirt at a time like this?* But at least someone had hope. He was not so sure he had any left. Things kept getting more and more complicated. Now he had new tasks. A lot of things had to work right for his mission to be a success.

From here, they walked in silence. They still had a short distance to travel and did not want to be spotted while flying around. Ferani stayed behind to watch the zakeri as was his duty as caretaker. Major Nazario noted how nimble the Undaari were as they hiked through the forest. And surprisingly light footed. He worried he would not hear them coming if they were trying to sneak up on him. This made them a dangerous foe should his people ever wrong them, and history reminded him, they probably would.

He found himself struggling to keep up with the long Undaari strides but managed. The oxygen rich atmosphere gave him the boost he needed to push himself harder and longer than usual. The lower than Earth gravity did not hurt either. Despite this, he found himself to be winded once they reached their destination. He saw that the others were struggling at least as much as he was, the civilians covered in sweat. They were not in the same type of shape as the peacekeepers.

Their destination was a large clearing in the woods. Monkley stayed back with Jaina and Brandon while Nazario, Garren, Kiva, and Jarreck moved forward to investigate. Nazario looked out into the clearing and noticed that the camp had been cleared out. Fires still smoldered; the Noxxons had only recently moved on. They entered the clearing together, keeping their eyes open for trouble.

Jarreck examined the tracks, trying to determine where the Noxxons had gone. Though it was dark outside, the forest created enough ambient blue light that they could still see reasonably well. Nazario found the forest glow to almost be that of a celestial body. Neither Jarreck nor Kiva used artificial light to search, so Nazario decided that his team would not either.

They were looking through the remnants of the camp when they heard noise from the forest. It was not from the rest of his squad. Eyes scanning the tree line, Nazario determined the sound was emanating from the forest right where Jarreck had placed the Noxxons' path. Nazario looked to Jarreck for answers, but the moment Nazario and Jarreck locked eyes, both Undaari vanished, leaving him and Garren alone. *We've been tricked!*

The next moment, two enormous, armored beings emerged from the forest and walked into the clearing. Though shorter than the Undaari, these things were still a full head taller than him. These were intimidating warriors straight out of nightmares. These must be the Noxxons.

Nazario and Garren froze; they had nowhere to hide. Without other options, they readied their exosuit's right arm mounted blasters. Yellow eyes, peering through metal helms, locked on Nazario. He felt his heart stop as the metal clad monsters roared out and charged. One carried a massive axe in its hand while the other wielded a large mace. Nazario had little doubt that either of those weapons could end his life in a single swing.

Nazario and Garren began firing their Valor blasters at them, but the white energy blasts were just absorbed into the armor and black rocky skin of the Noxxons. Nazario realized how ineffective their weapons were. All their technology and they were about to be slaughtered by creatures from an iron age. He hoped a stronger setting might make a difference as he charged his Valor arm cannon to its max. This setting was only used for emergencies when trapped. Fitting.

Before he could fire, one of the Noxxons fell over, a gnarly, meter-long arrow had appeared in his neck between plates of armor. The other one hesitated as it saw its partner fall. Yellow eyes scanned around for the unseen threat. The monster elicited a loud growl, baring sharp yellow teeth.

Jarreck appeared out of nowhere, curved blade drawn. The Undaari grabbed the second Noxxon by the head from behind, forcing its face upward. He reached around and quickly slit its throat through another gap in its armor. Blood splattered over Nazario and Garren as the Noxxon had been nearly on top of them. Jarreck let the Noxxon fall to the ground next to its comrade.

# Chapter 9
## Threats

Jarreck eyed the humans apologetically and explained, "I'm sorry if we scared you or made you feel abandoned. Our strength is in our stealth and speed. The Noxxons value their brute force."

Major Nazario stared back at him. Jarreck could see a flash of anger across his face for just a second.

Finally, Nazario replied through a clenched jaw, "You definitely had me thinking we'd been betrayed, but I'm glad I could count on you."

Jarreck nodded. "Your weapons seem weak and ineffective. There are vulnerable points in their armor that you must learn to focus on."

Nazario pursed his lips.

"Those blades you carry are impressive. And I think it's time for some answers. Who are these Noxxons exactly? What were they doing here?"

Kiva reappeared next to Jarreck, right in front of Nazario. The man nearly jumped out of his armor.

She answered for Jarreck, holding her blade up, "These are called sigridir. They are carried by every Undaari warrior and are designed to cut through the thick skin of the Noxxons... who were here searching for some ancient artifact that I *thought* was just myth, until recently." She looked at Jarreck before continuing, "The area is secure. There are no other Noxxons nearby. It looks like they took the artifact back East toward their territory."

Jarreck flashed Kiva a stern look before scolding her, "Kiva. You shouldn't have told them that."

"What exactly is this artifact?" Nazario asked with furrowed eyebrows as his eyes bounced between Jarreck and Kiva.

Jarreck continued to glare at Kiva while responding, "It's none of your concern, human. It's an Undaari issue that we'll handle. You've already learned more than I should've allowed."

Nazario took a deep breath before responding, "Look Jarreck, you don't have to trust us, but without us here with you right now, you won't be able to complete your mission. We could just head back to the archives if you'd prefer. Personally, I'd rather try to help you and keep this mission going."

Jarreck was very reluctant to respond, but after consideration chose to answer his question. It was not as if he had much choice under the circumstances.

"I'm not sure about the specifics of the artifact, but that thing is likely related to the old magic. Those arcane magics were banned due to their extremely dangerous nature. They couldn't be contained once unleashed, and even worse, they were used to create the most powerful weapons ever conceived. Thankfully, the key to opening the artifact, and others like it, was lost decades ago. There's no way to regain this ancient knowledge."

Nazario asked with growing concern in his voice, "How do you know the key is lost and hasn't been recovered by the Noxxons as well?"

Jarreck looked down and turned around. He locked watery eyes with Kiva.

Taking a deep breath, he replied, "Because I was there when they came for it. My father was the last Master of the Ancient Text. He had the key, and it was destroyed in the fire that burned down my childhood home."

Both Nazario and Kiva looked at Jarreck in surprise.

Kiva responded, her voice raised and full of pain, "The myths are true then? And you knew about them? The ancient texts actually exist?"

"Yes, but there's no longer a Master of the Ancient Text. No more Keeper. I'm sorry I never told you before but seeing as the Noxxons have discovered our darkest secrets, I suppose it's time. When the Noxxons murdered my father nearly sixty years ago, most of those secrets died with him."

Jarreck shifted uncomfortably. His eyes were focused on Kiva. He was not speaking to anyone else. Given the circumstances, he did not care that the others were there. *Especially if the Society is compromised.* He was responsible for the humans, whether he liked it or not, so they might as well know what they were getting into if they were going to tag along.

He continued his tale, "I was sworn to secrecy. Only two others in our Society ever knew about this. The Master of the Ancient Text was passed down in secret through my family. I was too young when my dad died for him to pass it along. I knew of my dad's role, but never learned the secrets."

Kiva shook her head. "No! That *can't* be true! That means that our past Societies truly committed those atrocities! They really wielded the Alackai as a tool of terror and dominated all the people in Undaalan! That means that people really do fear us. There really is a darkness in our past."

"Yes, but a darkness that's been locked away. We're no longer concerned with the wars waged in the past. The First Society fell from within. Dralvic failed to take over the Second Society. It no longer pertains to us. The Society needed to move forward in the light and become the beacon of the Undaari. We're the guardians against chaos now and have learned from our mistakes. When our Society was formed for the third time, we chose to keep the knowledge of the arcane arts locked away for good, and to focus on our ability to protect our lands."

"This is horrible. I really thought the Society stood for something good. We could lose everything, our Society, our people, our lands, everything. What if someone else has taken up Dralvic's mantle, trying to take over the Society? How could we stop the Society from committing such ruthless acts again if the arcane arts resurface? We need to do something!" Kiva yelled frantically, her tears unchecked.

Brandon approached the Undaari and Majors as they spoke with Monkley and Jaina right behind him. He had witnessed the attack. His heart still pumped hard from seeing the Noxxons. He looked at the Undaari and noted how upset they were over the events that had just transpired. He had heard their conversation and felt bad they were having to deal with such an ordeal. It seemed humans were not the only ones experiencing trying times.

Brandon spoke up nervously, "We can st-... stop them. Whatever happened in the p-... past doesn't dictate what will happen in the future. Our people, too, have a d-... dark history. But we have grown stronger from it. It's n-... not too late."

Jarreck shot Brandon a dirty look and spat, "What help could you possibly provide? Your weapons are useless. You're more of a hindrance than an assistance. We don't even know where they've taken the artifact."

"M-... Maybe we could help with that. Our ship has t-... technology that can track the energy signatures of your magic. We c-... can figure out where it currently is," Brandon offered, trying to control his stutter better.

"And we can follow their trail in the meantime," offered Nazario.

"Are you sure about that? We've already seen how ineffective your technology is," Kiva commented sourly.

Brandon moved over to the dead Noxxons and pulled a scanner out of his backpack. He scanned their bodies, adding to his growing database for this planet. Brandon looked back at Kiva and responded to her comment, not stopping his actions.

"We were able to m-... measure a lot of the energy on this p-... planet prior to our approach. We shouldn't have any issues with tr-... tracking this artifact if it's imbued with the A-... Alackai as well."

He could feel her eyes on him as he documented this species. This might be his only safe opportunity to capture the Noxxons. He noted their yellow eyes and overgrown teeth that extended out of their mouths like tusks, ending in sharp points.

They seemed foreign compared to the Undaari and other life in the area. Everything else was so colorful, but these things were more like obsidian. Their hands were large enough to squeeze a human head; a visualization he had difficulty getting out of his mind. These things were terrifying.

Jarreck watched him with a cocked eyebrow.

His shoulders sagged in defeat before he replied, "Well, let's give that a shot. Their fortress is on an island off the eastern coast of the mainland. I can't imagine where else they'd take it. Numitor Island is heavily guarded, and we would have little chance of recovering the artifact once it's there. If we knew their route, it would be easier to catch them. We need to move quickly if we're going to stop them."

Nazario nodded, "Monkley, can you escort Jaina and Brandon back to our ship? Be careful, and radio us once you make it back. Keep us updated on everything. Go ahead and send another update to the *Jericho*. They would be interested to know what we've discovered here."

Monkley nodded and saluted Nazario, "Peace never dies."

Monkley turned and stepped off for the woods. Garren trotted over to walk with Monkley. Brandon and Jaina followed close behind. Monkley leaned over and whispered to Garren. Brandon could barely overhear Monkley's brief conversation with Garren from the back of the group.

"How come you get to have all the fun?" Monkley asked.

"Because I'm still your boss and want to enjoy myself while I still can," Garren jokingly replied.

"Next time, we fight together. I wouldn't want anything happening to you in your old age."

They both laughed. Garren stopped walking and Monkley gave him an unprofessional two fingered salute. Monkley smiled and turned, leading Jaina and Brandon back to the zakeri. Garren made his way back to Nazario. Jaina broke the silence as they walked, speaking quietly to Brandon.

"That was terrifying. Those Noxxons are the scariest thing I've ever seen in my life. It's no wonder the Undaari fear and despise them so much."

Brandon's head shook as he replied, "Those things are m-... massive. Without our technology, humans would never be able to fight them. They look like they c-... could crush us like a grape. I feel terribly for the Undaari."

With a blank face, Jaina said, "I wonder exactly how long they've been at war. It sounded like thousands of years. I couldn't fathom thousands of years of war."

"Me n-... neither. On the flip side, the history of this planet is m-... marvelous. There are thousands of years of it. I c-... could study my whole life and never learn it all."

Jaina smiled and replied, "Agreed. I'm fascinated by all the diversity and life and culture. I never could've imagined this is what we'd find when we got here or that we would even find alien life. Actually, I suppose that *we're* the aliens on this planet. I just hope that we can assist the Undaari through this time so that we can have the opportunity to learn more about them. Hopefully, their Alackai is the answer we need to save the rest of our people."

Brandon nodded in agreement. He was not a fan of the Noxxons but loved everything else about this place so far, including making a new friend.

"The Alackai is *incredible*. It's in-... inconceivably powerful from what I've seen so far. There truly is a chance that if we learn how it works, we can p-... power our ship enough to get it here."

Brandon could no longer contain himself. His anxiety gave way to excitement as he rambled on even more, "I have to say it again; this world is straight out of a fantasy n-... novel from centuries ago. The Noxxons are like orcs or trolls. There's magic here. The zakeri are like griffins. The genre may have nearly died out, but like I said, I've always had an affinity for it. Now we're living it. I know our p-... people are going through hell right now, but I can't help but smile and be excited about all this."

Monkley kept his eyes forward and did not contribute to their conversation, ever the professional peacekeeper. Jaina continued to engage in the topic. Brandon was thankful for her. He needed the distraction from the reality of things. It helped him keep his nerves in check.

Jaina asked as they continued to walk, "Where did you learn all this stuff? I didn't think anyone really liked that stuff anymore."

"I had a large c-... collection of physical books from this genre back on Earth. I brought a few of my favorites with me on the *Jericho* to pass the t-... time. They had always helped me find an escape when life got tough. Maybe after we save our people, I could show them to you? You m-... might even appreciate them more now."

Jaina showed the tiniest of smiles on her face as she answered, "Maybe I will. After living it, I'm curious to see if they got it right."

He felt a warmth in his stomach as he explained, "These books are always filled with d-... death and fighting, and that's terrible, but I still can't help but be excited. Elves are most often the good guys battling the evil trolls and orcs. The orcs and tr-... trolls are often brutes that are physically imposing, yet dumb and wild. The comparisons are endless."

Jaina let out a small laugh as they walked. "So, you're saying the authors from hundreds of years ago actually got it right without realizing it?"

"Well, if you'd have t-... told me that we would get to our destination and find intelligent life, I would've been shocked. But I never in a million years would've g-... guessed that our fantasy stories would've been reality, and that we'd see them firsthand. The most exciting p-... part though, is the Alackai. I've always dreamed of using magic."

Ferani must have heard them from behind a tree as they approached, since he responded shortly, "Do not think the Alackai is yours to take." He stepped out for them to see. "She has a will of her own and chooses who can use it. She's only ever blessed the Undaari and won't be meddled with."

Brandon replied apologetically, "I d-... don't wish for you to think we're t-... trying to steal it. We simply hope that the Alackai c-... can help us protect our people as well. We are hoping it can g-... guide us to find a new home."

"And where exactly do you think your people will live in our lands?

It sounds like you have far too many people to live alongside us."

Brandon looked at Ferani in realization and prodded, "D-... Do your people know about the other landmasses on this p-... planet?"

Ferani replied, "The Noxxons control it, but it's far too small for your people."

"No, there are other c-... continents here, massive ones, far larger than this one. They appeared uninhabited though; no one lives there. We c-... could settle there and be friends from afar."

Ferani was clearly confused as he looked down on them, "There are no other lands. No ship has ever sailed off to explore and returned."

"I'm sorry, b-... but you've been misinformed. There are t-... two other continents. Ones that we could occupy for our p-... people without imposing on you and the Undaari."

"As long as you don't try to interfere with our people, I have no issues with that. I cannot say the same for the rest of us. We already have too many others in Undaalan," Ferani said as he glared at the humans.

"We won't interfere. In fact, w-... we need to go to our ship so that we can help your people. It's near your c-... capital city in the forest," Brandon said.

The four of them squeezed onto the back of a zakeri. Ferani let out a series of whistles before guiding their zakeri into the air. Brandon watched as the other two zakeri lifted off without riders and turned east toward Nazario and the others. *How do they understand commands so well?*

# Chapter 10

## Trap

Nazario took the rear guard as he and Garren followed Kiva and Jarreck. Jarreck led them eastward, following the trail of the Noxxons. It was rather cool at night in the forest as they walked. Nazario felt relaxed strolling through the woods. It was serene. *How did our people destroy such wondrous places back on Earth?*

As they walked, he noticed the Noxxons were not difficult to follow. That many large brutish people trampling their way through the forest left a pretty clear trail. The Noxxons didn't seem to value nature like the Undaari. This eased his concerns that the Undaari might be deceiving them about the nature of the conflict. He could see the first rays of sunlight through the treetops to their rear. *Is it morning already?*

His gut started to churn. The hairs on the back of his neck stood up as his eyes darted around.

"Jarreck, is it common for enemy soldiers to leave such an obvious trail in enemy territory?" he asked.

Jarreck stopped, eyes scanning the woods in the low light.

"The Noxxons are savages and don't bother with stealth, but this is excessive, even for them. So no, no it isn't," he responded.

Jarreck disappeared and Kiva immediately followed suit.

"I don't like it when they do that. Be ready," Nazario whispered to Garren before taking cover behind a tree.

Moments later, Nazario heard rustling noises coming from ahead in the forest. At least twenty Noxxons came into view through the trees, charging hard and fast for them. Nazario swore he could feel the vibrations through the ground from their stampede. He took a deep breath to steady his heart.

"Wait until they're close.  Full charge.  Don't miss."

Garren nodded his acknowledgement.  There was no chance they could hide.  The Noxxons obviously knew they were being followed.  It was a trap.  He prepped his suit's Valor arm cannon, ensuring it was still set to full power.  Their suit batteries could not sustain that power level long term.  It was a necessary risk though.  He wished he could have tested this out before his life depended on it.

The Noxxons were close, only about twenty meters away, when Nazario and Garren simultaneously blasted the two Noxxons in front.  It had the desired effect, lifting the Noxxons off their feet and throwing them back into the knot of Noxxons behind them.  Each flash of white energy melted through the thick metal armor leaving a ring of orange around the hole.

The craters in their chests were still smoking when Nazario and Garren fired their next rounds.  They struck down the next two as well, leaving four dead Noxxons in seconds.  If they could keep their distance, they might have a chance to survive against such odds.

The rest of the Noxxons stopped in their tracks, the charge breaking roughly fifteen meters away.  Nazario knew their hesitation would not last long.  The next moment, Jarreck and Kiva appeared next to their enemies, flanking the Noxxons.  They wrapped their curved blades around the necks of two Noxxons, dispatching them swiftly.  They moved quickly, killing two more before the Noxxons could react.

The Noxxons recovered surprisingly fast and closed the gap with both flanks.  Close quarters combat was an undeniable strength of the Noxxons.  Though more skilled and better equipped, the humans and Undaari were not going to survive very long against greater numbers of bigger, stronger adversaries.  Speed was their greatest ally in this fight.  They were able to dodge most of the blows that the Noxxons aimed at them, if only barely.

The Undaari had their curved blades swinging fast and hard, while the humans had their long, serrated, Titanium-Carbon Fiber alloy knives slashing.  Another two Noxxons went down, gutted, but things were beginning to deteriorate. Though the Noxxon numbers had been cut in half, they gained the advantage late in the fight.

Neither he nor Garren could fire their Valor canons safely in close quarters.  They would risk injuring or killing themselves or their new allies.  The Undaari had difficulty penetrating the defenses of so many enemies at once and were beginning to physically tire.  Both pairs of fighters faced off with several larger opponents.

Things were already beginning to look hopeless, when one of the Noxxons landed a heavy blow to Garren's left arm with its mace. His bone and Reliant sleeve shattered with an audible *crack*. He went down with a scream. Nazario lost his footing, as he turned to his comrade, and fell under the assault of the Noxxons. The four Noxxons assaulting the humans charged in for the kill, when a loud, ear-shattering scream pierced the sky.

Turquoise flashed across Nazario's vision. Two zakeri slammed down into the Noxxons. One tackled all four Noxxons attacking the humans at once. Its sheer size knocking them to the ground. With its razorlike yellow claws now extended, it shredded three of the Noxxons, while its massive jaw clamped down on, and ripped up, the fourth.

The other zakeri crashed into the six Noxxons attacking the Undaari, sending three sprawling to the ground, while the other three recovered and fled. The fierce predator made quick work on the three Noxxons it had caught. Blood covered its face and enormous paws.

Nazario had not moved an inch since the surprise arrival. Zakeri were creatures he now feared. He stared in awe as the winged beast chewed up the Noxxons that had almost killed him. Blood covered the forest floor around him. Garren groaned next to him.

A few meters away, Jarreck looked at Kiva and let out a sigh of relief. Nazario watched him turn and pursue the fleeing Noxxons. Jarreck quickly drew his bow from underneath his cape and loosed an arrow at the retreating Noxxons. The arrow penetrated a Noxxons neck, right where Nazario assumed its spinal column would be.

Before it had even hit the ground, Jarreck fired a second arrow, piercing the knee of a second Noxxon fleeing. He fired again, hitting it in the waist. He closed the gap and slit its throat before it could defend itself.

The final Noxxon managed to escape through the woods, while Jarreck finished off the second Noxxon. Jarreck returned to his party and knelt to catch his breath. He reached up to pet the zakeri in front of him, scratching under its chin.

"Good timing, my friend."

Nazario heard Garren groan again, drawing him back from his stupor. He moved quickly to administer first aid to his companion. The Reliant Exosuit had highly sophisticated, compact first aid kits attached to their hips. He splinted Garren's arm and injected a serum directly to the wounded area. This serum anesthetized the injury and stimulated the healing process. Nazario knew it would only take a couple days to heal completely.

Jarreck stood up and warned, "We need to move quickly, before more Noxxons show up. How's your friend?"

"He'll be fine. We can get moving now," replied Nazario.

Jarreck had fought with a ferocity that he had never seen before. Nazario did not want to make enemies with these people. He would do pretty much whatever they wanted until this mission was over.

Jarreck nodded and smiled.

"That's good news. I see your weapons aren't totally useless in battle. You both fought well."

Jarreck boosted Garren onto the rear mount behind Kiva as she pulled him up. Jarreck and Nazario mounted the second zakeri. They lifted off and headed north.

Nazario noted a large river to their right as he clung to Jarreck. It looked like a major source of water for the entire forest. They flew high over the dense forests for a while before they reached a fortress in the middle of a lake, which fed into the river.

Commander Braylon sat back in his chair on the Command Deck. It had been three days since Major Nazario had taken the *Inquisitor.* They had received reports from the other three ships that had gone searching for resources, but not his. He kept checking with Captain Hunter, their Communications Officer, even knowing he would be first to know when they received a report.

General Titus entered the Command Deck and walked straight up to Braylon. "Sir, can I speak to you privately in your office for a moment?"

"Of course, General," Braylon said enthusiastically. "Anything to distract myself from all this waiting around."

Braylon stood and followed the General into the office. After he walked through the doorway, he realized there were others in his office already. His eyebrows raised as he noticed they were all armed. General Titus closed the door behind them and folded his arms behind his back, blocking the entrance.

"Commander Braylon, you are unfit to command this vessel. Your incompetence has jeopardized this mission and left me with no other choice than to relieve you of duty. You will not be allowed to leave this office until we have done what you've failed to do and saved everyone. If you cooperate, we will make this easy on you. I do not covet your position, so once this is done, you may return to command. Questions?"

Braylon's heart sank. *This can't be real.*

He pleaded with his General, "Wait, what? Why are you doing this? No one will stand for this."

General Titus' deep voice responded, "Everyone who needs to be involved is already on board with this course of action. We have already received word from Major Nazario. There is a powerful energy source on ZX-746. There is civilization there as well. I will not let you mess this up for our people like you have everything else. Do what I say, and no one will ever have to know how close you came to dooming us all. Your family included."

His gut knotted up. "My family? Are they okay?"

"They're safe… for now. But I would *prefer* your cooperation. That will make this much easier."

Braylon's shoulders fell as he slouched forward.

"What do you need?"

General Titus strode back onto the Command Deck, leaving one officer to guard the Commander's office from the outside. His chest was puffed out and his head held high. He wore a half smile across his face. His navy-blue uniform was just as crisp and clean as ever.

"Alright everyone, here's the deal. Commander Braylon needs privacy to think about how we proceed. He has requested that no one disturbs him until further notice. Please ensure that Colonel Jansen and the *Plaintiff* are scrambled quickly to go assist Major Nazario."

He looked around the deck before his eyes locked with Captain Hunter's. Captain Hunter gave a barely perceptible nod back to the General.

# Chapter 11

## Help

Jaina, Brandon, and Monkley were greeted by Sergeant Piers when they landed at the *Inquisitor*. It was morning now, and Piers was eyeing both the colorful zakeri and the tall Undaari man in the new light as they approached. Jaina waved to the Sergeant.

"Sergeant James and Reigns are scouting the perimeter, ensuring no unwelcomed guests," Piers said instead of a greeting.

Ferani stayed with the zakeri while the humans boarded the ship and moved to the Command Deck. Once they reached the controls, Piers fired up the ship, bringing everything to life. Brandon turned on the ship's sensors. As the ship powered up, Jaina noticed a flashing light on Nazario's console indicating an incoming message.

She pressed the button to acknowledge the message. It had come from Commander Braylon.

MAJOR NAZARIO, WE HAVE A SECOND SHIP HEADING YOUR WAY, THE *PLAINTIFF*. THEY WILL BE THERE SOON TO OFFER EXTRA SECURITY AND WILL BE CARRYING HEAVY WEAPONRY. THEY SHOULD BE ABLE TO REMOVE ANY THREATS AND SECURE THE ENERGY SOURCE, SO WE CAN SAVE OUR SHIP. TIME IS OF THE ESSENCE. COLONEL JANSEN WILL BE TAKING POINT ON THIS MISSION FROM HERE.

Jaina looked up at her companions. There was a distinct lack of trust behind that message. She thought of their tenuous relationship with the Undaari.

"This isn't good. We can't just drop in a military force at this point. They could be taken as a threat or invasion force and betray what little trust we've built with the Undaari, especially with the Noxxon threat already. They can't have been briefed on the Undaari, yet. That message wouldn't have reached the *Jericho,* so soon. They just know there's intelligent life here controlling a vital power source."

Brandon looked over at her with confusion written all over his face as he asked, "But w-... wouldn't the extra assistance be helpful for fighting the Noxxons?"

Jaina shook her head. *This* was why she was so important on this mission. Diplomacy was her specialty.

"We can't allow them to march in here and wage war for the Alackai. I've seen this before. Military assistance would be construed as both an invasion and us forcing Undaari dependence on us. That would ruin everything we're working for. We're not just securing a power source; we're securing a home. We would never repair the damage. We have to stop this."

Brandon's face was drawn as he responded, "We can't d-... do anything that would ruin our chance to get to know the Undaari! They're way too important. Without their help, it c-... could take years to learn how to use the Alackai, if ever!"

Sergeant Piers glared at her. "We can't disobey direct orders."

"*I'm* a civilian; I don't take orders from the peacekeepers. And *you* are obligated to disobey unlawful orders. Murdering innocents sounds like an unlawful order to me," Jaina countered stiffly.

She never liked the idea of just following orders or using war to solve issues.

"*I* will not be the one to stop this... but I won't stop you either... if you have a plan," Piers added.

Jaina thought for a minute before asking, "What would prevent them from landing on the planet?"

"There isn't anything that would get them to disobey a direct order if they're already on their way. They wouldn't be scared of getting into a fight with a comparatively primitive species. Not to mention, they're scared of losing the *Jericho*," Piers said.

"There m-... might be one thing that would at least buy us some time. An infection. Something d-... deadly. Something that'll make them think twice about landing," Brandon chimed in.

Sergeant Piers nodded, "That might work, at least for a short period. But they would wise up pretty quickly. We might get an extra day or two."

"Then let's do it. Their ship is larger and faster than ours is. We only have a few hours before they reach us. They're risking a lot coming here. I don't think many of our ships have enough fuel to make a round trip. We'll need someone to play the victim. Sergeant Piers, do you care to volunteer? You won't have to say anything," said Jaina.

Sergeant Piers nodded with a frown on his face.

Darkness was already beginning to fall as they descended on their zakeri. Nazario still got a marvelous view of the fortress as they circled it before landing. It was forbidding, yet elegant. Functional, yet impenetrable. The outer wall was black and scarred in blue; each cyan vein glowed faintly in the fading light. It was electrifying.

They landed in a courtyard at the center of the fortress. The inner structures were constructed of the same white marble-like stone that was in Ambrecia, but with more of the obsidian stone as accents. There was an energy to this fortress that he could not comprehend. He looked around at his three companions before settling on Jarreck.

"How is it I can feel energy radiating from this place?"

Jarreck responded with a smile, "It's the Alackai. This fortress was constructed by our Society centuries ago, during the beginning of the Second Society. After that Society collapsed, the Undaari Army took over, continuing its mission. It has protected the river along our border and prevented the Noxxons from invading our territory ever since. This, my friend, is Entfall."

"I should've learned by now that it was the Alackai," Nazario admitted.

He was awestruck, imagining how powerful the Undaari would become if they had access to more advanced technology. This was a species that could grow to unmatched potential with the Alackai. He knew that a positive relationship with these wondrous people would be beneficial for both parties.

Kiva had more to add as they walked the zakeri into the stables, "The Alackai has never failed Entfall. Its magic runs deep preventing Entfall from ever being breached. This place is our greatest hope against the Noxxons."

They exited the stables and were immediately greeted by burgundy caped guards. The guards escorted them straight to the heart of the keep. As they neared the main hall of the fortress, Nazario looked at Kiva.

"Speaking of the Alackai, I keep forgetting you have magic. You can create fire with your bare hands. So why didn't you use that to fight the Noxxons in the forest?" Nazario asked, not hiding his confusion.

Jarreck answered for her, "The Society has taught us to be conservative with our gift. The Alackai is meant to guide and protect us, not wage a war. Besides, it's painful to use. The more power you draw, the more pain it inflicts on the user. We only use it against others in true desperation."

"It felt pretty desperate there for a moment. It seems like using the Alackai would be able to end fights quicker and save Undaari lives," he replied, still not understanding why they would not use their biggest advantage over the Noxxons, even with the risks.

War was painful already. Jarreck glared at Nazario, but Kiva smiled.

She leaned over and whispered, "I never agreed with the Society's view of this either, but it really can be painful."

Nazario was surprised by their different reactions to his observation. He was sure Jarreck was rolling his eyes, though he could not see it. Nazario did not push the conversation any further. His eyes stayed on the Undaari woman for a second longer, before he looked back to his surroundings.

They were escorted into a great chamber that was clearly the seat of power at Entfall. There was an ancient throne at the rear of the chamber, but it sat empty and covered in dust. Their escort was not heading there anyway.

Their destination was a large table on the side of the chamber, which was occupied by many Undaari warriors. It looked like a war table and was abuzz with life. At the head of the table was a fierce looking female who also bore a burgundy cape. As Nazario scanned the chamber, he realized that nearly all the Undaari here wore burgundy capes.

Jarreck walked right up to the female and greeted her with a warm smile and firm grasp of her forearm. Both of their aqua eyes lit up as their muscular arms embraced. Nazario was mesmerized by the sight and power exchanged between the pair.

Jarreck turned to Nazario and Garren and said, "This is Master Jerykka, Warden of Entfall, Shield of the Undaari."

As he examined Jerykka in that instant, he could feel the hairs on the back of his neck rising again. This woman had an aura of strength and confidence emanating from her that was overwhelming. She was muscular and toned with eight abdominal muscles rippling across her core. She wore the same leathery armor as the other Undaari warriors, with the addition of an oversized metal pauldron on her left shoulder. Everything about her told him that she could kill him in an instant without a second thought.

Nazario realized the women in this culture were obviously not treated differently than men, unlike many other cultures. Between Kiva and Jerykka, he had met very strong, respected women among the Undaari who held positions of power. He swore they carried themselves better than anyone he had ever met before. If he had been intimidated by Titus during the Colonial Rebellions, he did not know what to call his feelings now.

Nazario realized he was staring but could not look away. She was dangerous but beautiful, a lethal combination. Everything about her screamed warrior, yet she was undeniably attractive.

She wore her pitch-black hair in braids on the left side of her head, before it joined the rest of her mane, and wrapped around her head and neck to her chest. She too had a sleeve tattoo on her arm, but she had another intricate tattoo that covered a large portion of her left side, which could be seen on her abdomen and left thigh.

He did not understand how every Undaari was in such impressive shape. It was like every one of their people were perfect physical specimens. Even Jarreck, an aging old man, was impressively handsome. He could only hope to look as strong and attractive when he reached a more advanced age.

He processed all this information in just a moment before striding forward, trying to stand tall and firm, so as not to let anyone know how intimidated he was. He was enamored by this powerful person. He shook her hand while she stared him down. Garren shook her hand after.

She looked at Jarreck after releasing the handshakes and asked, "What is this? I've never seen beings like this before."

Jarreck nodded and answered, "They're called humans and they've come to us from beyond the stars. They're interested in learning about our culture and people. However, considering the times, they've offered their assistance with the current threat in exchange for an alliance. There are a few more of them around here."

"From beyond the stars, you say? How incredible. Please tell me that they're stronger than they appear. I can't imagine any of them being able to fight on their own."

Jerykka's eyes questioned the reality of it. Kiva smirked as Jerykka looked the humans up and down. Nazario suspected none of them had thought much of the humans at first either. He found himself wanting to prove himself to these people. He felt that he had handled himself well so far in their fight against the Noxxons.

Jarreck replied, "They've stood side by side with us in battle against the Noxxons. Without them, we might've been overwhelmed. They fight with courage and are rather resilient."

"Noxxons?" Jerykka's focus shifted immediately. "Where were you? We haven't seen Noxxon activity in years. But we've started to hear rumors of movement near our borders. Nothing has been substantiated yet. I've dispatched scouts to check it out. They should be returning soon."

Jarreck looked over at the war table, the center of which was dominated by a large terrain map of their lands. He pointed to the southern reaches of a vast forest.

"Here in the heart of the Lenakai Forest, just east of where I grew up."

"Impossible. The Noxxons haven't penetrated our territory in millennia. We would've detected their presence."

"I was shocked as well. Kiva and I investigated it, though. There were nearly eighty of them in a camp. I don't know how they got there, but they knew where they were going. They were excavating in the forest."

"Excavating for what? How could they have gotten there? Our borders are protected."

Jarreck looked away for a second and took a deep breath before responding, "I probably shouldn't tell you, but I need your help. It was an artifact from the First Society of the Scar. I don't know what they hope to accomplish with it, since Noxxons aren't touched by the Alackai, but they have the artifact. I have no idea what might be in it that they could use."

It worked. Brandon and Jaina looked at each other and let out a sigh of relief. Jaina knew Brandon had been worried that his idea would not work. *Considering how smart he is, he's not very confident in himself.*

Colonel Jansen would keep orbit above the planet, without landing and risking exposure. She was not willing to risk infecting their crew with whatever Sergeant Piers might have. The ruse would only last a couple days at best. She would grow impatient and the desire for action would outweigh the desire for caution.

In the meantime, Jaina asked the *Plaintiff* to perform detailed mapping scans from orbit while they waited. That would fill in any gaps they had missed in their own scans, as well as scan for additional details, such as energy signals across the land. Hopefully, the artifact emitted enough energy to be detected.

Jaina did not have many options to ensure the peacekeeper strike force in orbit did not compromise their mission. She decided to trust in the *Jericho's* leadership and sent a transmission directly to Commander Braylon, begging him to reconsider his plans. She explained the importance of the Undaari, both to the planet and as allies for the future.

Once she finished recording the transmission, she saw they had received the data from the *Plaintiff*. Hopefully, they could find the artifact and its path. They needed to do their part to help the Undaari. This would have been for nothing if they were unable to find it.

Jaina looked over at Sergeant Piers as he walked up, freshly cleaned of his 'sickness.' She nodded to him, letting him know it worked, without saying anything. She watched as Brandon went through the data they were receiving from the *Plaintiff*.

Brandon clicked a few buttons to bring up a 3D rendering of the lands in the middle of the Command Deck. Everyone stood up and gathered around the rendering. As they examined the beauty of the land, Jaina realized they needed more context to understand how it was all laid out, so she retrieved Ferani from outside. As he entered, Ferani looked around slowly, eyeing every inch of the ship. Jaina had forgotten that no Undaari had laid eyes on the *Inquisitor*.

She brought him over to the map and together, they examined it. The landmass was relatively small, maybe the size of Texas back on Earth. There were grass plains to the south and deserts ending in beaches to the east. The north had a snowcapped mountain range spanning the width of the continent while forests covered the remainder, extending from the center into the west where the land ended in cliffs.

Brandon looked at Ferani. "C-... Can you show us where we've traveled so far? Along with any m-... major landmarks or cities?"

Ferani nodded. He showed them their capital city, Ambrecia, confirmed their current location, and traced their previous path. He pointed out the overall scope of the Undaari lands, which included the entirety of the forests and made note of Entfall. He also explained the plains to the south were controlled by another race called Yaxkin, and Numitor Island off the east coast was the stronghold of the Noxxons.

Brandon began to input more information into the system. The forest lit up in celeste colored light along with the tallest peak of the mountain range. The bright blue was laced all over the land. He looked up at the others.

"The b-... blue is the energy reading from the Alackai. It's everywhere. There are a few points that light up p-... particularly bright though. The brightest being near the peak of the t-... tallest mountain, along with Entfall and some exceptionally wide trees scattered throughout the forest. This explains how the Undaari c-... can access the Alackai so readily. It's literally everywhere, especially throughout the forests they live in." He looked up from the map. "There is one outlier th-... though."

He pointed to a large blue spot southeast of Entfall, in the desert at the eastern edge of the Lenakai Forest. It was just north of a lake town Ferani had called Ermaca. They appeared to be following the forest line north, rather than east like Jarreck had previously guessed. It had moved northeast from where they had last seen the Noxxons.

"This is likely the c-... current location of the artifact."

"That's Noxxon territory, though mostly uninhabited," Ferani warned. "That's right where it butts up against our lands. We should be able to make good time and catch them unaware. I would suggest we make for Entfall first."

Brandon and Jaina nodded. She relayed the data gathered to Nazario so he could plan with Jarreck. Jaina also found out that they were already in Entfall, preparing their next move against the Noxxons. Jaina led their group back out to the zakeri after grabbing some fresh supplies and a couple of Peacemaker blaster rifles. They might need extra weaponry in the coming days.

Linnea finally returned to him. Vreeham had been impatiently pacing on the roof, watching the skies. She had been away for longer than expected. The stately winged ropen landed on his shoulder with a screech from its beaked mouth. There was a note attached to her talons. Vreeham removed the note as she nuzzled him, seeking affection for a job well done.

With an absent-minded pet on her pink neck, he read the note:

*He's no longer in Ambrecia. He has others with him. You have failed.*

He would need to take more active measures it seemed...

# Chapter 12
## Awakening

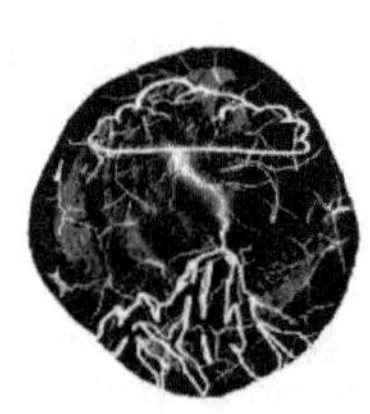 ingdon awoke from a very uncomfortable and restless sleep. He was still trapped in his cage on the back of the cart. He had been a captive of the Yaxkin for two years now. He was nearly fifteen but had lost count of the days since he had been captured and would never know which day was his birthday.

He still had some five years before he reached full maturity, so he had a significant amount more to grow. As it was, Lingdon was already the same height as many of the vertically challenged Yaxkin that he was slave to.

He had learned a lot about his captors during his slavery. He found the Yaxkin to be repugnant people with little morals, but he had no choice but to play nice. He needed to get to know them if he wanted to escape. They were abusive and cruel, not only to their slaves, but to each other. He hated them for all the pain they had caused him and other Undaari living on the borders.

He hoped to escape and pass himself off as a Yaxkin until he could get into the Lenakai Forest. Yaxkin were the shortest of the races in Undaalan, barely up to the chests of most Undaari. Their skin was darker than the Undaari and their eyes much more sensitive.

He could pass as one if he kept himself covered in one of their green cloaks. Since they operated in the sunny plains to the south, rather than the shadowy Lenakai Forest, the Yaxkin wore shaded goggles to protect their eyes. He would need to steal a pair of those as well.

The difficulty in the disguise was their beards. His face was completely hairless as was natural for Undaari, so he was unsure how to pull off their long, grey, braided beards. They were just ugly creatures. Lingdon always wanted to punch his Yaxkin slavers in their large noses.  It might limit their strong sense of smell whenever he tried to run.

He had been planning his escape for a while, but they rarely wandered into the forests.  When they did, conflict usually followed so he was never released from his cell.  Their senses were always heightened during combat anyway.  He needed them to be more at ease for his plan to work.

The Yaxkin had wandered into the Lenakai forest two years ago when they raided Lingdon's home and slaughtered his family in cold blood.  They were not generally slavers by trade, but sometimes they enjoyed the fruits of their conquests.  Lingdon was unlucky enough to be one of those fruits, *or lucky,* depending on how he looked at it.

His family had moved to the southern part of the Lenakai Forest decades ago but had moved to its edge only about three years ago.  His father had been worried about something, but Lingdon never knew what.  They were near enough to a small lake town called Danon, that they were able to get all their supplies and news, but far enough away to live secluded and escape the pressures of their family responsibilities.  He had never learned those responsibilities, though.

Lingdon often dreamed of his old life while sleeping on the wooden floor of his cage.  He was jarred by a wheel hitting a hole in the road.  The carts were pulled by large pack animals called sigrunes. He steadied himself as he looked out at the creatures.  They were short and strong with thick grey hide, only having hair along their spine, which could harden into spikes when threatened.

Lingdon loved these animals.  They were the only thing that had made him smile during the past two years.  They were slow animals but could pull large weights with little effort.  His favorite task was caring for the animals.  While the Yaxkin were cruel to each other, they cared for the sigrunes well enough; they were hard to replace.

He always found them to be odd looking, but thought they were adorable. Massive, floppy ears with a long trunk for a nose gave them strong senses out on the plains.  They had two spiral horns coming out of their foreheads that the Yaxkin often decorated to show their wealth.  The goofy creatures had helped him keep his sanity during slavery.

Lingdon checked his surroundings, hoping to figure out where they were today. *We're still in the Manterian Plains.*  He could not be sure what part just yet, but they were always on the move, allowing him to learn the territory well.  The Yaxkin clan that held him was one of the very few that traveled across the entire southern reach of Undaalan.  They had no territory of their own, unlike most clans.  He was going to need to know the area if he ever managed to escape.

After a short period of scanning, he realized they were nearing the Panteri River.  This was one of the biggest landmarks in the area.  It was a tributary of the Entfall River.  If the opportunity were ever afforded to him, this would be a great place to make his escape.

Today, he could feel the wind more tenderly on his cheeks.  He could smell a new freshness in the air.  Unless he was imagining it, he could see farther and sharper than before.  Every vibration of the cart reverberated through his body.  Things were different today.  He had much more energy running through his veins than he ever remembered.

His dad had taught him many survival skills; hunting, fishing, fire starting, shelter building, and fighting.  His dad had also taught him a couple of other unique skills.  These skills were impossible for him to use at the time, but his dad always told him that one day, he would be grown enough to begin to use them.  His heightened senses told him it was this day.

The Yaxkin convoy stopped near the river.  It was midday.  They were going to be preparing their boats to cross the wide river.  Travelling from coast to coast for their trade, they were well practiced at river crossings.

The Undaari did not support the slave trade, so the few slaves that this Yaxkin group had, were always kept hidden during their trades.  The Noxxons, however, highly valued Undaari slaves and that was where they were heading.  For some reason, the Yaxkin liked him and had chosen to not trade him, but he was not sure that he would continue getting that lucky.

One of the Yaxkin came and opened his cage, setting him to work on the boats.  There were many guards standing around, keeping a watchful eye on him and the other slaves as they worked.  Few Yaxkin worked on the boats.  Lingdon watched his owner as he moved through the camp.

His master carried a particularly brutal torture device to use when his slaves displeased him.  Lingdon had felt the sting of the Flingtail only a few times, but that pain was burned in him forever.  The device was a long cord with teeth and claws from the animals his master had killed embedded along it.  It would literally bite into the skin on impact, wrapping around the victim, squeezing, and burying deeper into their skin the more they struggled.

He had quickly learned to always follow commands, not requiring many lessons from his master.  Lingdon became one of the more trusted slaves, the masters rarely focusing on him. He did this on purpose; defiance gained him nothing, but compliance gained him limited freedom and privileges. That would give him an advantage when the time came to escape, as he was one of the few slaves not kept in chains outside the cages.

He unloaded the boat gear from the carts and set to work assembling the rafts, along with the other slaves. It would take several hours to complete the process. They would likely be camping on the far side of the river tonight. This usually meant fresh fish for dinner, but Lingdon was not hoping to find out.

Once all the rafts were assembled and the carts with their sigrunes loaded onto them, they pushed off into the river. The Yaxkin slaves continued to do the hard work, using poles to steer their rafts across the lazy river. It was dusk, so the slaves lit the colorful oil lamps on their rafts.

Each raft carried Yaxkin to oversee the slaves as they transported all the good across the river. There was only one Yaxkin on the raft with Lingdon. He had made sure to be one of the last rafts to push off. This was his opportunity to escape. He quickly formulated a plan.

The water would get a little rougher when the raft neared the center of the river. That would be his chance. He was standing near the sigrune as he steered the raft into the rough waters with the long pole.

As the craft began to rock in the choppy waters, he pretended to fall, grabbing the lamp hanging from the cart, tearing it from the bracket and smashing it on the raft. Orange and red flames spread immediately, but they were on a river, so the wood was too damp for the fire to last long. His Yaxkin passenger came rushing over to help put out the flames.

Lingdon prayed his hasty plan would work. He had not practiced the movements his father had taught him since he was enslaved. His passenger was busy with the fire and did not notice as Lingdon traced his hands through the air. Lingdon could feel the power build up in him. Power that his father had always told him existed, but Lingdon had yet to feel. He knew this was going to work. But then it did not.

Lingdon was not sure what had happened. He had done everything his father taught him. *Was I wrong?* He had felt the power inside him. He shook his arms out and tried the movements again. He could feel it more clearly this time. His passenger looked up, visibly confused by Lingdon's actions.

Lingdon completed the movements and this time, it worked. He shot purple fire from his hands, adding to the blaze. His passenger witnessed the entire thing, but before he could call out, the sigrune bucked from the flames, kicking wildly, and knocking the Yaxkin into the water. If the Yaxkin found out Lingdon had caused the fire, they would not believe he accidentally fell off his raft in panic and drowned. He needed them to think he had died, otherwise, they would chase him down.

That left Lingdon with only one choice. Before he had a chance to doubt himself, he dove into the water after the Yaxkin. A moment later, he clutched onto the Yaxkin and dragged him under.

Physically, Lingdon was slightly taller than this Yaxkin and becoming stronger, too. The Yaxkin was still in shock from what he had seen and reacted too slowly. Killing the Yaxkin was not his first choice, but he had to prevent his captor from alerting the others.

Lingdon got behind his victim and wrapped an arm around his neck. He squeezed the Yaxkin's throat and held him under water. His opponent struggled against him, clawed at him, and attempted to unsheathe his knife.

The Yaxkin managed to slash once at Lingdon's leg with his short blade before going limp. Lingdon's own lungs had been full entering the water. As an Undaari, he was naturally a more gifted athlete, able to hold his breath much longer. He came back up, screamed for help once, then went back under water.

He pulled the Yaxkin's green cloak and goggles off before he began to swim, allowing the current to carry him far away. He swam as fast as he could so that no one would see him escape in the deepening darkness. Many of the other Yaxkin would be too focused on getting the flames out, preventing their spread, to worry about the slave.

He swam downriver, unable to fight the current. He wanted to swim for distance rather than direction anyway, so following the current got him to safety fastest. It was the opposite direction he wanted to eventually go, but any direction away from his slavers would be a good thing. He needed to eventually get north to Ambrecia, where his father was from, not south.

Lingdon could feel his breath running out. His disguise created drag in the water as he swam. He was getting exhausted but had not reached his goal yet. Burning grew in his lungs. There was a bend in the river coming up that he wanted to pass.

That point was his goal so that he would be out of sight before he surfaced. His body was beginning to convulse as he fought to keep his head under water. The knife wound on his leg ached. He had lost a lot of blood. His heartbeat was increasing rapidly. He just needed to hold out a little longer until safety, releasing his disguise to help move faster.

He reached for the surface, ready to feel the cool night air. He could see the moonlight through the water. He stretched an arm out. He kicked hard again. His body accelerated the last short distance to escape the cold waters.

Then everything went black.

At Entfall, Major Nazario relayed the information he had received from his team to the Undaari. Jerykka's scouts had returned as well, carrying terrifying information. Noxxons were amassing on the border.

Jerykka moved over to the war table and began moving pieces around to account for the new information. She started planning how to counter the Noxxons and prepare for what seemed like an inevitable assault. She called Jarreck and Nazario over to discuss the situation further.

"There are Noxxons massing here, not too far from Entfall."

Jarreck's face emptied of blood.

"That's less than half a day's march from here. How many are there?"

Jerykka frowned and replied, "Based on reports, their forces will number seven thousand, once they've fully gathered. We might have a couple days before they've done so and are ready to strike."

"We must send word to Ambrecia! You need the Undaari Army!"

Jerykka raised a flat hand before Jarreck could continue and countered, "What I need most is time. We need to prepare the keep. We aren't ready for a sustained siege. If we can get everything prepared, we can hold out, even without the Army. You could help me with that."

She pointed to their location on the war table. Jerykka wanted to act before the Noxxons were ready. There was little hope of defeating the Noxxons in the open field, but she could delay their attack with a quick strike and retreat. They needed to buy more time. Entfall was not prepared for war. She needed to be their Shield.

Jarreck shook his head, "I'm sorry. It's a good plan, but I can't join you. My mission, and only true purpose in this war effort, is to track down the artifact and prevent the Noxxons from using it. If they manage to unlock its power, no manner of Undaari war effort could stop them."

Jerykka countered, "But isn't this battle the same mission? The artifact is heading straight for them."

"It will pass right by them.  They can't use it as it is.  My instincts say the Noxxon army is not their destination.  They will continue to transport the artifact along the tree line as they use the desert to make better time.  Based on the new information provided by the humans, I believe they're trying to bring it up the Scarred Mountain to the Heart of the Alackai.  Forbidden territory."

Jerykka recoiled at the notion, "Why would they bring it there?"

"I believe that's where this artifact was forged.  A lot of old magic was conceived there.  Perhaps that's how they hope to unlock its power.  I'm not sure what rituals would be required, but since they were able to locate the artifact, they likely know everything they need.  This is probably their only option to open it without the key," Jarreck explained slowly.

Jerykka nodded her understanding, but had one last question, "What does this artifact even do?"

Jarreck responded, "I can only speculate at this point.  However, knowing how old it must be, it could be one of several possibilities.  The old arcane arts had many texts and weapons which were hidden away long ago, due to their destructive potential.  It may hold instructions for their use.  This information, in the wrong hands, could be catastrophic to our world."

Jerykka's heart sank.

"What weapons could they be?  How could they even use them?"

Jarreck shook his head.

"I'm not sure.  There are old weapons that were lost in the history books.  Things like the Black Scythe, the Scarred Staff, the Skovi Sigridir, and the Lightning Bow.  There are several weapons that my father used to tell me tales about.  I haven't found any information about them outside of his stories.  The Society hid away that knowledge so that things like this *couldn't* happen.  No one should even know about this stuff who wasn't alive back then."

Jerykka did not understand.

She questioned him rapidly, "Then how could they have found out?  What do they hope to accomplish?  Are we actually in danger?  What about Entfall's magic?  Would that be enough to protect us?"

It took a minute before Jarreck responded, "Whatever's in the artifact, is likely the key to recovering this old magic, but the specifics are unclear.  Entfall hasn't been threatened by anything since Dralvic fomented civil war within the Society eons ago.

"But if the Noxxons can figure the artifact out, that could change.  They were Dralvic's greatest fear and *why* he turned on the Society.  He didn't want them to gain access to the Alackai.  What's worse is I don't believe it was the only artifact locked away.  The knowledge they contained was too dangerous for everything to be hidden away together."

Jerykka continued to question, "I still don't understand how they could've found this artifact or recovered it from the Lenakai Forest.  What prompted all this?"

Jerykka was growing desperate for answers.

"I *wish* I had the answers, Jerykka, I'm sure that in time, we'll find them.  Hopefully, not too late.  I've just barely begun to hear whispers of possibilities.

"What's most confusing is that the Noxxons have never been able to use the Alackai.  The Undaari were the chosen race to have direct access.  If the Noxxons, with their brute force and savagery, have found a way to use these weapons or the Alackai, it could be the end of the Undaari."

"But how would they be able to access it?  It's not in their blood."

"Things change, Jerykka.  There could be old spells that may grant them the ability to use the Alackai.  We're ignorant to believe that the Alackai can't choose to open itself to the Noxxons.  We don't know what the ancient texts hold or what knowledge was lost.  There may be something that gives them the ability to use the Alackai."

Jerykka could not accept this.  The Noxxons could not have possibly gained such power.

Head hanging low, she quietly asked, "How are we going to stop them?  Is there any chance their mission will fail?"

Jarreck shook his head again.  "I wouldn't count on it.  They clearly have the intent, so they *must* know something we don't.  That's why it's so vital we stop whatever they're planning.  They're preparing for a massive offensive.  But perhaps the Alackai sent us help to counter this new threat."  He turned and looked at Nazario and Garren as he finished his thought, "But we must act quickly and flawlessly."

Jerykka understood the weight of his words.

"We'll execute the surprise attack without you.  You need to stock up.  Take whatever supplies you need and stop them from using the artifact.  Do you need any warriors?  We don't have many to spare, but you can take whoever you need."

Jarreck waved off the suggestion and said, "I'll only take the humans, Kiva, and Ferani.  The humans are in my care and have shown heart.  They're also something the Noxxons are unfamiliar with, which may give us an advantage.  Besides, I don't wish to take away from your defenses.

We'll take the zakeri to get ahead of them and lay a trap. If all goes well, we'll secure the artifact and bring it back to Ambrecia for safekeeping."

Jerykka smiled at her friend. "I hope that'll be enough. My attack won't happen until close to sunrise. I always find it best when fighting against superior numbers to catch them sleeping. You need to rest. We all do. It sounds like there will be a *lot* of conflict in the immediate future."

Jarreck nodded and conceded, "Unfortunately, you're right. You still need to send word back to Ambrecia. The King needs to know about the threat marching on Entfall. If the scouts' reports are accurate, you'll need to have reinforcements, like it or not. We already know you're outnumbered and the Noxxons have learned some new tricks. We'll rest here tonight and give the other humans time to return. In the morning, we'll head out."

Major Nazario chimed in, "Is there anything you need from us in preparation? What can we do to help out?"

Jarreck replied, "Nothing. We'll take care of everything. Just rest and be ready to go. Make sure you have everything you need, provisions and all. There are supplies here if you need."

Nazario's face twisted a bit.

He turned to speak to Garren. "I wonder if their food is edible. I hope Brandon can determine that."

Garren tilted his head in a sort of curious acknowledgement.

Jarreck asked, "Do you have different food in your homeland?"

"Our food is different, but that doesn't necessarily mean we can't eat yours. We never expected other life in the galaxy to look this similar to us, so the food might be edible. Brandon can test it to be safe."

Jarreck replied, "We'll see once they return. In the meantime, I would suggest securing other weaponry as well. Your weapons are powerful, but they don't seem reliable for close combat. It would be wise to carry something else just in case."

Major Nazario nodded in agreement and turned to Jerykka, "Can someone escort us to your armory so we can accomplish that?"

Jerykka called over one of the guards and had him escort the humans to the armory. The guard would be able to assist them with all their needs.

She looked at Jarreck and asked, "Are you sure they're all you want with you? I worry about your life. We can't afford to lose you."

Jarreck smiled back at Jerykka, firmly grasped her forearm in an embrace, and smiled slyly. "Are you sure it's not just you? We'll be fine, they're stronger than they appear. They held their own against the Noxxons,

I promise.  I don't particularly like you being out there against so many Noxxons, either."

Jerykka smiled back but ignored his final comment.  She would never sit back while her troops were out in danger.

She started the customary farewell, "Alackai's Grace guide you—"

"Master Jerykka," a guard called out.  "We've found something.  It's an Undaari man, a young one.  Our scouts found him washed up on the shore of the Panteri River far to the south.  He's barely alive."

She looked over, confused, "Was he attacked by the Noxxons?"

"He's injured and unconscious, but it doesn't seem to be from the Noxxons.  He's being rushed to the medical wing."

Jerykka nodded and turned back to Jarreck, "Care to join me?"

"Naturally.  This could still be related to the Noxxons."

Night had completely fallen.  Jerykka left the humans in the care of her Undaari guard to find accommodations for the night.  *I hope they're as tough as Jarreck says they are.*  She would be departing soon, but Jarreck's mission with the humans would not start until the next morning.

# Chapter 13
## Failures

*C*ommander Braylon was at a loss. *Is this really a mutiny?* He could not believe what had happened. He understood that people were scared, but this felt extreme. They had lost their home and were now stranded in the middle of space, but they were not without hope. *It's my fault they're stranded, too. If I hadn't stopped the ship, we could've made it to the new home world.*

He could not blame the General completely; the situation had grown dire, but all hope was not lost, yet. It had only been five days since the *Inquisitor* departed for ZX-746. And Nazario had a potential lead on a solution.

Braylon trusted Nazario but had wanted a peaceful resolution. General Titus was a seasoned veteran who had helped quell the rebellions with ruthless efficiency. He knew how to dismantle a leadership and establish new dominance. If anyone were to save them through force, it was him.

Commander Braylon felt that General Titus' actions were admirable but misplaced. He had gone too far. This was too sensitive of a situation for rash actions. Braylon had to free himself and take control back before General Titus could forcibly take the land from these aliens to secure resources. *We're technically the aliens here.*

Braylon shook his head from behind his desk. Titus had enacted this mutiny the moment he heard there was an energy source on the planet. Realization dawned on Braylon. Titus had this contingency ready well in advance. He was a warmonger.

Braylon's internal monologue went into overdrive as he tried to work through the details of his situation. There had to be a chink in the armor around Titus' plan. He needed to find it and exploit it. If he processed through everything he knew, he was sure to find it.

Titus' plan might work to save the million humans remaining on the ship, but it was morally abhorrent. Titus had not given Braylon the opportunity to create his own plan. The present course of action would lead to an all-out war on their new planet. They could not lose more people. Not to mention, without understanding the energy source on the planet, and its possible instabilities, this attack could result in the destruction of said resources. *How could Titus not see the dangers of his actions?*

The first ship that had been sent was armed to the teeth with troops but hesitated in its mission due to information received upon arrival. THERE MAY BE A DEADLY DISEASE ON THE SURFACE. Braylon suspected that was a ruse; Major Nazario would have sent back word earlier if there were a true concern. The ship was now scanning the planet in more detail to prepare for an orbital attack. Now, General Titus was having a full squadron mobilized to bomb the planet and clear out any resistance.

The civilian population would have no idea that this mutiny had even happened. General Titus was using the Commander to ensure cooperation by making him give the orders. Braylon had no choice but to comply as his family was under threat. He was lucky enough to bring most of his family on this trip; he could not lose them now. He had his husband, his two kids, his parents, and his brother. They were his entire world and the reason he had accepted this position. They had wanted to explore even more than he did.

Titus had stationed guards in their domicile but told the family it was for their protection during the protests, so they had no idea they were under threat. Only a few among peacekeeper leadership were even aware of the mutiny. It was truly a professional job, but still wrong and dangerous. Braylon needed to convince the others to let him go. They needed to understand that this was the wrong course of action.

Unfortunately, only General Titus met with him, so he was unable to speak to anyone else. He had to admit that Titus had really thought this through. If Braylon could discover those who did not fully support the mutiny, he was sure they would listen to reason and help him escape. His computer access had been limited to prevent him from communicating outside his office. *Perhaps I can feign an illness myself.*

As he tried to formulate an escape plan, General Titus entered the office. His large muscular frame dominated the space. There was a distinct possibility that General Titus was the most physically fit seventy-five-year-old in the human population, even before the apocalypse. His experience and physical prowess were the only reason he had been able to continue serving at his advanced age. He could still outperform the younger troops on fitness tests.

Titus' navy-blue uniform was as crisp and clean as ever. His thick grey mustache was always perfectly trimmed. He maintained the same level of professionalism throughout any situation, no matter the stress level. That was why Braylon had leaned so heavily on him. It also may be why Titus thought he had the clearer mind to get them through this. Braylon envied his stress management skills.

Titus continued to stand at the door with his arms crossed behind his back as he spoke, "All right Braylon, here's the deal. The squadron is spinning up right now. I respect your rank and don't want to create an enemy. I'm just the only one willing to do whatever it takes to save our people. Once the squadron is gone, you're free to return to your family.

"All communications are shut off ship wide, so there'll be no way to call off the mission. Spend time with your family until the mission is over and we have secured the necessary resources. If you try anything stupid, you and your family will be jettisoned in an escape pod and left to die alone in space. Understood?"

Commander Braylon pleaded, "This is wrong. You are starting a war with the natives of our new home. You are committing a meaningless genocide. How can you give these orders in good conscience? There is another path. Let our team, the team *you* selected, complete their mission. They can do it. We have time."

Titus pointed a knife-like hand at the Commander. "Wrong, Braylon. It's not meaningless if it saves the last shred of humankind. We're out of time. We have it under good authority that the resources on the ship are dwindling faster than expected. People are panicking and protesting throughout the streets. There have been threats of riots. We had to implement martial law. If we don't resolve this situation quickly, we'll lose our chance to save our people, because they'll have torn themselves apart!"

"General, I beg you. End this and we can save everyone in a peaceful manner. Do you think these people will continue to follow you if they know you wiped out an entire civilization?"

"That's the difference between you and me. I *don't* seek to lead these people. I'm here to do what is necessary, *no matter the cost.* Once they're saved, you can have control back. They can hate me all they want. I don't care what they think about me. They may see me as a psychopath and a criminal, but they'll have that choice because they'll still be alive."

"What about your men? Surely, they do not support genocide. How do you think they will feel after they realize they murdered innocent people? If they betrayed me, they could betray you."

"Fear drives a man unlike anything else. Their values and morals go out the door when the fear for their survival is this elevated, especially when their families are at risk. No one is questioning me. Everyone is on board and eager to complete the plan. This is happening."

General Titus turned on his heels and exited the office without looking back. The door was barred from the outside. Braylon had to develop a new plan. He would not be able to stop the squadron from departing. But maybe he could call off the attack before they reached the planet. Preventing genocide was his priority. There had to be a way to communicate with them.

There were some very smart people on this ship. Someone had to be able to develop a work around and get communications out. Unfortunately, he only personally knew of one individual who could accomplish this, but he was part of General Titus' takeover. That would not work. He did know someone who might know someone, though. He just had to be careful.

All three moons floated high above the Noxxon camp on this cloudless night. It was a rare sight when all three were dancing in the sky together for all to see. They bathed the camp in the gentle blue light of the twins and the purple light of their brother, accompanied by stars shining brightly. It was a perfect evening. *A perfect evening for battle.* Jerykka considered the night sky a good sign and blessing from the Alackai.

She stood on the wooded hill overlooking the Noxxons from the north. There were nearly three thousand Noxxon soldiers at the camp below already. Campfires were lit throughout, and the smell of charred meat reached her nostrils. Savages. Most warriors had already settled in for the night, but the night watch was still gathered about the fires and walked the perimeter.

Jerykka only had sixty Undaari warriors with her to assault this massive encampment. As she surveyed the Noxxons, she went over the plan again in her head. This attack should slow down enemy preparations more than anything. Her assault would come from the flank opposite of the

Undaari fortifications, nearest the supply tents.

Her warriors were ready; it would be a quick attack. Their weapons and assault patterns would make it seem like six hundred were in the assault. They would not stick around for long. If they were there for more than a few minutes, the Noxxons would establish a strong counterattack and overwhelm them easily.

Her scouts had reported that the army could reach as many as seven thousand Noxxons once it was fully mustered. That meant this army was still building and supplying, though only a couple days away from an assault. Their attack would be horrific. This was the largest force the Noxxons had gathered in centuries. Yet the Undaari Army numbered more, so why attack now?

Her stomach sank as she thought about the impending death heading for Entfall. Jerykka knew Entfall had never fallen to an enemy force in a straight fight but could not help but think this time might be different. Her six hundred troops would have their hands full with these numbers. With extra time to prepare, she had little doubt her warriors would survive.

The fact the Noxxons were being so bold shook her to her core. This concerned her even more than the thought of losing the keep. *There has to be more to this. Even the Noxxons wouldn't sacrifice themselves for no reason.*

She suspected they had something up their sleeves that she could not anticipate. That made the Undaari preparations crucial to survival. She thought back to Jarreck and his fear about the artifact. There was more to this than any of them knew. They needed to do everything to ensure Entfall continued to shield the rest of the Undaari territory. She *had* to give them more time to prepare.

The last of the Noxxons had long since retired to their tents and the guards were no longer displaying much discipline. There was still a short while left before sunrise. She could feel the air getting colder and the sky reaching its darkest. This was the ideal time to strike.

*It's time.* Their movements were silent as they approached the enemy. Forty Undaari warriors hurled barrels full of sakari oil down the hill right into the heart of the Noxxon fires. Archers volleyed flaming arrows into the tents like fire rain.

Jerykka's plan flowed with perfection. Brightly colored fire spread throughout camp and destroyed Noxxon tents, while sewing chaos among their ranks. If they were lucky, they could take out a few hundred Noxxons as well. The Noxxons were sure to be set back several days in preparation.

Her Undaari would have more time to ready their defenses. They might even get some reinforcements from Ambrecia.

She surveyed the camp as new rainbow flames erupted. A mesmerizing cleansing of the corruption below. Shouts echoed through the night as the Noxxons were abruptly awoken by the fire. Burning flesh replaced the smell of cooking meats. The oil-laden barrels exploded, spraying more flaming sakari oil across the field. Jerykka and her Undaari warriors reached the perimeter of the camp with sigridir drawn. The cold metal cut through the Noxxons who had not been able to equip their armor.

Arrows continued to rain down on the Noxxons further into the camp as they emerged from their tents. The Undaari were quick, accurate, and lethal. They caught their enemy by surprise and cut their way into the Noxxon camp with ease. Blue, green, purple, and red flames burned through the corner of the camp and reached the supply tents.

The Undaari fought for several minutes before the Noxxons gained their footing, sounding their drums to signal a coordinated counterattack. The Noxxons in the center of camp had time to regroup and don their armor. A couple Undaari fell in battle, and Jerykka knew they would not be able to stand much longer. She signaled for her warriors to fall back with a high-pitched whistle. They had to retreat before the Noxxons could overwhelm them.

The Undaari warriors fled the battle quickly, disappearing into the darkness. The Noxxons pursued them, but as their hunt began, the last squad of twenty Undaari attacked from the south. These caught the Noxxons with their backs to them. The Noxxons were more prepared to fight this time, but still lost several troops quickly.

This second attack was only meant to be a distraction with one goal. The Noxxons turned back, unsure of where the Undaari were attacking from or how many there were. They fortified their defenses in the confusion rather than pursue their attackers. The southern Undaari squad would retreat quickly and make for Entfall immediately.

Jerykka's troops would hide in the woods up north, a safe distance away and well hidden. Pursuit should not follow. She wanted to monitor the chaos in the fresh light to assess how the Noxxons responded and what damage had been dealt. Jerykka needed to know precisely how delayed the Noxxons would be after this attack.

As they crested the hill to the north, Jerykka's stomach sank. They were met by two thousand Noxxons charging the wooded hill. This was the next battalion of Noxxon troops that had gathered to join the camp. They were much closer than she had anticipated. They must have heard the battle from a distance in the still night and charged.

There was no evasion to be had. The Noxxons were on her instantly. She drew her blade, desperate to get the Noxxons off her. Several Undaari warriors were killed immediately. Jerykka had been leading from the front of her squad. There was no escape for her. She screamed for her troops to retreat to the river as she fought against the overwhelming force.

A few Undaari managed to elude the Noxxon swarm. The rest were engaged in close combat or slain. As Jerykka fought the Noxxons, she felt a searing pain in her thigh. Without faltering, she continued to hack and slash at the Noxxons. She did not need her leg to hold her ground.

She created just a breath of space with her sigridir and raised her hands in front of her, calling upon the Alackai. She wildly flung cerulean flames at the Noxxons around her. They fell back several paces creating room for the trapped Undaari to break away.

As she ran, the pain in her leg spread. She had managed to ignore it thus far, but it refused to be forgotten. She could feel the dampness as blood ran down her leg and she limped along after her comrades. Her heart pounded rapidly, threatening to break out of her chest as she bled. Then she felt more shooting pain, this time from her opposite leg. She fell over with a scream. She glanced down at her legs and found a thick, Noxxon arrow protruding from it. Both of her legs were disabled.

Two other Undaari were killed by arrows to their backs. Tears flowed from her eyes as her mind raced. *What have I done?* Jerykka scrambled to her feet, struggling to block out the pain. *I have to slow down my pursuers.*

Using the Alackai, she conjured a wide wall of blue flames between the Undaari and the Noxxons. It would only slow them down for a few seconds, but the Undaari were faster when healthy. *At least the others could get away.*

The other Undaari ran for their lives as ordered. The sun was rising in their face. Jerykka could not keep up. She was getting light-headed. The pain was overwhelming. Her legs grew cold as they lost more blood. This mission had failed. The Noxxons were far more prepared than she had expected. Their attack was imminent.

Jerykka was knocked forward to the ground as another arrow pierced her shoulder. *This is it. I've failed the Undaari. I've failed Jarreck.* Her mind was no longer on escape, focusing instead on her failures.

She could not move her injured arm anymore. She slowly dragged herself with her uninjured limb toward the nearest tree and hid in the shrubbery.  She used what little energy she had left to camouflage herself with the Alackai.

*Maybe I'll get lucky.*  Jerykka quieted her breathing and tried to relax. She could hear the Noxxons charging again.  Her cerulean wall of fire was fading, as was her strength.  They were closing in on her.

She had left a large trail of blood.  The Noxxons screamed in excitement. They lusted for her blood.  Their metal armor clanged as their drums sounded.  They had found her trail.  Her thoughts were with Jarreck and Entfall as her vision turned to blackness.

# Chapter 14

## Recon

Jarreck and Nazario had their team ready. The other humans had returned from the *Inquisitor,* and they were topped off on supplies and weaponry. Jarreck's hastily assembled team was prepared to take flight on their zakeri with the first light of the day. The first squad of Undaari troops returned from Jerykka's attack as they made their way to the stables.

Jarreck overheard their report; it sounded like the attack went off without a hitch. At last contact, they had seen Jerykka's two squads heading toward their overlook on the north side of the camp to monitor the aftermath. He was glad everything had gone well. That was a burden off his mind as they began their mission.

The two zakeri took off from the stables with Jarreck, Nazario, Garren, and Ferani on the first. Kiva flew the second with Jaina, Brandon, and Monkley at the rear. It was a tight, uncomfortable fit but a relatively short flight. Ferani refused to risk more zakeri life than necessary, so they did not take all three.

Once they reached altitude, they headed directly east to the edge of the Lenakai Forest keeping just north of the Noxxon Army. The tree line would be their guide once they turned north. From the air, they could safely scout out the Noxxon troops escorting the artifact to the Scarred Mountain. Once they had position and pace, he could calculate an ambush point.

Jarreck's mind wandered as they flew. He was still curious about the boy the scouts had found. He had clearly been through a lot and was barely clinging to life. There were very few Undaari down in Manterian Plains; most of them were slaves. It had taken the scouts two days to transport him back to Entfall, yet he had never regained consciousness.

Jarreck refocused on the mission.  He could ill afford distractions. From their high altitude, their view stretched great distances across Undaalan to the curved horizons.  They followed the green expanse of forest speckled with pinks, purples, and blues.  Flowers were in full bloom.

To their south, he could see the smoke plumes from the Noxxons. To the north, he could just barely make out the Black Peaks in the distance with the Scarred Mountain at its heart.  That mountain loomed over the range, casting its dark shadow across many others.  It was an imposing sight.

Without conversational ability due to the wind, his mind continued to drift.  He stared off in the distance toward the Scarred Mountain.  It was said to be the birthplace of the Alackai, but it had become forbidden territory to most.

There was rumored to have been a powerful creature there protecting the Heart of the Alackai.  No one knew if this creature ever truly existed or was just part of the legend.  It was said it had been initially awoken by the First Society, though it was not until the Second Society's reign that the Heart had become forbidden.

He had been one of the very few ever granted permission to enter this place.  He had not seen evidence of any creature at the time, but he had been wrong about so much recently that he could not be sure of anything anymore.  Still, Jarreck doubted that any creature could survive that long, and he did not want to find out.

That meant preventing the Noxxons from reaching this sacred place.  They could never be allowed to corrupt its purity.  Jarreck's mind snapped back to the present as he spotted dust rising ahead.  Jarreck dropped their altitude.  Their view of the Black Peaks faded in the distance. He still kept a healthy altitude as they tracked the movements of the Noxxons below.

He watched the squad of brutes below, easy to follow; they never traveled stealthily.  They consumed and destroyed everything in their path. *That's why they can never be allowed to use the artifact.*  There was a reason the Alackai had never gifted them.  They would destroy the entire world, themselves included.

Once Jarreck had confirmed the Noxxons' course and speed, they descended into the forest.  They landed a safe distance to the north, well back in the tree line.  From there, they could erect a camp to operate from that allowed them quick access to an ambush site.

Jarreck took Nazario and Garren to scout the Noxxons, leaving Kiva in charge of the remaining group.  Kiva and the others should not face any threats and could rest in anticipation of the upcoming battle. Ferani would be able to feed and rest the zakeri.

"Have either of you held a knife before?" Kiva questioned them.

Both Brandon and Jaina looked up at Kiva and shook their heads. Brandon felt embarrassed to be so inexperienced. He was not looking forward to the possibility of being involved in this but knew the importance of being there and showing a willingness to sacrifice for the Undaari. Jaina had made it abundantly clear.

"Very well, after we set up camp, I'll teach you a few rudimentary drills," Kiva said.

Brandon reminded himself that they were building relationships far more important than just themselves. *This is what it takes to gain access to the Alackai.* If they could not stop the Noxxons, the people on the *Jericho* would never be able to call this planet, Undaaleria, home. Funny how they had to save someone else in order to save themselves.

While the war may be chaotic, this was an extraordinary opportunity to learn more about the history of this world and the culture of the Undaari. They could see their behaviors and customs while building a lasting friendship. And they could earn enough trust to examine the Alackai up close.

Brandon and Jaina had been equipped with the handheld Peacemaker blaster rifles they had brought from the *Inquisitor*'s armory. They did not have any sort of armor, so the Undaari had given them leather suits, which were generally for their younger Undaari learning combat for the first time.

They were also given large Undaari knives that were attached to their hips. Brandon felt very awkward in his new gear and looked over at Jaina, who was fidgeting with her armor. The only part of their original outfits they still wore were their Acumen visors. *This leather is rather luxurious, though.*

As they set up camp, Kiva continued her questioning, "What did you do in your homeland?"

Jaina answered first, "I'm a diplomat. So basically, I learn about the history of people as well as their languages, customs, and courtesies in order to build positive and lasting relationships."

Brandon knew that was a highly rehearsed answer, but his was not much better. "I'm a biologist. I study the world and its ecosystems to help advance t-... technology and make life easier for our people. I've dabbled a bit in astronomy as well to learn about theoretical worlds. We b-... both have a lot to learn about your home. It's truly marvelous here."

Kiva smiled. "We have people who seek knowledge as well. It has grown in value and become coveted in recent years. Our own Society seeks to maintain an accurate history of the world and learn all the secrets of the Alackai. It possesses far more books and records than were available in the Temple archives. Perhaps, when this is all over, you can work alongside our Society in these matters. Until then, we have to make sure you survive."

They finished setting up the tents and fire pit. Brandon looked at their work with admiration. He had never camped before. Most people had not since the only forests left were orbiting satellites beyond the skies with paid admission. He glanced at Jaina with a smile, then saw Kiva drawing her blade from behind her. He took a step back and reached for his new knife.

Kiva spoke to them, "I don't know how to work your weapons, but I can teach you a little bit about our knives to make you more comfortable."

Brandon relaxed and took his hand off the hilt of his knife. Kiva began running the pair through a couple simple drills and exercises with their weapons. Stances, thrusts, slashes.

Ferani sat back with Monkley and the brightly colored zakeri. Brandon could occasionally hear Ferani laughing as they trained. From the corner of his eye, he saw Ferani grinning widely and pointing toward him. The two zakeri seemed to be fixated on him as well, their cyan eyes unblinking.

They practiced for what felt like hours. Brandon was in awe of how precise and skilled Kiva was. He was worn out, though Kiva barely seemed to have broken a sweat. Brandon's face was flushed. He looked over and saw Jaina appeared just as tired as he. Neither of them were the most physically fit of people.

As they took a quick break, Jaina asked, "How do you interact with the Alackai? I've noticed that it's pretty ingrained in the plant life around, but how are you able to use its power?"

Kiva looked at her, surprised, but answered, "We gain its energy through the food we eat and our meditation. The Alackai is all around us and chooses who it wishes to carry its responsibility. Then there are the Entai. They give those of us who are Graced direct access to her strength."

Brandon side eyed Jaina before inquiring, "What are the Entai?"

Kiva answered by pointing to a relatively small tree in the distance, barely visible through the thick trunks of the forest. It stood in a clearing, alone. Kiva led the two humans to the Entai, leaving Ferani and Monkley behind with the zakeri. Monkley had made no reaction to the opportunity.

Brandon examined the unique tree as they stood at the edge of the clearing. Its bark was white and scarred with cyan veins, like the stonework at Entfall. It was much shorter than the surrounding trees, but its foliage was far wider, filling the clearing. Its green leaves were tinged with the same blue as its scars, as though blue blood ran through its system.

"These are the Entai. There are many throughout the Lenakai Forest. We can meditate upon them and draw strength."

"I've seen these b-... before," said Brandon as answers became clear. "Our mapping showed them bright and clear as a focal point of energy. They're literally a d-... direct port to the power of the land."

"Hm," Jaina said as she lifted her hand to her chin. "This might be weird, but can we see?"

Kiva thought for a moment and smiled, "An unusual request, but considering the circumstances, we can make that happen."

Brandon's smile grew again. He forgot about Ferani laughing at him and focused entirely on Kiva. *She is so much nicer and open than Jarreck.*

Before Kiva walked away, Brandon heard a screech from above. He looked up to see something flying overhead.

"I didn't know there were birds on this planet. I haven't seen any."

"Birds?" Kiva asked.

Brandon pointed to the pink creature soaring through the air.

"Ahh, a ropen. They're exceedingly rare. The Alackai has blessed us with its sighting."

Kiva stepped away from them and walked up to the Entai's trunk. She placed her hand upon the bark and touched her forehead to it. Brandon watched intently, eyes unblinking. Kiva closed her eyes for a few moments in what appeared to be a silent prayer. She sat down at the base of the tree, bringing her feet in, soles touching, and raising her arms, palms skyward, by her sides.

Each crack in the Entai's bark illuminated as a cyan glow spread up from its roots to its leaves. Tendrils of energy made their way up from the roots of the Entai and connected with Kiva, like blades of grass growing up through the ground. It was an awe-inspiring sight to behold. Brandon was shocked by how clear and active this physiological process occurred.

Brandon pulled out a leather wrapped paper journal from one of his pockets as well as a charcoal pencil. He sketched Kiva and her interactions with the Entai on a blank sheet of paper. He was fast with his art and quite talented, not taking long to finish his drawing of Kiva's meditation. Outside of his studies and reading, this was his greatest passion. It cost him a fortune to find a real paper journal, but it gave him comfort in trying times and helped him relax when stressed.

Brandon whispered to Jaina, unable to contain himself any longer, "I c-... cannot believe how she's able to interact with the natural energy sources of this planet. I would k-... kill to get some readings with my equipment in the future."

"Just remember, you might have to," Jaina cautioned.

She tried to imagine what it would be like to experience the Alackai. Despite all the technological advancements humans had made, nothing was as wonderful or magnificent as this. She looked over at Brandon and then down at his journal.

"What are you doing? Is that an actual paper journal?"

Brandon looked back at her in surprise, "I al-... always have one of these with me. I find p-... peace in drawing and writing by hand. It's far more rewarding and memorable than d-... digitally recording everything. And this is too incredible not to document with art. I've been doing this throughout our tr-... trip; have you honestly not noticed?"

Brandon's cheeks filled with blood as he flipped through the pages of his journal and showed her a few examples. Jaina saw drawings of an Undaari, a Noxxon, the Ambrecia palace, and a zakeri in his journal. There were several more pages full of drawings, but she missed their contents.

Jaina's eyes met his as he showed his work.

She quickly averted her gaze and spoke quietly, her voice cracking, "I suppose I haven't been looking at you all too much. Maybe I should be paying more attention to you. But there's just so much going on around here."

Jaina had a newfound appreciation for Brandon. She admired his passion and tradition. She could not hide a smile as her eyes lingered on Brandon for a few moments longer than she intended. She knew he was a man who was unapologetically himself and used his own strengths for the betterment of others. *He is quite a sight with his big smile and all that excitement spilling out.*

Jaina looked back up toward the Entai and watched as Kiva

finished her meditation. The teal glow faded from the leaves and scars. Kiva had taken nearly half an hour. She stood up and motioned them over. She had a worried expression on her face but smiled as they approached.

"What did you think of that?" Kiva asked.

Brandon nearly shouted, "That was the most incredible thing I've ever seen! I don't understand how you're able to c-... command the Alackai like that, but I truly hope I get to study this further in the future."

Kiva smiled, "Perhaps one day. But we don't command the Alackai, rather, we listen to her guidance. We must return to our friends, though."

Jaina was no longer listening to the conversation. She felt drawn to the Entai. It was as if gravity was drawing her in closer and closer. She was enamored by its beauty and power, as well as the act she'd just witnessed. She was helpless to resist. She slowly approached it and reached a hand toward it. She heard Kiva tell her that she should not touch the Entai, but the voice sounded distant.

Jaina was focused. Her hand made contact with the Entai. It was truly magnificent. She could feel its strength and energy. It had a warmth that she did not understand. She could feel it radiating from the tree into her very soul. Kiva placed a hand on her shoulder, drawing her attention back to her companions.

"Sorry, I just kind of lost myself there for a moment. I don't know what happened. The Entai is just so magical. So entrancing."

# Chapter 15
## Friends

Jarreck, Garren, and Nazario moved quietly through the forest. They had been following the Noxxon movements all day, while maintaining a safe distance. They neared the clearing that the Noxxons were now cutting out of the edge of the forest for their camp. His blood boiled as he saw his precious forest mutilated.

It was hard to get a good view of the camp from the ground level. Jarreck decided to climb a tree to get a good look at everything. He had Nazario climb an adjacent tree and left Garren at the base of the trees to watch their backs.

Peering through the dense green foliage, Jarreck barely managed to make out the details of the Noxxons' encampment. It appeared small and not too concerned with an attack. There were only two Noxxons standing guard, but the artifact was nowhere to be seen. They had stopped almost precisely where Jarreck had predicted.

There was a large tent in the center of camp with a few smaller tents surrounding it. *That center tent is probably where the artifact is.* There was little else around the camp. Jarreck estimated there were only about thirty Noxxons in the camp. That was less than he had expected but would still be more than enough to repel their attack. They had to be smart.

Jarreck and Nazario looked at each other across the limbs of the great trees and nodded. They had both seen everything they needed to. He climbed back down and saw Nazario following his lead. The trio made their way deep into the woods. They compared notes and filled Garren in on what they had observed.

Nazario brought up a hologram of the area from the ship's database using a device on his wrist. Nazario explained that his ship had processed the additional information from the *Plaintiff* and built a map. Their gear had a lot more functionality now. He showed Jarreck how to manipulate the floating image.

Using what was essentially a virtual sandbox, Jarreck drew up their attack plans and began explaining his idea. He wanted to attack just before sunrise, taking a page out of Jerykka's book. The Noxxons' guard would be lowest right before waking up. They would use the zakeri to give them the boost they needed against the superior numbers, despite the inevitable protest from Ferani.

They were not supposed to use the zakeri for battle due to their rarity and value, but they did not have much choice in these circumstances. They would ride them into battle, then quickly send the zakeri away. Jaina, Brandon, and Monkley would be up in the trees, shooting their energy weapons from a distance, separated from the fight.

Nazario insisted the civilians not be in the middle of combat and suggested the rifles would be easy enough for even the most inept novice to be an effective combatant. After they finished planning, they set out to return to the others.

Kiva sat back on her rock. Jarreck wanted them to rest a while before the mission. He had said it would be beneficial to relax and not focus on the upcoming battle. She had started a fire with the sap of the sakari flower, nestled below a pink leaved tree that appeared as if it were crying. They could cook their food and relax around prismatic flames. Kiva looked around at the team as the sun hid behind the horizon.

Jarreck sat across from her next to Nazario. Garren was to her left and both Brandon and Jaina to her right. Ferani was lying by the snoozing zakeri and Monkley had set up a hammock in the tree. Her eyes settled on Brandon and Jaina. They were avoiding eye contact with the others and had their heads hanging down, staring into the hypnotic fire. *Is this going to be their first fight?*

"Would it help if we talked more? I'm sure you have more questions," Kiva asked, directing her own question at the pair of civilians.

She wanted to help put them at ease. Jarreck looked over at her with squinted eyes but said nothing. Kiva saw the excitement in their eyes behind their glass visors. She had not experienced them like this before.

She understood that this was their first opportunity to learn a significant amount about the Undaari.  They cared far more about that chance than the upcoming fight.  She could see their shoulders relax.  Brandon and Jaina both spoke with a new burst of energy, taking full advantage of her offer.

Jaina fired off the first question, speaking as much with her hands as her mouth, "I heard you talking about other Societies earlier.  How many were there?"

"There have been three Societies of the Scar.  The First Society wielded great magic in the first war with the Noxxons but later died out due to political issues.  The Second Society rose later and tried to be neutral.  They built Entfall but fell into a civil war due to the continued conflict with the Noxxons.  Some wanted to maintain neutrality while others wanted to use the Alackai to protect the Undaari.  Jarreck and I are part of the Third Society and ours has lasted longest."

"Are m-... members of the Society the only ones that can use the Alackai?  What d-... do you even call yourselves?"

"We are called Skovi.  There are three sects within the Skovi: Shields, Swords, and Shades.  Jarreck and I are Shades.  Everyone within the Society is blessed with the Alackai, but not everyone Graced by the Alackai joins the Society.  Most of them are never properly trained in its use, though.  Master Jerykka is one of those who are Graced but not part of the Society."

"Why didn't she join?  And when did the war with the Noxxons start?"

"I cannot speak for Jerykka.  As for the Noxxons, it was during the time of the First Society that they'd been discovered.  While doing research up in the mountains near the eastern coast, a Skovi stumbled upon a few living together in a small tribe.  That Skovi barely escaped with their life and reported the new creatures back to the Council.

"But the Council ignored the threat.  When the Skovi went back to investigate later, he found that their numbers had doubled.  He was again attacked.  This time, he was killed by the Noxxons, but not before igniting a hatred among them.  We've been fighting them ever since," Kiva explained.

"But if there were so few Noxxons, how has the war dragged out so long?"

"Their numbers grew rapidly, and they began hunting the Undaari.  The First Society put them down with the Alackai, but a few escaped to the island that has since become their fortress.  On Numitor Island, their numbers increased, and they eventually attacked again.  Each time they're defeated, they survive on the island, just to come back stronger.  It's a stronghold we just can't seem to overcome."

"So, if the First Society was so p-... powerful with the Alackai, how did they fall?"

"Actually, Kiva, I should take this one," Jarreck jumped in. "This part isn't taught so well. They say that the First Society failed due to political failures. In reality, they ruled the Undaari with their power, using the arcane arts, and destroying any who disagreed with them.   They fell when one among them stood against the cruelty they inflicted and managed to create an even more powerful weapon through the will of the Alackai. The records of their names have been lost; I suspect intentionally."

Kiva's heart sank.  She had no idea the truth behind the First Society.  Jarreck had only recently revealed to her that the arcane arts had even existed.  Now learning what they did with them, it was too much.  She felt tears fall down her cheeks as she listened to Jarreck reveal more.

"Shortly after, the Second Society was formed.  The Noxxons again rose against the Undaari, as their species was untouched by the Alackai. They began another war and the Society tried to stay impartial.  Without the help of the Society, the Undaari turned to the Yaxkin for help and built a tenuous alliance with their former enemies."

Jaina and Brandon were both staring at him intently.  Kiva noticed that even Nazario had perked up to hear this tale.  The dancing firelight added a dramatic edge to the story.

"Some within the Society felt it was their duty to quell the Noxxon uprisings.  They tried to use the old arcane magic to wipe out the Noxxons. This led to a civil war within the Society that ended in its collapse.  It was enough to scare the Noxxons from battle with the Undaari.  They did not wish to deal with the power that they could wield.  The Yaxkin feared the Alackai as well and fled to the Manterian Plains."

"The Second Society had arcane magic as well? I thought their civil war was purely based on the Noxxons."

"I'm sorry, Kiva.  I taught you the story that the Society wanted everyone to know.  I was lucky to have learned the truth.  Nevertheless, while they had the best of intentions, twenty-one Skovi of the Second Society nearly destroyed all of Undaalan.

"They succumbed to the temptations of the arcane arts in their attempt to save the Undaari from the Noxxons.  Dralvic led their sect and tried to recover some of the old weapons. He called their group the Saviors of the Undaari.  Said they were the only ones willing to do whatever it took to save Undaalan from the Noxxons.  He and his sect were all killed in the ensuing civil war."

"I can't believe it.  I knew the Society wasn't as pure as they preached, but this is worse than I'd feared.  And now the arcane arts are threatening to tear apart Undaalan again, aren't they?"

"It's unfortunate, but yes, it would seem so.  That's why we must be successful in the morning.  You knew the story that the Society wanted you to know.  Now you know their secrets as well.  Kept locked away for the safety of our people.  The Society is different now, Kiva.  They can be trusted to protect the Undaari."

"I trust *you* Jarreck, not the Society.  But I will do whatever it takes to stop the Noxxons."

"That's all I'll ask, for now.  I'm sorry to have been the bearer of bad news, but perhaps we can get back to their questions. I feel that it's been beneficial to learn about each other and relax.  That was very wise of you."

Everyone sat in silence, processing the litany of information.  Kiva could not believe that the Society had lied about such important history.  She was ashamed to be part of it.  She was unsure she even wanted to continue being a Skovi once this was over.

"What about *your* Society?  You said it's lasted longer than the previous two.  It sounds like they have their flaws but are trying to be better. How is it different?" Jaina inquired.

Kiva smiled and wiped her tears before proceeding, "I'm not so sure that it's better right now.  But I appreciate the support.  From what I've learned, the Third Society was formed under Undaari rule in secret nearly a millennium ago.  The King at the time understood the importance of the Society for the Undaari's interactions with the Alackai.  This time, it was kept secret and loyal to the crown.  They were no longer independent.  This Society was given a clear role to play within the Undaari culture."

Brandon's eyebrows twisted.  "Wait, n-... no one knows your Society exists?"

Kiva shook her head.  "They do.  After a few centuries working from the shadows, a new King finally allowed them into the light.  The Undaari people were initially scared of their power and the rumors of their past.  The name Dralvic still lives in infamy among our people.  But the previous wars had happened so long before that there were little remaining records, just whispers of what had happened.  The Society had to be extremely careful not to intimidate the people while keeping the peace. They had to show that they were servants of the Undaari and the Alackai, not the other way around."

Jarreck jumped in, "That fear is why our Society fought so hard to erase their history.  No one among the Undaari knows the strength of the Alackai anymore.  They knew of its obvious existence, but few had any real connection.

"We were tasked to help the Undaari reconnect with the Alackai's Grace by bringing knowledge and research back to the people.  Our people needed to be involved with the Society to keep from fearing its power.  They would revolt if they suspected the Society of gathering power like the last two iterations.  Now we're run by a Council that answers directly to the King."

Jaina shook her head, her voice low, "That's awful.  It's so sad to hear about power hungry people hurting others.  I'm glad your Society's much more sensible.  How does the Alackai choose who she blesses?"

Jarreck shrugged his shoulders.  "No one knows.  The Alackai is wise and chooses who she sees fit.  My father had been a member of the Society.  It's run in the blood of the men in my family for generations now.  No one in Kiva's family had ever been touched before.  It was a surprise to them, but she took to it with a natural fire.  She's powerful with the Alackai's Grace, even if she doesn't believe it."

They all looked at Kiva.  Kiva shifted her body and looked away.  *I had a good mentor, but I'll never be as powerful or wise as him.*  She wished he would stop saying this stuff about her.

Nazario eyed her for a moment before finally joining the conversation, "You seem pretty wise, Jarreck.  Why aren't you on the Council?  I feel like you could solve this Noxxon issue in no time if you were."

Jarreck beamed.  "Unfortunately, it's not that simple.  The Society's Council is still kept hidden, even though the Society isn't.  There are five Councilors in total, including the High Councilor, who is our official leader and advisor to the King.

"The Council remains anonymous from the people so as not to be influenced in their decision-making.  The King and his advisors are the only people outside of the Society that works directly with the Councilors.  I'm not ready to sit back yet."

Jarreck looked around the camp and into the night sky.  Small flares rose off the vibrant fire in front of him, eliciting little puffs of smoke.

After a few moments and a deep breath, he continued, "What's more, the Councilors are all elderly Skovi whose bodies can no longer handle the Alackai.  The Alackai's power is damaging to our bodies.  Once we get too old, we can no longer sustain it.

"The Councilors are old and wise, but unable to seek power for themselves. Even if there was a position open on the Council, I'm not at that stage in my life, yet. I still have a little fight left in me. Besides, they stay secluded, guarding the knowledge of the Alackai while making decisions for others to follow."

Nazario replied, "I understand that. I'm not ready for a desk job yet either. I want to keep working in the field with my team. I hate to think of what might happen to my people if I wasn't on the ground with them."

Jarreck and Nazario locked eyes. Kiva could see a mutual look of admiration between them. She smiled and was thankful Nazario had taken the attention away from her. *I wish we could just stay here forever.* She tried to not think about the morning when their little peace would break.

Kiva heard laughing behind her and turned to find the source. The others around the campfire did as well. Garren was gleefully scratching a zakeri's turquoise belly and giggling to himself. The great creature lay on its back, purring with one of its hind legs scratching air. Garren froze and turned to face the group.

"What?"

"You're awfully giddy over there," laughed Nazario.

"You guys are getting to relax and have fun over there with your little history lessons. I'm doing what I want to relax."

Kiva's eyebrow raised and the group continued to stare at Garren.

"My parents were vets," he continued. "They would be quite beside themselves getting to meet such a magnificent creature. Leave me alone!"

The group collectively laughed and turned back to the fire. Kiva could see a glint in his eye as he went back to playing with the animal. She was beginning to enjoy the presence of the humans. They seemed to genuinely appreciate the Undaari culture.

Jaina broke the silence, "If all this knowledge was hidden away, how come you know so much about it?"

Jarreck's head fell. Kiva knew the answer to this, but she would never tell his story for him.

Nazario jumped in, shaking his head slowly, "Jaina, no. I'll fill you in later."

After a deep breath and lifting his head slightly, Jarreck responded, "It's okay, Nazario. I appreciate your concern. She missed this when we discussed it earlier."

Jarreck made eye contact with Jaina before continuing, "There was always one who maintained the knowledge of the past, to protect it from being discovered. This knowledge was passed down directly to their replacement. That knowledge died with Ambrosi'Jace, my father. He was the last Master of the Ancient Text and never got to pass the knowledge along.

"He was murdered by the Noxxons, who were searching for the information, when I was just a child. I knew of the role, but never gained its knowledge. What little I do know, my dad told me as fairy tales. There are barely snippets of information in our records. I learned what I could to try and make my dad proud."

Jaina frowned, "I'm so sorry about your father, Jarreck. I know it must not have been easy growing up after losing him. But if it matters, I'm sure he's proud of you. I haven't known you long, but you seem like a very honorable man."

Jarreck smiled weakly and straightened his posture, "Thank you, Jaina. I really needed that. I just wish he were here. He would know what to do in this situation. He could at least give us more insight on this artifact."

Brandon replied, "I'm sure that he c-... could, but I don't doubt that you will make the right d-... decisions. We won't even need to know what this artifact is for, because we're going to recover it tomorrow!" he said optimistically.

They all smiled after Brandon's comment.

Jaina timidly asked, "Do you really think our little group can succeed tomorrow?"

"Fellowship," Brandon corrected.

"What?" asked Nazario.

"We're more of a fellowship than a group."

"I see," replied Nazario with a raised eyebrow.

"Well, whatever we call ourselves," Jarreck said, "I have faith that the Alackai will guide us to success tomorrow. We can't afford to lose."

Kiva looked around at everyone's face. She enjoyed the warmth of the fire. She let out a large yawn. Everyone turned to look at her and her cheeks rushed with blood.

She quickly spoke, "Do you have any more questions? It's getting late and we need to get some rest."

Brandon responded, "Just one more. Earlier, you m-... mentioned something about Swords, Shields, and Shades. What are those?"

Kiva answered, "They're the different specialties of the Skovi. The Shields study the histories and knowledge accrued by the Society. They

practice defensive magic as well as act as diplomats to resolve conflict with their wisdom.  The Swords are the warriors.  They are trained to end conflict when the Shields can't prevent it.  There are ten of each."

The humans were all staring intently at her.  She looked over at Jarreck, who nodded, encouraging her to proceed.

"We're both Shades, stealth warriors, trained to move through the shadows and gather information.  Shades are chosen from the ranks of the Shields and Swords, so they have talents of their previous sect, in addition to their new training.  There are only five of us.  Jarreck was a Shield whereas I was a Sword."

Jaina smiled at Kiva, who returned the smile.

Jaina said, "Thank you so much for taking the time to teach us about your culture.  I know it's really helped us to relax.  Your people are so wonderful.  Hopefully, we can become great friends after this is all over."

Kiva glanced at Nazario before replying, "This has been an interesting experience for sure.  I can't help but wonder what your arrival means for us.  But I would like new friends."

Nazario locked eyes with Kiva through his visor, "A friendship would be nice.  For both our people."

Jaina spoke again, "You've told us so much about yourselves, is there anything you want to know about us?  I feel like we owe you so much already, just for your hospitality and giving us a chance to prove ourselves."

Jarreck's eyes narrowed as he watched the humans.  Kiva looked over at him for a moment before looking back at Jaina.  She had been holding in all her questions.  She was not sure when she would get a better chance to have them answered.  *We might not even live beyond tomorrow.*

"Where do you come from?  And how did you get here?" Kiva asked.

Jaina answered her questions, "We're from a planet called Earth. It used to be green like this place, but our population grew too great, and we had to clear out the trees to make room.  Our planet is covered in nothing but buildings and cities.  We even expanded into the sky with hovering cities and neighborhoods.  Some even orbited in space.

"We nearly destroyed all our plant life but managed to save it by creating artificial forests that float throughout the heavens as well.  We failed to protect our planet from ourselves, so we needed to start over.  We flew through space in a gigantic ship to get here."

The translators had difficulty keeping up with this information as the Undaari did not have words to explain a lot of their technology.  She got the gist of their story, though.

Kiva's face was drawn. "You destroyed your forests?  Are you trying to do that here too?"

Jaina shook her head frantically, "Oh no.  We *learned* from our mistakes, but it was too late for Earth.  We won't repeat that cycle.  We could learn a lot about conservation from your people.  We wish to grow alongside you, not destroy your world.  We could even live on the continents on the far side of this planet."

Kiva and Jarreck both looked at Jaina with confusion on their faces. "What other continents?" she asked.

Brandon replied, "There are t-... two other continents on this planet that are even bigger than this one.  I don't think they're t-... touched by the Alackai, though.  There were no energy readings coming from them."

Kiva sat back.  She looked over at Jarreck who appeared just as dumbfounded as her.  *What are they talking about?*  She had been enjoying getting to know the humans but was confused by this last revelation.  She did not know what else to say on the topic.

Kiva looked around the camp again and could see that the humans were relaxed and smiling.  The distraction had been welcomed.  She had interest in Nazario, and their military as well, but decided to leave those questions for another time.  She did not want another nasty surprise tonight.

Nazario was curious about something else, "Are the blue capes just a fashion statement?  Or do they serve a purpose?"

Jarreck laughed, "Capes have significance among our people. Different colors represent different things.  We wear blue because that is the cape of the Skovi.  It matches the Alackai's Light.  The King's guard wears white.  Jerykka and her elite guardians of Entfall wear burgundy.  Army Commanders wear black and the King wears gold."

Major Nazario was impressed.  "I have to say, I'm envious.  The capes are elegant yet make quite a strong statement.  I had been hoping to get my hands on one."

"Perhaps, when all of this is over."

Jaina asked another question.  "I remember the King's name being Ambrecia'Cepheus.  Did they name the capital after him?"

Jarreck shook his head.  "No, no.  The Undaari value their history and homes.  We're named after the city we hail from then our given name.

We only use full names in formal settings. I'm Ennika'Jarreck and this is Ambrosi'Kiva. We generally refer to each other with our given names."

Jarreck looked at Nazario and asked, "What's with the metal suit and why does it glow so brightly in the center?"

"These suits are designed to support us as we carry additional weight and prevent us from tiring quickly. They store built in weapons and computers to give us access to vast amounts of information for our missions. They make our lives as peacekeepers much easier and allow us to survive more should we find ourselves in combat."

Nazario pointed to his UPC Sigil as he continued, "In the center of my chest is a holographic projection of our galaxy. It's the sigil of our government, the United People's Commonwealth. All the stars you see in the night sky form this galaxy.

"We call it the Milky Way and are from this star that's bright blue. Your planet orbits around this other star that is now shining bright red. I realize this is a tiny display, but if your entire planet was represented by this tiny dot, just look how many other dots are between your planet and ours. That shows how far we've come to be here with you."

Nazario gestured to the skies, and they could see thousands of stars twinkling down on them. An arm of the Milky Way was fully evident across the sky shimmering in pink and purple light. Jarreck's eyes lit up as he followed Nazario's gestures into the heavens.

Jarreck quietly said, "Maybe the Alackai brought you here for a reason after all. Thank you for the information. It's time we settle in for the night and get some rest. The battle tomorrow will be fierce."

Nazario stepped away from the warm fire and settled into his sleeping bag on the grassy ground. He thought about how much had changed over the last week. They had only been on this planet a few days. They had not even known that other sentient life existed in the galaxy a week ago. Now they were risking their lives to save them. The human population's fate rested in his hands and his decisions.

If he failed to save this newly discovered species, then he would be letting the people back on the *Jericho* down. They would likely never be able to reach the safety of this planet and build a new home. Just a few months ago, there were a trillion humans in the galaxy, now there were a million left, all depending on him. *Five million*, but he was unsure as to the fate of the other four ships out across the galaxy, all fighting for survival.

He had not allowed the reality of the situation to truly hit him yet, but he could feel it building inside. He had to keep himself distracted from those thoughts and focused on his mission. When this was over, he would need a long vacation to process everything that had happened.

Garren struggled to fall asleep as he lay in his hammock, strung between two trees. Despite his body's relaxed position, his heart raced. Monkley shared a tree trunk with him as his hammock hung nearby. Garren tossed and turned as a cool evening breeze struck him. Sleep would evade him tonight. He switched sides again, this time to face Monkley.

Monkley's eyes were open. Garren nearly jumped out of his hammock.

"Monkley!" he hissed. "You scared the crap out of me. Why aren't you asleep?"

"Why aren't you?" Monkley answered with a question of his own.

"I can't. These past few days have been too chaotic. And tomorrow... tomorrow we might end it all."

"Thankfully. I'm ready for this to be over so we can get the *Jericho* here. Every day we're here is a day closer that ship is to tearing itself apart. The unrest aboard that ship was already concerning when we left."

"I suppose that's true. But I must admit, there's something about this place... Something freeing."

"Freeing how? Besides the obvious wilderness we find ourselves in."

Garren hesitated, "For the first time since we left home, I feel alive. The action here has been exhilarating. But it fills me with guilt. I'm having the time of my life these last couple days despite everything that has happened."

Monkley let out a small laugh, "It's been quite a rush. Even with you stealing most of the fun."

"You're a good friend Monkley. Without you, I might not have made it this far. I was on the precipice before this mission."

"Just taking care of my boss. I'm not quite ready to take over Recon. Not when the job is about to be so boring."

"Ha! Boring will never be in the job description."

"If you do your job tomorrow, it will be."

Garren smiled and rolled over. Talking helped his heart. He finally felt relaxed. The darkness was comforting. There wasn't as much glow in this section of the forest.

"Thank you," he whispered.

Monkley had been his rock.  He could not fathom how this mission would have gone without him.

# Chapter 16
## Surprises

Commander Braylon remained calm as he was escorted to his residence in the heart of the Haven. He knew the fleet had just been launched and was on its way to Undaaleria. That's what the reports had said the name of the planet is.

He had finally been allowed to hear the reports from Sergeant Piers and Jaina after the fleet had departed. The continent with the coveted energy source was called Undaalan. That was all much easier to say than ZX-746 or trying to describe the continent. He was sure the humans would try to rename it, though, if they took the planet by force. Unless he did something to protect it from genocide.

Braylon took a mental count. It had only been six days since Major Nazario departed with his team. Only three days of imprisonment. The fleet would be there by the eighth day. It took communications roughly twenty-four hours to reach their destination. That meant he only had one day, a little less than twenty-four hours, to get a signal to the fleet and stop their attack.

None of the civilians knew about the Undaari, nor the mutiny. General Titus had made sure to keep them all in the dark. He was not bound nor gagged as he was marched home. Titus just made it clear that if he spoke, his family would be in danger.

Braylon so desperately wanted to speak. He was not ready to sacrifice his family, though. Braylon wanted to hold a ship wide conference to tell everyone the phenomenal news, but the General prevented that. Everyone deserved to know the truth.

Titus clearly had a plan in place for the mutiny well before taking action. Braylon suspected that he had been planning it as early as their pit stop to set up Bastion's Hope.  The people would be against the current course of action if they knew the truth, which was why Titus had prevented him from speaking out.  Braylon felt that all they needed was hope but none remained.

As he neared the city, the cause of Titus' concern became more evident.  Titus had not been lying about the fears of the people and this showed why he chose to act.  The outskirts of the city were made up mostly of shops, a designated commerce sector, and it had been vandalized and pilfered.

Braylon slowed as they passed through this nearly abandoned section.  His face was blank as he surveyed the damage.  He had seen some of the vandalism from the monitors but seeing it in person hit him differently.  Guilt knotted his stomach as his escorts urged him to move faster.  The civilians were terrified. They were doing everything they could to ensure they lived as long as possible, even at the expense of others, to include hoarding supplies and goods.

Martial law had been instituted to prevent violence from breaking out, though it may have done more to incite it.  Braylon could feel the tension in the air.  He could see citizens peering at his delegation through their windows.  The people no longer acted civilized; their decisions had grown rash.  Braylon was devastated by how far they had fallen.

As they reached the interior of the city, there was a shift in the environment.  While there was less vandalism and next to no structural damage, people crowded in the streets, protesting across the city center.  There was a lot of graffiti across the skyscrapers calling out the military leadership for their failures.  The peacekeepers stood back, monitoring the situation, but would not intervene as long as the people stayed nonviolent.

The graffiti and the signs held above the protestors showed that many thought the peacekeepers were keeping citizens suppressed to save themselves.  *Keeping the civilians in the dark is dangerous.*  They deserved to know the truth of the situation.

Debris and trash were flung his way as the protesters saw his detail approach.  The peacekeepers moved in to push the crowds back and allow him to travel safely.  Nine of his guards formed a protective ring around him while the tenth stood at his side.  *The protestors are blaming me.*

Fights broke out in the crowds as they pushed back against the peacekeepers who were trying to restore order.  *I must find a way to right the ship and save these people.*  He had a general idea but was going to need a lot of help.

He feared the guards would keep a watchful eye on him within his domicile. He was not likely to be allowed to leave 'for his safety.' It would be dangerous trying to get help, but he was willing to do anything to save the *Jericho* and its people.

His security detail led him to the central tower of the city where his quarters were located. While his large detail consisted of ten peacekeepers, only three entered the elevator with him. The rest stayed on the ground level, securing the entrance. No one wanted the protesters to attack him, not even Titus.

Braylon wondered if these soldiers even knew about the mutiny. He was sure their leader had to have some sort of idea. He considered confronting him directly, but that was risky. He was not sure who he could trust and if these troops were in on the mutiny. They would report his attempt to convert them to Titus which would remove any freedoms he might have. If he had no other options, he would take the risk, but escaping was more important than ending the mutiny. He needed as few eyes on him as possible to stop the fleet.

Once they reached his level, near the top of the tower, they all exited the elevator. Only one of the guards entered his apartment with him, stating he was doing a security sweep. Braylon greeted his husband with a big hug. He looked around tentatively, but their two kids did not seem to be home.

He continued developing a plan in his head while he waited for the officer to complete the search. His brother was who might know someone who could help, but he had not talked to him since the selection process for the mission. He was not even sure how to contact him with communications down. He would have to go to his brother's assigned room several buildings away and hope he was home. Braylon needed to find a way past the guards.

The guard finished his sweep and approached Braylon.

"Sir, I have completed my sweep. Your home is secure. We'll have two guards outside your door and eight more in the lobby. If you need anything, please let us know. Hopefully, this will all be resolved quickly."

Commander Braylon nodded his understanding, and the guard stepped outside. He was surprised they were not staying inside to watch him. Titus must think he had already won. Or perhaps these peacekeepers thought this was a legitimate security mission. Either way, he made his way around his home, inspecting for surveillance devices before he smiled at his husband.

He relaxed his shoulders and focused on Taylor for the first time since entering his home.  Braylon had not found anything obvious, but suspected he was still being monitored.  His eyes scanned around the apartment again for the kids before he led the way to their bedroom.

Taylor looked at him knowingly and spoke in a soft tone, "The kids are with your parents.  What's going on?  You shouldn't be here with everything going on.  Not with all the chaos."

Braylon hugged him tightly again and relaxed.  He changed out of his navy-blue uniform into more casual clothes.  He did not have to be the Commander with Taylor.

"You know me all too well.  Things have taken a turn for the worst. I'm not in charge anymore.  General Titus has mutinied and *says* he's trying to save everyone, but his methods are dangerous and risky.  People are scared and rioting.  It's a mess right now.  But there's hope."

Taylor took a step back, eyeing him as if he thought this was an elaborate prank.

His voice was elevated when he finally asked, "Wait, what?  You're serious?  How can he do that?  What are you talking about?"

"He thinks it's the only way to save everyone.  He thinks I've messed up too much.  I'm not without error, but he's misguided.  More importantly, we've made the biggest discovery in human history, but it's being overshadowed by the events on this ship.

"We found a new power source; one that can save the *Jericho*.  But it belongs to an alien race living on ZX-746.  Titus thinks I'll mess this all up. I don't have much time to talk, though.  I have to act quickly in order to prevent genocide and save everyone.  I'll give you the rest of the details as soon as I can."

He motioned with his finger to be quiet and say no more.  Taylor slowly sat down on the bed with a blank look.  Braylon did not want General Titus to impose any more restrictions on him.  He had an idea.  He walked away as Taylor's eyes followed him out of the room.

Jarreck and Nazario rode their colorful zakeri just above the treetops with their counterparts, Kiva and Garren, on the second.  Monkley, Jaina, and Brandon sat in position high in the trees overlooking the Noxxon encampment, while still maintaining a safe distance from the action.  Ferani had stayed back at their camp awaiting the return of the two zakeri.  He would attend to their needs and ensure they were protected once they got back.

Nazario could just see tinges of pink and orange on the horizon behind them as they flew. Sunrise was only minutes away and would erupt like fire across the sky. The Noxxons would be waking any minute now.

The zakeri and their riders dropped over the treetops into the heart of the Noxxon camp. Turquoise feathers and yellow claws crashed down into the tents where the Noxxons slept. Jarreck leapt off the zakeri's back and started spreading his cerulean fire, trapping Noxxons in their burning tents.

Nazario took note of Jarreck's new tactic as he slid off the saddle. Not wasting any time, he unleashed full powered energy blasts from his Valor arm mounted cannon. He fired directly into the crowds of Noxxons trying to escape their tents. There were only a few Noxxons standing guard outside, but they had no opportunity to defend the others. Blasts of white energy pierced their heads and chests from a great distance, leaving small rings of molten orange metal around the wounds.

Kiva jumped off the second zakeri, sigridir drawn, and cut down other Noxxons fleeing their tents. Garren dismounted, covering her rear. The two zakeri clawed and bit their way through several Noxxons. The two ferocious felines tore apart several half-armored monsters trying to flee the destruction being inflicted.

The tents were ablaze with sapphire flames and the Noxxons were screaming in horror. Half their number already lay in bloody piles across their camp. Those still fighting were unprepared and falling quickly. The zakeri had done their job. Jarreck whistled loudly and the two winged cats shot into the sky, escaping any counterattack.

Once the zakeri were clear, bolts of energy rained down into the camp more densely, providing cover fire. Jaina, Brandon, and Monkley used their energy weapons from a distance to help suppress the Noxxon counterattack. These energy weapons were more powerful than the built-in arm cannons on the Reliant Exosuits. They were dedicated to combat, whereas the arm cannons were more versatile and used for other purposes as well, like cutting and welding.

Cerulean fire continued to spread through the camp as Jarreck and Kiva were using the Alackai to keep the Noxxons down. Nazario could see their teeth clench as they wielded their magic. Kiva had taken her former master's lead in using their greatest weapon.

Garren and Nazario were back-to-back now, blasting away at the Noxxons while wielding their Undaari blades to keep the Noxxons from closing in.  The Noxxons were falling quickly to their overwhelming power and surprise.  A smirk formed across his face as he watched his team —fellowship— lay waste to these cruel beings.

Nazario watched as the Noxxons reeled, just a few warriors still fighting.  Some moved as though they were going to retreat. Weapons were being dropped. *This is working!*

A great gust of wind blew through the camp, extinguishing the blue inferno.  From the still smoldering central tent, a massive Noxxon emerged. Nazario's heart sank.

This was no normal Noxxon.  The monstrosity stood nearly half a meter taller than the others around it.  Taller even than the Undaari.  It did not simply have rock-like skin like the other Noxxons.  It appeared to be made of actual obsidian rock cracked with red scars.  Its eyes even glowed bright scarlet as it stared him down.  Long yellow horns grew from its forehead giving it the appearance of a monstrous demon.  He had been wrong before; *this* was something straight out of a nightmare.

This thing was an abomination.  Nazario's body shuddered in spite of himself.  It had what looked like four giant, scarred, black stone spikes stabbed into its back and carried a massive onyx staff that matched them. Nazario felt true fear for the first time on this planet; this thing's mere presence caused terror in the heart of those around it.  Nazario cowered back from the monster.

Garren was the quickest to react.  He began firing his arm cannon at the new threat, still set at full power.  The first blast glanced off its shoulder, then the second off its other shoulder.  The attacks barely fazed it. It did not need armor to protect itself; it barely wore anything but a few pieces of metal and some chains.

The creature placed its staff directly in front of it and absorbed the next two blasts.  It started moving more quickly, swinging its staff around and pointing it directly back at Garren.  It conjured crimson flames and blasted them at the man.

Jarreck was faster though, moving quickly and using his magic to raise a cerulean shield of fire in front of their group.  It was not strong enough. The red fire ripped through the shield and knocked them all to the ground, leaving their skin singed in places. The smell of burning flesh stifled their senses but seemed to feed the large Noxxon's blood lust.  It howled in excitement.

The abomination quickly twirled its staff again, moving impossibly fast for its size.  It conjured a vermilion ball of fire in the air that followed the path of the staff. As the monstrosity brought its staff down toward Garren, the ball of fire followed, raining crimson flames down on the man. The scarlet ball crushed Garren with explosive force, killing him instantly. Nazario's heart stopped as he witnessed the horror.

Jarreck screamed fearfully, "Run! We can't stand against this thing!"

Nazario jumped in front of Kiva to shield her as she ran. He fired off a couple more shots at the threat, but they were completely ineffective. Nazario ran for the trees without further hesitation, adrenaline coursing through his body. He knew when to not argue. Not even the Colonial Rebellions had left him this shaken.

Kiva vanished, using the Alackai to hide herself and escape. Jarreck called upon the Alackai to blast cyan fire at the Noxxon, knocking it back a step and causing hesitation in its actions. That was apparently all the time Jarreck needed to disappear and escape. The group fled quickly. Nazario could hear a deep, rumbling laugh fill the air as they fled.

The massive thing did not bother to chase them. It slammed its staff down, calling the attention of the remaining few Noxxons. They turned from the fight as the group fled and got ready to move out. There were less than ten Noxxons left to gather their supplies before they continued their long march north toward the Scarred Mountain.

Jarreck, Kiva, and Nazario made it to the trees where their companions had been stationed. They bent in half, hands on their knees, trying to catch their breath. The others climbed down the tree, exiting their stand. The two zakeri were circling the base, protecting the team, rather than returning to their camp. Jaina was the first out of the tree, fear and shock still covering her face. She was practically screaming at Jarreck as she shoved a finger into his chest.

"What *happened*? What *was* that thing? You said the Noxxons *couldn't* use the Alackai!"

Jarreck slowly shook his head, still panting, "I have no idea. No Noxxon has *ever* been granted the power of the Alackai. That thing was unnatural, but it explains why they're pursuing the ancient knowledge. They've discovered how to use it. I don't understand how it works or what happened, but it *must* be stopped. The Noxxon threat is even greater than I feared. That abomination was more powerful than any Skovi I've ever known."

Kiva looked at her former master, still bent over, "How is this even possible? Did you see the spikes in its back? They were made of the same stone that protects Entfall. That Noxxon was made into a weapon."

"I saw, but I don't know how. They *had* to have found other texts. Maybe they've been experimenting with the black stone in their fortress. I didn't even think there was much left to mine. I don't think this was something that the Society ever thought was possible. This is something different, something much darker. They *must* be defeated, and the knowledge destroyed so that the Noxxons can't make more. Otherwise, all of Undaalan will be wiped out."

Monkley was the last one out of the tree. When he reached the base, he recklessly charged back toward the Noxxon camp. Nazario grabbed him, pulling him back. Monkley struggled against him, throwing Nazario's hands off. Nazario jumped on Monkley, tackling him to the ground.

"I have to go back! I'm not leaving him!" Monkley shouted, still struggling to free himself.

"We won't," said Nazario as he pinned Monkley down. Jaina and Brandon rushed forward to help.

"If you go back now, you'll die, too," said Jaina.

Nazario spoke to the Undaari, still struggling to hold Monkley back, "We need to recover Garren's body. I'm not sure about your traditions for the fallen, but we don't leave ours behind."

Jarreck nodded at Nazario. "Neither do we. We'll make every effort to recover his body shortly. We must give the Noxxons time to clear out first. We don't want to face that abomination again."

Nazario loosened his grip on Monkley and stood up. Monkley got to his feet quickly, jaw clenched, still shooting daggers at Nazario. Nazario placed his hand on Monkley's shoulder, silently supporting his team member.

Kiva looked over at Nazario. He looked back at her and could see she was still breathing heavily as she shifted closer to his side. He had been worried that she would get hurt. He did not want to lose anyone else. *I can't believe I lost Garren.*

Jarreck turned to Kiva, "In the meantime, Kiva, the Council must be made aware of these events. Both our Council and the King's advisors. Take Jaina and Brandon with you. The King seems to like the humans and wants an alliance with them. They can help with the diplomatic side of this. After we recover Garren's body, Nazario, Monkley, and I will head back to Entfall to warn Jerykka of this new threat."

Everyone nodded their understanding. Kiva, Jaina, and Brandon mounted their zakeri and took flight immediately. Nazario and Jarreck watched them disappear from sight and lingered a little longer. No one wanted to wait longer than necessary before returning to the Noxxon camp. They did not bother to return to their own camp, distracted as they were.

Nazario eyed Monkley as the Captain paced through the forest. There was a rage inside him unlike anything Nazario had ever witnessed. He knew the two had been best friends for years.

"We'll get him Monkley, I promise," Nazario offered.

"That's not good enough. Those Noxxons will pay for what they did. Garren didn't deserve to die. He was finally recovering."

"He didn't die in vain. He died to save the lives of everyone on board the *Jericho*."

"I know that, but it's still not enough. He deserves to be honored and remembered."

"He will be given the highest military honors, Monkley. Everyone will know that he gave his life for them. He'll be immortalized in Remembrance."

"That's the least we can do. And I'm going to kill that thing."

A few minutes later, they mounted the zakeri and lifted off. Jarreck flew to a high altitude before flying over the camp. No one wanted to risk being in range of any attacks if the Noxxons were still around. Thankfully, the Noxxons had already moved on. They landed in the camp and searched through the remnants. The dead Noxxons had been left to rot, along with the ruins of their tents.

Garren's body, however, was nowhere to be seen. It appeared the Noxxons had taken it. Nazario's fists clenched as his body tensed up. He let out a loud scream that startled Jarreck. Nazario fell to his knees, his entire body shaking. Jarreck placed a hand on Nazario's shoulder to calm him.

"NO!" Monkley screamed from behind them.

Nazario turned to see Monkley kicking a dead Noxxon body. The realization that they had lost Garren's body had hit Monkley, too, even harder. Nazario did not bother to stop him. The man needed to get his frustrations out.

"We'll get him back. For now, we *have* to regroup. Let's get back to Entfall and plan from there. This is far from over, my friends," Jarreck stated.

Nazario nodded. It took a few more kicks before Monkley turned away from the Noxxon and joined them. They mounted their zakeri and lifted off, making their way to Entfall. It was not a long trip.

As they landed in the courtyard, Jarreck could tell something was wrong. There was panic in the air; people were scurrying about quickly. This was not like his arrival in Ambrecia. He could feel the difference immediately.

Without bothering to bring the zakeri to the stables, he led the way through the chaos into the main hall. Jarreck grabbed the first person he saw and demanded to know where Jerykka was.

"Sir, Master Jerykka never made it back. She and most of her men fell in battle. They were trapped by the Noxxons. Only a few of her warriors managed to escape and warn us. Worse, the Noxxons will be here by nightfall. Intayr is preparing the defenses in her absence."

Jarreck nearly fell over. He grabbed Nazario by the shoulder, trying to steady himself, his other arm grasping his chest. It was difficult to breathe. *Jerykka can't have fallen. I need her. We all need her.*

She was their Shield against the Noxxons. Without her, he did not know how Entfall would survive the attack. Without Jerykka, Entfall's strength would crumble. If Entfall fell, so would the entire Undaari people. He looked over to Nazario, tears in his eyes.

"Help them, please."

He struggled to stand straight, still grasping his chest as he walked out the back of the hall without looking back. Tears ran down his cheeks like a river. He made his way through the fortress. He had a destination in mind, slipping through a secret passage. It was the only place he felt he could go to grieve this loss. He was one of only two living people, other than Jerykka herself, who knew of this passage. His former master, Councilor Gierdahl, had shown him this place during his training.

It did not take him long to reach his destination. Down in the depths of the keep, there was a large chamber with a single Entai growing strong in the center. The entire cavern was made from the same black stone that the outer walls were. Jarreck fell to his knees in front of the Entai. He placed a hand on its bark and rested his forehead against the tree.

Through the tears he managed to whisper a request, "Alackai, please, guide us through this tragedy. Save us from this threat. I don't have the strength to do so without you. Please..."

He pleaded to the Alackai, desperate for an answer. He lost himself in her, feeling her strength well up inside him as the tendrils of cerulean energy came up through the ground and connected with him. He could feel a renewed warmth and energy inside of him.  No answers were provided to him.  The Alackai never spoke directly to those she Graced; however, she was able to convey one thing: Hope.

He released the last of his tears and stood, examining his surroundings.  This space had once been a naturally formed cave where the Entai found root.  There was a wall with a massive stained-glass window built into the side of the cavern that had once been the mouth to the cave.  This Entai was the true heart of the keep.

His muscles were refreshed and bulging under his armor.  Energy was coursing through his veins.  His heart was walled off, finally able to focus on the task at hand.  He bowed in thanks before the Entai and made his way back to the main hall.

When he reached the war table, he found Nazario standing with the other Undaari.  Nazario had one thing to say as he walked up.

"They're here."

# Chapter 17

## Pleas

Kiva landed their zakeri in a flurry of feathers inside the central courtyard of Ambrecia, dismounting in a flash. She led the humans to the entrance of the palace. There, she instructed the guards to take the humans directly to the King. She let them know she would be there shortly but had to report elsewhere first.

Kiva returned to the zakeri, gently holding it under its boulder sized face, scratching its chin lovingly. She whispered instructions to it, then whistled, signaling for it to return to the stables. Normally, she would escort the zakeri, but they would not be long. It could rest there until she called it back. Kiva used the Alackai to vanish, making her way to the Society's secret headquarters.

She used the Alackai to open the door and enter unseen. It had only been a few days since she followed Jarreck through this door to warn the Society about the Noxxons finding the artifact. A lot had happened since then. She could not believe how extraordinarily desperate these days had been.

Once she was inside, she allowed herself to become visible again. She made her way to the Council Chambers. Kiva knocked once then entered without waiting for the traditional summons. The entire Council had already gathered, and the chambers were completely full. It appeared the entire Society was gathered here except for Jarreck and herself.

High Councilor Vreeham looked up at Kiva as she entered. The Council Chambers fell silent.

"Ah, Kiva, we were beginning to think you and Jarreck were too busy with our visitors to arrive when summoned," Vreeham chided.

She looked up at the High Councilor, not hiding her surprise,

"We've received no summons, High Councilor. Nor is Jarreck with me. He's still in Entfall, assisting with their battle preparations. I had not intended to stay."

High Councilor Vreeham raised a hand to silence Kiva.

"It doesn't matter why you're here. We've gathered to discuss the rumored Noxxon threat. There has been a call for aid from Entfall. We're determining what course of action would be best for the Society to follow moving forward. Our priority must be to protect Ambrecia and the King."

"It's no rumor. The threat is re—"

The High Councilor again interrupted and continued speaking over her, "We do not feel that Entfall is in any real danger, so sending the Society there would be pointless. Besides, the Society does not serve Entfall, it serves the Undaari and their King. That means we're needed here in Ambrecia."

"High Councilor, I *must* protest. The Society *is* needed at Entfall. We can't let—"

Again, the High Councilor cut off Kiva.

"It's not up to you. The Council has decided. The Noxxon threat has been exaggerated. Master Jerykka is creating panic for nothing. She's fearful of failure. Her ineptitude has led her to be underprepared, but Entfall shall continue to stand. After the Noxxons have been repelled, we may have to recommend replacement.

"*You* are being reassigned to be the King's Skovi protector. You are no longer needed in Entfall wasting time with Jarreck. We're asking you to keep the humans nearby. The King is intrigued by them, though they seem like a poor distraction to us. They don't provide the Undaari with anything of value."

Kiva yelled at the High Councilor, "I belong in Entfall! With Jarreck! You don't understand. I'm only here to warn you the Noxxons have learned how to use the Alackai. They've discovered some ancient artifact. Entfall is in serious danger and if we can't stop them, they will destroy all of Undaalan."

Another Councilor scoffed at her, "How *dare* you make up lies to get your way. Jarreck was never one to heed the Council, but *your* insubordination will not be tolerated any longer. Do as directed or you will lose your place among the Society. Jarreck is a senile old man who you should distance yourself from. Our place is here in Ambrecia, protecting the King and his people."

Kiva waved her hand at the Council in dismissal. She charged out of the chambers.

As she reached the door, she turned back and yelled at the Council, "I cannot standby and allow the Noxxons to destroy everything we hold dear. My place is in Entfall with Jarreck, protecting our people, not hiding here in ignorance! And the humans have proven far more useful in this struggle than anyone on the Council!"

She stormed out of the chambers and down the passages without bothering to wait for a response. She used the secret staircase to make her way to the palace near the King's Court. She was going to warn him, then take the humans back to Entfall where they actually had a chance to do something.

She reached the throne room, charging in without waiting for the white caped guards to open the doors. She barged past and they drew their weapons, chasing after.

The King looked up, surprised by her abruptness. Jaina and Brandon turned around, startled. The King smiled when his eyes fell on Kiva. The King's smiled quickly faded, though, worry covering his face instead.

He waved off the charging White Guards and asked, "What happened, young Kiva?"

She looked up at the King as she approached. She slowed her charge, trying to calm herself. The King had always been like a father to her, but he was still King. She had lost her real dad in an accident when she was young. A storm had rolled in, creating large waves that knocked him from the cliff walls of Ambrosi, leading down to the docks. He was washed out to sea after returning from a fishing trip.

King Cepheus had appeared at the funeral to support her and her mother. He had just lost his wife and child in an unrelated incident and had taken special interest in Kiva. He had moved her and her mother to Ambrecia and looked out for them after. Despite their bond, she needed to maintain customs.

She remembered something that Jarreck had always told her during her training. *No matter how tough the times or frightful the situation, always pay the proper respects to our King. Without him, the Society would be nothing. He is our greatest ally, and we must remember the pressures he faces already. Without that respect, it's hard to keep what you say in mind with the weight of the kingdom already there.*

She hesitated, then bowed before the King.

"My King, the Noxxon situation has grown dire, and the Society won't listen. I fear their ignorance will cost us greatly. The Noxxons have learned how to use the Alackai. We don't understand it, but their power is great. I'm lucky to even be alive. The humans lost one of their own protecting me. If we can't stop them in Entfall, I fear that we won't be able to stop them at all."

The King nodded and smiled at her softly. He stood up and walked over to Kiva, placing a hand on her shoulder to comfort her.

"Our guests have filled me in on the situation, and I agree with you. Entfall is the shield of the entire Undaari people, not just Ambrecia. The humans have proven their strength. We must take action to ensure *everyone* is protected. Take the humans with you. I trust you to do what is best for our people. You *always* have my deepest trust. I will speak with the Society's Council and my advisors. They're not as brave as you, young one. Now hurry, I can imagine the Society is not happy with your actions. Alackai's Grace guide you."

Kiva smiled. She wanted to hug him but held to their customs. He was a wise and fair King. Jarreck was also wise with his teachings. He knew best how to take care of his people and one day, would make an excellent Councilor. *If we survive.* She bowed again to the King.

"And her Light protect you."

The humans bowed as well, and all three departed. They walked through the doors and exited the palace into Ambrecia's central courtyard. Councilor Gierdahl was waiting for them. She let out a high-pitched whistle to call their zakeri back.

She looked directly at him and angrily stated, "I'm going to Entfall. The Society is wrong."

Councilor Gierdahl smiled knowingly. "I know, Kiva. I'm not here to stop you. I just wanted to let you know I convinced the Council not to lay down punishment until this ordeal is over. I wanted you to leave without the weight of that on your mind. I support you, but I follow the Council, ignorant as it may be sometimes. You know our history. They're scared to act for fear of negative reaction. I'll try to get you support in Entfall. Give Jarreck my best; he was one of the strongest students I've ever had. Alackai's Grace guide you."

The zakeri landed by Kiva's side. Kiva's eyes narrowed with suspicion, but she returned the Councilor's smile.

"And her Light protect you."

She mounted the zakeri with the humans and took flight. Right after they reached their cruising altitude, Jaina leaned in close to Kiva.

"I have an idea."

Jarreck made his way to the ramparts of Entfall. He needed to see the invasion force for himself. Nazario was by his side, along with Intayr and Monkley. When they reached their vantage point, he was able to see the sprawling strength of the approaching Noxxons.

They were still far off in the distance, but closing in. The Noxxon army was tearing down the entire forest on the approach to Entfall, clearing a wide path. Judging by their current pace, they would reach the shores of the lake before nightfall.

Jarreck wondered what their plan of attack would be. Surely, they would charge along the natural land bridge to the gates, but that was a serious choke point. As large as their numbers were, the Noxxons could not hope to defeat Entfall this way. *They had to have another plan, some sort of trickery.*

He turned to Intayr and nodded. Jarreck and Intayr, with their respective cerulean and burgundy capes billowing in the wind, turned, and led Major Nazario back to the war table to continue preparing their plan.

They left Monkley on the rampart with orders to observe and assist wherever he could. The man was bouncing on his feet, ready for the fight to begin. Jarreck would return to the ramparts with the others, once the Noxxons reached the shores.

Jarreck could see Monkley's jaw still clenched as he glared out at the Noxxon horde. He felt bad that Monkley did not get the chance to grieve the loss of his close friend. Grieving was important in Undaari culture.

Jarreck spoke once they reached the war table, "Let's not pretend that the Noxxons intend to knock down the front gates. There's more to it than that. They're brutes, but they're not totally dumb. They'll have a plan, and we must anticipate it. They've already proven there's far more to this invasion than just brute strength."

Nazario and Intayr nodded.

Intayr slowly began to speak, "No one knew this fortress better than Master Jerykka. I wish she were here to help. She would know exactly what to do. I only just transferred into this position from Ambrecia a few moon cycles ago."

"Who knows this place best of those remaining? Perhaps we could use more help," Jarreck asked.

Intayr thought for a moment, "That would have to be Rentari, the Captain of the White Guard. The King insisted that a detachment of his King's Guard be stationed here to protect the Warden. I'll have him brought here. He's been at Jerykka's side for years."

He called a guard over and instructed him to retrieve the Captain from the ramparts. It did not take long for Rentari to report to Intayr. When he approached, Intayr greeted him. Rentari was geared up and ready for battle with his white cape trailing behind him.

He nodded at Intayr and asked, "What can I do to be of service?"

"We need to know everything about this keep as far as weaknesses and access points. The Noxxons will surely seek to exploit them while feigning a head on attack. We're unsure what they might find or of any weaknesses that may exist. Without the Warden here to help, we're turning to you for advice," Intayr explained.

"I'm afraid that the Warden didn't often allow me to accompany her. I stood by her side at the war table, but she never liked that the King stationed us here, as though she couldn't protect herself or Entfall. She most often used us as supplementary patrols along the exterior of the keep, or out on missions to protect some of the small villages in the area. There are secrets here that only she knew. But I'll do my best to assist where I can."

"We'll have to assume that if you don't know of it, then neither will the Noxxons. Show us *everything* you can think of," said Jarreck.

Entfall was built to withstand any known enemy. The outer wall was tall and impenetrable. It had an inner wall as a secondary line of defense with a courtyard separating the two. Inside the inner wall were the workings of an entire city.

It had shops, housing, and stables for their animals surrounding an inner courtyard. Finally, there was the main fortress structure, which had the tallest walls and fewest entrances. There were several defensible positions throughout the keep giving the Undaari an advantage over superior numbers.

The group talked for another hour, discussing avenues of approach and possible targets for the Noxxons. There were docks on the north side of the keep for fishing boats. There were also a few hidden side gates to allow troops out for flanking movements. They stationed guards inside these gates just in case the Noxxons discovered them.

They added additional roving overwatches across the entire rampart. No troops would be allowed to abandon their post to assist elsewhere, no matter how intense the battle became. They did not want to risk the main battle being a distraction that allowed the Noxxons to sneak in through another route.  There would also be roaming guards along the interior of the wall, just in case.

Jarreck looked over their plan.  Intayr nodded his head in satisfaction.  That was the moment a sentry entered the main hall to inform them that the Noxxons had reached the shores.  Jarreck led their fellowship after the sentry up to the ramparts.  They could hear the beat of the Noxxon war drums clearly before they even reached the top of the walls; they were deafening.

He could feel his heartbeat quickening with the drums as he reached the lookout.  Jarreck's jaw dropped when he saw the sheer size of the Noxxon army.  It had already been intimidating to hear the drums beating in unison; seeing the horde just intensified the fear.  He watched the Noxxons halt at the shoreline and begin setting up camp, clearing out the trees around them.  The sun was setting, and visibility would not last much longer.  As the sky changed color to pink and orange, the sun's dying rays fell on the most horrific scene.

In the center of camp, Jarreck saw the body of Jerykka strung up by her arms.  Ropes were tied around her wrists, suspending her high above the Noxxons on a wooden, rolling platform.  She was hanging freely and dripping blood down her legs and off her toes.  Jarreck's heart sank, and his gut twisted around like he was going to puke.  He could feel the collective misery of the Undaari as their last hopes drained from their bodies.

There was another Noxxon abomination with a staff moving toward her. *There are more of these Staff Bearer things?* It slammed its staff on the ground and flames erupted on the platform, illuminating it.  The crimson firelight presented a clear view of Jerykka in the dying light.  Every wound was visible, and blood covered much of her body.

As the flames tickled her feet, they began to twitch.  Her head rolled back in pain as she regained consciousness. *She's alive!* The Staff Bearer yelled and another Noxxon approached the platform, brandishing a whip.  It began lashing Jerykka, eliciting screams that could be heard over the drumbeat.

"No!" Jarreck screamed, his voice cracking and body shaking.

They were torturing her in front of the keep.  Worse, they were too far away for the Undaari archers to put an end to her misery.  This act was clearly meant to ruin the morale and strike a serious blow to the Undaari resolve.  The Noxxon whipped her until she passed out again from the pain, blood flowing freely from the fresh wounds across her abdomen and back.

Jarreck was sickened by the brutality. His rage boiled up quickly. He surveyed the entire Noxxon camp, developing a quick plan. He noticed the Noxxons building boats from the trees they had ripped from the ground.

Jarreck looked at Intayr, "My place isn't here. I'm getting Jerykka back. I need your best archer to come with me. Someone who knows this may be a one-way mission."

Captain Rentari took a step forward. "You're looking at him."

Nazario also stepped forward, "You're crazy if you think I'm not joining you as well. I know her importance to your people. I'm here to help and can do a lot more out there than stuck in here."

Jarreck did not argue. He took one last look at Jerykka and saw the flames dying down around her. He turned and made his way down the ramparts. Rentari and Nazario followed him closely. He went straight for the docks. He would not make it down the bridge alive. The Noxxon camp extended right up to the edge of it.

He would take a small boat to the lake's edge, just north of the camp. The drums were still beating and would mask their approach on the water. The drums would continue throughout the night, to keep the Undaari from sleeping.

Jarreck's rage at the Noxxons was spilling over. Nazario looked at him worriedly, holding one of the new rifles his people had brought.

"Jarreck, my friend, you're *literally* crackling with electricity. I'm concerned that you'll set our boat on fire."

Jarreck looked at Nazario, his eyes glowing already.

"I'm keeping it in, but it's close to boiling over. The Noxxons will regret their actions. I'll enter the camp alone, in full stealth. Rentari, I need you to stay back. You're here in case I fail to rescue her. Her suffering ends tonight. Nazario, stay with him and watch his back."

They both nodded. He was thankful they did not argue. He could feel the Alackai's energy spilling out of him. He was about to explode, and they were not going to hold him back. They approached the shore, paddling quietly, and pulled the small boat onto land. Rentari and Nazario hid it in the woods under some shrubbery while Jarreck walked off on his mission, vanishing from sight.

# Chapter 18
## Family

Commander Braylon made his way through his housing unit to the back patio. He opened the door and unfolded the small deck, giving him an astounding view of the Haven. It was unfortunate that he had not gotten the chance yet to enjoy the cityscape, but the current state of things made that difficult. He scanned the nearby buildings and saw that most patios remained sealed, ready for space flight. He figured most people had not been able to relax and enjoy their homes on the dropships either.

He would not be able to exit his domicile the conventional way for fear of being caught. He eyed the surrounding buildings and determined there may be a viable path to make his escape. If it were anyone else, he knew this option would be impossible.

As he stepped out of the confines of the patio railing and got his footing stabilized, he felt a familiar comfort. His muscles still remembered powering their way through the most difficult obstacle courses in Basic Training. He had enjoyed them so much that he elevated his rush through free climbing buildings and cliffs. From the patio, he exited the housing unit and began to climb down the exterior wall of the central tower.

He looked over his shoulder and checked his surroundings, trying to move quickly. There was an adjacent building that he could get to if he got a little bit lower. His building was right in the heart of the Haven; there were still people protesting far below. Each building had antennae and protrusions that served various functions depending on the building; most were for flight after the buildings were ejected.

One of these protrusions was close enough to the adjacent building that he could jump the distance. It was a long jump but should be doable.

He would not be able to escape notice if he climbed his building to the bottom, but if he got into another building stealthily, his chances were much better.

Nimbly making his way down the building would be tricky, testing his skills. The surfaces were extremely smooth, built to reduce friction on atmospheric entry. His sweaty grip was tenuous at best, but he managed a steady pace. He wanted to move faster but knew that moving smoothly without error was the smarter method. Speed could kill him and doom his mission. The winds were rattling him around as the air was circulated across the Haven.

Braylon neared the protrusion he was aiming for. As he stood there, back to the wall, he began to mentally measure and calculate the jump. It was farther, and lower, than he remembered in the diagrams. The drop was two stories. *This is going to hurt.*

It was his only chance though. His own life, as well as the fate of the entire Undaari people, rested on him making this jump. He took a deep breath to steady himself, pushed off the wall and sprinted forward the few steps to the edge and leapt cleanly.

He hung in the air for what felt like minutes as every worst-case scenario rattled through his head, before coming down on the adjacent building. When he landed, his feet struggled to gain a strong grip on the smooth surface; they slipped out from under him. He landed on his back and slid off the protrusion. *This is it. This is how I'm going to die.* He desperately grabbed for anything to root himself to the building.

His momentum continued to carry him forward. As he crashed head-first into the exterior wall of the building, stars erupted in his vision. He began sliding down the side of the building, its frictionless surface doing nothing to slow him down. He could not stop himself; the Haven platform coming quickly.

He got lucky, in a sense, and fell into an antenna array. Most of the antenna shot out perpendicular to the building, however, a small arm stuck out vertically. This arm saved his life as it lanced forcefully into his right shoulder. His luck came as the impalement secured him to the array and prevented him from falling any farther.

The pain was excruciating, as it penetrated his body next to his clavicle all the way through to his shoulder blade. Blood dripped out of the wound, down the antenna. Slight movements assured Braylon that he was still able to move his arm. His mission was not over, but the difficulty just increased exponentially. He was certain that the antenna had missed anything vital and thankful that this antenna was not currently powered.

He lay there a moment, trying to steady his breathing. He needed to calm his racing heart if he was going to get going again. He was not out of the woods yet; he still had to get inside this building and work his way down from there. He spotted an open patio another two stories below him and twenty meters to the side. It was going to be a particularly difficult climb with his new injury.

Braylon took another deep breath, then pushed himself up, pulling his shoulder off the antenna. He groaned as the antenna appendage slid out of his wound. Blood began flowing freely, streaming down his arm and body. He did not have anything to staunch the bleeding.

As he moved, he realized how precarious his perch was. He could still use his injured arm, but it was shaky and slick with blood. He slowly slid his way closer to the exterior of the building at the root of the antenna.

He eased his way along the exterior of the building toward the patio. He worried about the blood now covering his hands as it reduced his already strained grip. His reach was limited, but that did not stop him from fitting his hands into the grooves and grabbing onto any protrusions.

He lost his grip with his blood-soaked hand as he shuffled on his toes in the tiny crevice along the exterior of the building. He swung around, slamming his back on the wall, only maintaining his grasp with his dry hand. His climber's forearm saved him from plummeting into the crowds of unobservant protestors below. He regained his footing and inched along the sketchy path.

He was growing lightheaded when he finally reached the patio and entered the dwelling. He looked around and was surprised to find no one was home. Probably protesting him below. Braylon let out a sigh, relieved to have survived his descent. His body was still shaky from the experience. Sweat beaded along his brow.

Braylon made his way to the bathroom and patched up his shoulder. He could ill afford to lose more blood. There was a basic first aid kit under the sink and plenty of towels. He stole a fresh hoodie to cover his injury and hide his face before exiting the front door and making his way to the elevator. He felt bad for the occupants who would have to clean up. Braylon moved more quickly now. He had already lost too much time during his climb.

He entered the central elevator and descended to the main level. He wore normal civilian clothes, face hidden under the hood, hoping it would help him blend in. Many protestors had hoods covering their faces, not comfortable with revealing their identities. He did not have far to go to reach his brother's building. The peacekeepers monitoring the protests were too busy to notice him as he moved through the crowded streets.

If he could just tell the people what they had found on the planet, things would be far different. He would make sure they knew; they *deserved* to know the truth of the matter. That would fix things. Two buildings away, he entered the elevator and made his way to his brother's domicile.

He hoped his brother was home as he rang the doorbell. He was not a fan of the government and may be out protesting as well. He found himself holding his breath as he waited. He had no one else to turn to for help. The door finally cracked open after a long agonizing minute. He finally released his breath.

"Kevin! I'm so thankful you're here."

Braylon's Academy formalities stayed hidden away as he spoke to his brother with much more familiarity. The Commander barged through the door and moved to hug Kevin, who stepped back, dodging him.

"What are you doing here, *Leonard*? Did you see what's going on with the people outside?"

"That's why I'm here. I need your help."

Kevin hesitated a moment, then stepped aside to let him enter fully.

"I may not be out there risking an attack from your people, but I'm still thoroughly upset by the treatment we've received. You have no right to lock us down like this. This had better be good, *Leonard*," Kevin said, continuing to iterate the Commander's first name with distaste.

Braylon smiled. "I need your friend, the one you've been telling me about. What's his name?"

"Do you mean Lance? The guy you originally *denied* for the mission until I begged you to reconsider?"

"He had a poor record and couldn't pass a background check. My hands were tied, but, as it turns out, I need someone who's used to working outside the law."

"Well, I don't think I want to expose him to you. He's probably too busy anyway."

"Kevin, get over yourself! This is about so much more than our petty disagreements. We've found intelligent life and General Titus is on the verge of wiping them out! I'm trying to save them *and* our people, and right now, that depends on Lance's help."

Kevin tried to punch him, his eyes were red, his jaw clenched. The

Commander was well trained and reacted quickly. He easily dodged the blow, closed the gap, and jabbed Kevin in the gut. Braylon moved to end the fight by swinging around to grab Kevin from behind and taking him to the ground with a chokehold. He could feel dampness through the dressing on his wound.

Braylon spoke with pity, "You've never been able to beat me, brother, so why keep trying?"

"If I don't stand up to bullies like you, who will?" Kevin countered.

Braylon sighed and relaxed his grip without letting go.

"I'm no bully. You have this stigma against peacekeepers. I'll always love you brother, even when your arrogance leads you to make stupid decisions. Now take me to Lance. We have lives to save. Or are your prejudices more important than that?"

Kevin conceded, tapping his brother's leg.

"Fine, it's a bit of a trek, and we'll have to hope he's even home. We can't call ahead because all communications are down. *That* was a great call."

"That wasn't me. That's what you don't understand. I'm not in charge of what's been happening," Braylon said, desperate to make Kevin understand the reality of the situation as they both stood.

Kevin was obviously confused. "What do you mean you're not in charge? This is *your* mission. You're the *Commander*." Kevin's face fell before he continued. "Wait, did you say something about intelligent life?"

"I told you, things aren't as they appear. And yes, I did. Now we must hurry. I'll give you the rest of the details on the way."

Kevin nodded and led the way. Lance was in the lower portion of a building some distance away. They made their way into the service tunnels below the main platform before they spoke. As they walked, Braylon explained everything to his brother. He told him about the mutiny, about the Undaari, about the General's plans, and about his own plan to reveal the truth to the people.

Kevin was clearly dumbfounded. This was a lot of information for anyone to handle at once. Braylon gave his brother a few minutes to process the information as they walked.

Braylon continued, "I need Lance to reestablish communications with the fleet heading to the planet. They don't know that I'm no longer in charge, since I was the one who had to give the order. Another order from me should stop their mission. We *can't* let these people be wiped out. After I stop the fleet, I need Lance to get me into the local communications system.

I can get word out to our people about the planet. I believe that would calm the protests."

"I had no idea, Leonard. I'm sorry. I sorta lost control of myself in my apartment. I just had so much anger pent up that I wasn't listening to you. Here I was thinking that you'd screwed us all over and were trying to establish martial law for power," Kevin stated guiltily.

"Despite your preconceived notions about me and the peacekeepers, I would never do something like that. I believe in our people."

Lingdon awoke from a strange dream. He had been back in the forests near his home with his family. It was an ethereal experience in which his father, who looked younger than he remembered, brought him for a long walk into the depths of the woods. They chatted for what felt like hours. During these talks, his father confessed his failures in his youth and explained that he had doomed all of Undaalan as a result. He had fled from his failures to their new home in the woods.

His father explained that Lingdon has a special power within him. While he had been unable to train him, his father was proud of him and his ability to naturally use this gift. He explained that this was a gift from the Alackai that only a few others had ever been granted. He stated that it ran in their family and had always been particularly powerful with them. He must trust the Alackai.

Lingdon did not know what it all meant, but he felt that it had been more than just a dream. As he sat up in his bed, the medics rushed over to him. They began performing various tests and questioning him about his condition. Lingdon was confused, the last he remembered he was swimming downriver away from his Yaxkin captors.

"Where am I? How did I get here?"

"Please relax, young sir. You're safe. You're in Entfall. Our scouts found you and brought you in. We didn't think you would survive. You're very fortunate that you were found when you were. Otherwise, you might not be here today."

"Entfall? I've never heard of it. I need to get to Ambrecia, the capital. I can find help there. That's where I was planning to go. My dad's from there."

The medic looked at him worriedly, "Now isn't a good time to be leaving the keep. It's not safe outside. We're dealing with a serious situation."

Lingdon looked at the medic, confused, but stood up anyway. He ignored the medics and exited the medical bay. He did not know where he was going, but as he walked, he could see there was a lot of activity around him. He began following the crowds and found himself in a large hall. He was unsure where he was, but people were clearly panicking.

There were a lot of people gathered around a large table off to the side of the hall. As he walked by, one of the soldiers around the table looked up and noticed him. He gestured to a second man who turned and addressed him.

"You shouldn't be here. Report back to the medical bay... unless you are going to help out," a fierce looking, burgundy caped Undaari spoke to him.

"Help with what?"

Lingdon realized everyone around the table wore burgundy capes.

The first man glanced at the second, then explained, "We're under attack from the Noxxons. We could do with every able-bodied fighter we can... if you know how to fight."

"I've never fought before in my life," Lingdon said, looking away. That was not *technically* true now. "I need to leave here. I shouldn't even be here. I was heading to Ambrecia. I need to find someone to help me."

"Well, you must've gotten quite lost. No one can leave the keep right now. We're under siege. Unless you have some way to walk through a Noxxon army unharmed, you must return to the medical bay, or find a way to make yourself useful. If you can't fight, then help move supplies and prepare the keep," the second Undaari said.

"A Noxxon army?! Can we even survive an attack like that?" Lingdon asked fearfully.

He had not escaped them after all.

The second Undaari answered again, "No force has ever defeated Entfall. We'll be safe here. We just have to ride this attack out. You may leave once it's over. For now, stick by my side and run whatever errands I require. I know the Warden had an interest in you, so it would be wise to keep you nearby. My name is Intayr."

"I'm Lingdon. I'll do whatever you need. I don't have much choice in the matter. I'm not much of a fighter, but I can be of service. I guess I owe your people my life, anyway. It's the least I can do before my journey continues," he said, trying to be brave and stand tall.

# Chapter 19
## Rescue

Major Nazario and Captain Rentari silently made their way through the lush forest, north of the Noxxon camp. They carefully avoided any Noxxon scouts patrolling the woods. As they wound their way through all the obstacles, Nazario began smelling the fires of the Noxxon camp. Through the dense forest, he spotted them burning everything they chopped down if it was not being used for construction. Their camp would be well lit. Nazario could not tell where Jarreck was, even with the firelight. *I wish special ops could do that.*

When they got closer to the edge of camp, they noticed the Noxxons were burning down some of the surrounding trees as well. There was too much moisture in this forest near the river for the fire to spread out of control, but it shrouded the area in dense smoke. Between the smoke, the bright flames, and the constant drumbeat, Nazario did not see how anyone in Entfall would sleep that night.

The Noxxons were enlarging their encampment, giving a wide berth between it and the tree line. Nazario and Rentari struggled to find a safe place to hide close to the Noxxon camp. Nazario turned to Rentari.

"Do you think he can actually rescue her?"

"I don't know Jarreck very well, but the look in his eyes while we were in the boat shook me. I wouldn't want to be the Noxxons right now."

Nazario smiled. Jarreck always left quite the impression on everyone. *I could learn a lot from a man like that.* He looked out over the Noxxon camp, trying to determine where Jarreck was.

"Can you really end Jerykka's suffering if Jarreck fails?"

Rentari glanced at Nazario for just a moment before looking back toward the Noxxons. The lack of answer was answer enough. Despite the cool evening air, he could feel a bead of sweat forming on his temples.

Jarreck silently ruminated as he made his way to the edge of the Noxxon encampment. He paused a moment, trying to discern the quickest path to the heart of the camp. He had to be careful of that Staff Bearer, though. Its location remained a mystery as he proceeded. Jarreck was not sure if it would be able to detect him. It would be difficult for most Noxxons to notice him, but he could not be sure about this new threat.

There were thousands of Noxxons between himself and Jerykka, and he had to be careful not to touch any of them. He may be difficult to see, but he was still physically there. He stepped softly, even though the constant thump of the drums would mask any sounds he made. There were throngs of Noxxons bustling around preparing for the assault.

As he moved through the camp, Jarreck noticed that the Noxxons were not well supplied. Jerykka must have really hurt their stores. The Noxxons did not seem ready for a sustained siege; their attack was premature. He took stock of the wood being cut and burned down around the camp. He could not possibly be more angry than he already was, but he could feel a new pain in his heart over the destruction. *Such a pointless waste.*

He kept his hand on the hilt of his sigridir as he passed by the Noxxon fires. His eyes darted across the Noxxon faces as he moved silently. The heat from the fires was not the cause of the sweat now dripping down his face. The Alackai was coursing through his body, ready to be unleashed.

As he neared the center of camp, he could clearly see the platform, now only illuminated by torchlight. Jerykka hung motionless, suspended high above the camp. He saw several Noxxon guards surrounding her, ensuring she could not escape.

Several large tents were erected nearby, no doubt where the Noxxon leadership would be located. Alarms would sound the moment he initiated his attack. This would be no easy task. His eyes scanned the camp as he positioned himself near the platform. He would approach from the front where he could get the best angle on the sentries.

He slowly circled around the platform as he began to focus his magic. There were five guards on each side of the platform, standing ready. He did not hold back, allowing the Alackai to flow on its own, without the use of the usual hand movements. He felt the power well up again within him; his skin crackled with electricity.

His camouflage fell as the blue flames formed in his hands. The Noxxons looked up and stumbled back from the sight. They could not have expected anyone to infiltrate the camp and attack right at its heart.

Jarreck unleashed his power on all ten of the Noxxons surrounding Jerykka. The bright cerulean flames, streaming directly at the Noxxons, ripped through their bodies as if they were paper. The flames behaved differently than he had ever witnessed, acting of their own accord, intertwined with streaks of lightning.

The guards did not have time to react or even call out a warning. Jarreck redirected the flames to the ropes suspending Jerykka. He jumped up onto the platform and caught her as she fell from her restraints.

She was barely alive and covered in her own blood. He knew of no one else who could have survived such torture and pain. *I couldn't have done it.* Even underneath the blood and mud, he admired her strength and tenacity. He would not lose her.

His head popped up as his ears twitched. He could hear metal clanging over the drumbeat. The Noxxons would be on them in moments. He placed a hand on Jerykka's chest and called upon the Alackai, channeling her strength into the unconscious woman.

He hoped to give her a surge of energy. This boost could be dangerous for her and would not last long, but it was his only hope for getting her to safety. He could not carry her and fight the Noxxons at the same time. She awoke abruptly, eyes snapping open.

"Jarreck! Where are we?"

Before he had the chance to reply, the Staff Bearer emerged from the closest tent and slammed its staff down, causing red flames to erupt around them. The two Undaari were trapped. The Staff Bearer closed in on its quarry. Jarreck filled with rage again. He was not going to allow the Staff Bearer to harm Jerykka anymore. He set her down and charged without hesitation.

His skin crackled again as he called upon the Alackai. Sparks danced on the skin of his arms. He drew his blade, wielding magic and metal. He could feel the energy surging through him, more powerful than he had ever experienced before.

He unleashed his full strength at the Staff Bearer as he closed in. The Staff Bearer raised its staff to shield from Jarreck's magic, but Jarreck's might was stronger. The aqua flames penetrated its shield blowing it backward and searing its shoulder.

The Staff Bearer howled in pain.  Fear flashed across its glowing scarlet eyes.  It recovered quickly, calling on its dark magic and swinging its staff wildly to counter Jarreck.  It twirled the staff in a blur of movement, attempting to slam it into Jarreck, bringing its magic crashing down with it.

Jarreck was faster though, moving at the greatest speeds he had ever attained in his life.  He ducked the attack and closed the distance.  He swung his blade low, trying to take the abomination out at the knees as he passed.

The Staff Bearer was far more nimble than the average lumbering Noxxon, though.  Its strength and agility appeared bolstered by the corrupted Alackai.  It jumped over the blade and brought its staff crashing down on Jarreck.

However, he was already moving and used his magic to deflect the blow.  The drumbeat doubled its pace.  He turned and charged again, using his forward movement to slide between the great Noxxon's legs and get behind it.  He unleashed everything he had in a powerful blast.  Blue flames erupted from his right hand encased in the lightning.

The fire dug into the Staff Bearer's back, disintegrating its few pieces of armor, and tearing out two spikes from its back.  The Staff Bearer fell forward onto its face.  Jarreck closed in, blending the Alackai's energy with the black metal of his blade.

The monstrosity let out an ear shattering roar as it rolled over and aimed its staff at Jarreck.  Crimson flames streamed forward directly at Jarreck. Jarreck called up a shield to dampen the blow, but was shoved back, barely maintaining his footing as he slid.

Before Jarreck could attack, the Staff Bearer was up and charging. Jarreck ducked the staff that was swinging at his head.  Crouching under the Staff Bearer, he slashed his magic infused blade into the inner thigh of the Staff Bearer, cleaving flesh down to the bone.  The Alackai's energy allowed metal to cut deep through the rocky skin, toppling the Staff Bearer.

The Staff Bearer crashed to the ground, screaming in pain.  The crimson flames surrounding the battlefield started to fade out. Jarreck could see the masses of Noxxons waiting behind the dying fire.  There were hundreds of Noxxons swarming around the arena, armed to the teeth.  Even if he defeated the Staff Bearer, they could not escape.  He would have to fight through the Noxxon horde waiting for them.

Jerykka was very weak, still lying on the ground, but she managed to use the Alackai to feed the Staff Bearer's fire circle.  The Noxxon warriors were still cut off.  She called out to Jarreck, warning him they would soon be overwhelmed.

Jarreck looked at her then back to the Staff Bearer. *I must destroy this abomination.* He called everything he had into his hands and blasted the Staff Bearer. Aqua flames and lightning erupted from Jarreck's hands into the monster's chest. It vainly attempted to shield itself, but the steady stream of power ripped through its shield and began tearing it apart, melting its flesh from bone.

Two more Staff Bearers emerged from an adjacent tent. They lifted their staffs in unison and blasted red flames at Jarreck. *How many of these things are there?* He dodged to the side, narrowly avoiding the flames. Jarreck landed on his knee, staring down the monsters. He could not believe there were more. *How had the Alackai allowed this?*

Jarreck breathed heavily now. He could feel the Alackai's strength receding, having put everything he had into taking down the first Staff Bearer. He had failed to kill it but maybe he could still save Jerykka.

He turned and sprinted toward her, using what little energy he had to spread more flames around and delay pursuit. He scooped Jerykka up and used the Alackai to camouflage not only himself, but her as well. This would be difficult to maintain for long, but he hoped it would buy them enough time to escape.

He was fleeing with Jerykka in his arms when one of the Staff Bearers broke through his blue flames. It slammed the butt of its staff onto the ground and a wave of vermilion light emanated out. The light spread quickly, engulfing everything around. When it caught up to Jarreck, it revealed them, rendering his camouflage useless. He had created some distance from the Staff Bearers, but they were still surrounded by the Noxxon army.

Jarreck turned, standing tall to face their enemy. He would not fall without a fight. *Rentari, now's the time.* Jarreck set Jerykka down on her feet. Standing side by side, the two Undaari, in a sea of Noxxons, turned back toward the Staff Bearers. Jarreck gathered his strength, in plain sight of everyone, unable to hide. He had to fight.

The Staff Bearers slowly closed in and began twirling their staffs around. The Noxxon army encircled them but did not attack. Crimson flames grew around them. His cape provided little protection from their heat. Jerykka took Jarreck's hand. She leaned in and touched her forehead to his, closing her eyes.

"At least we'll die together."

He replied, "I'm sorry I failed you, my love."

"Don't question yourself now, Jarreck. Our paths never allowed us to stay together for long."

Jarreck smiled back at Jerykka in response. He was ready to face his end with Jerykka by his side. If he had to die, he was glad she was there with him. She had always been an anchor in his otherwise chaotic life, even though he did not get as much time by her side as he wished. He could see the light beginning to fade in her eyes. He knew he did not have much energy remaining either.

The Staff Bearers had closed the gap and were about to attack when one stumbled backwards, an arrow protruding from its neck. It was clearly caught off guard and had not been protecting itself. Shock reflected in its eyes for just a moment. It recovered quickly, tearing the arrow from its neck. It screamed as blood poured from its wound. Its red eyes grew brighter.

Before it could bring its staff back to bear, Jarreck and Jerykka unleashed everything they had left against it. The distraction was enough to get past its defenses, knocking it back just a step. The Staff Bearer steadied itself, using its staff to regain its balance. Jarreck and Jerykka had no strength left, leaning on each other for support.

The second Staff Bearer circled around them. Both of the evil beings raised their weapons in unison. Jarreck and Jerykka were caught between them in the middle of the Noxxon army. Staffs burned with crimson fire as the Staff Bearers attacked.

However, before the crimson flames even left the staffs, large bolts of white energy rained down from the sky all around them. Explosions sent dirt flying into the air. Jarreck was just as confused as the Noxxons appeared to be. The Noxxons looked around at each other then up into the sky.

The Staff Bearers were able to shield themselves from the attack, but the Noxxons surrounding the arena were blasted back. More light rained down on the area, clearing out a wide path. Jarreck looked at Jerykka.

"Should we run for it?"

Jerykka leaned against him. "We wouldn't make it. We're too weak. I can't run anymore."

Jarreck nodded. He looked up into the sky with sudden realization. There was a large light in the dark sky where the blasts were emanating from. It changed directions and began moving toward them. This thing was only attacking the Noxxons.

"It's the humans!" he exclaimed. "That must be their ship they've been speaking of."

The ship landed right in front of them. A door opened on the side and both Jaina and Kiva were standing before them. They were accompanied by two more humans. Jaina yelled for them to run on board. Kiva jumped off the ship with Sergeant James. James grabbed Jarreck and Jerykka, helping them to the ship. Kiva spread more cerulean flames around, ensuring their escape.

Another human remained at the door with his weapon up, providing cover fire. They quickly boarded the ship and were airborne again. It only took a minute to reach the keep and land at Entfall. Jarreck barely had time to marvel at the ship before they landed. Through half closed eyes, he noticed that it managed to fit snugly in the courtyard as he was rushed off.

Undaari medics were waiting for them. Jarreck pleaded with them to save Jerykka. He explained that she was fading fast. He did not have energy either. He saw them pick her up before his vision blackened.

Nazario watched the events rapidly unfolding before him through the scope of his Peacemaker. He had just been about to pull the trigger on a Staff Bearer when the *Inquisitor* arrived. He nearly yelled out a cheer as the ship cleared the camp.

His emotions were mixed. He was angry that they had risked his ship, but he appreciated their ingenuity. *They shouldn't have done that. I'll have to chat with Sergeant Piers when we get back.*

He let out the breath he had been subconsciously holding. He could not help but smile in spite of himself. He was truly worried they were going to lose Jarreck. That man was the epitome of what Nazario wished he were. Jarreck had achieved the impossible against incalculable odds, rescuing the Warden. *Without Jerykka, our new allies won't survive very long.*

He looked over at Rentari, "It's a good thing you missed."

"I never miss," Rentari replied with a wink. "We must hurry, though. The Noxxons will launch a counterattack quickly. Once the attack begins, we won't be able to get back into the keep."

Nazario nodded. Before he turned to head back, he took one final look into the Noxxon camp, surveying the chaos. He watched in the firelight as the two uninjured Staff Bearers ripped the spikes out of the third. The third fell apart like ash without the dark magic sustaining it.

The remaining two Staff Bearers buried the extra spikes into each other's backs.  Their bodies jolted and their muscles flexed as additional power rushed into them.  These two were even bigger now.  Nazario's heart sank as he witnessed the sacrifice. *We have to get out of here.* He turned and followed Rentari back to their boat.

# Chapter 20
## Recovery

espite the short ride back to Entfall, both Jarreck and Jerykka had lost consciousness by their arrival. Kiva looked at her former master. He had accomplished something no one else would have even considered. He had saved the Warden and possibly all the Undaari. Jarreck had gone toe to toe with the Staff Bearers. She could not comprehend the tenacity her former master had portrayed or the power he had wielded.

Jarreck was always powerful, possibly the toughest in their entire Society, but he had never acted like this before. He always strictly complied with the rules laid down by the Society. The Warden's importance in the upcoming battle was undeniable, but she had never seen him act with such disregard for his own life. Kiva could never truly appreciate what her master achieved tonight, but she knew that without him, the Undaari would not survive. This had reinforced her decision to defy the Council and return to Entfall. They were not infallible.

She stepped off the ship behind James and Reigns who were carrying Jarreck and Jerykka. Kiva looked around the courtyard as she followed and noticed the Undaari warriors were warily examining the ship from a distance. Its dark metal hull stood in stark contrast to the white stone courtyard of the keep. She smiled as her brethren ogled the ship. Brandon, Jaina, and Piers stayed behind on the *Inquisitor*.

The medics rushing to aid their Warden were professionals, not allowing their shock to inhibit their ability to care for their patients. They placed Jerykka and Jarreck on stretchers and carried them off to the medical bay. Once the medics had control of the two unconscious Undaari, James and Reigns returned to the ship.

Kiva followed the medics into the main keep but stopped in the main hall to update the leadership on the events that had transpired. They laid out the entire defensive plan for her, seeking any input she may have. It was a rudimentary plan, leaving them heavily reliant on archers to slow the Noxxon advance. They pulled several squads of archers from the front lines to cover side entrances. She worked with them for a short while, using the knowledge she had gained while flying over the Noxxon camp to help adjust the defense.

Once she had exhausted her usefulness, she informed them she felt she had been away from Jarreck for too long. It seemed Intayr had a solid plan of defense. They had adjusted the distribution to maximize the front lines in hopes the side gates could be watched from a distance. Hopefully, they would be able to hold out while the Warden recovered. She would be able to rally the troops and patch up any holes once she was back on her feet.

Kiva made her way up to the medical bay and saw the medics busily attending to their charges. The medics would be able to patch the two up, but they would need additional care to fully recover their strength. Restoring the Alackai's energy was a whole other challenge.

Kiva had known that the Alackai had blessed Jerykka, but she never understood why Jerykka had not joined the Society. She suspected Jarreck knew more on this topic than he had previously mentioned. She noticed a white cloaked man in the med bay hovering protectively over the Warden.

She watched as he placed a hand on her shoulder and told her, "Next time, you don't leave without me. I won't allow you to come to harm again."

Kiva walked up to him as he spoke with the Warden. She could see that Jerykka was still unconscious. That did not deter the man from speaking supportively to her.

Kiva told him, "I've always admired her strength. I know the King has the weight of the entire kingdom on his shoulders, but she carries their shield high. Our people would be lost without her."

The White Guard smiled at Kiva. "I know she would truly appreciate your kind words. My name is Rentari. I only just got back. This was my first priority. My companion and I narrowly managed to evade the Noxxons and make our way back into the keep."

That's when Kiva realized Major Nazario was in the room as well, sitting back in the corner watching over Jarreck. He stood up when he saw her.

"What took you so long?" he asked.

Her eyes lit up as she rushed toward him. She had feared something bad had happened to him when she arrived in Entfall, and he was nowhere to be found. She had grown fond of the human.

She pulled up last second, foregoing an embrace and breaking eye contact. She enjoyed his company and found comfort in his presence but was not sure about his customs. He was strong like her master. He cared about his companions like Jarreck did as well.

"I had to check in with Intayr and get them up to date on the Noxxon army. How are you?"

He smiled. "I'm well. I thought Jaina and Brandon would've come up here by now. I see I must make my way to them. Are they still on my ship?"

Kiva nodded. "They stated they were dealing with something before coming up. I don't know what it's about."

"Thank you. Can you send word when these two wake up?"

Kiva agreed. Nazario gave her a warm smile and placed a hand on her shoulder before he departed the medical bay. Rentari looked over at Kiva.

"Have you been working with these humans for long?"

She smiled. "Since they first arrived. They've shown true bravery in the face of the Noxxons that few are capable of. There's a lot more to them than you would guess from their size."

Rentari nodded. "He owes our people nothing yet stood with Jarreck and me on a suicide mission against thousands of Noxxons. Jerykka wouldn't have survived without them. She's our one true hope in the upcoming battle. As much as I've trained and learned here, Intayr and I know but a fraction of this keep's secrets."

"I've never been more worried for the Undaari in my life. Not until now. But the humans have given me hope. They've changed the dynamic of this war." Kiva's eyes strayed after Nazario as she continued, "Without them, if I'd have seen the Noxxon forces attacking our borders, I would've given up. Jarreck didn't fully trust them at first, but he's grown to respect them. He hopes the Alackai brought them here for a reason."

Rentari smiled but did not add anything else to the conversation. He continued to sit loyally by the Warden's side. Kiva walked over to her old master and placed a hand lightly on his shoulder.

"You're getting old if you haven't recovered from that little scuffle yet."

"Maybe I just value my sleep," Jarreck whispered weakly, a wry smile forming on the corner of his lip.

He slowly opened his eyes and sat up.

"Thank the Alackai. Master, that was *very* foolish of you. I thought you valued restraint and smart action."

Jarreck chuckled a little. "There was no time to think. Things are changing too quickly. Sometimes it's wise to act without thinking. I might never have gone if I'd have thought about it logically." Jarreck looked over to Jerykka, worry all over his face. "How's she doing?"

"The medics have done all they can at this point. Her body is as healed as they can make her for the time being, but she still hasn't woken. It hasn't been long. We only returned a short while ago. The night is growing old. Now we just wait."

Jarreck shook his head. "We don't have time to wait, there's another course of action. The Noxxons will likely begin their assault by daybreak. They don't want anyone to rest. They'll wait until we're tired from being on alert all night before they strike, dragging the battle out as exhaustion sets in. As long as Jerykka's patched up and safe to be moved, I can assist her healing. Help me."

Kiva helped Jarreck stand up. Rentari stood as well, hand raised in front of him.

"Jerykka is in no condition to be moved."

"Ah, her White Guard Captain. I assure you; I will not allow harm to come to her. You should trust me by now. We don't have time to wait, though. I can help her recover, but not here."

"If I had not witnessed what you did to save her, I wouldn't."

Rentari bent over and picked up Jerykka, cradling her in his arms. "Where are we going?"

"Just follow me."

They exited the medical bay, despite the medics' protests. Jarreck led the way, leaning heavily on Kiva, walking through the keep into the main hall. As they crossed the hall, everyone turned to watch them. Some of the Undaari rushed forward to assist. Jarreck simply waved them away.

A young Undaari boy rushed forward despite Jarreck's gesture and said, "Sir, that symbol on your clasp. I need your help. I think you're who I've been searching for."

Jarreck brushed passed him without a second glance.

"I don't have time to help you, boy."

They carried on without further interruption, Kiva doing her best to support Jarreck, but he was growing heavy. They hurried through the back passages, deep into the keep.

Rentari sounded impatient as he asked, "Where are we going? There's nothing down here."

Kiva did not know where they were going either. Jarreck continued walking a little further before stopping. He turned back to face Rentari.

"Please trust me."

He touched a seemingly random stone and a hidden passage opened.

"I know where I'm going. Only someone gifted by the Alackai can open this passage. It's well hidden and protected for a reason."

Kiva continued to support Jarreck as they walked, Rentari following with Jerykka still in his arms. It was not long until they reached chamber that was home to an Entai. She had never seen an Entai inside before, it must have been standing here before Entfall was even built. Through the tall stained-glass windows at the far side of the chamber, she could see the first signs of light on the horizon. Kiva stopped at the entrance of the chamber as she took in the sight.

She spoke to Jarreck, "The Society created this place, didn't they?"

Jarreck smiled as he led Rentari toward the Entai. "They built all of Entfall, Kiva, you know that. But this cavern is the reason they chose this location, building Entfall around this Entai. They had wielded immense power and this chamber was the heart of it all." Jarreck turned to Rentari. "Please lay her down at the base on the Entai. We'll need privacy. Please wait outside these chambers. We'll come out when we're done."

Neither Kiva nor Rentari argued as they quickly exited the chamber. Kiva understood his plan and desire for privacy. This would be a difficult task to handle.

Alone now, Jarreck knelt beside Jerykka. She still had not stirred. He needed her to come back.

He gave her a kiss on the forehead and whispered, "I'm sorry."

He sat back in front of the Entai and began to meditate. It did not take long for the Entai to respond and reach out with its tendrils, connecting with him. He could feel the rush of the Alackai surging into his body. He felt her Grace and power fill him.  He began to think about Jerykka.  She was in no condition to meditate herself, so he asked the Alackai to reach out to Jerykka on her behalf, unsure if the Alackai would answer his request.

As he meditated, he fell deeper and deeper into the Alackai.  His connection had grown stronger the last few times he had communed with her.  He was unsure why their relationship had evolved, but he could not deny that she had blessed him with the strength to face the Noxxon threat.

He began to feel the presence of another.  The Alackai had drawn in Jerykka as well.  She would be strengthened by her Grace, too.  He was thankful the Alackai continued to bless her, despite her turning away from the Society.

He was beginning to suspect the Alackai did not value the Society as much as the individuals she had blessed.  This had become more apparent in his battle with the Noxxons.  He had not felt pain while wielding the Alackai after disregarding the Society's rules.

Jarreck continued to be drawn into the Alackai, deeper than he had ever been, until there was nothing but whiteness around him.  Jerykka was there beside him in the vast white emptiness.  He had never had an experience like this while communing with the Alackai.  It was surreal. Dreamlike even.  He looked at Jerykka, eyes meeting, neither hiding their shock.

"Well, this is new," said Jarreck, unsure of what was happening.

Jerykka nodded, "Is this real?"

"It feels like it, but I don't know where we are."

He embraced Jerykka tightly, nearly crushing the air out of her.

"I'm sorry for failing you.  I'm sorry I didn't go with you.  And I'm sorry for having to rush your healing like this, but we don't have much time before the Noxxons attack."

"You have *never* failed me.  You had your own path to follow. Without you, I wouldn't have had the strength to survive."  She fell into his embrace.  "I wish we could just stay here forever and forget the turmoil going on.  But I know we don't have much time.  The Noxxons will attack quickly after our escape."

"You lied to me, though.  You said we would die together.  But it seems like we've lived to fight another day.  Unfortunately, our time here together is limited," Jarreck laughed with a sly smile.

She smiled and kissed him deeply.

"Well, we might as well make the most of it."

Before she could continue, the white emptiness began to fill with trees. They were immersed in a dense green forest. Jarreck looked around, trying to discern the meaning of it. He eyed Jerykka who seemed just as shocked by the events unfolding around them.

"What's going on?" Jerykka asked.

Jarreck shook his head in response. He began walking, leading the way through the forest, hand in hand with Jerykka. The sky had an unusual purple hue to it.

As they walked, it became colder, steadily growing wintry. Large snowflakes fell gently over the forest, even though it was summer last he checked. It was a still, peaceful night. They continued in silence, allowing the Alackai to fill their bodies and keep them warm.

Before long, they began to hear loud noises in the distance, but it was too far away to clearly discern their source. They changed direction to seek out the source of the clatter. As they neared, the sounds became recognizable. It was the unmistakable sound of blade and steel clashing in battle. Shouts accompanied the metallic clanging. Jarreck's pace quickened as they raced to investigate the action.

He stopped suddenly. They were nearing the commotion. Jerykka looked at him questioningly. Jarreck held up a hand to silence her before she could ask anything. He looked around slowly, eyeing the terrain, confirming his suspicion.

"I know where we are," he whispered.

Before waiting for a response, he began sprinting toward the sound. He already knew what he was going to find. They came to the edge of a clearing with a cabin standing at its center. Outside the cabin, two Undaari fought for their lives against a swarm of Noxxons. They were holding their own for the time being.

Jerykka started to charge forward to help the Undaari, but Jarreck grabbed her and held her back.

"This is *not* our fight. We're here to observe."

"What do you mean observe? Those Undaari need our help!"

"Jerykka, we're inside the Alackai. These events aren't really happening right now. They've *already* happened. The Alackai wants us to see them for some reason. We must observe carefully so we don't miss anything."

"What if we're here to change the past?"

"Nothing can change the past, Jerykka," he said with a growing knot in his stomach.

He had spent many restless nights wishing he could change the very events he was now witnessing. He held back every urge in his body to rush forward and assist the Undaari struggling before him.

"We can only learn from the past," he continued, "so that we may avoid repeating the same mistakes. There's an Entai over there; that's probably how the Alackai witnessed these events. We should move there to get the full view."

As they reached their new vantage point, they were able to discern a male and a female Undaari, battling against the Noxxons. Jarreck and Jerykka crouched behind the Entai as they watched the two Undaari fight. They were very skilled in combat, fending off overwhelming Noxxon numbers, despite being casually dressed. There were Noxxon bodies everywhere. The fresh snow was stained crimson with their blood. The cabin caught fire in the fight. The female Undaari desperately fought her way back toward the cabin.

During the fighting, the Noxxons were able to overpower the female as she approached the doorway. As she fell, the male fought harder, making his way to her, trying to protect her. She was still fighting from the ground, but there was a large gash in her leg, keeping her off her feet. The man could not reach her.

Jarreck focused on his breathing as Undaari blood mixed with Noxxon in the snow. The man continued fighting harder, desperate to survive. The Noxxons were falling fast, the two Undaari might actually survive. Another Undaari emerged from the forest. *They're saved!*

The newcomer wore the Society's cape and clasp. The male Undaari recognized the new man and screamed for help. *How had the Noxxons won if help arrived on time?*

As the call for aid sounded, another group of twenty Noxxons emerged from the forest, running into the battle while ignoring the third Undaari. Jarreck felt a pit in the bottom of his stomach. The Skovi newcomer watched from a distance as the Noxxons fought the two Undaari.

Several Noxxons charged into the house around the female. The female stood up, despite her injuries, and pursued them. Shortly after, they heard the woman scream from inside. Jarreck almost screamed himself, his heart pounding in his throat.

The male outside looked back at the cabin as the flames spread. One of the Noxxons smashed the man in the head with a hammer, knocking him to the ground. The other Noxxons captured the man and put him on his knees.

Jarreck was at a loss for words. He did not understand what he was seeing.  It made no sense that this Undaari man, this Skovi, would betray his people and align with the Noxxons.  His heart raced.  He needed answers.

All he wanted in that moment was to rush forward and cut the traitor down.  His body was tensed as he held back his urges.  He was here for a larger purpose.  He had to look closer at the bigger picture in front of him.

These new Noxxons that followed the newcomer were a little taller than their brethren and wore less armor.  Jarreck's confusion grew as he noticed the Noxxons were all branded on their right shoulder with a familiar symbol.  He could not place his finger on where he recognized the symbol from, but he knew he had seen it before.

The Undaari began to question his captive, "Where are the Ancient Texts?  I know you know their location."

The captive refused to answer as blood trailed down his body.

"Where is the key that opens the Black Tablet?"

Again, there was no answer.  The Skovi grew angry and smacked the Undaari man.

"Don't make me kill you, Jace.  You could join me as we help set the Society free from the King's rule.  We would never die.  We could rule all of Undaalan together and unite all the people.  No more war, no more fighting. One kingdom under our command.  We could rule for eternity."

Jace spat at his captor.  The Skovi wiped his face.

"So be it.  I will find what I'm looking for.  We'll tear this house to the ground, stone by stone, and find the answers."

That was the first time Jace showed any fear.  He struggled against the Noxxons holding him.  The Undaari punched him hard in the temple, knocking him back to the ground, a satisfied grin crossing his face.

"Kill him."

Jace, barely conscious, reached a hand toward the Entai and weakly whispered, "Jarreck," before a Noxxon slit his throat.  *No!*  Jarreck was in shock.  Reliving the darkest moment of his life took its toll.  Hate filled his very soul toward the Noxxons and this traitor.  Confusion was there as well.  *How did his father know he was there right now?*

Jerykka looked at him, eyebrows twisting, realization flashing across her face.  "Those were your parents, weren't they?"

Jarreck nodded, tears in his eyes.  He had known he was going to witness his parents' deaths before they had even reached the clearing, but he had still not been prepared for it.  Nor had he expected the implications. He continued watching in horror.  This nightmare would not end.

The Skovi dismissed the remaining Noxxons and watched the cabin as it burned. Jarreck noticed that the branded Noxxons only numbered ten at this point. There were another ten regular Noxxons still alive as well. His parents had fought hard. There had to be at least thirty Noxxon bodies spread throughout the clearing.

The fire had raged during the interrogation. It only took a short while longer for it to burn out. The Undaari traitor entered the house and after what felt like hours, exited. He wore a look of frustration and anger as he looked around the clearing. He had just taken a step toward the woods when his ears perked up.

He turned to see an Undaari boy crying by his dead parents. A victorious smile crept along the traitor's face. He approached the boy, feigning concern. The boy ran back inside, then returned moments later and walked away with him. They did not follow the Noxxons east, rather, they walked north, toward Ambrecia.

Vreeham could feel his blood boiling. His orders had been ignored. And it seemed Gierdahl had encouraged the disobedience. That councilor was a wild card. The other three were in line, but not Gierdahl. Another loose end that needed to be tied up. The cancer was spreading.

What was worse was that Jarreck's antics had risked everything. He did not think before he acted. A costly mistake that came close to unraveling the Society. It was time to be more direct. No more distractions. The man needed to be removed before he ruined everything.

*You must be quick. There is another way in. Under darkness, let light be your guide. Take the boats.*

He tied the message to Linnea. With another screech, the ropen leapt into the air. Her pink wings carried her at incredible speed as she quickly disappeared into the sky. Hopefully, she wasn't too late. If her note were not ignored, they could rid themselves of this nuisance and the Society would rise to its glory.

# Chapter 21
## Defense

The Noxxon war drums had slowed their pace after the *Inquisitor* escaped the battlefield. Their rhythmic beat still reverberated across the walls of Entfall, but their attack felt less imminent. Monkley moved about the ramparts helping the Undaari with their last-minute preparations. His heart still ached over the loss of his best friend, but he was determined to bury the pain with this battle. As he stared over the ramparts at the Noxxon horde, he could feel his rage building inside like a typhoon. *It's time for payback.*

He fell in with the White Guard, knowing they would be in the thickest parts of the battle. He had not felt the thrill of war since he was a young lieutenant. There had been a few skirmishes that popped up in the colonies after the rebellions had ended. Some citizens of the newly formed UPC refused to accept the new governing body.

The drumbeat quickened. He looked out behind the fortress and saw the sky beginning to brighten. A smile crept across his face as he stood next to the white caped Undaari warriors. His heart pumped faster, matching the cadence of the drums.

From his perch on the outer wall, he could see the Noxxons forming ranks along the shoreline at the edge of the bridge. He silently tallied the Noxxon numbers in their squads, platoons, companies. There were only five thousand across the lake from the keep, a formidable army, but a full two thousand short of expectations. *How did Jerykka's scouts miscount so badly?*

He could hear the Undaari Captains readying their archers. *Time to get it.* He rested the barrel of his Peacemaker energy rifle on the wall as he knelt behind it. The Noxxon horde began to rumble forward.

He settled his sights on a Noxxon in the front rank and took a deep breath to steady his heartbeat. He released his breath, staying on target. His finger squeezed the trigger. The Noxxon's head exploded in a white burst of light, splattering the others around it.

The Undaari on the rampart loosed their arrows. Death rained down on the front line of the Noxxons. As the dead fell, the Noxxon army roared in hatred. As one, the entire army charged down the bridge. Monkley fired his energy rifle at will. The Undaari defenders sent volley after volley of arrows into the Noxxon horde.

But the Noxxons pulled shields off their backs and held them above their heads as they closed in on Entfall's gate. The shields rendered the archers ineffective, granting few arrows passage to strike the Noxxons underneath. Noxxon archers had larger bows allowing them to stand out of Undaari archer range and still send arrows back into Entfall. The Noxxons had freshly built catapults firing large boulders at the walls, though they shattered harmlessly against Entfall's black stone.

Monkley had more luck with his energy weapon. He could still strike with pinpoint accuracy between shields. Warrior after warrior perished from his attacks, but there were too many to make a difference. He began targeting the Noxxon archers along the shoreline, desperate to slow down their march.

A White Guard standing next to Monkley fell to his death over the ramparts after a Noxxon arrow struck him. He could hear the screams of other Undaari warriors being massacred in the light of the new day. The drumbeat kept pounding away as the Noxxons continued to advance.

Despite their best efforts, the Undaari barely slowed the Noxxons charging down the land bridge. They reached Entfall's ramparts after just a short period of time. They threw grappling hooks and ladders up against the wall. Some hacked away at the front gate, but that proved fruitless. Entfall's defenses were undamaged by the Noxxon weapons.

Undaari warriors cut at the hooks and ladders, trying to prevent the swarm from scaling the walls. Arrows continued to strike down the Undaari defending the walls. They were forced to remain under cover as long as they could, only popping out to attack for seconds at a time.

Monkley struck down another Noxxon archer and ducked back under cover. He watched an arrow strike the wall where he had just been. Sweat was beginning to trickle down his forehead. He took another deep breath before popping back out. Another Noxxon archer fell under his attack. An alert sounded on his rifle: LOW BATTERY. He only had a few shots left.

A Noxxon warrior hopped over the wall just a couple meters away from him. Monkley drew his knife and charged before the Noxxon could get its footing. He slashed at its inner thigh, eliciting a scream, then threw his shoulder into its stomach. The Noxxon fell back off the ramparts and crashed into the horde below, smashing two others.

He locked eyes with Garren, who was fighting nearby. Monkley froze for a second as he saw his friend again. Another Noxxon came over the wall behind Garren and raised its large mace over him. A split second later, it fell back with Monkley's knife stuck through its eye. Monkley recovered his knife and wiped it off on the dead Noxxon. When he looked back at Garren, he realized that it was a burgundy caped Undaari defender.

The Undaari man said, "Thank you, I owe you my life."

Monkley shook his head and replied, "Don't thank me yet. This isn't over."

Another Noxxon came over the wall and was met by a swarm of other Undaari fighters. Monkley pushed the image of Garren from his head and returned to the fight. Though the Undaari warriors were falling, the Noxxons were falling at a far higher rate. A boulder flew over Monkley's head and crashed into the keep. It found its mark against the inner wall, leaving a large crack. *That wall isn't as tough as the outer wall.*

Monkley popped back over the wall and shot a Noxxon operating one of the catapults. They were starting to do damage. They might not be effective against the outer wall, but they could still kill the Undaari defenders and destroy the interior of the keep.

The battle dragged on all day. Monkley worked alongside the White Guard, matching them in kills. He was covered in Noxxon blood from those he killed on the ramparts. *Thankfully, they're not able to scale the ramparts in large groups.* His rifle ran out of power, so he was left with his Valor arm cannon and knife. He picked up an Undaari sigridir as an added precaution, though it felt oversized in his hands.

Thousands of Noxxons were at the walls, trying to breach the fortress. Monkley looked over to the other White Guards as the sun reached for the eastern horizon beyond the Noxxons.

"Do you have anything heavy we can drop on them? Or flammable?"

"There's not much here. We didn't have time to prepare or gather resources from the neighboring towns. There may be a few barrels of sakari oil in the storeroom, but that won't do much against this many."

"It's better than nothing. Can your men get them up here? We need to slow the Noxxons down."

The Undaari nodded and brought several warriors with him to gather the oil. Monkley continued to fight the Noxxons as he waited for the White Guard to return. He was growing weary, moving slower with each foe he fought. It was not long before they returned, carrying three barrels. They were joined by Sergeant James and Reigns.

"This is all we have left," the White Guard said.

"It'll have to do," Monkley said before looking at the newcomers.

Reigns shrugged at Monkley's gaze, "What? We got bored watching the ship. Piers can handle it, we wanted to help."

Monkley smirked. He would have to share the fun with the Sergeants. They both carried fresh Peacemakers. He directed them to the corner of the ramparts to take up an overwatch position. They would not encounter many Noxxon warriors there but could still pick away at the enemy.

Monkley took a quick peek over the ramparts, examining the horde below. He directed the White Guard to the thickest groups of Noxxon warriors. They dumped the barrels over the wall. The heavy objects crushed several Noxxons below and shattered, splashing oil across the ground. Monkley looked at the warriors and nodded. They dropped flaming torches over the edge of the wall.

Rainbow-colored flames erupted across the Noxxons fighting below, illuminating the horde in the dying sunlight. Screams echoed across the night over the sound of the drumbeat. The onslaught slowed, giving Monkley and the other Undaari a short break to sit down and catch their breath. He glanced over the rampart, watching the brightly colored flames dancing over the dying. In any other circumstance, the fire would have been beautiful.

As his breathing and heartbeat slowed, he heard shouts starting to echo from the side wall of Entfall. He swore he heard Garren's shout. *The Noxxons must have shifted their focus.*

He fought through the exhaustion to stand and sprinted along the ramparts to assist. He could not rest while Garren was still fighting for his life. He loved the fight. They both did. They had fought side by side many times out in the colonies against insurgents and even pirates. Monkley was not going to allow him to have all the fun, no matter how drained he was. He could see several Noxxons on the ramparts ahead of him engaging the Undaari.

Monkley was to the back of the Noxxons, their focus on the Undaari. With all the action and drums beating, he had no issues sneaking up behind them. He cut them down quickly using his new sigridir. When they fell, he was greeted by cheers from the Undaari.

For a split second, he saw Garren among the Undaari, then he disappeared. *Just my imagination again. Garren's dead.* He allowed himself a small frown just before another Noxxon crested the wall and knocked him to the ground. The Undaari warriors nearby made short work of the lone Noxxon before assisting Monkley back to his feet in the early night.

He took a deep breath as other warriors flooded the area to defend against the Noxxons. They shifted to account for the Noxxons' new focus while the flames burned at the base of the front wall. Monkley began hearing more shouting from the opposite side of the keep. The Noxxons were attacking from the docks now, too. He took another breath before running back along the ramparts to the other side.

There were only a few Undaari archers on this portion of the ramparts trying to slow down the Noxxons' new attack. Over one hundred Noxxons had docked at the boat yard in the darkness. The gates into the keep were not well fortified at this position. Burgundy caped Undaari gathered around the gate to defend the keep.

Monkley descended the stairs, joining the ground troops. He wished Garren were actually there fighting alongside him rather than these ghosts he kept seeing. He had always been a great leader and friend. Rather than waiting for the Noxxons to break down the small side gate, Monkley led a charge against the Noxxons out onto the docks as he felt Garren would have.

He knew Garren would hate to sit back and wait for the enemy. Monkley burst through the gate with twenty Undaari behind him. He fired his Valor arm cannon into the crowd of Noxxons gathered on the docks, knocking several back. He clashed into the Noxxon forces wielding the sigridir. The Undaari were right behind him. The archers above continued their volleys.

Monkley single-handedly battled a pair of Noxxons. Breathing heavy, he continued to outmaneuver the lumbering barbarians. His arm cannon had run out of power as well, so he only had the sigridir and his knife to fight. If he were not careful, he would kill the battery of the Reliant Exosuit as well. That would leave him immobilized.

He slashed at one Noxxon then dodged the other. He drew in one Noxxon and narrowly avoided its attack, causing it to hit its partner. He used his blade to cut into the back of the first Noxxon. The other Noxxon kicked out at him, connecting with his chest and sending him flailing.

That Noxxon closed on him while the other Noxxon was on the ground writhing in pain. An arrow ended the injured Noxxon's life from the ramparts, leaving Monkley on his back with the other Noxxon still bearing down on him. It raised its battle axe to strike down Monkley. He held the sigridir up in a vain attempt to shield himself. But then the Noxxon's head exploded in white light, spraying brain matter all over Monkley, its body falling on him as well.

He scrambled out from under the warrior. Wiping blood off his face, he looked up and saw two energy rifles firing into the crowds of Noxxons on the docks. Shaking his head and letting out his breath, he charged back into battle alongside the Undaari.

It was a long, arduous battle, but the Undaari eventually prevailed on the docks. They took heavy casualties as nearly half died. Monkley fell over in exhaustion, trying to catch his breath. *I need a break after this.* He relaxed for a few moments in the darkness, still hearing the sounds of metal clanging in the distance.

He saw the moons in the sky before letting his head roll to the side as he laid there. There was Garren again, standing off to his side, watching him. Then he was gone again, just as fast, and behind him, in the distance, Monkley saw something on the water. *Am I imagining this too?* Whatever it was, it disappeared around the rear of Entfall. *That's probably not a good thing.* He stood up quickly, steadying himself against lightheadedness, then rushed back into Entfall.

Negren was just finishing up for the day at the quarry. He turned to his father to show off the quality of what he had accomplished. There was a large amount of rock in his cart. He felt he had managed to crush them to relatively uniform size for future use. He was thirteen years old and just old enough to start his apprenticeship with his father.

In the Undaari culture, the young begin a yearlong apprenticeship with one of their parents at age thirteen, then switch to the other at fourteen. Like many young Undaari, Negren did not particularly find his parents' jobs that exciting and wanted a new challenge. His mother was a healer. It was an interesting job, but there was little work here other than quarry accidents.

He could not wait to turn fifteen so he could pursue a more technical craftsman job. He loved the rocks, but he wanted to work them into their final form, not gather them. He wished to explore beyond his small hometown of Entrea.

Entrea was nestled at the base of the mountain range, west of the Scarred Mountain and the Entfall River. Its purpose centered around the quarry. There, they gathered most of the stone and building materials for the entire Undaari Kingdom. They had a strong sense of pride and purpose in the village, but it was too small and comfortable for him.

He wanted to explore the rest of the kingdom and find new challenges. More often than not, when Undaari got to apply for their journeyship at age sixteen, they chose a career field shared by their parents, making it easier to gain acceptance and a position.

But for Negren, being an artisan would give him the opportunity to explore. He would be helping to build new buildings and statues with the rock that his home and father had gathered. That was his dream.

His father looked over his work and smiled, "You've done adequate work. You're talented for how relatively shortly you've been working the quarry. You still have a long way to go, though."

He smiled at his father. It was tough love.

"Gee, thanks, dad."

Rendon laughed. "You'll never guess what I found on my dig today."

Negren looked up at his father with wide eyes.

"Black stone. The first deposit we've seen in decades. There isn't much, but it's cause for celebration."

Negren squealed with glee. He had never seen black stone before. His father had been promising to bring him to Entfall one day, so that he might see its walls. He envied the artisan who would get to shape the black stone into something wondrous.

"Come, my son, we must get home. We'll discuss your work more in the morning. Your mother will have dinner ready soon. I believe she has prepared your favorite meal tonight. I think she has some big news for you."

Negren grew even more excited. "Am I finally getting a little brother? I've always wanted a brother. Three sisters can be a little unfair sometimes."

Rendon beamed at his son. "I can't spoil the news for your mother. You'll just have to wait and see."

Together, they mounted their massive family graca. Negren

rubbed the thick mat of green fur on the animal's neck. He had always found gracas to have the most adorable faces with their long, hairy beards making them look like old men.

He sat up in front of his father and looked between the graca's massive, paddle shaped antlers. In the curves of their antlers, plants grew wild, adding to the camouflage of their mossy looking fur. Negren was proud of the saplings growing in its antlers; he had spent long hours helping the graca grow the rich plant life.

They were the strongest animals in Undaalan, and common near the mountains, which was why the Undaari in Entrea had domesticated them. They were highly useful in the quarries both for transport and work. Not many of the local Undaari could afford a graca, but their family had done well in the quarries. Negren was excited and energetic. He just wanted to dance around in his saddle.

Negren heard his father laugh behind him as they began to ride home. They lived on the far side of town. As they reached the central square, Negren could see a bright red glow beginning to emanate in the distance ahead of them. He heard screams from that area as well. There was a fire spreading.

Before they got too close, they saw an Undaari man running toward them screaming, "Noxxons! Noxxons!"

Before his father could react or inquire further, an arrow struck the man in the back, and he toppled over. His father jumped off their mount and told Negren to flee.

"Son, get to Ambrecia. Alert the guards there. We need help. Go, now, quickly. I'll get your mom and we'll meet you there. I love you."

Negren could not understand what was happening. His heart was beating rapidly, and his body began shaking. He did as his father told him. He turned the graca around and began to ride as fast as he could through the town; the enormous antlers made it difficult to navigate through the tight walkways.

His heart pounded even faster inside his chest as his eyes shot all around him, searching the town as he rode. He had not gotten far when he turned back to see his father. Rendon had drawn his knife but a swarm of Noxxons overcame him. There were hundreds of them tearing through his home. They were setting everything on fire and destroying all in their path.

His father was dead and likely his entire family. He had to escape and warn the King. He had never seen Noxxons before, but they were even scarier than he had ever imagined. He was racing toward the edge of town trying to escape. He could not understand how they had gotten there. Entfall protected all the Lenakai Forest.

Other Undaari were fleeing the devastation as well, but most were not mounted. He had a chance, whereas they did not. He could see everyone dying around him. He had never witnessed death before, and it would scar him for the rest of his life. His spine shuddered as he rode on. Despite being mounted, the Noxxons were moving in a frenzy, able to keep pace as they destroyed Entrea.

He finally broke passed the last building and was able to direct his graca to a full sprint. He had escaped. He turned back and saw his entire town on fire. No one else seemed to have made it. If he were not able to reach Ambrecia himself, no one would be able to warn them before the Noxxons were at the gates.

He turned forward again before he felt his mount fell out from under him. A large arrow had struck the graca in its hind leg. It toppled to the ground. As they stumbled to a halt, the graca rolled over top of him, crushing his legs, and pinning him to the ground. He could not free himself.

He lay there in pain, desperately trying to find a way to escape his fate. Moments later, an enormous Noxxon approached him. It had a large staff in its hand and walked up to him nonchalantly.

It took one look at him and pressed the butt of its staff into his chest, preventing him from inhaling. He struggled to breathe and vainly attempted to push the staff off him. He could not speak without air. His heart pounded faster, sweat pouring from his head. He pleaded with his eyes to be released. Tears streamed down his face.

He had failed. *I'm sorry.* He hoped that his family knew he had tried. No one in Entrea had survived. Ambrecia would be caught unawares. He lost consciousness quickly, unable to breathe anymore. The Staff Bearer asphyxiated him without hesitation then continued to lead the Noxxon swarm toward Ambrecia.

# Chapter 22
## Backdoor

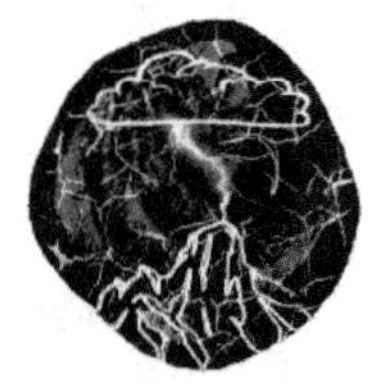

Jarreck awoke from the vision suddenly. It took several seconds to reorient himself to the ancient Council Chambers. It was already night again as he looked out the stained-glass window of the chamber. He stood and watched as Jerykka stirred.

As her eyes opened, he asked, "How are you feeling?"

He helped her stand as she responded, "Much better. My strength has been restored and my wounds are healing well. A little tender, but I'll be fine."

Jarreck clasped her by the hands and looked her directly in the eyes. As their eyes locked, both sets began to glow blue. He lingered on her eyes for a few moments, then turned and led the way out of the chamber, leaving words unsaid. *Now isn't the time.* They reached the exit and met with Kiva and Rentari who still dutifully stood guard.

"How long were we in there?" Jerykka demanded.

Kiva replied, "Oh, thank the Alackai. It's been forever. You were in there all day. Night has just fallen again. Should you be walking already?"

"We're fine. Well refreshed, thanks to the Alackai. Jarreck was smart to take us there. I appreciate your concern."

The winding passages took some time to navigate, but the group hurried back to the main hall. As they entered, cheers of joy resounded throughout the chamber. The defenders of Entfall began moving with a renewed fervor. The four made their way to the war table and met with Intayr, who had the boy from the river by his side. Nazario was there as well.

"It's begun," Intayr informed them.

Jerykka nodded. "Are our defenses in place?"

"As best as I could without your input. I've been trying to coordinate everything from here. Their attack began at sunrise. The battle has raged all day. It's been a brutal assault, but we're holding against the onslaught."

"You've done well. We need to make adjustments here and here, but you seem to have everything else covered as well as can be hoped," she said.

She pointed to a few places on the sandbox where she felt they needed to make the adjustments. There were some hidden entrances she made note of. They planned and issued orders for a few more minutes, shoring up their defenses. They began receiving reports of attacks at various new locations, but the defenses were holding and rapidly adapting to the Noxxons.

Jerykka was only willing to spare sentries to watch over the secret entrances. She suspected no attack would come there but felt it better to be safe. Jarreck did not blame her after what they had witnessed. Unfortunately, they could not afford to station entire squads to defend them. If any Noxxons were seen approaching, the sentries were ordered to abandon their post and get reinforcements.

While Jerykka was making her plans with Intayr, the boy from the river approached Jarreck again. "Sir, can you please help me? My Father had the same clasp as you. I was heading to Ambrecia to find someone, but I think you might be who I'm looking for."

Jarreck shook his head at the boy. "You're mistaken, young one. I don't know your father. My place isn't in Ambrecia and I'm too busy with the events unfolding around us to help you."

The young Undaari was clearly disappointed. "I understand. I just thought that..." was all he said as he trailed off.

Jarreck turned to address the Warden, "Jerykka, I can't stay long. The events we saw, they complicate things. I have to act now since the Noxxons are even better informed than I had previously expected."

He was surprised when she spoke in agreement. "I know. What we saw was unbelievable and truly complicates everything. It also means that Entfall may not be as secure as I had hoped; the Noxxons may have information they shouldn't. Help me secure the castle, then go on your mission."

"I can't argue with that, what do you need?"

They continued to coordinate the defense of Entfall throughout the night. Jerykka insisted they take shifts resting, and even tried making her way out to the ramparts to relieve her troops. The other leaders followed her example. The night dragged on as the Noxxon forces tried to breech their defenses. Though few Undaari fell in battle, they were being worn down far quicker than the Noxxons. Late into the night, Jerykka reconvened their group at the war table.

"Are we missing anything? They've attacked from the front, and we just repelled them from the docks. That seems too simple, but no other movement has been noted. There has to be more to this attack than that. I haven't even received reports of those Staff Bearers yet. It's been dark out though, so it's hard for our sentries to catch everything. With the new light, it'll be easier to watch."

Nazario raised a question. "Are there any entrances from the rear? Like escape tunnels? It seems like classic misdirection to attack from the front then sneak around back."

Jerykka replied, "There's one secret entrance to our rear, but it's impossible for the Noxxons to access. It exits miles to the west. They cannot cross the Entfall River while Entfall still stands."

Nazario was confused. "You keep saying that, but how do you know they can't cross it?"

Jerykka took a deep breath. Recalling a memory from long ago, she recited:

*"Swift river flows with glowing aqua energy. Washing away all signs of corruption. Powerful, yet nourishing, giving life to all around it. Saving the world from devastation. Spirits of the past lending their protective magic. Impassible without the Alackai's permission. Protector of life, love, and the Undaari. Shielding the culture, heritage, and giving spirit of those from the Lenakai Forest."*

The human kept staring at her expectantly.

She rolled her eyes and explained, "The Entfall River is protected by the Alackai. As long as Entfall still stands, the Alackai's magic will protect the river. There are three retractable bridges along the river, each protected by a city. Eilenar just north of us is the first. Ennika and Aberash are to the south. Those are the *only* places where they could cross, but we would know about it."

Jarreck nodded in support. Nazario stopped his line of questioning. Another human entered the hall as she spoke again.

"Besides, that entrance is known only to me. At least it was, until my request for aid. I gave the King its location so that the Society could help. Even with a traitor, the information couldn't have made it to the Noxxons since I sent that message. And it still requires the Alackai to access."

Jerykka shook her head as she turned back to their sand table. *I don't care how valuable Jarreck finds them, they are insufferable know-it-alls.* She looked at Jarreck who was also examining the war table closely. *It's too simple. The Noxxons must have something else planned.* She was about to speak when the other human joined the group.

The human newcomer spoke directly to her. "I'm sorry to interrupt, but are you sure there are no rear entrances? I don't mean to question you, but in the moonlight, I thought I saw something out on the water. We had just repelled the Noxxon attack on the docks. I didn't get a good look, but it looked like a boat of Noxxons. It was heading behind Entfall."

Jerykka shook her head again with frustration, "I know this fortress better than anyone. There are no entrances there."

Nazario looked at his human counterpart, "Monkley, are you sure about what you saw?"

Monkley responded to Nazario, but was staring off in a different direction, as though speaking to someone else, "I know what I saw! I wasn't imagining anything."

Jarreck did not take his eyes off the table as he finally spoke. "There's something we missed. It might not be a traditional entrance, but it's something that could be breached easy enough. Something that's not defended."

That was when it hit Jerykka as well. She looked back to where they had been, only hours before.

"Rentari, gather the White Guard from the ramparts. Bring them back to the chamber we just came from. Hurry."

"Yes, Master Jerykka."

Jerykka spoke to Nazario next, "We'll take care of this. You and your subordinate can get some rest if needed, then go help on the ramparts."

Nazario nodded and led Monkley back out of the hall. Jerykka turned to Jarreck, and they both departed with Kiva trailing after. She left Intayr behind to continue coordinating the war effort. As they hurried,

Jarreck began filling Kiva in on what they feared, and what they had seen in the Alackai. Kiva was shocked.

"How do you know this is even true?"

Jarreck answered her concerns, "It's one of those things where you had to be there. The realism behind it, coupled with the accuracy of my memory. The Alackai would not lie to us. It also filled in the gaps about how the Noxxons were able to gain access to our knowledge."

"Who was the Skovi?" Kiva asked.

Jarreck hesitated for a moment, "It was High Councilor Vreeham. Back when he was young. He called the artifact the Black Tablet. He's the one who rescued me. It all fits."

"But if he wanted that information, why involve the Noxxons?" Kiva questioned with wide eyes.

"That's the last missing piece to the puzzle. I'm not sure of the purpose behind his actions or his eventual goal. We won't be able to find out until after this battle is over. But knowing this information, we can be more prepared. He doesn't know that we know, and it should *stay* that way until we have the last pieces of the puzzle."

Kiva nodded her acknowledgement, and they walked the rest of the way silently. Jerykka knew this would be the Noxxon's next move, but she was hoping it was not too late. Monkley had only barely seen Noxxon boats on the water. The battle had been raging for hours now. The Noxxons were likely waiting for the focus to be entirely up front.

They reached the hidden entrance to the passage, and she reopened it. Jerykka had the Alackai coursing through her body. She could see the cyan glow in Jarreck's and Kiva's eyes as well. They drew their black blades and proceeded, Jarreck taking point down the narrow passage.

They slowly made their way through the passage, eyeing every nook and cranny. Every shadow and hallway they passed. They reached the chamber and the Entai without encountering anything. Jerykka was relieved they were not too late. Jarreck lowered his sigridir and relaxed a bit. He cautiously made his way toward the stained-glass window.

As he approached the Entai, getting closer to the large window, a crashing sound echoed across the chamber. It originated from behind the Entai. In the next moment, three Noxxons charged from behind the Entai. Jarreck raised his blade quickly, fending off the attack.

Jerykka and Kiva rushed in quickly to assist. Three Noxxons were not much of a threat to the three of them. Two Noxxons fell quickly. Before they killed the third, a Staff Bearer emerged from behind the Entai. It quickly brought its arcane magic into the fight, blasting everyone back, including the last Noxxon. It spread its crimson fire around the chamber.

Before Jerykka knew it, a second Staff Bearer entered the chamber, followed by another dozen Noxxons. They were swarming the trio. The Alackai had given them strength, though. Jarreck and Jerykka fought back with fervor, focused on the Staff Bearers. Kiva engaged the Noxxons, keeping them off the others and watching their backs.

The battle grew fierce. Noxxons were falling fast to Kiva's sword and fire. She was easily the most skilled in physical combat, having been a Sword previously. Cerulean and crimson flames danced everywhere. Jerykka was less trained with the Alackai, but naturally powerful. She let the Alackai flow freely as she fought. She beat back a Staff Bearer, gaining the upper hand.

The second Staff Bearer switched targets, charging her quickly. It swung its weapon with great force at Jerykka. She saw it at the last second and ducked the attack. However, she was too slow to avoid its second strike as it twirled its staff back around.

Fire ripped into Jerykka's side, sending her careening across the chamber. Jarreck quickly jumped between her and the Staff Bearers, their four spikes glowing brightly in their backs. He fought back, taking them both on at the same time while shielding Jerykka. Jerykka flipped back to her feet, fighting through the pain, and reengaged the Staff Bearers.

She yelled to Jarreck, "After all these wounds, I'm going to need quite a hot bath and some relaxation."

Jarreck smiled as the battle intensified. "Well, if you'd actually carry your weight in this fight, maybe I'll draw that bath for you and take you on a vacation."

Jerykka decided to use the Staff Bearer's tactics against them and changed targets in the heat of battle, landing a deep slash into Jarreck's Staff Bearer. That Staff Bearer fell with a howl. The attack left Jerykka's back exposed. Her own Staff Bearer jumped forward, trying to drive its staff into her. Jarreck was quicker though, changing targets. He used the Alackai to shield Jerykka and blasted the Staff Bearer back.

Jerykka caught Kiva fighting out of the corner of her eye. Kiva continued to fight the Noxxon warriors on her own. She favored her sigridir rather than the Alackai during her fight. She slid between Noxxons, using their leverage against them. As she dodged one, she threw it off balance into another. She slashed between their plates of armor. Throats were ripped out, flesh reaped from bone. The Noxxons were no match for her speed and skill.

Jerykka tried to close in on the downed Staff Bearer to finish it like Kiva was finishing the Noxxons, but before she could strike, it bounced back up, swinging its staff around. The Staff Bearers were deceptively quick, faster than normal Noxxons, the corrupted Alackai giving them unnatural strength and speed. Jerykka was fast, too. She ducked under the staff and closed in. Before she could attack, the Staff Bearer kicked out, planting its foot in her chest, toppling her backwards and knocking the wind out of her chest.

Jarreck was too busy fighting his Staff Bearer to witness Jerykka fall. He kept working to find an opening in the defenses of his opponent. Her Staff Bearer rushed in. Jerykka closed her eyes, waiting for the staff to crash down on her, trying to shield herself with the Alackai.

Contact never came though. Instead, she felt warmth washing over her. She quickly opened her eyes to witness a purple energy hurl the Staff Bearer back. It was not a flame, more like a beam of light. She was uncertain how else to describe it.

This new attack caught everyone off guard, the entire room froze with shock. The Undaari boy from the river was standing in the chamber now, with his hands raised in front of him, channeling this new energy into the fray. It was not enough to kill the Staff Bearer, too erratic and uncontrolled, but it was powerful, nonetheless.

Jerykka watched as Jarreck rushed over to the Entai. *What is he doing?* The Staff Bearers were recovering from the surprise attack, turning their focus on the newest threat. Jarreck placed a hand on the Entai and closed his eyes. The Staff Bearers charged the boy, who still stood at the entrance.

Everything was happening in slow motion as Jerykka watched it play out. The Entai began to glow, its tendrils reaching up to Jarreck. His eyes brightened further as energy channeled into his body. Kiva was still fighting the last few Noxxons. The boy was not moving as the Staff Bearers closed the gap with him. Jerykka started to stand, but it was too late.

Blue flames encased in lightning erupted out of Jarreck's outstretched hand. The Staff Bearers were wielding their weapons, conjuring crimson flames. As they swung their weapons toward the boy, the cerulean flames from Jarreck caught them. Jarreck was screaming as he channeled the Alackai from the Entai. The Staff Bearers struggled to shield themselves against the fresh onslaught. The blue flames ripped through their shields, wrapping around them like flaming tornados.

The Staff Bearers emitted a chilling howl as their obsidian rock skin was melted from their bone. No one in the chamber dared move as they watched the Staff Bearers disintegrate. It was over just moments after it began. Jerykka watched as Jarreck fell over, curled into a ball, unconscious.

She rushed to his side, begging him to still be alive. Kiva turned for a moment but had to reengage the last few Noxxons in the chamber. The Noxxons still had not moved after witnessing their leaders' destruction. Kiva ended them with just a few strokes of her blade. They did not even fight back.

Jerykka did not look up as the remaining White Guard finally reached the chamber with Rentari at their head. They swarmed in, fifteen strong, sweeping the chamber for threats and establishing a security blanket at the window. Jerykka's heart ached as she examined Jarreck, barely managing to direct the White Guard to protect the Entai at all costs.

Jerykka knelt next to Jarreck and began cradling his head, tears filling her eyes. Her body rocked back and forth as she pleaded for his life. Jarreck's body was bloody and burnt, smoke still rising from his skin. She prayed to the Alackai, begging for his strength to be restored.

Jerykka looked to Kiva, voice cracking as she screamed for answers, "What happened?! What did he do?!"

Kiva was having difficulty breathing, coughing through the smoke and stench filling the chamber.

She responded solemnly, "He channeled the Alackai's might directly from the Entai. That's forbidden by the Society as it almost certainly leads to a painful death. Our bodies aren't capable of handling that level of energy. He sacrificed himself to save us, or at least he was willing to. It appears he's still breathing, but as to the damage he sustained, I cannot speak."

Jerykka was horrified by what he had done. She pulled Jarreck in tight, her tears falling on his head. She could not slow her rapid heartbeat. She rocked more vigorously as she cradled Jarreck.

Rentari moved closer to Jerykka and placed a hand on her shoulder to comfort his Warden. "What can we do, Master Jerykka?"

She shook her head. She did not have an answer. For the first time as Warden of Entfall, she did not know what to do. Jarreck's breathing became raspy, slowing further. She looked at Kiva, pleading with her eyes for an answer that did not exist.

She was not at a loss for long. Tendrils from the Entai grew from the ground again and grasped Jarreck. It appeared the Alackai had not forsaken him.  She jumped up, releasing him, allowing him to be enveloped by the Entai.  Energy began to flow into his body and his skin began to heal slowly.

After several long, agonizing minutes, Jarreck blinked, coming awake.  Jerykka watched as he moved haggardly, as though he had aged twenty years in just minutes.  He slowly sat up, trying to steady himself.  The Entai withdrew from his body.  Jerykka threw herself on him in an embrace.

"Don't you ever do that again.  You don't get to sacrifice yourself for me, we either get through this together or we die by each other's side."

Jarreck smiled and jokingly responded, "Well that doesn't seem fair.  How am I going to have a hero's burial if I fail to save your life?"

Jerykka smacked him for his comment, and then kissed him deeply, no longer caring if anyone knew of their connection.  After a few moments, she pulled back and smiled.

"I'm thankful the Alackai didn't forsake you for pulling such a *stupid* stunt."

Jarreck replied, "I feel that the Society's understanding of the Alackai may be flawed in ignorance.  I don't understand why the Alackai has been so kind to me.  We shall see over the coming days."  He then turned to look at the boy, still frozen at the chamber entrance, and asked, "Who *are* you?  I've never seen such power bestowed upon anyone by the Alackai."

"I'm Lingdon."

"Well, Lingdon, is there anything else about you?  I could do with a little more than that."

"Oh, right, sorry.  I'm seeking help understanding this power.  I saw the symbol on your clasp.  My father had the same one, so I thought you were the person I needed to find.  The Yaxkin murdered him and took me as a slave.  That is until a few days ago when I escaped and was brought here by your scouts."

"Well, Lingdon, I must apologize.  Had I realized this was the help you needed, I would have made an exception for you.  Things have been chaotic around here."

Jerykka noticed Jarreck staring into Lingdon's eyes with a look of curiosity.  She followed Jarreck's lead and noticed purple specks in his cyan irises.  Her eyebrows rose and eyes widened.  She turned back to Jarreck but did not interrupt.

"Stick by my side, Lingdon, we'll get you taken care of.  You have my word."

"Thank you, sir!"

"Please, my name is Jarreck, this is Kiva, and this is Master Jerykka, Warden of Entfall.  We must head back to the main hall and return to the battle."

Jarreck, Jerykka, Kiva, and Lingdon made their way back, leaving Rentari and the White Guard to continue the defense of the Entai.  Lingdon stuck to Jarreck's side faithfully.  Jerykka smiled, remembering when Kiva used to follow Jarreck around like that.

Through the stained-glass window, Rentari could see the sun cresting over the horizon.  A new day had dawned as the pink and orange light shined in on the Entai.  In the new light, the White Guard found the Noxxon boats and scuttled the craft to ensure no more Noxxons had landed.  He would not allow the Noxxons to attempt another attack here.

# Chapter 23
## Resourceful

*M*ajor Nazario found Intayr on the rampart walls over the front gate of Entfall. Nazario carried a fresh Peacemaker energy rifle with him. He did his best to assist the Undaari with breaking the Noxxon horde that was bearing down on them all. Night faded away as the sun ignited the skies above Entfall.

Intayr was responsible for coordinating the Undaari defenses from the ramparts now as their numbers were gradually depleted. Despite their strong defensive posture behind the tall black walls and their ranged weapons, the Noxxons were taking control of the fight with their ever so slow grinding. The Noxxons had archers and catapults on the shore that were wearing the Undaari numbers thin. Noxxon bodies littered the ramparts alongside the Undaari dead. They would never surrender, despite their odds of survival.

Nazario was not sure how much longer they could realistically hold the outer wall. They had to have killed hundreds of Noxxons throughout the night, but it barely seemed to have made a dent in their forces. The Undaari were growing exhausted as well. They needed another plan in order to ward off the invasion. That was when he got an idea. He could take a page out of Jaina's ill-advised book.

He departed his station without a second thought, leaving his energy rifle with Intayr. He knew it would be more effective than the bow Intayr had been using. He wove his way through the chaos and into the inner courtyard of Entfall. Boarding the *Inquisitor*, he moved straight for the Command Deck.

When he reached it, he found Jaina and Brandon on the radio trying to communicate with someone. He looked over at Sergeant Piers who stood observing from the digital sand table in the center of the Command Deck.

"Who are they talking to?" Nazario asked.

"The *Plaintiff*. They're impatient and wanting to enter the fray."

Major Nazario sighed. He had forgotten about them.

"This isn't a battle humans are waging. We're here on a diplomatic mission and will assist only as necessary to solidify relationships, but we cannot wage a war. We don't know what sort of damage we can cause."

"You don't have to tell me," Piers responded.

Brandon looked up from the communications console where he was working with Jaina. "We also d-... don't know what our weapons might do to the Alackai that is laced throughout the planet. It could ignite the p-... power source and severely damage the environment. Anything more p-... powerful than what we have on the ground already is too dangerous. They could not only destroy the people and land but eliminate the only hope for saving our p-... people."

"Are they not listening to this logic?"

Jaina looked at him now. "Well, unfortunately, we already lied to them to keep them from landing a few days ago. We told them that Sergeant Piers got infected with something, and that no one could land safely. They backed off, but they've since called our bluff. They don't believe our new warnings."

Nazario shook his head in frustration. "When did that happen? You seem to have forgotten to mention this detail. You should've informed me so I could handle this. Let me speak to them."

He strode over to the communications console and waited for Doctor Jimenez to hand him the headset. Brandon was hesitant and clearly wanted to say more but bit his lip.

When Nazario received it, he addressed the *Plaintiff*, "Colonel Jansen, this is Major Nazario. Please stand down. The situation planetside is being handled. Any involvement from your crew could jeopardize the mission and our relationship with the natives. Please confirm."

It took a few moments to receive a reply. "Major Nazario, things are out of our hands now. The *Jericho* has sent a small fleet to take control of the situation under the direct order of Commander Braylon. Once they arrive, we'll all enter this conflict. We understand your request but have our orders. They should arrive within twenty-four hours."

"Jansen, this is unacceptable. Lives are at risk. Not just our own. There is a war happening down here. We don't need to unnecessarily risk more lives.  Our small task force is better equipped to secure the power source and save our people."

"It's not my choice.  These orders come directly from Commander Braylon.  We're on standby until the fleet arrives.  Additionally, just so your conscious is clear, no more lives will be at risk.  We'll be performing an orbital bombardment to wipe out the enemy forces and clear our path to recover the power source ourselves."

"You'll kill friendlies with an attack like that!  It will ruin *all* diplomatic relations on our new home.  We don't even know that this energy source will work, or how volatile it is.  That attack could destroy *everything!*"

Nazario was baffled at the decision to attack from space.  It did not seem like something Commander Braylon would order.  It was too ruthless.  Too callous.  It wreaked of Titus.  Had Braylon let the General influence the decision?  He could feel anger welling up inside him.  This decision could cost humankind everything.  He would not allow the rest of humanity to fade into darkness.  They still had a chance.

He cut off communications, knowing it was just a waste of time. *How could anyone be so stupid? We have to stop this.*  He had no idea how to accomplish this, though.  He had to warn the Undaari.  *Maybe we can evacuate their people so only the Noxxons are destroyed.*  The Undaari might appreciate that enough to maintain diplomatic relations.

He looked over to Jaina, shrugging with his palms up, "What do we do?  How do we maintain diplomacy?  Do you have any ideas?"

Jaina shook her head.

Brandon answered the questions, "Un-... Unfortunately, since they won't listen, the only person who can stop them is Commander Br-... Braylon.  We can't communicate with him fast enough to get him to order a stand down.  The only way t-... to show them that there's no need to b-... bombard the planet would be to win this war before the fleet arrives.  Even then, who knows, they're pretty intent on recovering the Alackai as quickly as p-... possible.  They may still attack the Undaari t-... to ensure there's no resistance."

Nazario looked up, his previous idea taking new light in his head. "Jaina, Brandon, go find Jarreck and Jerykka.  Warn them about this attack.  Recommend evacuation, we don't want to lose any Undaari lives.  Sergeant Piers, I need you on the weapons console.  We may have just enough weaponry to force the Noxxons to retreat.  Where are Sergeants James and Reigns?"

Sergeant Piers replied, "They got bored guarding the ship.  They went up to the ramparts to fight alongside the Undaari and Monkley."

"I'm going to need them to strap in and take positions at the airlocks, to give us a little more firepower. We're taking the *Inquisitor* into battle against the Noxxons. It's the only chance we have of ending this war before the fleet attacks."

Jaina squinted her eyes at Nazario. "Didn't you just scold us last night for doing this exact same thing?"

Nazario rubbed the back of his neck. "I suppose I did. I would like to say things are more desperate now, but we both know that's a lie. I'm sorry. We have to get going though. Hurry to Jerykka."

They had their orders; Major Nazario hoped it would be enough. It would take some time to finalize preparations. He could not imagine how poorly this situation might turn out if the human attack happened.

Commander Braylon and his brother made their way through the service tunnels underneath the city's main platform. The empty pathways allowed them to move unseen and make good time toward their destination. Most workers had abandoned their maintenance jobs during the protests, leaving a clear underbelly. Braylon was finally able to relax a little but felt cut off from everything; there were no windows down here, no breezes from the recycled air circulators, no city noises.

"Lance is located near the outskirts of the city. He was one of the last people to get a room on the ship, so there was little left for him. He has to maintain a grocery store to justify his presence here. Working a menial job was the only option left. If you'd have gotten him one of the slots I originally requested, he could've been much closer to us and wouldn't have to work outside his field just to be allowed on the mission. He could be fully focused on assisting with the situation."

"You've made your point, brother. I'll work on trusting you more in the future. Just understand my side of things, he was considered a criminal. It would have looked very poorly to pull so many strings just to get someone like that on the primary mission for the expedition. I was pushing things to even get him approved how I did. I can't maintain my position if I'm using it in ways that look as though I'm abusing it."

"Whatever you say, Leo. You can keep making all the excuses you want, but I know you look down on both of us. If the situation weren't so dire, I wouldn't even consider helping you out of your own mess."

"I would expect nothing less of you. We must hurry, though."

Braylon increased their pace as they wound their way toward Lance's grocery store. It was still a dropship like the other buildings, but the outskirts were smaller for commerce and had considerably less amenities. They weren't originally meant for housing, but several had their storage rooms converted to living quarters for their staff in the last phase of construction of the *Jericho.* Things were more crowded than originally anticipated.

They could not quite reach all the way to the outskirts through the underlying service areas. They had to go up to the main level for the final leg of their journey. It was a risk, but Braylon knew there would be limited people in the area. Everyone had gathered near the central spire to protest him. They ascended to the main level and continued their hike to Lance's shop.

As they approached, Braylon noticed that even though the riots were in the heart of the city, their effect was felt all the way to the edges. In addition to the graffiti and vandalism, there was garbage strewn everywhere. No one had bothered to clean up after themselves. People did not care about anything when they thought they were going to die. It was a mess, but at least there were no witnesses around to worry about.

They entered Lance's store. It was nothing more than a small market with mostly empty shelves. The people had raided it for supplies during their panic. No one sat at the counter watching over the looted store. They made their way to the back of the store to the elevator. It would take them down to the living quarters.

The floor was very cramped when they exited the elevator. It was clear that this had once been a single large storage room. Now it contained several small living quarters formed by makeshift walls. These could not be comfortable living arrangements. Braylon had no idea there were quarters this tightly packed on the ship; these must have been added last second. He felt worse about not getting Lance onto the mission earlier.

Kevin led the way to a room in the back of the floor and knocked firmly. There was no answer, so he tried again. When there continued to be no answer, Kevin looked at Braylon with a worried expression.

"I fear he may be away. We would have no way to track him down."

Braylon took a step forward and knocked as hard as he could.

"I'm going to kick this door down if he doesn't answer. Maybe we can figure out where he went. This is an emergency."

"I would emphasize the importance of privacy and citizen rights, but you're not going to listen anyway."

Braylon shook his head, annoyed with his brother. He took a step back and aligned himself with the edge of the door. He kicked at it, straight on, with the bottom of his foot, leaning hard into it. The door opened a split second before his foot reached it and he tumbled into the room.

Lance jumped back, shocked.

"What the heck? Who are you? Kevin?"

Kevin was quick to answer, "Sorry for barging in Lance. This is my brother, Leonard. We have a slight emergency and need your assistance."

Lance's shock quickly turned to excitement. "The Commander?! It's my pleasure to have you! I'm so sorry for letting you fall."

He rushed forward to excitedly shake hands with Braylon as he stood up. "Thank you so much for getting me onto this mission. It's truly the opportunity of a lifetime! I'm sorry for the mess. Had I known I would be entertaining you, I would've tried to clean up. Please come in!"

Braylon was equally shocked and pleased with Lance's reaction. He was worried that Lance would hold resentment toward him, as his brother did.

"It is a pleasure to finally meet you, Lance. My brother has spoken incredibly highly of you. We need smart, capable people like yourself for this undertaking, especially now, in the worst of times." Braylon's Academy formalities resurfaced as he spoke to Lance.

Lance's expression flattened as he responded, "It's a truly horrible time. Thankfully, I had no one left behind on Earth; I was the last of my family. But enough about me, what brings you here? I'm sure you're not just here to meet your brother's friend. Not with everything else going on."

"Unfortunately, you are correct. We are dealing with emergency after emergency. You were brought for your technical skills, but I am here because of some of your more illicit ones."

Vreeham read the note again. A shiver ran down his spine. He was not ready for what was to come. Linnea's razor-sharp talons dug into his shoulder. She was not happy being ignored by him.

*You have failed us. Do not fail again. Distract them. We are coming.*

He did not want to see them. He just wanted the Society to thrive as promised.  What had he done?  Had he done the right thing trying to save his people?  Vreeham stared out onto the plains approaching Ambrecia. Solitary strolls along its wall were the only thing that settled his mind these days.

# Chapter 24
## Desperation

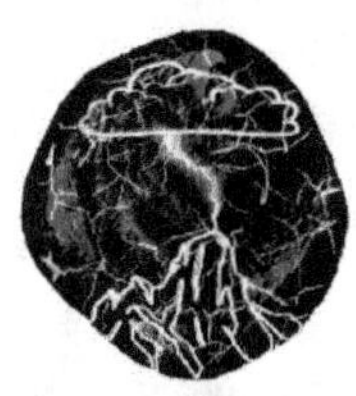 Jarreck had never seen Jerykka standing so fiercely, her muscles rippling as she issued orders. They were back around the war table and Jerykka was coordinating the continued defense. He could feel an aura of strength about her. He had always admired her tenacity and ability to inspire and strengthen her troops, but she was on a whole new level with the events unfolding around them. Jerykka made fleeting eye contact with him but looked away quickly when she caught him staring.

"What are you looking at, Jarreck?"

Jarreck had not realized he was staring at her, but quickly recovered, simply stating, "I'm just at a loss as to what the Undaari would do without you. What I'd do without you. You've truly proven why you're the Shield of our people. Unfortunately, I believe we're at a crossroads. We must part ways. We won't win this war here. Even if we managed to repel this assault, there's something far worse coming. We have to stop it before it gets here."

Jarreck could see the disappointment in her eyes. The regret that he filled her with. They had coordinated the war effort from here throughout the day, long after he had intended. He knew they were on limited time. With the pace the Noxxons had been traveling with the artifact, they would reach the Scarred Mountain as early as the morning.

When she finally spoke, however, it was not in disagreement, "I know. I wish this weren't the case, though. I'm going to need you here by my side if Entfall is to survive."

"We only need you to hold out long enough for us to stop the Noxxons from gaining control over the Black Tablet and the arcane magic.

If we can thwart that plan, I hope the Noxxons will retreat."

Jerykka nodded. Jarreck did not want to say goodbye again, knowing this very well might be the last time. *She didn't try to stop me, though. Even she knows it's time for them to part.*

If they were to die, he would have preferred them do it side-by-side fighting for their people, not split across their lands on a mission no one would ever know about. But if he did not leave now, he might never have the strength again. And his selfishness would cost them everything.

"What aid can we provide you on your journey?"

Jarreck shook his head, "None. We must travel quickly and lightly. I'll take Kiva and Lingdon, along with a few humans, to try and stop that Staff Bearer before it reaches the Black Peaks. I've spent too much time back here. They've gotten too close to the Heart of the Alackai already."

He stepped forward, reaching to grasp Jerykka's arm one last time in farewell. She grabbed his arm in return but pulled him into her embrace and hugged him deeply while whispering quietly, so only he could hear, "Please come back to me."

Her eyes did not glow upon their embrace, instead only a glimmer of a tear formed in her eye, then it was gone.

"Alackai's Grace guide you."

He smiled softly and replied, "Her Light protect you."

Jarreck turned to Kiva who stood ready, and Lingdon who looked nervous, but excited.

"It's time to go, we must head to the stables and meet with the humans. Quickly now."

The *Inquisitor* soared above the battlefield. The afternoon had set in by time they were ready to execute his plan. Major Nazario surveyed the battle through the viewscreen with augmented reality analytics overlayed with the live view to determine the most effective places to attack the Noxxons. As he piloted the ship, he directed his gunners through the intercom system.

Sergeant Piers manned the small armament station for the ship's lone built-in energy cannon. James and Reigns each had their own Peacemaker energy rifles and were stationed outside the airlocks. Each was tethered so as not to accidentally fall. He swung the ship low over the bridge giving them clear shots at the front of the Noxxon assault.

Their weapons blasted into the knots of Noxxons massed around the stronghold's walls and charging up the bridge, but barely seemed to make a dent in their numbers. It hardly even seemed to slow the Noxxon attacks, just created a momentary pause as they turned and examined the new threat. Despite the firepower above them, the Noxxons continued their attacks with a renewed fury. More and more Noxxons spilled over the walls before the ship could kill them.

Nazario and his men made several passes over the bridge trying to dissuade such a direct assault, but their weapons were not inflicting the level of damage he had hoped for. They did not seem to instill the fear he needed their alien technology to create. They did manage to distract a lot of Noxxon archers, as they began trying to down the ship, rather than the Undaari on the ramparts. Their arrows bouncing harmlessly off its black metallic hull.

He decided they would have to change their attack if they wanted the Noxxons to retreat. Something had to scare the brutes. He wished they had taken a battlecruiser now, with more firepower, even knowing that would not have been practical.

The ship in orbit was a bomber class, its weapons overpowered for this precision. But it sure would be enjoyable watching it rain down on these cruel beings, even with the close quarters. Besides, they had already decided its weapons may cause unintended consequences and could not be called upon to render assistance. That was a whole other bag of worms he intended to keep closed. As easy as reinforcements would make this mission, this was how it needed to be done. For diplomacy. For their future.

He surveyed the lack of damage his ship was inflicting. Hitting large stationary targets would be much easier than trying to hit individual Noxxons from the air. Their numbers were too great to pick them off, even in large groupings. Nazario was a veteran of the rebellions and understood the art of warfare. They might not be able to beat the Noxxons in a straight fight, but maybe they could outlast them if he managed to destroy the last of the Noxxon supplies.

He brought the ship around to the main Noxxon camp. He took a high-altitude approach as he searched for high value targets. If they could destroy some strategic assets, perhaps they could break this attack. Even a short retreat might be enough to get the bombers to stand down.

Nazario identified a few tents that were still guarded, as well as a lumberyard where the Noxxons were assembling wooden war machines from the forest around them. It appeared they were nearly complete with several wooden monstrosities, which would tower over the Undaari defenses. Those would be his target. He was surprised these had not been finished before they launched their assault.

They circled the camp one more time, then passed low and quick over the lumberyard, leaving a trail of fire, and burning the war machines as they crossed the camp. The Noxxons attempted to defend their equipment, but only had arrows with which to do so. Nazario brought their ship around for another pass. This time their target was the largest tent in the center of the camp, presumably their supply point.

As they made this pass, he could see the Staff Bearers emerge from a smaller tent to the rear of the large camp. Nazario made note of the three Staff Bearers and their tent. He continued to call out targets to his gunners. Their weapons fired into the large supply tent, setting it ablaze.

Next, he would turn his ship on the Staff Bearers now that he knew where they were. He hoped that their weaponry and altitude would prove to be more than enough to take them down. They were the leaders of this assault force, but *why haven't they joined the fight yet?*

The *Inquisitor* swung in low from the rear of the camp. He intended to hit the Staff Bearers hard and incapacitate their leadership. The sun was setting directly behind them, making it difficult for their enemy to see their approach. As they closed in on their quarry, he noticed there was no fear from the Staff Bearers as they stood their ground. They did not frighten as easily as their counterparts.

He watched as the three remaining Staff Bearers all turned to face the *Inquisitor*. He called for his men to target them and prepare to fire. He realized the Staff Bearers made no attempt to flee, rather, they each lifted their staffs straight into the air. Light began to emanate from above them. Nazario felt the blood drain from his face. They were going to attack, and he had seen what their weapons could do. He screamed for the gunners to fire, not knowing how the magic might affect the ship.

His men fired their weapons in a deadly barrage as the Staff Bearers unleashed their attack. All three Staff Bearers combined their attack into a single energy blast. A massive ball of crimson flames came hurtling toward the ship. Nazario attempted evasive maneuvers but was unsuccessful.

The attack struck the side of the ship at one of the airlocks as it turned away. The blast shook the ship to its core. Nazario nearly lost his seat as the ship rattled. Alarms blared on the Command Deck as the system reported significant damage. He called to his gunners for status updates. He received no reply from Sergeant Reigns.

Nazario knew they could not continue the assault. He would be lucky to even land the ship safely. His plan was another complete failure in a long list of his failures. He gave the ship full throttle to escape the battlefield then veered back around to the fortress. It would take some skill to land inside the tight confines of the courtyard again safely. Worse, he feared their ship might not be space-worthy anymore after that attack. They had limited maintenance supplies on board.

Nazario reduced the throttle as they came over the ramparts. The ship sank rapidly, nearly clipping the top of the fortress walls and slamming to the ground. The ship skidded to a halt in the small inner courtyard. He unstrapped from the pilot seat and rushed to check the damage. He ran to the hatch where Reigns had been. It was still intact from the inside, but as he opened the door, he found a large burnt hole in the armor of the ship next to it. Reigns was nowhere to be seen.

He stepped through the hatch and saw the end of Reigns' tether still attached to the ship. The other end had broken. He screamed and slammed his fist into the hull. *I can't keep losing men! No one else is going to die under my command!*

It was an inevitable reality of war, but not one he had ever accepted well. He thought back to Garren. He thought back to the company he had lost in the Colonial Rebellions. *After this, I'm retiring.*

Taking a deep, steadying breath, he examined the damage to his ship. The hole in the armor appeared to be superficial and did not penetrate the hull completely. It had damaged some of their sensors in the area and he could see exposed wires. It could have been much worse. He could not risk losing the ship and knew that given another chance, the Staff Bearers might succeed in destroying it. He still needed it to return to the *Jericho.*

That was it. *That was my only chance to stop the orbital bombardment and I've failed everyone.* He turned away from his ship to find himself face to face with Jerykka, her sigridir drawn and eyes glowing cyan, as the night set in. He stepped back from her. Jaina and Brandon were at her side, cowering away from the angry woman.

"I'm sorry, Master Jerykka, our mission failed. We couldn't force the Noxxons back. Our people are going to destroy the entire battlefield, Entfall included, in order to clear a path to recover the Alackai."

Jerykka frowned. "Jaina and Brandon have informed me of their plan. This is most unfortunate. I did *not* expect your people to become our enemy as well."

She stepped closer, towering over him.  Nazario shook his head, averting his eyes.

"That's not their intent, I swear.  They're just scared.  Scared like your people are now.  I may have intentionally withheld information about our people for their own protection, and I apologize, but considering the circumstances, you should know it wasn't done with ill intent."

He still could not meet her piercing gaze as she leaned in closer, ready to strike.

"It's time we fill you in on the rest of the details.  I'm sorry we didn't tell you everything before, but we're still not your enemy.  Please listen and trust me now.  Trust that I still value our friendship and care about your survival.  You're going to want to consider evacuating Entfall to save your people from what's coming next."

She stepped back, narrowing her eyes further, returning her blade to her hip.  Jaw clenched, Jerykka shook her head.

"We will *not* abandon Entfall under any circumstances.  If we die, we'll die here with honor.  We will defend this keep until our last breath.  In the meantime, I wish to hear these details you mentioned before I make my final decision on what to do with you.  I would prefer to only fight one enemy today.  Let's return to the war room and discuss this further."

"Whatever you wish.  But where is Jarreck?  I would have expected him to be at your side."

Jerykka pointed to the stables housing the zakeri.  "They're preparing to leave.  He has Kiva with him.  Their duties require them elsewhere.  They would prefer to have you there, but I'm not willing to trust you with their lives."

"I'm sorry, but I must go to him.  I know how important his mission is.  Jaina can stay to explain everything.  Brandon can help, too.  They're much better at this sort of thing anyway."

"Absolutely not," she declared.

"Jarreck is my only hope of stopping this attack now.  Ending this war will end the threat from my people.  I will take James with me and leave Piers to work on patching up my ship.  It can be used to evacuate some of your people, should you reconsider."

Jerykka sighed deeply.  With a frown, she waved him off.  She turned and walked toward the main hall.  He watched her go, hoping her frustrations did not signal the end of their alliance.  Brandon made to follow her, but Jaina hesitated.

She looked up, confused, and asked, "What about Reigns?"

Nazario slowly shook his head. "The Staff Bearers killed him when they did this to the ship. He was standing right there on the platform."

Jaina teared up and nodded. Brandon grabbed her hand in support. He turned away and looked toward the main hall. Jaina took a deep breath and followed after Jerykka, still holding Brandon's hand.

Nazario grabbed James from the *Inquisitor* and led him to the stables. He saw Jarreck, Kiva, and another young Undaari male. Jarreck looked up and acknowledged Nazario with a nod. Kiva smiled at him.

Jarreck introduced the boy. "This is Lingdon. He'll be joining us. I feel he may have a larger role in the events to come. We're heading to the Scarred Mountain. The Noxxons may have already reached it with the Black Tablet. We've spent too much time here. We must go. We cannot allow them to unlock its secrets."

Jarreck mounted the first zakeri. Nazario held up his hand as he ran forward.

"Wait, Jarreck, there's something else going on. Something you need to know. We told Jerykka already, but haven't had the chance to fill you in," he started, but almost did not finish when his eyes met with Kiva's. She would hate him, but he had to continue, "We have to force a Noxxon retreat tonight, or else my people in space will destroy everything here, including Entfall. They will end this war, no matter the cost."

Jarreck turned and dismounted the zakeri, storming up to Nazario, his eyes glowing cyan.

"What are you talking about? Why would your people attack us?"

Nazario was embarrassed but explained the situation in detail and why they would ever consider such a course of action. Jarreck grabbed Nazario by the chest of his exosuit and slammed him into the wall. Nazario could feel heat against his chest.

He pleaded, "This came from those above me. They're scared. They're in trouble. Please. This isn't how the humans normally behave."

He knew that was not necessarily true but what else could he say?

Jarreck's hand became encased in blue flames. "You knew your people would do this! I *knew* you couldn't be trusted. You were just a distraction from the Noxxon threat!"

Nazario shook his head. "No, my friend. My people have died to help you. My people just need help. They need the Alackai—"

Jarreck threw Nazario to the ground and drew his sigridir. The Skovi towered over the human. James rushed to Nazario's side, but Nazario waved him away. Kiva turned away as Jarreck stepped toward Nazario.

Nazario held his hand up defensively.

"We can still stop the attack.  We just have to force a Noxxon retreat."

Jarreck swung his blade down at Nazario.  Nazario rolled to the side dodging the attack.  Jarreck kicked him in his side, and he tumbled across the ground in front of the stables.  Gasping for breath and feeling the ache of his ribs, Nazario looked up to find Jarreck charging.

Jarreck closed the gap quickly, leaping in the air, driving his blade down at Nazario.  Nazario hopped to his feet, barely sidestepping the attack.  Nazario used Jarreck's momentum and wild attacks against him by slamming his shoulder into Jarreck's side, sending him tumbling.

Jarreck yelled in anger as he fell but jumped to his feet an instant later.  Both his hands were engulfed in cerulean flames.  He stepped toward Nazario who was still trying to catch his breath, sending the flames streaming at him.  Kiva jumped in front of the attack, calling the Alackai to shield them.  She withstood the attack, wincing in pain as she used her magic.  The flames lit up the courtyard as they battled in front of the stables.

"Stop, Jarreck!" she screamed.

He did not stop.  Jarreck moved to get around Kiva.  Kiva countered with flames of her own, yelling out as she unleashed her own fiery attack.  Jarreck swatted away the flames and focused on Kiva.  After a moment, the energy faded from his eyes.

"Please, Jarreck.  We need their help.  I trust him," Kiva begged.

Jarreck eyed Nazario distrustfully.  The flames around his hands began to fade.

"The Alackai isn't yours to take.  She chooses who she helps," Jarreck muttered, looking at the ground.

"I know.  We don't wish to take it.  We just want to ask her to save us.  To beg for her help.  We thought if we could help you, she might help us.  My people are just impatient out of fear.  I promise.  I've already lost two friends to this war, don't make me lose another," Nazario said, reaching a hand toward Jarreck.

"I can't speak for the Alackai, but if I had other warriors who could join me, I would leave you behind.  What did you have planned?" Jarreck asked, meeting his gaze but not taking his hand.

"Well, they're finishing the construction of their siege equipment now," Nazario said, lowering his outstretched hand.  "They're going to use them soon.  Their Staff Bearers have been hanging back as well.  If we can take out the siege equipment and cut off the Staff Bearers from the battle, maybe the Noxxons will retreat, or at least slow their attack. They can't penetrate these walls without the siege equipment or their masters."

Jarreck contemplated Nazario's observations. "Perhaps when they begin moving their siege equipment into place, we can set it ablaze and cut the Noxxons on the bridge off from those still crowding the shore. That might create enough panic for us to push them back. At least for a little bit."

Jaina was open and honest about everything that had transpired with the humans. She spoke about everything from their assigned mission, to the destruction of their solar system, and finally to being stranded in space without hope of survival. She was careful not to leave out any details. She wanted to ensure that Jerykka would understand the gravity of their situation. Sympathy was what they needed most now to maintain a relationship.

Jerykka *needed* to know why they were so scared. Now was not the time to hold back any cards. All their bargaining chips would be laid on the table and she would know of their desperation. Jaina hoped the translators would be able to convey their desperation effectively.

"Unfortunately, our people are scared for their lives. They fear that without some sort of new energy, they'll all die up in space, the last of our kind. We don't seek to take the Alackai with ill will; our people are just trying to survive. No one is thinking clearly right now."

"The Alackai is of *no* use to your people. You're not of this world, only the Undaari can access this gift."

"*They* don't know that. They're desperate. And there may yet be a way we can use it, just to rescue them. The Alackai is powerful and wise and surely wouldn't wish an entire people left for dead. Especially if you help you fend off the Noxxons. We wanted a peaceful solution to foster an enduring partnership with the Undaari. I still wish to seek a peaceful solution between our people. I abhor all the fighting. If there were another way to save you, I'd take it."

Brandon stood by Jaina's side in support. He nodded as she spoke. His eyes darted back and forth between the two women as they discussed the implications of the upcoming attack.

Jerykka shook her head while eyeing Jaina. "It would seem that your people are not as wise, nor as compassionate, as your team. We'll have to reevaluate our friendship in the future. But for now, you and your companions have proven yourselves to me. There may yet be a way for us to survive this attack. How long until it happens?"

Brandon finally spoke, "N-… Not long, they should arrive by morning. Once they arrive, it will take time to finalize pr-… preparations. They'll relay to us once they've arrived to g-… give us a chance to escape ourselves. I can p-… pass that warning along once it's here. Our ships really c-… can wipe Entfall off this planet, the Noxxon army along with it, without ever setting foot on the g-… ground. Please reconsider evacuating."

Jaina looked at Brandon for a moment. *His stuttering has gotten worse with all this tension.* She looked back to Jerykka, watching her ponder their words. She felt her heart thumping in her chest as she anxiously awaiting the decision. Jaina agreed with Brandon. The Undaari *should* evacuate.

"This fortress has defended against larger hordes and more powerful magic than this in the past. We'll find a way now. It still has some magic remaining in its old bones. The Alackai has gifted her strength to build these walls and she will continue to protect them."

"Is there any chance of a peaceful resolution to your war with the Noxxons?  Is there anything that they've wanted from the Undaari? Something that could be negotiated now to sate their thirst?" asked Jaina. *Diplomacy will be far better for this planet than continued war.*

"The Noxxons are savages without reason. Their hatred for us runs in their blood. There is no reasoning with them ever. They would kill our messenger if we even tried to talk."

"It just seems that with the millennia of war, peace would be the preferred option. They must be tired of dying. There *has* to be a way to strike a peace without driving the other to extinction. Both people have a right to live. Peace is *always* worth the risk."

Jerykka shook her head vigorously.  "I've told you that it's impossible. But we can survive your people's attack here. As we will survive theirs."

Jaina was worried about this plan.  "I'm not sure that will be enough, but we'll stand by you. I hope to prove our commitment to future relations. Prove that we don't want to fight. Peace is always an option. But if war is where we're at, I'll do my part to see its end. Besides, I could not live with myself if war broke out between our people. I must go back to our ship, though, to monitor communications. I'll let you know as soon as they're here."

# Chapter 25
## Counterattack

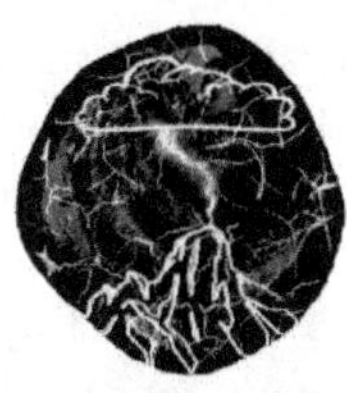Back in Ambrecia, the Undaari King had received word of the Noxxon attack on Entfall. He convened his advisors, including High Councilor Vreeham and Councilor Gierdahl of the Society. Councilor Gierdahl was not a true advisor, but the King valued his opinion, nonetheless. They had known each other a long time. Together, they met to discuss dire matters. The King could not march their army to Entfall without the support of his advisors.

Councilor Gierdahl stood up and spoke to the assembly, "We must send the Undaari Army to Entfall to crush the Noxxons at our doorstep. Their transgressions cannot be tolerated. We must not allow them to gain entrance into our lands. Every Undaari must be protected, not just those here in the capital. Between the Society and our army, the Noxxons will be rid of once and for all."

There was arguing amongst the advisors at this. The King was unsure which course of action to take. His thoughts were with Kiva, but he had to listen to his advisors as well. A good King must. He longed for his warrior days when he did not have to play politician.

High Councilor Vreeham stood next. Among all his advisors, he had always trusted Vreeham the most. He had been by his side since before he was King. No one had done more to take care of him or help him grow into the King he was today.

With a heavy voice, Vreeham stated, "With all due respect, Gierdahl, if we send the army to Entfall, no one will be left here to defend Ambrecia. If we fail to defend Entfall, then nothing stands between the Noxxons and Ambrecia. Besides, this threat is nothing new. The Noxxons have attempted this several times before. Their army will crumble against

Entfall as it has previously.  We would be creating panic for no reason if we even muster the army.  It would be better to leave them at their homes with their families."

Gierdahl fired back, "Jarreck and Kiva have risked their lives to bring us warning so that we may act in time.  They did not do so for us to cower here behind the walls of Ambrecia.  They're out there fighting as we speak, and the Society should support them."

"Jarreck and Kiva are borderline traitors, Gierdahl.  You've seen their actions and know they've defied the Council's orders.  They seek nothing but to undermine the Society.  I would hazard to say they may even be working with the Noxxons based on their wild accusations.  How can you continue to defend them?"

"I defend them because I know them.  They are the most determined and loyal Skovi within the Society.  They would never betray us.  Besides, I would rather trust them and send aid in time than sit here and find out they were right when the Noxxons march up to our gates."

Vreeham laughed loudly, "The Noxxons at our gates? So foolhardy.  But if it's as grim as you say, then Entfall wouldn't last until our troops reach their shores.  What would you have us do?  Mobilize the army and leave them vulnerable?  Or worse, have them miss the Noxxons altogether?  Send our Skovi and have them slaughtered?  The true threat comes from within.  Not the Noxxons."

"Better to try than do nothing, High Councilor.  We should trust in Jarreck.  We must send aid to Entfall.  And we must excise the cancer that is their new corruption of the Alackai."

"Ahh yes.  Thank you for reminding me of Jarreck's boldest claim to date.  He states that the Noxxons have magically gained access to the Alackai.  What an absurdity.  He is not to be trusted.  The old man has lost his mind and should be thrown from the Society.  Would save us all a massive headache."

"He is no senile old man," argued Gierdahl.

"Regardless, his claims are baseless.  Even Jerykka, who called for aid made no such mention of Noxxons using the Alackai.  Their army will crumble against Entfall.  You'll see.  In just a few days we'll all be laughing over the Noxxon failure while drinking glasses of raza."

There was some nodding among the other advisors.

Gierdahl countered, "It's time for the Society to stand again, alongside the Undaari.  They need to join those brave warriors defending Entfall and assist in securing it.  The Undaari Army should march as well.

It's more than a match for the Noxxons. Why not just ensure this becomes nothing more? We don't have to send the entire army, just enough to fortify Entfall."

Some other advisors nodded in agreement to this.

Vreeham fired back, "I fear that may not be the case. Seeing the Society lead a war effort may frighten our people. It could create undue panic. It would be best to not validate the Noxxons. Their existence is a corruption on our lands; we shouldn't even acknowledge their existence."

The advisors were split.

Councilor Gierdahl made a final, desperate plea. "If the Undaari Army doesn't march to Entfall, then we could be allowing the Noxxons to enter our lands. They would raid every one of our villages before reaching Ambrecia. We would be abandoning the rest of our people to their will. They would be slaughtered and enslaved. Assisting Entfall is the only course of action that makes any sense. Surely you all see this."

There were some grumblings of agreement. The King watched the ebb and flow of the arguments over the advisors. The advisors had seemed split before, but now their volume and echoes were favoring Councilor Gierdahl's plan of attack. The High Councilor sat quietly for a moment, pondering.

When he began speaking again, it was in a low, soft voice, "One last proposal then. We send the Skovi Shields to bolster Entfall. The Shields are a small force and could sneak into the fortress and strengthen its defenses just as well as the Undaari Army could. Only they could do it with less risk of life, without creating fear across our lands.

"I don't particularly agree with mustering our army, better leave them at home with their families. But since you have support, then I suggest we place our army nearby in Eilenar. From there, they could assist both Eilenar and Entfall. They won't be marching to war, but they'll be nearby to cut off any further Noxxon incursions. We can defend the river without raising alarm."

There were some nods amongst the other advisors. *This is a solid plan, too.* It seemed to be the best of both worlds. The King continued watching the debate. He knew that the High Councilor had argued well, but the crowd still favored Gierdahl. The High Councilor looked away from the other advisors, turning directly toward the King.

"My King, I have stood by your side for decades. I have never let you down before and I will continue to be your most trusted servant. We cannot risk our people's sense of security. They will panic and our lands would fall into chaos.  If our people see us mobilize our entire army to fight the Noxxons at Entfall, they will see it as desperation and fear for the future.

"We could station the army at Eilenar to conduct a training event, since they haven't been mobilized in some time.  That would avoid creating a panic over such a minor threat.  And the Society cannot act in the open for the same reason.  If they were to march with the army, the people would assume we had taken control and panic even more."

The King placed his hand on his chin as he contemplated the options.  He wanted to assist Kiva as he had promised, but he could not go against his advisors.  He may be King, but he was no absolute authority.  And he did not trust himself with such power anyway.  His eyes wandered across the other advisors in front of him.  They were as worried about the people as he was.  His eyes settled on Councilor Gierdahl.

Gierdahl stood up and spoke briefly, "The decision is yours, my King.  I wish only to ensure all courses of action have been considered before your wisdom decides.  Any action is preferred to inaction."

The King stood at that moment.  "Deploy the Undaari Army.  We will follow the High Councilor's plan.  We do not wish to create a panic, but we must ensure that our lands are secure."  The King turned directly to Gierdahl and added, "You have spoken wisely, and I do *not* disagree with you.  In that regard, send the Shields to assist Kiva in the defense of Entfall.  If they move quickly, they could bolster the defenses and guarantee the army is not needed in action.  We will not abandon Kiva and the rest of our people in Entfall.  Send Swords to our other cities.  Make sure they're safe."

Night had fallen over the keep.  The battle at Entfall was bathed in the blue moonlight of the twin moons.  As Jarreck and Nazario moved along the lower bank of the bridge, Jarreck could hear the battle raging above.  They had snuck out of a secret entrance on the north side of the keep.  Jarreck could smell the Noxxon blood soaking the bridge as they moved.  They traveled the narrow path with their backs to the bridge wall, avoiding detection.

The siege equipment was slowly rumbling toward the bridge.  There were still hundreds of Noxxons along the shoreline, waiting for their chance to attack.  The Noxxons on the bridge were continuing their attempts to scale the walls with ropes and ladders.  It was slow moving.  Others were trying to break down the gates, which was even slower.  The bridge was littered with bodies as the Noxxons pressed forward. Jarreck could still smell the burnt Noxxon flesh from the sakari oil the night before.

Catapults still fired stone projectiles, but they had little effect against the fractured obsidian walls. Archers slowly picked off Undaari defenders. Noxxon war drums still filled the air with their incessant beat. Jarreck's heart raced with them. He could hear the screams of Noxxons and Undaari coupled with the clang of metal. The Undaari were fighting a one-sided battle. Jarreck was still unsure why the Staff Bearers had not entered the fight yet. *Perhaps they are waiting for something. Whatever that might be, it would be terrible.*

They neared the shoreline, unseen. Jarreck heard the siege machines creaking as they neared the bridge. There were several towers with internal staircases to allow Noxxons to scale the walls quickly. There was also a massive, wheeled battering ram. They would try to go over and through the walls. Jarreck suspected the Staff Bearers were waiting for a breach before they began to fight. Then it would be over for the Undaari.

As they hid there, waiting for the siege equipment to reach the bridge, Jarreck thought back to his conversation with Nazario. Had Nazario not lost warriors of his own, and put himself in harm's way to protect Kiva, Jarreck would have killed him already. If it came to a choice, he feared Nazario would elect to abandon the Undaari.

Jarreck was glad that Nazario was with him, though. His support had made this war more tolerable. Nazario had proven himself a friend of the Undaari, but Jarreck still felt deeply wounded by the actions of his people. He would not allow Nazario to lose anymore friends.

Jarreck peered over the lip of the bridge, spying the war machines. This would be the easy part of their current mission. After their attack, they would flee into the forest and make their way north toward Eilenar. Kiva would be there, waiting for them with two zakeri.

Then they would have to face that Staff Bearer again. A shiver ran down his spine as he remembered how helpless he had felt. Though they had fared better in recent battles, he had yet to kill one without the aid of an Entai. This mission would be terribly dangerous and still, Nazario had volunteered. Jarreck tried to push the mistrust and suspicion of Nazario from his mind. He needed the human right now. Even more, they were friends now.

The siege equipment rolled into position. The wood was still fresh and moist, so the Undaari archers had little chance to ignite them. Jarreck would use the Alackai's cerulean flames instead. He moved quickly, calling up the Alackai. He felt stronger with its use, and closer to her. Things had changed during the course of this war. The pain had gone away once he had stopped using the restrictive hand movements of the Society.

His blue flames struck the base of the rolling tower. He spread the fire quickly, using it to prevent the Noxxons from counterattacking. As the flames grew on the tower, it began to weaken. It was Nazario's turn to attack. He blasted his Valor arm canon at the top of the tower. He needed to knock it off balance. As bursts of white energy collided with the tower, it began to lean. The wheels at the base began to crack as the center of gravity shifted.

Within moments, the tower came crashing down. It fell onto a second tower. The second tower crashed off the opposite edge of the bridge and into the lake. Jarreck continued to spread his cerulean flames along the first tower as it turned into a raging inferno. The Noxxons on the bridge turned and screamed. They were cut off from retreat and nearly half the remaining forces. Many Noxxons panicked and leapt off the bridge to escape the flames. Disarray and chaos were seeded into their ranks.

Then their escape brought the Noxxons directly toward where Jarreck and Nazario were hiding. The Noxxons on the shore quickly spotted them as well. The barbarians charged into the water to surround them. Their escape route was cut off. *This is not part of the plan.* Jarreck drew his sigridir and brought the Alackai's flames to bear. Nazario drew his blade as well and fired the arm cannon into the charging Noxxons.

Jarreck fought for his life, Nazario at his side. Weapons slashed and energy crashed into their attackers, but the Noxxons were pressing in on them. They would not be able to hold them back much longer. As strong and skilled as they were, they could not resist such numbers. Hundreds of Noxxons were swarming them now, barely even paying heed to the warriors atop the walls.

The flames of the burning wreckage on the bridge were suddenly extinguished. The Staff Bearers had arrived. They used the Alackai to choke the flames out and clear a path for the rest of their Noxxons. All three Staff Bearers turned on Jarreck and Nazario.

Jarreck threw his blue fire at the Staff Bearers to slow them down. They walked through it like it was nothing, twirling their staffs in front of them as shields. As Jarreck watched the Staff Bearers approach, he noticed that on their red scarred, black, stony shoulders, they were branded.

He recognized the brands from his vision. And from some other place in his memory. These were the same Noxxons who had killed his father.  They had grown stronger since that day.  Taller too.  Somehow infused with the Alackai.  Jarreck could not imagine winning this battle. Escape would be difficult, but it was their only option.

They had fallen back into the water of the lake, thigh deep.  Jarreck pulled Nazario close to himself, then used the Alackai to create a massive column of cerulean flames around them.  The Noxxons stepped back, shielding their eyes from the light.  The Staff Bearers on the bridge paused as they monitored the flames dancing over the lake's surface.  They began to throw their crimson fire at the column.

The flaming aqua column began to grow unstable before it exploded outward.  Jarreck and Nazario had already dove under the lake's dark water, having appeared to vanish.  When they finally surfaced again, they had made it far out into the center of the lake.  No Noxxons were pursuing them.  Instead, their focus had shifted back toward their assault.

Jarreck and Nazario were no longer able to sneak up along the shoreline.  They still had a good distance to swim before they reached the safety of the north shore.  Jarreck's body was trembling as they swam, but not from the cold waters.  That had been entirely too close for comfort.

They could see the first signs of light on the western horizon. Jarreck worried they had taken too much time in this attack.  They needed to hurry to the Scarred Mountain and stop the Noxxons from opening the Black Tablet.  The attack on Entfall would never stop otherwise.

He led the way as they swam.  By the time they reached the shore, the sun had fully erupted over the horizon.  They were able to see the damage they had inflicted on the siege equipment, but it had not been enough to force a retreat.  It had barely even slowed the Noxxon attack. There were still two more siege towers and their battering ram.  Jarreck noticed another odd piece of equipment, now lumbering forward, but could not identify it.  He turned away from the battle and let out a deep sigh.  He looked at Nazario before rushing through the forest to reach Eilenar.

Morning had fully set in by time they made it to their destination. Their clothes were already dry in the heat of the sun.  They met Kiva at a tavern in town.  She was surrounded by Undaari enjoying their breakfasts. It seemed peaceful here as the Undaari began their days, unbothered by the war occurring just to their south in Entfall.

Kiva led them to the stables where they mounted their zakeri. Jarreck climbed on the lead creature with James and Lingdon, leaving Kiva to follow with Nazario.  Nazario climbed onto the zakeri and held on tightly to Kiva.

He still looked awkward riding the great animals, like he could never sit comfortably on them.  They quickly lifted off and began their journey north.  They pushed the zakeri hard.  This was probably harder than they should have gone, considering the distance they were covering, but this was no time to leave anything on the table.  They needed to make good time to close the gap.

# Chapter 26
## Shield

$\mathcal{L}$ance looked down to avoid eye contact, clearly intimidated and worried he was in trouble. He glanced at Kevin for just a moment before his eyes returned to the floor.

"What skills would those be?" he cautiously asked, nervously eyeing his computer against the wall.

"Do not mistake my meaning, Lance, you are not in trouble," Braylon said with a reassuring smile. "Your skills are necessary to save our people. I know about your past and your record, just as I know about nearly every single person on this ship. My brother is the reason that record did not stop you from joining our mission. And you are in a unique position to prove why you were chosen."

Lance's eyes narrowed. "So, I'm not under arrest?"

Braylon looked at him questioningly, then joked, "Why would you be under arrest? And why would I be the one to do it?"

Lance's eyes betrayed him, showing how nervous and shy he had just become.

He looked at Kevin, who simply nodded his head reassuringly, then he responded to Braylon, "I haven't exactly been following a lot of the martial law guidance and thought you were here to bust me."

Braylon smiled. "Not today. Quite the opposite, actually. I need your help to violate more of them."

Lance looked taken aback. "Why do you need help with that? You could just lift martial law and do whatever you needed to."

"You are right. I *could* if I were still in charge of the ship. As it is, there has been a mutiny. I am on house arrest but managed to sneak away. I need your help to stop a plan that will likely doom our people, and jeopardize our future relationships with a friendly, alien race, called the Undaari, on our destination planet."

Braylon continued on, apprising Lance of the situation. He watched Lance's jaw drop as the information hit him. Kevin nodded his affirmation. Braylon knew it was a lot of information at once for Lance to handle.

"This could still be prevented if not for our communications being shut off ship wide. I could call off the mission, but I have to find a way to reach the ships. Can you help?" Braylon asked.

Lance continued to look blankly as he processed all the new information. Kevin put his hand on Lance's shoulder to get his attention.

"We can talk about all these implications in the future, but we *have* to get communications established at the soonest possible moment. You're the best person I know for this sort of thing," said Kevin.

Lance snapped out of his shock. "Yes! I can do that! I just have to find a backdoor into the system. Important programs like this always have a well-protected back door, in case someone messes up the front door by accident."

Lance sat at his computer and started to work, then popped his head up to add, "Well, it's really more like a small vent way up in the attic, which isn't accessible without a hydraulic lift and specialized tools." He looked back at his console as he continued, "They didn't destroy the communications array, they just shut them down and locked everyone out, sealing the front door. I won't be able to unlock that door, but I could find us a lift to sneak in the back."

Lance resumed working without another word. He feverishly typed away at his console. He worked for a few minutes, occasionally exclaiming in frustration. Finally, he threw his hands up in defeat and looked over at the brothers.

"Internal communications are cake, and I have access to those. Our long-range, ship-to-ship communications, however, are going to be difficult. They're on an isolated network and aren't connected to anything else. I would have to be onsite in order to get into that system. Basically, they're in a completely different house in another town. I have to get to that house to get in."

"Where would we have to go for that? The Command Deck? Or the antenna itself?" Braylon asked.

"Well, either of those options would work, but they're impractical and dangerous. We don't have envirosuits to go outside and directly tap into the antenna, and with the mutiny, we would never make it to the Command Deck. There is a third option though."

Jerykka discussed her distrust of the humans with Brandon in the main hall as they looked over the war table. She was still considering evicting them from Entfall. Brandon pleaded for her to understand their intentions. Her trust in them had been broken, but she saw that Jarreck had still taken Nazario with him. She trusted Jarreck. She sent a messenger for Rentari.

Another human stumbled into the main hall. The one Nazario had left working on repairs for the *Inquisitor*. He limped over to her as she spoke to Brandon. He was out of breath by time he reached them. Brandon looked up at him as he approached.

"Sergeant P-... Piers? What's wrong?"

"It's time."

Brandon's face went vacant. "We have to move qui-... quickly. We must evacuate before they d-... destroy this whole place. We can get some Undaari out on our ship."

"I've already told you, we're *not* evacuating. We have another option. Entfall has never fallen because the Alackai has never allowed it. She will not abandon us now. We will survive the attack and let your people destroy the Noxxons." Jerykka stood strong, moving away from Brandon.

Brandon looked after her as she walked away and called out, "You d-... don't understand!"

Sergeant Piers and Brandon followed Jerykka, trying to dissuade her from staying. Jerykka ignored their protests as she walked. *Why do these humans think they know everything?*

"Master Jerykka," Brandon started, but she raised a hand to stop him.

"I've made my decision. You're welcome to stay, but do *not* incite fear or question my decision. *You* are the ones who don't understand. If you want to help, secure the ramparts."

Jerykka made her way to the throne at the head of the hall, leaving Brandon and Piers standing in the hall, dumbfounded. The throne was covered in dust as it had not been sat in for years. Jerykka had refused to ever sit there. She did not feel that it was the place of a Warden. Only the King of the Undaari should sit on a throne. Many Wardens had sat there over the years, but neither Jerykka, nor her predecessor, had been comfortable with the idea.

Despite her feelings, she knew it was her duty to claim the throne this day. The hall fell silent as she stepped up to it. She felt the eyes of her subordinates following her as she walked. Her people at the war table stopped what they were doing to watch. Everyone knew her disdain for the throne.

She ran her hands over the stone surface, brushing away some of the dust. As she sat down in place, she could feel warmth emanating from the seat. For a stone seat that had not been occupied for at least a century, it was surprisingly welcoming.

She knew why, of course, but it was still a shock. She smiled as she pressed her body against the stone. There was still life in Entfall. The Alackai was still strong within it. The throne was black and fractured, just like the walls she was seeking to protect. She sat there, steadying herself, preparing for what was to come.

Rentari approached her as she took a few deep steadying breaths. He was accompanied by the messenger she had sent just a few minutes before.

She looked at him. "It's time for me to call upon the Alackai to assist us. Take these humans with you and join Intayr up on the ramparts. We will get about a day to rest and recover with her Grace protecting us."

Rentari acknowledged her command with a nod and made his way up to the ramparts with Brandon and Piers. Jerykka sat back fully into the throne, allowing herself to sink into the hard seat. She closed her eyes and began to concentrate on the Alackai. She fell into a deep meditation. She could feel the warmth of the throne growing as the blue fractures across its surface began to glow brightly.

Up on the ramparts, Intayr still led the Undaari in defense of Entfall, using the magic rifle that Nazario had given him. He could not believe its power. He was not sure he would ever give it back. He saw the humans approaching and greeted them with a quick wave.

He continued to fire his new weapon into the Noxxons. They were nearing the wall with the siege equipment at this point. The rifle audibly alarmed in his hand: LOW BATTERY. He looked at the red light on the rifle. *What does that mean?*

The Undaari had killed countless Noxxons and destroyed two siege towers already, but the Noxxons seemed endless. The Undaari might not be able to hold out much longer. It seemed like every time they killed one Noxxon, four more took its place. The bridge was still filled with Noxxons marching forward while the shoreline was still covered in their archers. They never tired. Never ended. Just a mass of hatred, slowly crushing the Undaari.

The Undaari were hard to kill in their stronghold, but they had no reinforcements. Each death was a grievous wound to their forces. Their numbers were dwindling. Without some sort of miracle, they would not last another day.

The Noxxons were fighting harder than expected. Their focus and resolve unmatched by anything in their history. With the towers and uniquely designed battering ram making their way across the bridge, the tide of this battle would shift quickly in favor of the Noxxons.

Intayr could see something else in the distance that struck him as odd. In the camp, the Noxxons had built something else, something big out of the wood they had gathered from the forest. He had no idea what it was, but the front part resembled a bow. This thing was being built for a reason. It had to be part of their plan to penetrate Entfall. He was worried. The Staff Bearers watched it slowly roll through their camp.

He could see Monkley elsewhere on the ramparts, fighting like a true warrior on behalf of the Undaari. Monkley was right in the thick of it, risking his life. More Noxxons had made it over the walls, but they were few in number. Rentari came up the rampart walls with Brandon and Jaina. The four of them silently watched the Noxxons move their war machines into position.

Rentari was the first to break the silence. "Jerykka's about to call upon the Alackai to protect us. Everyone needs to step back from the ramparts. We need to pass the word around. She will give us all a break from the fight, before the Noxxons can push their weapons into action."

Intayr nodded and began to spread the word. Entfall's defenders took cover on the ramparts, no longer fighting against the Noxxons approaching. Only a few more Noxxons managed to scale the wall before Entfall came to life, and they were quickly dispatched. Intayr took a deep breath and stood.

He watched in awe as the cyan fractures in the black stone of the ramparts began to glow. The glow grew in intensity, moving from the base of the wall to the top. Intayr could feel the power emanating from the walls as the Alackai came to life.  After a few moments of the energy building, a bright cerulean wall of light rose from the edge of the ramparts.

No one had witnessed the power of the Alackai at Entfall in centuries.  It was awe-inspiring as the shield grew.  Intayr nearly wept at its beauty as the shield reached high into the sky and arched back toward the center of the fortress, creating a dome over Entfall.

The Undaari defenders stood and watched as the shield took shape and enveloped the stronghold.  Intayr turned to look out at the Noxxons.  Projectiles disintegrated on the shield as the Noxxon archers and catapults were still firing.  Their warriors on the bridge stopped moving.  The few that were scaling the wall had been scalded by the energy and fell to their deaths.

Once the dome had enclosed the fortress completely, it began to grow outward.  Intayr watched, slack-jawed, as it continued to grow to its full size, consuming the Noxxons still attacking the walls.  Their bodies disintegrated as easily as the arrows, leaving their armor falling to the ground.  The Noxxons on the bridge began to flee from its power back down the bridge to the safety of their camp.  The shield moved out from the rampart walls to encase the entire island that Entfall sat on.

Still, the shield continued to grow.  As it expanded further, any Noxxons that were caught fell victim to its power. The shield destroyed over a hundred Noxxons as it grew to full strength.  It only destroyed the living and the projectiles in the air; the bodies of the dead Noxxons and their siege equipment went unharmed. Cheers erupted from the Undaari as the Alackai grew to protect them.  Intayr smiled with relief as they would finally get their first break from battle.

The shield stopped expanding once it reached the end of the bridge at the shore.  Jerykka had said it would last a day.  It could only be held as long as Jerykka maintained her strength and concentration.  Intayr had heard her speak of it only once.  The shield was reserved for extreme circumstance.  The longest any Warden had ever managed to maintain the shield was a full day, sunrise to sunrise.  *Plenty of time to rest and recharge,* he though as he collapsed to the ground.

Jarreck and the others had not been flying long when he turned back to look at Entfall.  They had put a lot of distance between themselves and Entfall, but he could still see its tiny silhouette in the distance. He could see the blue glow of the shield starting to envelope the fortress and surrounding lake.  He knew what it meant and was glad they had made it out before the shield went up.  They never would have made it to the Scarred Mountain in time if they had not left when they did.

He slowed the zakeri in the air, just before the keep disappeared over the horizon.  They needed to make good time but paused at the unique sight.  Jarreck had never seen its shield in action.  Was not even sure it was real.  Nazario looked back for a second as well.  Kiva followed suit.

Just as Entfall was fading away in the distance, bright bursts of white light erupted around Entfall.  They all witnessed the destructive power of the human ships.

"The orbital bombardment has begun.  I really hope they made it out in time.  I wish we could have helped them more.  But we have our mission," Major Nazario yelled across their zakeri to Jarreck.

Jarreck replied, "Master Jerykka is wise and wouldn't risk her people or the keep.  There are strong defenses at that fortress.

Entfall had disappeared in a cloud of debris and smoke.  He turned back, feeling the dampness in his eyes, and focused on their mission.  It was the only thing that mattered now.  It only took a couple more hours to reach the Scarred Mountain.

# Chapter 27
## Messages

Brandon had grabbed Jaina from the ship as he made his way to the ramparts with Rentari and traded Piers back to work on repairs. He watched as the shield began to form and had insisted they examine it closer, together. Intayr and Rentari were sitting down to rest at the moment and Monkley made his way over to join them.

Brandon was standing on the rampart looking up at the shield with wide-eyed bewilderment. He could not comprehend the power of the Alackai or how it could create something so powerful, yet so beautiful. The shimmer of the shield was mesmerizing. He furiously took notes as he studied the shield from the ramparts.

Jaina spoke to Brandon, "I just don't understand how the Alackai is able to do so much. What's the science behind it?"

Brandon shook his head. "It's magic! I don't know if our science will ever fully understand it. From a b-… biological standpoint, it makes no sense, but we better survive this and save the Undaari so I can find out!"

Monkley brought them back to the present. "The orbital strike will occur within the next couple minutes. I'm not sure this shield can withstand the force, so better say any goodbyes now. Even if it can, it sounds as though this shield will only last for a day at best. At least the Noxxons should get wiped out in the blast. That might be enough to stop further attacks."

As Monkley spoke, Brandon noticed something in the distance. "It's hard t-… to see outside of the shield, but it looks like there's something g-… going on in the Noxxon camp."

Intayr and Rentari stood to join them. All five began to look out from the ramparts carefully. Brandon could just make out the three Staff

Bearers at the front of the Noxxon camp. They stood side by side. In unison, they raised their staffs, aiming them at the shield. Vermilion energy streamed from their black staffs, impacting the shield.

The shield did not waver. It appeared to be too strong for the Staff Bearers to penetrate. Brandon watched closely, eyes squinting at the sight to determine their effect. He saw no holes forming in the shield. It seemed to be holding.

Intayr pointed his finger toward the shield. "The shield's changing color. They're corrupting it."

Brandon noticed the change in hue. The shield over the bridge was indeed changing color, darkening, turning purple then red at the epicenter of their attack. The shield did not appear to be weakening though; the color was just as thick and vibrant, just different. Brandon realized it was starting to expand from the bridge, bubbling out, moving toward the Noxxon camp.

"They're hijacking the shield to protect themselves. How can they do that?" Rentari said in disbelief.

The shield expanded quickly, pulled over the Noxxon camp by their Staff Bearers. The expansion was a purple-red bubble that grew like a pimple from the pure cerulean shield created by Entfall. Unlike when the shield had originally formed, this new expansion did not harm the Noxxons as it passed over them. They were being brought inside the protection of the Alackai.

The expansion grew rapidly. The Undaari around Brandon began to panic; they were not going to get their reprieve from the battle. The shield had grown to cover over half of the Noxxon army, when the Undaari around him gasped and began to look above them. Brandon followed their gaze. Bright lights had appeared over them. The orbital strike had begun.

Moments after the flashes appeared in the sky, bright bursts of energy rained down on the shield. They impacted one after another in a ferocious onslaught that covered its entire surface. Fire spread along the dome-like shield and down its side to the water. The flames reached out toward the Noxxon camp, engulfing the Noxxons that had not made it under the shield's protection yet.

Brandon could see the waters around the keep begin to boil as the explosions reached them. They continued to spread to the shores edge. He had to cover his ears against the deafening sound. No one under the shield, Undaari, Human, or Noxxon, dared move. Like him, they were all scared of the destruction surrounding them, frozen as if their movement might collapse the shield. The bombardment and destruction only lasted for a few

long minutes.

The sky did not clear for several more minutes.  It was incredibly still inside the shield.  The silence was unnerving, even the drumbeat had ceased.  The sun began to peek back through the dust.  Monkley jumped up.

"When they realize Entfall's still here, they'll attack again!  They'll keep launching until everything is gone!" he shouted.

Jaina took off running.  Brandon followed after her.  His thoughts were racing as they ran.  The ships would figure out the keep had not been destroyed and the Noxxons had survived.  He hoped they might be able to persuade the fleet not to attack again.  He was not sure how long the shields would last if the attack continued.

Under his hood, Braylon made his way through the edge of the city and down below to its underside.  He would use the service tunnels again like he had used them to find Lance.  These would allow him to continue his mission virtually unseen.  He walked in silence, contemplating the events that led up to the mutiny and his near exile.  He shook his head and brought himself back to the present. *This will require all my concentration.*

As he made his way to the aft edge of the city, he went over the plan in his head.  It was simple enough, but still risky.  Lance had written a program to backdoor the communications lockout.  It was on the tablet that he had tucked away in his hoodie.  His destination was the Hub, an electrical substation that connected the Haven to the ship's main power systems.  There was a direct tie-in to the ship-to-ship communications there.  There would also be security at his destination, and he was unarmed.

He had no intention of harming his men.  He still did not know who he could trust.  He feared that if anyone noticed his movements in an odd place, word would reach Titus, even in innocent conversation.  He needed to either find a way around the guards or subdue them quietly, without injury.  He had nothing but a basic tool set and an earpiece that allowed him to speak to Lance and Kevin.

Thankfully, there was a distinct absence of workers in the lower levels.  He suspected that with all the protests, the rest of the workers were taking a strike against their maintenance tasks.  The lack of workers made it easier to move stealthily, but should he run across anyone, he would stick out like a sore thumb.  He hoped that the lack of workers meant a lack of security as well.  The peacekeepers probably had other priorities.

He wound his way through the lower walkways. He was nearing his destination when he heard a voice ahead. He kept his eyes open and crept along the path, hoping to see the voice's source before it saw him. When he came around a bend in the path, he saw a grey-uniformed guard speaking on the radio. The guard had his back to Braylon as he spoke angrily into his radio. There was an open panel on the wall next to another pathway. *I will only get one shot at this.*

Braylon stepped lightly, carefully approaching the distracted guard. He held his breath for fear of breathing too loudly. His heart raced in anticipation. He was just a step away from the guard. He carefully reached forward, fingers wrapping around the grip of the guard's Assent sidearm. He yanked it from its holster quickly and fired it into the guard's back before he could even react.

The guard slumped forward, crashing into the ground loudly. Braylon winced a little as he watched the stunned man fall flat on his face. He searched the guard for any useful tools. He was contemplating stealing the radio when something smacked him hard in the back.

Braylon tumbled forward next to the unconscious guard. He rolled over to see another security guard holding a large wrench. His back ached from the pain already. She closed in on him, cocking the wrench for another swing when she froze.

"Commander Braylon?!"

His hood had fallen.

"What? What are you do—"

Braylon fired the stunner pistol at the guard. She collapsed on the ground as well. He was unsure if he appreciated her not using her stunner or not. It would have taken him two hours to regain consciousness if she had, but it would not have been painful. He slowly stood up, trying to massage his back. His shoulder was throbbing. He needed to finish his mission so he could get proper medical attention.

Braylon moved the unconscious guards to a storage locker down the side passage and hid them from sight. He whispered an apology to the sleeping peacekeepers. He kept the stunner and took the radio so he could monitor the security communications, hoping to avoid other security personnel.

He continued moving toward the Hub; it was not far now. It was too vital a system not to maintain peacekeeper supervision, so having the Assent stunner comforted him. The Hub allowed the city to plug into the ship's communications, while being the only maintenance hardline access point on the ship.  To get to any other lines would require cutting through bulkheads.

Lance had reassured him that the communications system was still intact, just was simply turned off.  If he were right, this would all be over soon. With direct access, Lance would be able to turn it back on long enough to send a message without General Titus noticing.

Lance had pre-programmed the tablet device to do the job. Braylon had prerecorded a message that would be uploaded instantly and transmitted to the fleet. The program would turn the system on, upload the message, and shut it back down in a split second.  No one would notice anything.

He made his way to the substation.  There were no more surprises as he wound his way through the service level.  Once Braylon reached the Hub, he found only two guards watching the entrance.  They were relaxing back and joking around with each other.

He was disappointed in their lack of discipline. *What if someone were to attack this place?  Someone with ill intentions.*  Especially with everyone on strike or protesting up in the center of the city.  It was not a stretch that some disgruntled civilian would commit an act of domestic terrorism.  It was easy enough for him to make it there, he could only imagine what would happen if someone had ill will.  He would have to hold remedial training and briefings on discipline.  Once this was all over, of course.

However, he had to admit, they did make it far easier for him to accomplish his mission.  He rounded the last corner and saw a distinct lack of cover for the last thirty meters to the entrance of the substation. He could not afford to get into a firefight, but their carefree posture would allow him to get close.  Braylon would have to be careful not to alert the guards they were in any danger.  He walked slowly and calmly, like he belonged there.

The guards did not even notice him until he was halfway to them. They looked up as he approached but did not bother to stand until he was within ten meters.  He moved slowly, his stunner concealed.  As he drew close, he looked them in the eyes and smiled with a wave, attempting to be as open and nonthreatening as possible.  They did not put their guard up.

The peacekeeper on the left questioned him, "What business do you have here?  All the workers are on strike."

"Unfortunately, there is some emergency work to be done.  No strike can prevent me from completing it."

He quickly drew the Assent stunner from within his clothing.  Two short blasts knocked them both out. He needed to hurry now. He was unsure if there were more guards inside or if this was everyone. For this to work, he needed to ensure no one was alerted. Titus could not find out what he was doing. Without bothering to move the unconscious guards, he rushed through the doors into the substation.

He charged in, ready to return fire, but no opposition came. He walked through the substation, weapon ready, and made it all the way to the maintenance area without further incident. That was where he could plug in.

A guard exited the bathroom next to him as he walked.

"What the—"

Braylon stunned him without hesitation as he continued to eye his surroundings. Hopefully, that was the last of them. His blood was pumping, ready for anything else. He felt bad for attacking his men. They had not even had a fighting chance. Their lack of discipline was disappointing. Remedial training was definitely on the docket after this. He was surprised there were not more guards than the three but assumed they had been pulled from duty to help with the protests.

Through the earpiece, Lance directed him to the location where the tablet could be plugged in. He walked to the far end of the room and inserted it where told and turned it on. The tablet ran its program automatically and sent the message without incident. A green light flashed on the tablet a moment later. Lance confirmed the mission was complete.

"That was far easier than I expected it to be. Maybe luck is still on our side."

Braylon packed up the tablet and made his way out of the substation. He found it odd that his mission was completed so easily. *Maybe Titus didn't think I had the strength to succeed.* He had one more mission to accomplish before he returned to his family.

Brandon could hear shouting coming from behind him, up on the ramparts. The Noxxons must be marching on Entfall again. He needed to be quick so he could return to the battle, not that he had contributed much so far. He rushed across the courtyard behind Jaina and ran into the ship. It did not take them long to reach the communications terminal. Brandon saw they were already being hailed. Jaina answered it on speaker.

"*Inquisitor.* This is the *Plaintiff.* The fleet in orbit has received follow on orders from Commander Braylon. We are to stand down and provide any assistance you require from above. Major Nazario is in full command of all operations on the planet. We apologize for the strike and hope you managed to evacuate and remain safe."

This was good news. The best they had received in ages it felt like. He did not understand the change in heart from the Commander but was thankful it had happened. That had been a long sprint for nothing. They still had other pressing matters. Now, he needed to get back to the ramparts now.

The defenders would need all the assistance they could get. Knowing they were safe from the ships in orbit would help them succeed in the defense. It would be hard to survive both the Noxxons and the orbital strikes.

Jaina looked at him. "I'm going to check on Jerykka. She should know that it's over."

Jaina left without another word. He grabbed the last two Peacemaker energy rifles and nearly all the fresh batteries from the equipment locker on his way out. He raced back up the ramparts to rejoin the others. He handed one rifle off to Rentari and took the other for himself.

"We c-... can help slow down the Noxxon charge."

The Noxxons were formed up, staying behind the Staff Bearers. Their siege equipment had been left unharmed by the shield. It would only be minutes before the Noxxons were at the walls again. The Staff Bearers stepped forward, leading the march on Entfall this time. They were no longer going to sit back. They were still out of range of the Undaari arrows for the moment, but not the rifles.

Monkley suggested, "Maybe if we focus on the Staff Bearers, we can take one down, or at least limit their ability to maintain their shield."

Brandon nodded his understanding. He was not a fan of the fight but was willing to do whatever it took. *I discovered elves; I'm not going to let them be exterminated.* Brandon saw Intayr's eyes light up when he handed the Undaari a fresh battery. Monkley was smiling as he gave Rentari a quick lesson on the operation of the energy rifle. *Why does he seem to be having the time of his life?*

Energy rifles fired directly at the center Staff Bearer, one after the other, in rapid succession. The Staff Bearer reacted impossibly fast, raising his offhand to create a magical shield to protect himself. The rifle blasts were unable to penetrate its defenses. It continued to step forward at the head of the horde, a smile creeping across its face.

"We need to keep at it. That monster will tire eventually. Nothing has endless power," Monkley said optimistically.

They intensified their onslaught, firing faster. Brandon's finger grew fatigued to the point of nearly cramping. The Staff Bearer came within arrow range. Undaari archers released volleys of arrows at the monstrosity in conjunction with the white energy blasts. The Staff Bearer slowed its pace. *It's weakening.*

The Noxxon horde began charging forward with fervor. They had drawn even with the Staff Bearers at the edge of the bridge. The central Staff Bearer stumbled back a bit under their fire and lost concentration. Its focus on the shield above began to falter. The shield expansion began to fail. The other two Staff Bearers compensated as well as they could. These two each had five spikes in their backs.

The Noxxons charged hard, opening themselves up to arrow attacks, distracting from the Staff Bearer as they closed in on the keep. The expansion began to shrink down as the Noxxons moved forward. The two five-spike Staff Bearers continued to hold the shield, preventing it from collapsing too quickly and killing their warriors.

There were still over three thousand Noxxon soldiers attacking. More than half the original army; it was still a powerful invasion force. Now the Noxxons had their leaders and new siege equipment joining the fight. They still had two siege towers, an odd-looking battering ram, and another unusual piece that Brandon could not identify. They had brought it under the shield and were now rushing it forward before the shield collapsed entirely on them.

The Undaari forces had been whittled down. There were only about three hundred Undaari left. Cover became scarce as the catapults resumed their attacks while they rolled onto the bridge behind the towers. The Undaari archers shifted their attack to the Noxxons as they charged. The Noxxons raised their shields again to protect against the arrows.

Intayr was first to note the trouble they were in. "I'm not sure how long we'll be able to keep them out of the fortress. I've never seen equipment like that. Maybe we should try to destroy that instead."

"Finish off that Staff Bearer first. If we can collapse their shield, we might be able to take down a bunch of Noxxons with it."

The Staff Bearer struggled to shield itself any longer as they continued their attack. The rifles began to break through and strike the being. One blast struck its shoulder, breaking its armor off. Another blast struck its leg, causing it to stumble. The next blast struck it in the chest. It screamed in anger, trying to bring its shield back up.  Another blast found its mark.  It crumbled under the onslaught.

As the center Staff Bearer collapsed, the other Staff Bearers released their hold on the shield.  Their expansion collapsed, but the entire Noxxon army had made it inside Entfall's shield.  The remaining two Staff Bearers marched forward, callously leaving the third on the ground.  They brought up the rear of their force, raising shields with their hands to avoid the same fate as their third.

The Noxxon forces reached the rampart walls and moved their siege equipment into place.  The two remaining siege towers were stationed at the wall, allowing the Noxxons to climb their stairs and storm the rampart in waves.  There was little left to slow the Noxxons from overwhelming the rampart walls now.  The Undaari defenders bunched up around the Noxxon towers.  The battering ram was approaching the gate.

The Staff Bearers marched ever forward, slamming their staffs to the ground, firing crimson spheres at the Undaari on the ramparts.  Their magic fire blasted through the tops of the rampart, ripping Undaari defenders apart.  Brandon's stomach knotted up.  Entfall's walls could stand against the catapults, but not the corruption of the Staff Bearers.

Brandon found it difficult to keep fighting.  He saw Monkley firing his rifle into the Noxxon horde.  Intayr and Rentari had moved to assist with the defense against the towers.  Brandon covered his ears and sat down. *This is too much.  I need to get out of here.*  He began rocking on the ground.

Monkley reached a hand down to him.  "You got this.  The Undaari are depending on you.  And I need your help.  We have to take down those towers."

Brandon slowly reached his hand up and took Monkley's.  "H-... How are we su-... supposed to d-... do that?"

Monkley smiled.  "Those towers are on wheels.  Take out the wheels, take out the tower.  We have advanced weaponry."

The shield above began to disintegrate.  Jerykka must have used the last of her strength.  Entfall's last major defense fell.  Some of the Undaari archers moved to the courtyard, no longer able to find cover, and began blindly firing outward over the wall.

Brandon stood next to Monkley and followed his lead.  Their rifles still had battery left.  They fired together at the same wheel.  It took several shots before the wheel cracked.  The tower began to lean.  Noxxons began to yell on the tower.  They kept firing.  The tower paused for a moment, then collapsed back into the Noxxon horde, crushing several warriors.

The merlon next to them blew apart as the Staff Bearers targeted them. The two humans hid low below the parapets. Projectiles fell around them. They could hardly move any more. On hands and knees, they crawled along the battlements, escaping the focus of the Noxxons. Further down the ramparts, they poked their heads out.

The battering ram had reached the gate as the first tower fell. It was built like a trebuchet, using massive counterbalances to fling the ram into its target. They parked it at the door and cocked it, ready to slam into the gate. Their unidentified piece of equipment was staged on the bridge. The battering ram released its payload, smashing into the gates. Brandon barely noticed any movement of the massive doors. It would take a lot more to break through.

Monkley's face fell as he watched. Things were growing desperate. The Noxxons were still coming over the wall. Their equipment was beginning to do its work. The Staff Bearers continued to attack the walls of Entfall, slowly breaking down its defenses. The Undaari were beyond exhaustion as they died one by one, struggling to fight back. Brandon heard each scream.

Jaina made her way into the main hall. Her eyes locked on Jerykka. She was sitting on the throne as it glowed blue with the Alackai's power. Jaina could see her eyes still closed in concentration. She assumed Jerykka was meditating with the Alackai as Kiva had through the Entai.

Jaina hurried through the hall toward her. One of the burgundy caped guards moved to impede her progress.

"I *must* speak to Master Jerykka. It's an emergency."

The Undaari man looked at her, then back at Jerykka, and finally back at her. His jaw was clenched as he debated what to do. After a few more moments, he stepped aside, allowing her to pass.

Jaina approached the Warden slowly. She noticed signs of just how strained Jerykka was. Sweat was flowing freely down her face. Her eyebrows were furrowed in concentration. Her body was beginning to shake as her breathing grew haggard. *Will she even be able to hear me right now?*

"Jerykka?" she asked, softly.

Jerykka did not stir. Jaina got even closer, eyeing Jerykka. She was concerned what might happen if Jerykka was disturbed. Her breathing got worse as her body trembled more violently. Her skin was turning pale and drawn. She looked like death. *If she keeps powering the shield for no reason, it might kill her.*

Jaina closed the last few steps toward the shaking Warden. Jerykka was drenched in sweat on the throne. The glow was starting to fade around her. Jaina's own heartbeat began to quicken as she monitored her. She reached out her hand and touched Jerykka on the shoulder.

"Master Jerykka, please. The humans are no longer attacking. You don't need to keep the shield up."

Jerykka's eyes snapped open so fast that Jaina stepped back, startled.

"Jaina?"

The Warden's eyes closed again as she collapsed off the throne. She fell to a heap on the ground, wrapped in her burgundy cape.

"HELP!"

Braylon ducked back into the service tunnels. Eyes scanned for signs of peacekeeper activity as he walked, despite a successful mission. Uncertainty filled him. What if Titus had been right and he just ruined their only chance at making a home? The fear of failure quickened his heart far more than the anticipation of action had. All he wanted was to do the right thing.

He came around a corner and crashed right into something. Stumbling back, he realized it was a someone. An elderly man who was accompanied by a second, younger man.

"Commander?" the younger man asked.

"Uhh..."

"You're the Commander? I'm so sorry for knocking you around like that!" the older of the two said.

How had the elderly man been so solid? He looked far too frail to have nearly tackled him. Beyond that, he didn't recognize the man. He knew nearly every face on board his ship. Braylon's hand slipped to the sidearm. He could not afford to be reported. He eyed the men, judging their reactions.

"What are you doing down here?" he asked the pair.

"My son was just showing me around. I haven't seen such a marvel in my time. I hope to make myself useful."

"Everyone on this mission is useful, so I do not understand,"

Braylon said through squinted eyes.

"Excuse me, I must apologize.  I haven't had the opportunity to introduce myself.  I am Mr. Harmund, of the *Beagle*.  You rescued me after… after the world ended."

*I remember now.*  Nazario had brought them back.  Braylon had been meaning to meet their newest crew.

"It was really nothing.  I'm sorry, I really must be going," Braylon said.

"Now wait just a minute.  Let me buy you a drink at least.  I owe you something for reuniting me with my son here."

"I apologize, but I have urgent matters that require my attention.  I must go.  Things are far worse on this ship than they seem.  I only ask for your discretion.  Perhaps another time we can have that drink."

"Don't be too quick to force things, Commander," Harmund cautioned.  "I've seen a lot of failure from people rushing in."

"Trust me, this is not one of those times."

"Then I'll leave you with this: a gentle nudge can accomplish far more than a violent shove."

*Odd words for a time like this.*

# Chapter 28

## Heart

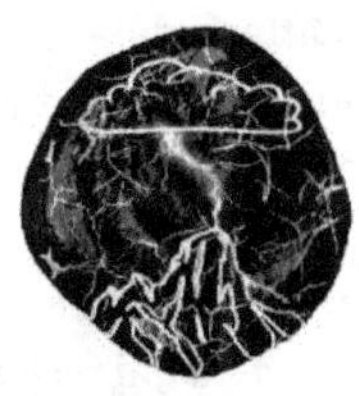 Jarreck led the squad through a hidden path along the Scarred Mountain. The sun was high in the air, beating down on the small fellowship. They had seen the Noxxons approaching the mountain from a distance while still in the air. He hoped to sneak up the mountain and lay a trap for them before they reached the mountain's heart. This time, he would not be caught off guard. The Noxxons had already played their hand.

And they had moved far slower than they should have. They already thought they had won, so were in no hurry to complete their mission. Their misguided arrogance would give Jarreck a second chance. If they could take out the Noxxons and secure the artifact, they could end this war before it burned down the entire countryside. He looked up the mountain at its heart.

It had been forbidden for anyone to go up the mountain for millennia, but exceptions were sometimes made in secret. It was where he had met Councilor Gierdahl to complete his training as a Shade. Gierdahl had not yet been made a Councilor, but he was being groomed for the next opening. His body had been nearing its limit with the Alackai. Councilors had special privileges and Gierdahl had already been granted many of them. Jarreck knew that the Councilor had expected much of him.

The Scarred Mountain was aptly named as it was made from the same scarred black stone as the walls of Entfall. It had been the source of most of the fractured black stone in Undaalan. Most of it had been mined out to build Entfall except for the highest reaches. They had not wanted to disturb the mountain's connection with the Alackai.

While Jarreck was curious how to open the artifact, he did not want to find out from the Noxxons.  He needed to ensure that it was never opened, even by himself.  He had a plan in place to try to stop the Noxxons.  There were only about ten Noxxons left in the group from what they could see from overhead. *This was their chance to end this war. There only real chance.*

The five of them with the two zakeri could easily take them, as long as they took down that Staff Bearer quickly.  Jarreck stationed James up above on the rocky mountain with a Peacemaker energy rifle.  Nazario had insisted they keep James as overwatch, away from the fight.  Jarreck intended to have Kiva, Lingdon, Nazario, and himself attack together with everything they had.  They would focus all their might directly at the Staff Bearer.

Then they would have the zakeri swoop in and attack the other Noxxons to cover their backs.  The zakeri could kill them all before the Noxxons were able to counterattack. Jarreck felt like it was a solid plan.  No one else had other suggestions.

They were staged and ready.  It took another couple hours before they heard the Noxxons approaching their hideout on the ascent. Jarreck's body tensed.  He saw the others shift, ready to spring into action.  Jarreck and Kiva vanished in front of the others, ready to strike the Staff Bearer from stealth.  The first of the Noxxons came around the bend.

There were four Noxxons in the lead, followed by the Staff Bearer. Four more Noxxons followed carrying the Black Tablet while one more Noxxon brought up the rear.  This last Noxxon was much smaller than the rest and cloaked, but this had barely registered in Jarreck's mind when the trap was sprung.

A white blast from James' rifle struck the Staff Bearer squarely in its head between the overgrown horns.  It stumbled back but did not fall. Before the Staff Bearer could bring up its defenses, Jarreck and Kiva appeared, spouting flames from their fingers and slicing at exposed body parts with sigridirs.  It screamed out as its eyes illuminated in bright scarlet hatred. Nazario charged in quickly to join the attack.  Lingdon, however, did not move or enter the fight, still hidden in the brush.

James continued to fire upon the Staff Bearer from his safe perch. The Staff Bearer somehow started to recover from the surprise attack. Jarreck's plan was not quick enough to kill it, though it was severely weakened. The zakeri slammed into the remaining Noxxons as a bright blur of feathers when they tried to counter, each shredding two Noxxons instantly with yellow claws. The Staff Bearer was reeling, struggling just to survive.

The small Noxxon at the rear slammed a staff of its own down upon the ground. The staff released an energy wave that knocked everyone, including the flailing Noxxons, backwards. Jarreck and Kiva bounced back up quickly and turned to face the new threat, cyan flames at the ready. Nazario recovered next. The small Noxxon removed its hood for all to see.

Except it was no Noxxon. Instead, the face they saw was Garren's. His face was not as it had been before though. It was pale and drawn, with glowing scarlet eyes. Jarreck noticed his cloak was clasped with the same symbol as the Staff Bearers' brands. When Garren spoke, he no longer sounded like himself. Instead, he spoke with a deeper, rough voice.

"Took you long enough. I've been expecting you, Jarreck."

Jarreck's stomach sank. It was a trap. Garren pointed his staff at one of the zakeri as it charged and fired vermilion lightning at it, striking it down. It exploded in a burst of turquoise feathers. The other zakeri quickly took flight and escaped, startled by the attack. It disappeared quickly, leaving them without a ride.

"I had been wondering when you would finally show yourself. I knew you were the only real threat to my plan. You take after your father," Garren spat at the ground with disgust. "Stupid naïve Skovi. The Society is fumbling around, too scared to act. They could not stop me."

Jarreck was in shock, his eyes narrowing as he spoke, "I don't understand. But I will *never* allow you to destroy the Undaari."

Nazario hesitantly asked, "Garren? How are you alive? Why are you doing this?"

Garren laughed. "This body no longer belongs to the one you call Garren. He was broken long before I came along. Long before I had him killed. I've fixed his body and claimed it for myself. This is the new body I'll use to conquer the Undaari and take my rightful place as ruler of Undaalan."

"Who *are* you?" Jarreck demanded.

"You *thought* I was killed. The *entire* Undaari people turned on me. For what? Trying to bring us forward and make us more powerful? This time, I will have a new weapon to ensure the defeat of the Society that turned on me." He gestured to the artifact lying on the ground.

The man paused to allow the pieces to connect in Jarreck's mind. When they did not, his smile faded to a frown. His eyes darted between his adversaries, as though he was waiting for one of them to speak.

"Well, *that* was very anticlimactic. I suppose that if you can't figure out who I am, I'll just tell you. It is I, Dralvic!" The man paused for effect, eyeing Jarreck. "The Second Society *betrayed* me. They did not understand the powers I possessed. I cannot be killed like some common Undaari. The Society almost allowed the Noxxons to destroy them. The Undaari are ignorant of both the strength of the Noxxons and the arcane arts. So now I'm back and will use these powers alongside the Noxxons to finish the Undaari."

"How is this *possible*?" Jarreck questioned.

He recognized the name in a rush of clarity. It all clicked together. The mystery symbol, the Noxxon's newfound knowledge, Vreeham's betrayal. It was all Dralvic, somehow back from the dead. Something that should have been impossible.

"You don't know me, Jarreck, but I know the Society. And I know your Councilors. I've heard of you and your honor. I had thought to take your body for my conquest, but this one will stand out more. Let the Undaari feel betrayed by their new 'friends.'" He paused for a moment before adding, "I knew your father, too. You'll fail just as he did. Once you're out of my way, there will be *no one* to stand against me."

Jarreck tried to strike Dralvic with blue flames. Dralvic was faster; he slapped away the attack with his staff. Dralvic laughed at Jarreck's attempt.

"You can't hope to defeat me."

"How can you use the Alackai with a human body?"

"The Alackai is one with my *soul*. It protected me when my body died. I've been able to move body to body, outliving each new host and growing stronger. The Alackai isn't in this body; it's in my *very essence*. And this time, I'll have a new weapon to aid in my quest."

Jarreck screamed out, vainly attempting to strike Dralvic. Dralvic was fast and stepped aside. He swung his staff into Jarreck's chest, slamming him down on his back.

"The Undaari did not want the power I tried to give them. But the Noxxons appreciate me. Do you enjoy my new friends? I managed to bring my Saviors along with me, well, some of them. Your father saw to that. But the Noxxons have been very appreciative of the power I granted them using the remnants of my Saviors. With the help of my new Naaji and this weapon," Dralvic again gestured to the Black Tablet, "we will rise to rule all of Undaalan." Dralvic laughed maniacally.

"You can't! We'll stop you!" Jarreck yelled desperately, struggling to regain his feet.

A blast of light came hurtling through the air aimed for Dralvic's head. Dralvic was ready. He knocked the blast aside and pointed his staff back at James in his sniper perch. Dralvic fired a blast of his ruby lightning and blew a crater in the mountain where James was hidden. There had been no time for James to run as his perch exploded in an avalanche of rubble.

Jarreck and Kiva tried to strike again in unison, yelling an anger. Nazario screamed as he charged in, Valor arm cannon blasting. These attacks too were struck aside. Dralvic fired his lightning directly at Kiva. Everything was happening quickly around Jarreck, but it felt like time was inching by.

He watched in horror as the lightning approached Kiva, without time to react. As she stood frozen, Nazario reacted, jumping in front of her and taking the brunt of the attack. They were both blown backwards, leaving Jarreck to fight Dralvic on his own.

Dralvic spun his staff around again and pointed it directly at Jarreck. He did not attack him though. Instead, he enveloped Jarreck in vermilion energy, trapping him, and lifting him into the air.

"You've started to learn how to actually use the Alackai, rather than follow the Society's restrictive teachings. I'm impressed. I would have thought that incompetent oaf Vreeham would surely have punished your boldness. Regardless, I have further need of your assistance before I allow you to die." He turned to the remaining Noxxons. "Get up, and grab the Black Tablet, we're moving on."

Lingdon stood frozen in the bushes long after the Noxxons had left. *Why was this time so much more difficult for me?* He was in shock. Something had felt wrong with the attack. A feeling in his gut had caused the hesitation. He had never used his power for attack, just to protect. *Now Jarreck is gone, too, just like my father.*

He had thought Jarreck was powerful and Dralvic made him look like a fool. When he finally had the courage to move again, he made his way to where Nazario and Kiva lay, still unconscious on the ground.

Nazario's body was badly burnt, still smoking, but he was breathing. Kiva had some burning on her extremities, but otherwise appeared unharmed. They both had been knocked out by the impact of the blast.

Lingdon tried to revive them, gently shaking the pair, but only Kiva stirred. She reacted quickly, seeing Nazario in that state of unconsciousness.

She did not bother to acknowledge Lingdon. She began calling upon the Alackai. Lingdon watched as she traced her hands along Nazario's chest, pouring the energy into his body.

As her hands moved, she saw the light in the center of his chest was flickering. Lingdon saw it as well. He watched as it faded out. Kiva screamed so loud that Lingdon had jumped back, covering his sharp ears. Tears were in her cyan eyes. He watched as her hands and eyes glowed, the cerulean glow flowing from her hands into Nazario's body.

"I can't save him, but I might be able to buy him some time. I must get him back to Entfall to the other humans. They may have something that can save him," she said before whistling loudly.

She continued, "What happened to Jarreck? Did you see anything?"

Lingdon avoided eye contact as he spoke, his arms wrapped around his own chest. "That Dralvic person took him. He said he needed Jarreck's help."

Kiva paused and looked up the mountain toward where Jarreck had been taken. Their zakeri landed, drawing Kiva's attention back. Without saying anything further to Lingdon, she flung Nazario over the zakeri's back and climbed aboard. Light had already faded to darkness, too much time had already passed since their injuries.

Lingdon watched as she took flight. He understood the importance of saving the human. It took him a moment to realize he was alone. He looked up at the mountain above him. He could see the blue fractures glowing faintly across its surface. Near the dark summit, he could see the pitch-black spot devoid of light where the entrance to the Heart was.

With no plan nor anyone to tell him what to do, he decided his best option was to follow after Jarreck and Dralvic. He hoped that he might get an opportunity to rescue him. *I've already failed him once; I can't do it again.* He had no idea how he would accomplish this. Dralvic was obviously far too powerful for him. But he had seen Dralvic take Jarreck hostage, not kill him, so he hoped Jarreck might still be alive. He would know what to do.

Lingdon worked his way up the path in the mountain, listening carefully. He did not want to let Dralvic know that he existed. If Jarreck was so easily defeated, he could never overpower Dralvic. He scanned the mountain ahead of him as he walked, following the narrow trail up toward the summit. He struggled to control his breathing. His heart pounded as he hiked his way up the Scarred Mountain. He had no other choice than to press forward.

Jarreck was still immobilized, floating along at Dralvic's will. He struggled against his bonds. Breathing was difficult against the orb of crimson energy, unable to even expand his chest. He did not understand this power. It was not something he had ever read about. That was evidence enough that this was truly Dralvic. Dralvic had known much of the arcane arts, and he was the last known user of them, even inventing new magic no one else had ever thought of.

Jarreck did not understand why Dralvic had not killed him. *What could Dralvic possibly need from me?* They completed their ascent up the Scarred Mountain. The Naaji was limping along, on its last leg. The remaining four Noxxons carried the artifact. Jarreck floated along next to Dralvic, still restrained by the red energy. Dralvic had not said a word as they walked.

When they entered the cave, Jarreck was surprised to find that it was not as dark as outside. The cavern was naturally lit by the same cyan fractures in its rock as the surface of the mountain had. The fractures glowed faintly, pulsating in the absence of sunlight. There were stalactites hanging over a small lake in the middle of the cavern, with a tiny rock island at its center. The cavern was unchanged from his previous trip decades before.

Around the cavern walls, were the statues of previous Society High Councilors carved into the stone. At the back of the cavern was an ancient altar. At its center sat a large orb, made from an unusual metallic stone, covered in purple fractures, and smoothed into a perfect sphere. It appeared that all the blue fractures originated from this orb. That was the true Heart of the Alackai.

"Bring the artifact to the altar," Dralvic said before looking at Jarreck. "Have you ever been here before?"

"Once. My master brought me here at the end of my training. It's forbidden to most."

Dralvic laughed sarcastically. "It's forbidden because the Society fears the power here. The Society has always feared the power of the Alackai. Ever since the First Society collapsed, they've placed strict rules that prevented it from coming to true power. That'll no longer be acceptable. The Alackai chose us, we should embrace it."

"You're nothing but a power-hungry monster. You've corrupted the Alackai and would doom our lands."

"My dear boy, I'm saving our lands.  There's *so* much you don't know or understand.  If I don't do this, then the Three Kingdoms will burn. The Noxxons would destroy it all, themselves included.  There will *always* be war between those that have and those that don't.  And now there's a new threat with these *humans*."  He said the last word with disgust.  "I'm bringing peace to Undaalan.  And *you're* going to help me."

Jarreck stewed in silent refusal.

"You're only still alive because you're *going* to help me."

Jarreck laughed sarcastically and shook his head.  "I'll *never* help you."

"Ah, not willingly for sure.  But I don't need your permission for your help.  And you will help me *twice* before you die.  I assure you."  Dralvic wore a large smile on Garren's face.

They had reached the altar at the rear of the cavern.  Dralvic directed the Noxxons to lay the artifact down at its base in front of the orb. He ordered the Noxxons and Naaji to step back from the altar and stand at the water's edge.  He turned to look at the artifact.  A triumphant smile covered his pale face.

"Do you know what's inside the Black Tablet?"

Jarreck shook his head.  He did not want to find out either.  Nor did he know how to stop Dralvic from opening it.  From what Jarreck could tell, they had already lost.  There was no one to stop Dralvic from taking over everything.  They had been betrayed but had not been given the chance to warn anyone about it.

"It's the key to my victory.  I'm sure the curiosity is eating at you by now.  You've been on our trail for quite some time.  Don't worry, you're about to find out.  But first, this is where I take your assistance.  Without you, I cannot open it."

"I told you; I will *never* help you.  I don't want to know what's inside of it.  I know that the artifact contains nothing but death and misery."

Dralvic laughed.  "You're a terrible liar.  But I am giving.  You will have your questions answered.  Rejoice knowing you're part of the greatest moment in history."

Dralvic continued to smile as Jarreck shook his head.

"I already told you.  I don't need your permission to take your assistance.  I simply need something that I believe you have on your person. You may not even realize what it is.  The High Councilor failed to retrieve it for me decades ago.  He suspects you've carried it close to your heart since."

Dralvic stepped closer to Jarreck and sniffed at his unmoving body.

"I can smell the stone on you."

He reached for Jarreck's neck and found a necklace hidden underneath his clothing. Dralvic pulled it out to reveal his father's old clasp. Dralvic smiled.

Jarreck was puzzled. *Why does he need my father's clasp?* He struggled against Dralvic's hold, trying not to lose the clasp. His curiosity did begin to pique as he struggled. This was his father's clasp. His father had always valued it. Jarreck had kept it as a memento to him and had never told anyone that he had it, not even Kiva.

"Do you know what this is? What this *really* is?"

"My father's clasp for his cape," Jarreck said, genuinely not knowing anything more than that.

"You truly are naïve, Skovi. Just like your father. He was the Society's Master of the Ancient Text. He held the key to recovering ancient and lost knowledge should the need ever arise. That was no metaphor.

"He wouldn't give the information to Vreeham when asked, so he lost his life protecting it. That was all for nothing. A true shame, too. Your father was smart and could've been a much more capable asset than Vreeham ever was. Vreeham can't do anything right. No matter. I was able to find the artifact without him. And now I have the key to open it."

Dralvic stepped away from Jarreck. He carried the clasp over to the obsidian artifact. The stone clasp fit snuggly into a small recess on the artifact. Dralvic traced a line along the center of its black stone. The fractures in the orb began to glow bright purple. The glow spread to the artifact through the ground, changing to blue; a line formed down its center.

Realization struck Jarreck harder than a boulder rolling down the mountain. This had been more than just a trap. Dralvic had intentionally been moving slowly, waiting for him to appear. If he had stayed in Entfall, Dralvic would not have been able to open the artifact. He would have needed to break down the black stone walls. Jarreck had cost the Undaari everything.

After a few more moments, the artifact burst open with a deafening boom, shaking the entire cavern. Stalactites fell into the lake sending ripples across its dark surface as Dralvic examined the contents of the Black Tablet. There were three objects inside: two ancient, thick tomes, and a scythe. Dralvic reached down and picked up the weapon.

"Do you recognize this? I would imagine you've at least heard rumor of its power."

"The Black Scythe. I suspected it was a possible relic inside the tablet. You can't use it. It was too powerful for even the first Society to use. It'll bring too much destruction to Undaalan. It's too dangerous."

Dralvic smiled. "It's too dangerous for anyone else. But then again, no one else could use it. There are certain magics required to unlock its power. Certain *arcane arts*. I discovered them long ago and have been preparing myself for this day for decades.

"They're what led me to discovering its secret. These tomes don't relate to the Scythe. They mixed the tomes around so as not to keep the keys to each weapon stored with them. The weapons they relate to are nothing compared to the Scythe, though maybe one day I'll gather them as well. I recovered the ones pertaining to this weapon eons ago. I'm the only person alive who could control this. And with it, the entire Society will fall."

"What arcane arts? That's *nothing* but a killing machine. There is nothing more to it."

"To everyone else, yes," Dralvic said knowingly. "But for me, it reaps the souls of its victims to feed me their life force. I grow stronger with every person I kill. I had to learn to do this on my own before I could use this weapon, otherwise it would reap my soul as well. That's how my essence has survived all these years. The Black Scythe would kill anyone else who tried to wield it."

The ground began to rumble, and the lake began to boil. There was a loud roar echoing around the cavern. Dralvic had a flash of fear in his eyes for a moment before he replaced it with another smile.

"And here comes the second way you'll help me."

"What do you mean? What is that?"

"Did you ever notice that your father's clasp had a symbol that was different than the one your Society currently bears? The clouds look different. That's because they're wings. The wings of the guardian who protects the Heart. Opening the artifact has awoken it from its slumber. It's coming, and you'll serve as a distraction while I leave with the Black Scythe."

Jarreck was unable to respond. A giant creature erupted from the center of the lake. The small island that had previously been there was the slumbering beast's back. Jarreck audibly gasped. The creature appeared to be made entirely of the cavern's black stone, though its fractures glowed purple like the Heart.

The creature leapt from the water and crashed into the Noxxons standing at the lake's edge. Jarreck struggled harder against his bonds, his heart pounding. The monster crushed the Noxxons like insects with its six enormous, clawed legs. The weight of its gigantic, rocky body shook the ground as it stomped around. It had to be the size of at least ten zakeri. Then the beast opened its massive jaw and bit down on the Naaji, ripping it cleanly in half.

Dralvic had already made his way around the lake and was nearing the cavern entrance. His hold on Jarreck weakened and finally released him. Jarreck quickly fled the creature while it was feasting on the Noxxons.

The guardian finished eating the Naaji and the crushed Noxxons then began to scan the cavern for its next prey. Jarreck figured that had probably been the first meal it had eaten in centuries, ever since it last awoke. Jarreck could barely catch his breath in the chaos.

The stone monster's purple eyes locked on Jarreck, and it charged at him. The creature leapt across the lake's shore, closing the gap in seconds. Jarreck desperately flung the Alackai's flame back at the monster. The creature slowed its attack, not visibly injured by the attack but taking its time to reassess its prey.

The monster moved forward more slowly, slithering it way across the rock floor and still reached Jarreck before he could escape. The creature's gaping mouth lunged toward Jarreck. They were near the mouth of the cavern when a dark shadow appeared in the entrance.

Purple flames slammed into the creature's face, causing it to miss its target and shriek. The creature cowered back for a second, before roaring loudly, opening its jaw and shooting purple lightning at the two Undaari in the cave's entrance. It missed its fast-moving targets, instead blowing a hole in the cavern, widening their escape.

Jarreck and Lingdon jumped out of the cavern and rolled down the side of the Scarred Mountain. Jarreck did not bother to slow his progress; they were trying to create as much distance between themselves and the creature as they could. Lingdon was keeping up with him, struggling to avoid crashing into any obstacles.

Jarreck caught a glimpse of the creature above. It was watching them from the mouth of the cave. It let out another roar then spread its massive stony wings, blocking the view of the mountain. It took flight in a huge rush of wind, flying straight down to the bottom of the mountain and waiting for its prey to come crashing down to it.

Jarreck and Lingdon rolled to a stop in front of the monster. It sniffed at them, daring them to attack it again. Neither of them did. Jarreck knew it would be a pointless effort. The creature coiled its long body back from them, ready to strike, its gaze focused on Lingdon alone. With a loud roar, its mouth encased Lingdon in a single bite. Without bothering with

Jarreck, the creature leapt into the air again, returning to its den.

Jarreck did not understand why the creature had let him live. Jarreck's body shook to his core. *I've failed Lingdon as well now.* The night was growing old. His surroundings were only illuminated by the two blue moons and starlight. Jarreck's mind raced as he failed to process the revelations from the cave. His mind felt numb under the weight of everything. Jarreck ran. He ran without thinking, unsure of his destination.

# Chapter 29

## Hope

General Titus ordered vigilant monitoring of all systems for outgoing signals. Should any signals be attempted, Captain Hunter, or whoever else was on comms at the time, was to ensure they were shut down immediately. As a result, Titus found himself extremely displeased when Captain Hunter entered his office.

"What do you *mean* a signal got out? How could you have allowed this to happen?" Titus demanded.

"I sincerely apologize, sir. There was nothing I could've done. All external communications were shut down. Somehow, they got turned on and shut back down in under a second. I didn't even have time to look at my screen before it was over."

"I don't understand. If communications only came on for a second, how did a signal go out?"

"It was a data burst, sir. I wasn't expecting that. You have to have a high level of technical expertise to even package one of those that efficiently. I didn't think there was anyone on board capable of that. I wasn't even sure that a signal had gone out. That's what took me so long to report. It happened nearly thirty minutes ago, but I had to run diagnostics on the system to even understand what had happened."

"Do you know who sent it and where the destination was?"

"Yes, sir. It took some digging, but I managed to get a copy of the signal. It came from the Hub and was sent to our ships at ZX-746. It was a cease fire order from Commander Braylon."

"Most unfortunate. Thank you for the information. Go back to your station. You no longer need to worry about monitoring comms."

"Yes, sir."

After the Captain departed, General Titus sat back in his chair. There was no pointing laying down punishment on Hunter at this point. The Commander had pulled off the impossible. Surprising for a gutless hack like him. *I shouldn't have underestimated him. Mutinies are much easier when the outgoing Commander is dead.*

Titus would have to wait and see if the fleet managed to complete his plan before they received the cease fire signal. It was a race against the clock now. They should still make it to the planet and commence their attack before the message reached them.

His rage boiled as he thought on Braylon's actions. He would never forgive the Commander if their people died in the emptiness of space. Their other scout ships had returned with no viable planets in range and no hope of providing an energy source to help the *Jericho* reach their safe haven.

He took comfort in the fact that he had made the correct decision. *I made the smart decision. I'm the one that gave the humans the best chance at survival.* Commander Braylon put too much faith in the team on the planet. In Nazario. He took too big a risk that they could save everyone by themselves.

The General stood from his seat at his desk and moved over to the shelving on the sidewall. He needed a glass of bourbon after that unfortunate event. Suddenly, Braylon burst through his office door, having not even been considerate enough to knock.

"Care for a drink?" Titus asked, unfazed by Braylon's sudden and discourteous arrival.

Without waiting for an answer, Titus poured a second glass for his uninvited guest. He turned around and set a glass down on the far side of his desk for Braylon then sat down in his own chair. He eyed Braylon as he stood in the doorway.

Commander Braylon did not move from the entrance. His squinted eyes were darting around the room as he entered warily. Titus watched as Braylon's eyes drifted from himself, to the glass of golden bourbon, to the UPC flag hanging behind the desk. There was not much else for the Commander to look at as he slowly made his way toward the desk. Titus waited patiently as the Commander took the seat opposite him.

The General spoke before Braylon was able to. "You know, I have to say, I respect your convictions. I didn't think highly of you when you were chosen to command this vessel. I felt that you were too weak, too emotional, too inexperienced for this responsibility.

"But the original mission was easy enough, so I bit my tongue at your appointment, suffering through your ineptitude despite my concerns. Hell, I even brought Nazario along, and the man withdrew his troops during a battle, nearly costing me a devastating loss.  But I understood his reasoning.  He had dedication and compassion for his troops.  You had none of that."

The General paused for a minute to monitor Braylon's reactions. Braylon did nothing but stare back at him, which only served to irritate him further, so Titus continued.

"However, your actions here have proven that you're stronger than I anticipated.  I wholeheartedly disagree with your choices here, but I've grown to respect you.  It would seem that we'll just have to wait and see whose plan wins out.  As long as our people are safe, then it doesn't matter to me who was right."

Finally, Titus got a response out of him.  "You cannot expect me to just sit back and wait.  Your actions were treasonous.  You should be arrested and locked away for the rest of your life.  You jeopardized the lives of *everyone* on that planet, as well as this ship.  You cannot possibly still feel as though your actions were right."

Titus responded angrily, raising his voice, "I believe that the safety of our people, and a home to continue on, is worth *any* price, to include the destruction of some primitive life, should it stand in our way!  Don't forget that *your* decisions put us in this predicament in the first place!  Do *not* question my motives.

"You only received command because you married the Sovereign's son.  That position should've gone to someone *far* more qualified.  Someone who could make the tough decisions that are necessary for our survival. Everything I have done was to save our people.  There is *nothing* left for us to discuss here."

"You are way too smug about genocide.  If the human race were not facing total extinction, we would be having a *completely* different conversation as to your fate.  Unfortunately for you, there *is* something to do here.  It takes priority over dealing with you."

Commander Braylon stood and moved to walk out of the room.

Before he was able to escape the uncomfortable conversation, General Titus said one last thing, "Try not to overwhelm everyone with *too* much information.  You saw how poorly they handled the prospect of only having two years to live.  Imagine how they'll react to the idea that we found intelligent life."

General Titus' blood boiled as Braylon ignored him and continued out the door.

The people were still filling the streets of the city in a never-ending sign of defiance. They had signs protesting the military control and despite martial law, they still had that right. They were entitled to peacefully protest and express their concerns.

Everyone in the Haven was still upset about limited supplies and the destruction of their solar system. Some were even spouting wild conspiracy theories that the government knew this was going to happen, and that was why the ships were built in the first place. Absurd, but not the craziest conspiracy theory to be passed around.

They left trash strewn everywhere and got into multiple brawls with one another, resulting in peacekeeper intervention. Most of the graffiti and looting had happened prior to martial law being implemented. Citizens were destroying their own city rather than working hard to help it survive. Tensions were at an all-time high.

As Commander Braylon watched his people on the cameras, he grew mortified. He did not want to admit it, but General Titus had a point with their reactions. Braylon felt that his faith in them would be justified. If he could give them hope, they would get back on the right track and set the ship right. These survivors were strong, and they would *never* give up as long as there was a glimmer of hope. He steadied himself in his office.

It was decorated with all the awards he had earned and pictures of his family. He realized how showy it must have been to the General. Another difference in their philosophies. He took another deep breath as he pushed his disappointment in the General from his mind.

His words today would either bring a new wave of cooperation to their passengers as he hoped, or they would bring chaos and new levels of rioting as the General feared. He pressed a button on his desk and the video system took control. It broadcast his face, with the UPC flag behind him, ship wide. Every projector above the city and every holovision inside it turned on to broadcast his message.

"Hope is the foundation of progress. Hope has led to every innovation, every advancement, and every idea that humankind has ever created. Hope for survival. Hope for change. Hope for a better future.

"If the last two months have taught us anything, it is how

important hope is for all of us. Your hope has been stripped from you. We have survived the worst events in human history. We are stranded in deep space with no prospects for the future. Your leadership has failed you."

He took a moment to let his words sink in.

He took a deep breath before continuing, "I speak to you today, to give you back the hope that was stolen from you. The hope that you all deserve to have. The end is not here. Not for us. Not humankind. We will survive. Not only survive but thrive on our new home of Undaaleria. That is the name of the planet we are destined for, formerly known as ZX-746.

"We sent a team ahead to scout it out. That team has made the most unbelievable discoveries in the history of the human race. They have found intelligent alien life. These people are not only clever and kind, but they have a powerful energy source. These people are known as the Undaari. They are living on our future home. It will be a paradise for us.

"The team is led by Major Nazario, one of our most decorated leaders and a veteran of the Colonial Rebellions. He has by his side, Ambassador Anderson's top assistant, Doctor Jaina Svensson. Together, they are working alongside the Undaari to establish diplomatic relations and trade. More details will become available as negotiations close.

"We should all be proud of ourselves for making it this far. We will not fade into the night. We will stand strong and unified. Humankind *will* survive. There is *hope* for the future."

He ended his broadcast and let out a deep sigh as he gathered his thoughts. *It's over now.* He hoped it had the desired effect. The people just need to stay strong and look forward a little longer. They will be saved. It was time for him to sit back and let others carry out their duties. There were still risks and uncertainties on the planet, but there was nothing he could do about it now. *Nazario must be successful.*

The General watched the broadcast in his office. It was a professional message, straight and to the point. No mention about the peacekeepers and their actions. No hint of the mutiny. No concern with the bloodthirsty aliens standing in their way. Only hope was portrayed to the people. There was nothing left for him to do. He stood from behind his desk and exited his office. He made his way down from the command tower to the city.

Like the Commander, he was considered important enough to be afforded the luxury of quarters in the city, rather than the barracks inside the control tower. He rarely used his quarters, as he deemed them too fancy, and usually slept in his office on a cot. He found it more satisfying to rough it and it reminded him of his younger days.

When he reached the Haven, he finally got to see the damage firsthand. The pictures had been bad, but this was far worse. His fears were affirmed. These people could not be trusted with their own care. They would have destroyed themselves if not for his actions. His disappointment in himself grew even more knowing Braylon had doomed them.

As he strode through the town, self-assured in his actions, he began to see a different picture. At the center of the city, he noticed that people were no longer protesting. He paused a moment as he looked closer and realized they were celebrating and embracing each other. *Maybe Braylon had been right.* He let out a brief smile as he walked through the crowds of singing people. Some of the citizens even tried to pull him into the celebrations, though he politely refused.

When he entered his apartment, he took his time to get undressed before moving to his bedroom. He laid down on his bed, alone. *Was I really wrong?* He could do nothing else so he might as well relax. He had not been truly alone with his thoughts since they had left Earth. He had needed to stay strong for the people. He could finally let himself process everything. He looked over at his bedside table and saw the only personal item he had brought with him.

It was a picture of his wife and children. He missed them now more than ever. They had been killed by the colonial rebels near the end of the war. The rebels had targeted a civilian city to send a message. His family had been living there, waiting for him to return from the war.

That event had changed him; it had cost the rebels the war. He had lost his reason to care about restraint. He had become ruthless, willing to sacrifice anything to achieve results. Titus could barely look at their faces in the photo. He was flooded with shame at what he had become since their deaths. His family would never have accepted his actions. He had dishonored their memory.

Commander Braylon had been right. Titus had lost himself years ago. Memories of the life he had enjoyed with his wife flashed across his mind. He could still see her smile as he played with his kids. He could still hear his kids' laughter. They were everything to him and he had disgraced them.

The Commander, this man who Titus thought was weak and a

waste of oxygen, had shown him true strength again.  All his brutality had been a result of the fear and pain of his past.  His heart felt as though a knife was cutting through it.  His muscles grew weak and convulsed.  He looked over at his personal side arm on his bedside table.  He could not handle what he had become.  He lost all control of his body as the dam broke and tears rushed down his cheeks.

# Chapter 30
## Shattered

$\mathcal{T}$he front gates were still holding.  For now.  The Undaari had been lucky to survive the night.  As the new day began, Intayr feared the Noxxon battering ram would begin making progress.  Over the ramparts, Intayr had seen the first dents in the metal appear.  Not only could he hear them, but he could feel the reverberations of the gate as the battering ram struck it over and over in a never-ending cacophony of banging.

He watched from the ramparts as the Noxxons' newest weapon was deployed.  The machine had two huge bows mounted on a rolling platform.  It had been loaded during the night, the ammunition arriving under darkness.

The contraption launched two massive, black stone arrows at the wall.  *Where did they get all that black stone?  There hasn't been a vein in centuries.*  The stone arrows struck the hinges of the gate and pierced the wall like it was nothing.

Intayr's breath got stuck in his throat.  The arrows had broken through the wall easier than the Staff Bearer's magic.  There were ropes connecting the arrows back to the platform.  A hundred Noxxons grabbed hold of the ropes and began to pull.

The final siege tower fell under the humans' attacks.  It came too late.  The Noxxons, with their siege equipment, were breaking down the wall.  It crumbled under their pressure.  There was nowhere left to seek cover.

The Undaari fled down into the outer courtyard as the ramparts were abandoned.  Intayr stood at the front of the Undaari warriors as they moved to defend the gates.  The gate would still serve as a choke point to slow the Noxxon advance.

After the outer wall, their next retreat would be into the inner wall. Their final line of defense would be inside the main hall itself. The Undaari had fought hard, but they would not survive without a miracle. Intayr had Rentari by his side. Monkley and Brandon were nearby. Monkley was a strong warrior and had proven that the humans would be strong allies in the future. *If there is a future.* Brandon had shown a willingness to do anything to build their friendship, but he was no warrior.

"Brandon! You have no place here. Get back to your ship and help out there."

Brandon looked at him from his position next to Monkley. Brandon looked at Monkley, silently pleading for advice. Monkley simply nodded at him, so Brandon did as Intayr had said. Intayr looked at Monkley, then was drawn back to the gates as another boom echoed from the battering ram on the other side. The noise drowned out the Noxxon drums for just a few seconds. The cracks in the wall were spreading like spider webs.

The Undaari were crowded behind the gates, taking a moment to catch their breath before the Noxxons broke through. It was clear that it would not take long for the Noxxons to overrun them in the outer courtyard. The inner wall would be easier to defend, but they could not just give up ground; there was not much remaining. Intayr could hear the Noxxons battering the gate again. It was deafening.

Intayr's blood was pumping fast. He was covered in sweat and blood from the long battle. He took a long, deep breath. The wall around the gate disintegrated as the Noxxons pulled the black stone arrows back toward them. The gate's upper hinges crumbled away as well. The gate began to lean and groan as the lower hinges struggled to hold it upright. The battering ram struck the gate and with a deafening clatter; it fell into the keep.

As the gate crashed in, the Undaari loosed their arrows. Monkley, Intayr, and Rentari all fired their Peacemakers. Though the Noxxons had taken extreme losses, they still outnumbered the remaining Undaari nearly ten to one.

The battle raged across the courtyard. Undaari archers moved back behind the inner wall and took up positions in the arrow slits. Their warriors on the front lines were far faster than the Noxxons, even after the long fight. Noxxons fell by the dozens, but nothing slowed their pace. The Staff Bearers were moving forward through their ranks, no longer bringing up the rear.

Once the Staff Bearers made it through the gate, all ranged fire was redirected at them.  The Staff Bearers shielded themselves and began blasting away at the Undaari warriors.  Crimson flames spread across the courtyard, eating away Undaari resistance.  Their screams gave life to the barbaric Noxxons who went into a frenzy and charged more intensely.

Intayr signaled the retreat, turning to cover his men with the aid of Monkley and Rentari.  The Undaari were falling quickly, their blood soaking the lawn and walls.  Intayr and his little team used the energy weapons to slow down the Staff Bearers.

Their focus was the Staff Bearer that had gotten injured under the shield.  It had somehow survived and was back in the fight, though clearly struggling to keep up with its brethren. Intayr figured if they could take this one down for good, it might give them a fighting chance against the remaining two.  The Staff Bearers had advanced near the front ranks of the Noxxon horde, within a stone's throw of Intayr.

As the Undaari retreated, their archers fired everything at the single Staff Bearer. It had already been struggling to maintain its shield.  The other two were taking more offensive stances.  They did not seem concerned with the life of the other Staff Bearer nor the Noxxons fighting for them; their crimson flames did not discriminate between Undaari or Noxxon.

Once Intayr, Rentari, and Monkley began focusing their fire on the same Staff Bearer, it stopped advancing.  It could not shield itself much longer.  The other two Staff Bearers continued advancing, allowing the cripple to take the brunt of the blasts, attacking the Undaari masses as they tried to flee to their next level of relative safety.  Crimson flames filled the courtyard in the ferocious and unforgiving attack, killing Undaari and Noxxon alike.

The third Staff Bearer fell back under the firepower.  It was blown away by the combined efforts of energy rifle and bow.  The crimson flames surrounding it had not hurt the Undaari efforts either.  Intayr cheered internally as their white energy blasts ripped chunks out of the weakened Staff Bearer's body.  It finally fell as it succumbed to its injuries, turning to ash.

The three remaining fighters had overstayed their welcome.  One of the Staff Bearers shifted its focus toward the trio and sent crimson flames at them.  Monkley and Intayr managed to dodge to the side; Rentari was too slow and was encapsulated by the flames, burning away with a shriek. Intayr and Monkley could do nothing to help him and retreated through the gates.

The heavy metal doors were barred from the inside. The Noxxon siege equipment was too large to bring through the remains of the first gate and these walls were even taller. The Undaari would be able to hold this wall much longer than they had the courtyard. Archers continued to pick away at the Noxxons who were bunching up. The outer courtyard was getting crowded as the last of the Noxxons piled in through the front gates and off the bridge.

Intayr ordered his soldiers to rotate out and take short rests. No warrior hesitated to follow the order. Intayr could see that everyone was exhausted, haunted eyes stared back at him from his fighters. He sent Monkley to check in on Brandon and Piers. Brandon had radioed Monkley with a plan to do something with the *Inquisitor.* Intayr did not understand their plan but knew it would help in the fight.

Intayr looked out over the inner courtyard behind him. He saw the *Inquisitor* lying in the center of the grass. The sun had risen high and was shining down on the ship. The gardens were untouched by the war. The shops around the exterior were still pristine. His eyes continued to wander for a second. The living quarters next to the fortress appeared peaceful, calling his name. He was beyond exhausted.

Intayr looked back out of his arrow slit and saw the carnage, as though it was an entirely different world than the inner courtyard. There were hundreds of bodies strewn across the outer courtyard. Everything was covered in blood. There were scorch marks all over from the blasters and Staff Bearers. The front gates lay on the ground, damaged beyond repair. The ramparts had crumbled and left rocky debris everywhere. A tear came to Intayr's eye as he surveyed the destruction and chaos created by the Noxxons.

He hated the Noxxons with a passion. They never brought anything but death to the Undaari. As he watched them fill in the remainder of the courtyard under archer fire, he realized they were preparing for something. They had gathered shields and held them above their heads to protect themselves from the arrows. The Noxxons were staged at the gate as though they thought they would be entering immediately. They were not even bothering to scale the walls. He did not understand how they thought they could already penetrate this line of defense.

As he watched, he saw the two remaining Staff Bearers point their staffs at the gates and create a focused stream of crimson fire. Intayr watched in horror as heat began to rise and wash over the inner walls.

There was nothing special about these gates that might allow them to withstand intense heat for long. Their long-awaited reprieve would not come. Again. They had to quickly form up and prepare for the next wave of Noxxons.

Kiva raced back to Entfall on the zakeri. She was not sure if it would still be standing but knew the other humans would be there if it were. She felt sorry for the zakeri. It was not meant to be pushed this hard. Kiva was scared for Nazario's life though. She had him across her lap so she could monitor him as they flew.

She was scared to lose him after everything they had been through. After he had saved her again. His breathing had become slow and shallow. She kept a hand on his chest, internally pleading for each breath to come. She felt something for the man, despite the freshness of their time together.

As she raced along, she was able to make out Entfall in the distance. It was still dark as she approached, though the horizon to her right was starting to light up. She was thankful that the humans in space had not managed to destroy it. Jerykka had been right.

She grew worried as she got closer. She could see fires spread all over Entfall's bridge and the surrounding shore. She could smell smoke from the destruction the Noxxons had brought. She could hear the echoes of battle from the air. Yet she could not help them as Nazario's life depended on her quick action.

She closed in on Entfall and quickly landed inside the inner courtyard, near the *Inquisitor*. There were medics nearby assisting with the wounded. She quickly pulled them aside to attend to Nazario, then went to the *Inquisitor* searching for the other humans. She found Brandon and Piers on board and informed them of the situation. Brandon quickly grabbed some supplies and rushed to the aid of Nazario. Piers had to finish the work he was doing before the Noxxons broke through.

Kiva stepped back out into the courtyard and could smell the blood mixing with the smoke from the battle. She could hear metal clanging and warriors screaming. She knew how Entfall was designed; they could defend these walls for a while before the Noxxons would breach them. She walked over to the zakeri and scratched its chin.

"Thank you for staying strong for us. I'm sorry for pushing you so hard. I have one more favor to ask. I hope you can understand me. If he's alive, please find Jarreck.  The Undaari need him if we hope to survive."

The zakeri took flight, quickly disappearing over the ramparts. She watched as it faded away in the new light of the morning.  She smiled, thankful for the zakeri.  It had carried them throughout Undaalan, from mission to mission.  Without it, they never would have even had the chance to stop the Noxxons.  She turned and strode into the main fortress toward the medical wing to check in on Nazario.

As she passed through, Kiva noticed the main hall and war table were next to empty.  There was no planning left to do.  Everyone was fighting for their lives.  The Undaari were in survival mode, struggling to keep the Noxxons at bay, and without help, they would not survive.  She needed to check on Nazario before she could assist.  She would not be clear headed knowing he was on his death bed.

When she reached the medical bay, she was relieved to see Brandon already there administering some of the human healing compounds.  Nazario was still unconscious but breathing.  She realized that Jerykka was in the bed next to him, also unconscious.  She looked over to the medics.

"What happened to Master Jerykka?"

One of the medics took a moment to reply, "Her body was drained beyond its limit while using the Alackai to shield Entfall.  She pushed herself too hard trying to protect her people."

"Will she recover?  She's still needed here."

"We don't know," the medic replied before getting back to work on her other patients.

Kiva was not happy with the news.  Jerykka was needed here more than ever.  More than anyone else.  Kiva was at a loss.  She looked over to Brandon, hoping for good news.  Brandon locked eyes with her.  She was not hiding her emotions very well.

Brandon smiled and warmly offered, "I b-... believe you got him here in time.  He's badly injured, but his armor took the brunt of the blast. It's t-... trashed and needs to be removed.  Despite how advanced our medicine is, it'll still take time for his b-... body to recover.  Judging by how the battle is going, we might not have time for him to heal.  He should not be t-... transported again.  He might not survive it."

Kiva's eyes teared up.  A smile broke across her face.  She was happy to not be losing this man.  She had grown comfortable having his presence in her life as they battled the Noxxons.  She sat there with him silently for some time, watching the man breathe.  She lost track of time before she spoke again.

She looked Brandon in the eyes, her voice full of energy, "If he needs time, I'll give him time. I've wasted enough sitting idly by as it is. I will *not* lose him."

She marched out the medical bay to the front lines. She hoped Intayr was still leading the battle. She would track him down on the ramparts.

But when she reached the inner courtyard, she saw the gates barred. The Undaari had fallen back to the inner walls since she landed. They had not lasted as long as she had hoped. The sun was high in the sky. She had spent more time than she realized by Nazario's side.

She was moving up the stairs into the inner ramparts when she saw the Undaari fleeing toward her. She was confused. Where were they going? They should have been able to hold this defensive position much longer as well. They could not have been there very long.

Intayr met her, grabbed her by the arm, and told her to flee. She did as she was told. When she got back down into the inner courtyard, she noticed the gate was glowing red hot and beginning to melt. *How is that possible?*

She knew the answer to her own question. The corrupted Naajis had devastating power. They were what allowed the Noxxons to make a move on the Undaari like this. They never would have stood a chance otherwise. Intayr pulled her onto the *Inquisitor* as everyone else took up positions around the gate, leading her back to Piers.

"Is it ready?" Intayr questioned Piers.

"Almost, but I need a couple more minutes."

"You don't have it; they'll be here in seconds."

Kiva knew she could give them the time and charged out. She began calling up the Alackai, ready to begin fighting the Noxxons as soon as the gate fell. As painful as it could be, it was worth it if they could hold out longer.

She had just reached the gate when it finally melted off its hinges and fell forward. The Noxxons were already charging. She threw blue fire into the Noxxon horde squeezing through the gate. Only a few could fit at once. The gate served as an excellent fatal funnel as she filled it with flames, allowing the Undaari to defend it effectively.

Her cerulean fire tore into the brutish Noxxons. Kiva flinched as she made her attack, feeling the magic tear through her body. The Noxxons acted without regard for their own safety, running into the flames. They were getting eaten alive, but she could only maintain the flames for so long before they would break through.

Undaari archers behind her were assisting with the Noxxons trying to break her defenses. Though Kiva felt strong and was able to maintain the flames, there were just too many Noxxons advancing to stop them all. A couple Noxxons made it past her defenses, but they were quickly slain by the Undaari warrior at her side. Intayr appeared at her side as well.

"It's ready. We must move out of the way."

Intayr grabbed her by the arm and led her to safety. The *Inquisitor's* engines fired up behind them. The ship hovered above the ground, about ten meters in the air. It swung about so that the engines were facing the gate. Its turret swung around to face the gate as well. It fired rapidly into the Noxxons amassed at the gate. White flashes of light decimated the Noxxon forces trying to enter the courtyard. They could not break past it.

At this point, nearly a hundred Noxxons had died trying to penetrate the wall. Their numbers were falling as they attempted to breach the final Undaari defenses. Intayr signaled a retreat for all the melee warriors at the gate. This was their best chance to seek safety in the main body of the fortress. The archers stood tall at the entrance to the main hall, covering their retreat. Monkley, Intayr, and Kiva assisted the archers with their energy weapons and the Alackai.

Piers joined them as well, apologizing for taking so long to get the ship ready. He explained that he had to complete repairs then get it set for a remote pilot from his suit. The ship would depart if the Noxxons broke through. He could not risk the ship falling into the hands of the enemy or being destroyed.

Intayr looked over to Kiva. "With those Staff Bearers, we won't be able to hold much longer."

Kiva watched as crimson energy began to fill the gateway, his words already becoming reality. The Staff Bearers were coming. Kiva and Intayr looked at each other. She could see the exhaustion on his face. They were falling back to make their final stand in the main hall when an Undaari warrior approached Intayr.

"Aid has come! Five Skovi Shields have made it into Entfall to support us. Commander Khasan is leading the Undaari Army here. They've gathered at Eilenar!"

"Shields?" Kiva exclaimed, looking for confirmation.

"When will they be here? We need them now. We won't last much longer," Intayr questioned.

The messenger glanced at Kiva for a moment before looking back at Intayr and continuing, "Yes, sir. Eight thousand strong. They've sent scouts ahead to assess the situation. Once they see the damage, they'll march with haste."

Intayr's eyes grew wide. He began moving quicker, encouraging his warriors. Kiva's chest began to flutter. *All we need is time.* They were going to survive.

She turned and saw the Staff Bearers step through the gate, shielding their army against the *Inquisitor.* Her heart sank. The army would still be hours away at best. She fled with the other warriors into the main hall. They would make their final stand there.

The Staff Bearers blocked the blasts of the *Inquisitor* and the Noxxons began to pour into the courtyard around them. They were quickly devastating everything in the area as they charged their way at the Undaari. Piers sent a signal to the *Inquisitor,* and it shot high into the sky, engines blowing back the nearby Noxxons. One of the Staff Bearers attempted to attack it with crimson energy, but the *Inquisitor* got away safely.

The Noxxons turned their sights on the main fortress. The Undaari closed the massive metal doors as the Noxxons charged. The Staff Bearers were at the front of the Noxxon line. The doors began to rattle as the Noxxon army began its final assault.

Intayr ordered the Shields to use the Alackai to protect the door and buy them time. Kiva was not sure it would be enough. Even if the Undaari Army made it before the Noxxons crushed them, the Undaari would have a tough time clearing the keep. The Noxxons could use much of the remaining defenses around the fortress to slow the army.

The Undaari defenders would gain a short reprieve inside the main hall while the Shields protected the doors. As long as their luck with reprieves did not continue at least. The Noxxons would burn down everything in the courtyard. They wanted to destroy everything the Undaari built.

The Shields created a blue wall of energy against the doors of the main hall. Kiva watched as they concentrated on the Alackai. She could see the pain in their faces. Their efforts would fortify and protect the gates from the crimson flames of the Staff Bearers as long as they could fight through the pain. Intayr turned to Kiva and escorted her back to the medical bay. She had a moment to check on her friends.

Jerykka awoke with a start. She bolted upright in her hospital bed, weak blue flames encasing her fists. The room was quiet. A single person moved about. A medic. She was in the med bay. The flames on her fists died.

The medic rushed to attend her. She began a series of tests, some rather invasive. She squeezed every muscle, shoved a finger down her throat, pried her eyelids open, and even tickled her feet. It was insulting to be treated in such an undignified manner.

"Enough. What's happening in the battle outside?" Jerykka demanded.

"I'm not so sure you want to know, Master Jerykka."

"I have to know."

"From what I've heard, the outer wall has been breached. But your warriors are still fighting. We haven't lost."

"They've breached?" she exclaimed as she moved to stand.

Her legs were not moving as fast as she needed. She swung them over the edge of the bed. She tried to use her arms to scoot herself off the bed, but they failed. There was no strength left in her muscles.

"You're not strong enough yet, Warden. You must rest."

"How can I rest when my people are dying out there?"

"You won't do them any good by getting yourself killed trying to reach the battle," the medic chided.

Reluctantly, Jerykka allowed the medic to push her back into bed with protest, "You don't understand. My troops need to see me if they're going to win."

"You have plenty of people under your command who are capable of inspiration. You don't have to control every aspect of battle for your troops to be at their best. You can trust them."

"I trust them more than anything, but they depend on me."

"It's time that they depend on themselves and show you exactly what they're made of. They're still fighting for you. They know what you sacrificed to give them a chance."

"How do I help them from here?" she begged, tears welling up in her eyes.

"You show them your faith in them."

"But how?"

"When you see them next, and you will see them soon, you guide them.  Let them see your faith and they will rise up.  A gentle nudge can accomplish far more than a violent shove."

Oddly, it made sense to her.

# Chapter 31
## Home

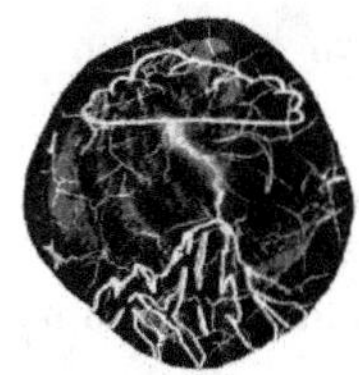

Jarreck had been running through the Lenakai Forest all night and well into the morning. He was still in shock from the events he had witnessed. He just wanted to forget everything and get lost in the woods where he would never have to deal with this turmoil anymore. They had lost.

He had been tricked and effortlessly defeated by Dralvic, and that was before he had even secured the Black Scythe. He knew of no possible way they could survive this. The Alackai had been corrupted by the arcane arts and nothing he knew of could save her.

As he ran, he began smelling the scent of smoke. He slowed his pace and examined his surroundings. He realized he had traveled a significant distance west along the base of the Black Peaks. The sun had risen high over the treetops. In the distance, he noticed that the forest had been trampled over.

He did not understand. As he moved closer to inspect, he saw the unmistakable tracks of Noxxons. They must have passed through this way, tearing a path through the trees. There had to have been hundreds of them. *How could they have come through here already? Had they defeated Entfall that quickly?*

He came to a stop to think. These tracks were at least two days old, probably more. This could not have been from the Noxxons attacking Entfall. There had to be another Noxxon force, and they were heading directly for Ambrecia. He ran toward the smell of the smoke. It did not take him long to come across the smoldering town of Entrea.

He fell to his knees in desperation. The entire town had been ravaged. Buildings were charred from fires. There had been hundreds of

Undaari living here. Their lifeless bodies were littered across the ground. The Noxxons had senselessly murdered everyone. He even saw a pregnant woman with her three young daughters who had all been shot in the back with arrows while fleeing.

Anger welled up within him. He screamed out in rage as tears fell from his eyes. He had never felt so defeated. Everything he loved and cherished was being destroyed. He did not understand how the Alackai could have allowed this to happen. He did not know what else he could do.

He sat there, on his knees, a broken man. As he contemplated his own failure, he heard flapping and looked up to see a turquoise zakeri landing next to him. It was the same zakeri that had brought them to the Scarred Mountain. He did not understand how it had found him, or what it wanted. He realized that Kiva and Nazario had been left behind on the mountain. He had forgotten all about them in his self-pity.

He stood up and wiped his tears. The zakeri approached him, cyan eyes peering deep into his soul. The feathery creature leaned down before him. Its behavior suggested it had been looking for him and wanted him to get on. Jarreck did as he was bid and mounted the zakeri. It quickly took flight. Jarreck expected to be carried back to the Scarred Mountain to retrieve Kiva and Nazario, but instead, the zakeri carried him south.

Jarreck's next thought was he was being carried back to Entfall. He knew how desperate things had been when he left. He was not even sure it would still be standing after the humans attacked. He hoped he had not seen Jerykka for the last time. Again, he was wrong about his destination. He was carried further west than Entfall.

He decided to stop worrying so much about his destination and began thinking about the events of the past several days. He could not believe that the Undaari were on the brink of destruction. What should have been the greatest event in Undaari history was overshadowed by the Noxxons. Meeting the humans who came from the stars should have been met with celebrations, not death. He did not understand why the Alackai had brought the humans there, if not to aid them in their fight against the Noxxons.

The zakeri began to descend and he was even more clueless as to their destination. He saw a clearing in front of them with an Entai overlooking the remnants of a cottage. He realized he had been brought back to where it had all started for him. *Why did the zakeri bring me here? How does it know of my connection to this place?*

Jarreck had many more unanswered questions. When they landed, he decided to take a closer look at everything that had been left behind. Flashes of his memories kept appearing before him as he walked. They were mixed with his vision from the Entai. He had been brought here for a reason. He knew the Alackai had a connection to all living creatures, even if they were not blessed with her powers. Perhaps she was trying to show him the way.

He slowly walked through the burnt remains of his family cabin. Everything looked as it did decades ago when the Noxxons murdered his family, except it was overgrown by vegetation. He meticulously searched through everything. He found the metal tin that his mother had baked his favorite fruit pie in the day she died. He found the remnants of his father's cerulean cape. He saw the bed that he slept in every night growing up.

Tears flowed freely down his cheek. It had been an emotional nine days for him. *Has it really only been nine days since I was here last, and Kiva had found me?* Their journey had taken them all over Undaalan working with many different people and learning of new races. Yet everything they had sacrificed had been in vain.

He searched through everything in the house. *There must be a reason I was brought here. I must have missed something.* When he reached the hidden compartment in his parents' room that had once hidden his father's clasp, he noticed something peculiar. The wood at the bottom was cracked and rotting. There was something shiny underneath it. *It's a hidden shelf, not the bottom. There's more underneath.*

He lifted the rotting wood to reveal a small metal box in the bottom. He carefully picked it up, inspecting it for any hidden details. He opened it, revealing a drawing of him and his parents from his childhood. Along with it was a short letter that his dad had written to him:

*My Dearest Son,*

    *You have always been the brightest light in my dark life. I have seen far too much chaos to believe that I will be around long enough to see you grown. I have left this letter in case I do not get to see the man you will become. I had always expected you to take my place within the Society after my passing. As you know, I was the Master of the Ancient Text.*

    *However, I have since distanced myself from the Council. I maintain the ancient knowledge but worry about the intent that the Council has moving forward. There has been trouble brewing within the Society and the Council has chosen to keep it quiet. I do not agree with their reasoning.*

*I will assume that if I am not around by time you mature that the Society will attempt to recruit you. I do not wish for you to join them. They are not necessary to be Graced by the Alackai. She does not value the Society like they would have us think. There are other paths to honor her Grace.*

*My only hope for you is that you grow to be strong and wise. To understand that there is more to the Alackai and her gifts than we could ever imagine. Always trust in her. She will never fail us, though she will test us beyond the limits we think we are capable of. She is never wrong.*

*Alackai's Grace guide you.*

*I love you more than you could ever know,*
*Your Father,*
*Jace*

Jarreck finished the letter. The events transpiring now were the ones his father had spoken of in the letter. If his father had felt that the Society was wrong, then it was. As Jarreck had started to suspect, the Society was not as pure or righteous as they preached. He had been questioning their position in the Alackai's eye. Kiva had been correct to doubt the Society. They did not understand the Alackai at all. Maybe he should have been learning from her.

He understood now, more than ever, why Jerykka had decided to end her training with the Society and go to Entfall. She was the smart one in the pair. He had always envied her freedom from the Society but could never abandon his oath to them. He still had a job to do.

He stepped outside the cabin, still unsure what his path would be. The sunlight was fading on him again. As he looked around, he noticed that his mother's garden had grown strong, even in the absence of care. He marveled at nature and how the Alackai encouraged it to grow. The Alackai did not need the Undaari, the Undaari needed the Alackai. The Alackai chose to bless the Undaari. It was up to Jarreck to return the favor.

He noticed the Entai standing at the edge of the clearing, like an ageless sentry. Another flash of memories took him. *How had my dad known I was there in the vision?* Jarreck walked over to the Entai out of curiosity.

He placed his palm on its white bark and leaned in, touching his forehead to the massive tree. He sat down under the tree and began to meditate.

He connected with the Entai immediately and was drawn deep into her Grace again. Once he was within the Alackai and the chaos around him had faded away, he opened his eyes. He saw that he was still by the Entai next to his childhood cabin. Only now, the cabin looked freshly built, still standing strong, untouched by fire. *Is this another vision of the past?*

He stood and looked around, cautiously taking in his surroundings. The sky had a familiar purple hue to it. He saw a man and woman standing at the entrance to the cabin. The man looked up at him and approached. Jarreck's confusion grew. *Why does everything have to be so mysterious?*

The man had a warm smile on his face as he greeted him. "Hello, my son."

Lingdon felt his body in disbelief when he realized he was still alive. He had thought the giant creature was going to eat him, but it never swallowed. Instead, it had carried him inside its massive jaw. Lingdon's heart was racing, but he could barely breathe in the cramped confines of the creature's mouth. He could tell that the great rocky beast had taken flight, but he was unsure as to their destination. He did not have to wait long for an answer.

The creature landed with a thud just minutes later. It crawled a short distance then opened its jaw, depositing Lingdon on the rocky ground. It was just as dark here as inside its mouth. He saw still water in front of him. He realized it was the lake inside the cave of the Heart. He did not understand why his life had been spared. The monster had attempted to kill or eat everything else. *Am I a snack that it's saving for later?*

He turned back to look at the stony creature and realized it was staring at him expectantly. It leaned forward and nudged Lingdon toward the water with its nose. Lingdon did not understand what the creature wanted, but he took a few steps toward the edge of the water. He looked back again. It was still looking at him intently. He decided it must want him to get in the water. He slowly stepped into the dark lake.

Lingdon feared the thing was trying to drown him but remembered it could kill him a hundred other ways without effort. His heart was still racing as he tried to discern his fate. This was not about him dying, or at least he hoped not. He continued walking out into the water until it was up to his waist. He turned to find the creature had curled around on itself, getting comfortable while watching its new pet.

That was what Lingdon felt like, a pet. More specifically a fish, as though he had just been brought home by his new owner. He was not sure what to do. His breathing slowed as he awaited his fate. As he stood there in the water, he realized it was not cold at all. He felt the moisture, but the temperature matched the cavern perfectly and was very comfortable. He did not know what else to do, so he sat down where he was, the water reaching up to his neck.

He wondered how he might escape this predicament. He wished Jarreck was here to help him. Jarreck would know what to do. But the rocky creature had stolen him away from Jarreck. *Jarreck probably thinks I'm dead.*

That was when the creature lazily reached a claw out to the lake and touched the water with its talon. The purple fractures along its rocky body began to glow for a second, then darkened. The light spread from its body into the lake, emanating along ripples from its claw across the entire surface. Lingdon now feared this was how the monster intended to kill him. He watched as the light grew and enveloped him. His heart rate increased again. *What's happening?*

As the light spread, Lingdon could feel a familiar warmth wash over him. He was not sure what was happening. He no longer had control over himself. His fear began to dissipate. His eyes rolled back in his head, and he lost consciousness.

When they reached the medical bay, Kiva was relieved to see Jerykka had regained consciousness. Nazario was still out in the next bed over. The medics were monitoring both, especially Jerykka, despite her protests. Kiva also noticed Jaina in the medical bay helping Brandon out. She realized that she had not seen Jaina earlier.

Kiva looked at Jaina puzzled. "Where have you been?"

Jaina looked up with her eyebrows furrowed. "What? Err... I had been trying to help out the Undaari elsewhere. I got caught up doing that and just made it here."

Before Kiva could question any further, Nazario bolted straight up yelling, "GARREN!"

Everyone in the medical bay jumped back, startled. Kiva rushed to Nazario who was breathing heavily.

She reached her hand out to his shoulder in comfort as she calmly asked, "Are you okay?"

His eyes rapidly shot around the room before settling on her.

"We have to save Garren. I have to go back for him."

"I'm sorry, but he's dead. We can't save him."

"No! He's alive. I saw him."

"Nazario... That wasn't him anymore."

"But it was his body. It's still his brain. He's just possessed. We can bring him back. I can rescue him. I know he's still in there."

Kiva was not sure she agreed but could not find a reason to argue. "That wouldn't be the craziest thing to have happened this week. I suppose we can always try."

His shoulders relaxed ever so slightly. "I shouldn't have survived. I have to take this as a sign I lived so I could save him."

Kiva smiled as she looked back at Nazario and placed her hand on his. He closed his hand around hers weakly, looking into her eyes. She hoped he was right.

Nazario told her, "Thank you. Without your quick actions, I would not have survived. I owe you my life."

Kiva smiled in return. "In truth, I already owed you mine many times over. You took that blast instead of me. It was the least I could do. But I wouldn't say no to spending more time with you after all this, though."

She was happy to have her friend back. She was not ready to lose him. Or anyone else. This war had already brought a terrible price. She hoped it did not continue any longer. She was prepared to do whatever it took to end it. She moved over to Jerykka after releasing Nazario's hand with a warm smile.

"Master Jerykka, are you all right?"

Jerykka nodded and weakly replied, "I will be. The medics said that I pushed myself too hard. I say that I wasn't able to push myself hard enough. I have failed those inside the keep. I'm too weak to even walk. I'm out of the fight. The first Warden to fail the Undaari."

"You haven't failed. And no other Warden has faced as terrible a threat as you have. You've *more* than proven that you're the strongest Warden that Entfall has ever known. You'll fully recuperate in no time!"

"It won't be soon enough, Kiva. My body is too weak. I can't possibly recover in time to help defend this place. I need you to take up the mantle and save us. We only need a little more time. The Undaari cannot fall."

Jerykka grabbed Kiva's arm with surprising strength. She looked Kiva in the eyes as her own eyes began to glow faintly. There was still strength in Jerykka, but it would take time to recover. The Alackai had drained her body. Kiva understood what Jerykka needed from her. She knew Jarreck would be disappointed if she did not help Jerykka. Then she remembered. *Jarreck's still missing.*

"Master Jerykka, I have bad news."

"What is it, Kiva?"

"Jarreck was taken. The person orchestrating everything was an old arcane arts user from the Second Society. His name is Dralvic and he's terrifyingly powerful. He said that the artifact contained a new weapon for him to use. He defeated us all without any effort. He created the Staff Bearers, the Naaji. He took Jarreck with him, and I haven't seen him since. I fear that Dralvic killed him."

It had not fully sunk in yet that her old master was likely dead. She did not know how to be strong without his guidance. She was lost. He had always been there to support her. Jerykka's grip on Kiva's arm tightened.

"He's still alive, Kiva. I know it. But you're stronger than you ever realized. Jarreck knew it, too. He knew you would be better than he ever could. He said you'd be the best of us all. He spoke about you constantly. Even if we've lost him, for now, we still have you, and that gives us a chance."

Kiva smiled through the tears and nodded her affirmation to Jerykka. Kiva began to pull away from Jerykka, but Jerykka tightened her grip.

"The Society has been holding you back, Kiva. Jarreck was beginning to suspect it as well. He told me as much. There's a reason you've always felt so defiant toward it. You must trust in the Alackai alone. She will guide you and empower you."

Kiva was not sure what the Warden meant but smiled her thanks. She turned and left the medical bay. Intayr had been watching them from a seat in the corner of the medical bay and jumped up as Kiva exited. He followed after her as she headed back to the main hall to assist with the final defense. She had already spent too much time away from the fight.

When they reached the main hall, Kiva saw that the defenses were still holding, but the Shields were already tiring. Their jaws were clenched and sweat dripped down their brows. They were struggling with the pain. She had not been gone that long.

Kiva could see Undaari warriors collapsed all over the hall, exhausted. They were trying to get some sleep and rest before the battle continued. *These defenders will not survive until the Undaari Army makes it.* There were only a little more than two hundred Undaari left and no more defenses once the doors were broken.

The Noxxon numbers had fallen too, but they still had nearly two thousand warriors and the two Naajis, last she saw. The Undaari would not be able to withstand those numbers. The Shields would be nearly useless in battle once the Noxxons penetrated the hall.

Intayr looked at Kiva, defeated. His eyes begged her for answers. Kiva was clueless though. She did not know how to save everyone; she just knew she needed to buy them time. Time enough for the Undaari Army to arrive and Jerykka's strength to be restored.

She surveyed the main hall again, looking for a clue. As she scanned the area, she noticed that the upper regions of the door had begun to turn red. The Staff Bearers were winning. She did not understand how they seemed to have such limitless power.

The Shields were unable to protect the entirety of the doors anymore. The doors were tall though, so they concentrated their energy on its lower regions. They could still keep the Noxxons from pouring through.

As she watched, the upper portions of the doors turned liquid, raining molten metal onto the floor. Noxxon arrows began to fill the opening. The Undaari shifted their positions to avoid the rain of death. Tables were flipped to provide cover. The Shields still managed to continue protecting the lower regions of the doors so the Noxxons could not march through. Undaari archers took up position and returned arrow volleys against the Noxxons.

Intayr gathered up his troops to defend the doors. The Undaari had to continue the fighting at the doors. They could limit the number of Noxxons entering the fight there. The Undaari man looked around at the others. Kiva could see the determination in their eyes. They were all ready to lay down their lives to protect Undaalan.

Kiva was looking around the hall when a thought flashed across her mind. She lifted her head up and examined the door. She knew what she had to do. What everyone had been preparing her for. It was her turn to put herself in harm's way for everyone who had saved her life.

It was time she repaid her debts to Nazario, Jerykka, Jarreck, and the hundreds of Undaari who had already sacrificed themselves for her. The Undaari Army could reach them at any time. She could ensure the defenders lasted long enough to be saved.

She began to call upon the Alackai, allowing her energy to course through her body.  She would no longer use the Society's methods.  She freed herself from the fear of loss knowing that her sacrifice would save hundreds.  She would heed Jerykka's advice.  And Jarreck's.

It was okay to die.  It was okay to not follow the Society's strict rules.  She released herself to the Alackai's will.  Her master had always said to not act without thinking, but she was thinking more clearly than ever.  *What good was having the Grace of the Alackai if I can't use it to save the people I care about?*

She thought of how Nazario had freely offered his life to save hers.  She remembered how Jarreck had risked his life to rescue Jerykka.  She knew how Jerykka had given of herself to save her defenders.

She would be just as strong as those she loved and respected.  She felt the Alackai's rush like never before.  It was as though its power had been held back by a spigot but could now flow freely.  There was no more pain.  She sprinted toward the door and leapt over the remains, sailing through the gaping hole at the top.

# Chapter 32
## Belief

 $\mathcal{C}$ommander Khasan, the Undaari military Commander, stood tall as he marched at the front of his troops. He wore the traditional armor of Undaari warriors, but his was dyed onyx to match his black cape. He led the entire Undaari Army on its offensive to rescue Entfall. His Commander's cape billowed in the wind as he awaited word from his scouts. They had not been gone long when they returned to report the Noxxons had broken through the walls and were overwhelming its defenders.

Khasan immediately redeployed the army from Eilenar, hoping they would not be too late. Eight thousand Undaari warriors would ensure the Noxxons would not escape Entfall, or harm anyone else again. He had five Skovi Shields at his side, marching with the army, to ensure they could handle any surprises that the Noxxons left.

The army cut through the forest with a practiced swiftness. He could smell the smoke before they reached the Noxxon warcamp. Once they broke past the forest edge, he saw the destruction the Noxxons had left behind. They had wreaked havoc on the surrounding forest, leaving a blackened scar before moving on to Entfall.

Khasan's heart sank as he surveyed the damage. The Undaari valued the life and sanctity of the forest, and the Noxxons had destroyed it just to insult them. He left half his army to remove the remains of the Noxxon horde and clean up the desecration. His army was too vast to function effectively in the confines of Entfall's walls anyway.

When they reached the bridge, he could see the smoldering remains of the siege equipment and the crumbling walls of Entfall. The Noxxons had brought death to Entfall, but Entfall had given death back tenfold.  The bridge was littered with hundreds of dead Noxxons.  Still, he saw no movement, no signs that the battle was still being fought.

Khasan needed answers.  Were any Undaari still alive?  Did they still fight inside the keep?  He marched down the bridge, eyes scanning everywhere, his troops on his heels.  They cleared the debris and bodies off the bridge as they closed in on the keep.

The hairs on the back of his neck stood up.  He slowed, expecting to be ambushed when they reached the gates.  *What is left of them.*  He surveyed the destruction up close.  He never imagined Entfall could be penetrated like this.  No one had ever been close.  It was supposed to be impossible.  Yet the front gate had been thoroughly demolished, ripped straight from the wall.  His entire army could not have done it.

As he cautiously moved forward, Khasan's senses pricked up.  He was watching for signs of an attack.  He passed through the gates, weapons raised, with his eyes darting across every inch of the ramparts and outer courtyard.  No attack came.  Khasan was surprised but pleased.  The Noxxons must not have claimed the keep.  *Entfall hasn't fallen yet.*

He looked at the Shields striding next to them.  They were using the Alackai to create blue energy walls in front of them to protect the Undaari. He could see their eyes narrowed in concentration. His ears caught the first sign of life.  Khasan could hear the faint sounds of battle in the distance.  There were screams and sounds of metal clanging.

"The battle must still be raging on.  There are no defenses in place here.  We must hurry," Khasan called to his troops.

They still had to march across the courtyard to the inner wall.  It was a large fortress.  As they passed through the outer courtyard, Khasan saw the bodies of the Undaari mixed in with the Noxxons.  The Undaari had given the Noxxons the fight of their lives.  Scorch marks covered the walls and blood soaked the courtyard.

Khasan's eyes scanned across the battlefield.  He gave a quick mental tally of the death toll.  There were nearly ten dead Noxxons to every dead Undaari inside the walls of Entfall.  The tenacity of the Undaari warriors protecting Entfall was unmatched. They were the greatest fighters in the Undaari kingdom.  If they had reinforcements earlier, they could have easily repelled the Noxxons.  *We were deployed too late.  Why had the King hesitated so long?*

The sounds of war echoed through Entfall.  There was still a battle being fought past the inner walls.  His pace quickened as they crossed the outer courtyard and closed in on the gate of the inner wall.  There was still a chance for the Undaari here to survive.  The army behind began charging through Entfall recklessly, passing through the smashed down front gate and filling the outer courtyard.

Khasan led the way to the gate of the inner wall.  He saw the large, melted doors lying on the ground.  He looked through the opening and saw the Noxxons charging out toward his men.  The Shields next to him took up defensive postures and used their blue walls to create a funnel into the Undaari front lines.

As the Noxxons erupted through the inner gate, Khasan realized that they were not charging, *they're fleeing.*  He was confused, but that did not stop him, or his men, from striking down the Noxxons as they approached.  There were over a thousand Noxxons fleeing the fight.  They were a broken army, not even carrying their weapons anymore.

The Army made quick work of the last Noxxons, not losing a single soldier themselves.  Khasan pushed through the gate.  He could still hear fighting from the inner courtyard.  He led the Undaari through the melted gates.  When they emerged, he saw an intense scene.  There were piles of dead Noxxons filling the courtyard around them.  Rain started to sprinkle on them as Khasan tried to make sense of what he was seeing.

Kiva landed outside the gates with a massive explosive force of blue fire.  Everything within ten meters was blasted back by a spherical eruption of cerulean flames.  Many Noxxons died from the sheer force of her power.  Even the Staff Bearers were knocked off balance, disrupting their assault on the gates.  They recovered quickly and turned toward Kiva as one.

She had to be the epitome of speed.  It was the only way to keep the Staff Bearers from landing any attacks on her.  Attacks she could ill afford to take.  She had to drag this battle out until their reinforcements arrived.  She ran like a blue blur, allowing the Alackai to fill her entire being and augment her movements.  She dodged their staff blasts, allowing the crimson fire to strike down the Noxxon warriors behind her.

The Naajis attacked wildly, showing little concern about the lives of their troops.  Kiva's movements were too swift for the Staff Bearers.  She had them spinning around trying to track her down.  She dodged from side to side, cutting down Noxxon warriors while the Naajis killed more with their wild attacks.

Whenever she saw an opportunity, she closed the gap with the

Staff Bearers. She used her blade to hack away at vulnerable spots in their all-but-impervious rocky skin. She could not overpower them in a straight fight but figured she might be agile enough to whittle them down slowly.

Their attacks became more random and intense, turning their horde into collateral damage while not allowing the Noxxons to press in. They tried to predict her movements and get ahead of her but were killing their own warriors by the dozens instead. Red flames danced across the courtyard as she dodged through them.

Her heartbeat slowed, as though she were strolling through the forest. She breathed as though she were lounging about. The Alackai filled her, sustained her, and strengthened her. Everything around her had slowed down.

One Naaji got lucky. Its crimson flames caught enough of Kiva to send her spinning. Her side was singed, but her armor and cape protected most of her. The other Staff Bearer closed in before she could escape. She changed tactics, charging the Staff Bearers, and bringing cyan flames about her hands and arms. Closing the distance, she used her sword and hands to fight in close quarters.

She ducked one attack. Struck with fire. Side stepped another attack. Slashed with metal. She had never moved so fast in her life. She felt like she had reached a new level within the Alackai. Jerykka was right. The Society had no clue how to use the Alackai anymore.

She felt the rush of energy. It was addictive. She had been given the strength to save everyone remaining in the keep. Everyone who had already sacrificed so much for her and the rest of the Undaari. As she moved, she continued to pick at the Naajis' defenses. She tried to stay between the two, letting their misses sail toward each other.

After several attempts, she finally got one Naaji to miss and strike the other. The Staff Bearer was sent flailing across the courtyard, its obsidian skin scorched and smoking. Kiva closed in on the injured Naaji, using her blue flames to create a vortex and trap it.

She clenched her fist, directing the flaming twister to close in tightly around the Staff Bearer. Its flesh cooked under the heat of her flames, like a fish over an open flame. The other Staff Bearer swung its staff around, crashing into Kiva's side and launching her into a knot of Noxxon warriors. She tackled several of the unexpecting brutes.

She felt her ribs crack on impact while her side was lacerated. She winced as she sprang back up. She felt the Alackai rush to her wounds, staving off the pain despite her blood flowing freely. She smiled as she stared down the Naaji.  The Noxxon warriors around her scrambled to attack her.  Their blades swung too slowly.  She created a wall of flames that threw them back, killing more.  Their numbers were thinning rapidly.

She began trusting more deeply in the Alackai.  She allowed her body to act as the Alackai willed.  The Society had been wrong about a lot. She could do anything with the Alackai as her guide.  She had the power to attain new heights and break down even the toughest of walls.

Kiva charged back at the Naajis.  The Undaari Army would be nearing the keep by now. *I've got this.* She called the flames back up in her hands, extending her power to the sigridir in her hand.  She went for the still standing Naaji as the second slowly recovered from her flaming tornado.

She leapt into the air and brought her blade down at its head.  The Staff Bearer raised its staff to protect itself.  Kiva's Alackai infused blade cut straight through its scarred onyx staff and buried deep into its shoulder.  It shrieked in pain, unable to comprehend what had just happened.  It tumbled back in awe, fear evident in its ruby eyes.  As it fell back, Kiva yanked her blade out, spraying inky blood everywhere.

She called up her cerulean flames.  The other Staff Bearer countered before she could strike again.  It pointed its staff at her, spewing crimson flames. She redirected her own fire to shield her.  She was pushed back by the blast but did not fall.  She withstood the attack, then began to step forward. Crimson flames continued to stream at her, but she pushed through them, deflecting fire into the crowds of Noxxons around her.

She closed the gap with the Staff Bearer, determined to eradicate this corruption.  She began building momentum and speed as she moved. She steamrolled through the second monstrous Naaji, slamming her shoulder into its gut.  It stumbled back but maintained its footing.  The Naaji on the ground howled at his warriors.  The Noxxons tightened around her. There were still over a thousand of the fearsome warriors.

Noxxons arrows began to rain down on Kiva.  She used her flames to shove the Staff Bearer back before turning her fire up into a shield to protect her from the Noxxon arrows.  She turned on the new threat and began wielding the flames around her.  She spread them through the ranks of the Noxxons.  She had lost herself completely to the Alackai.  She was barely aware of her actions anymore.  Everything her body did was pure instinct with the intent and determination to save the remaining Undaari and humans.

The flames ate into the Noxxons, striking them down quickly. Dozens of Noxxons burned away in seconds.  A panic began to build among

them.  The Naajis froze, their eyes opened wide.  It was as if they were overawed by the power she was wielding.

The Staff Bearers took a step back from Kiva, shielding themselves with their arms, as the scarlet glow of the corrupted Alackai flickered in their eyes.  Their attack faltered as they glanced at each other, seeming to seek reassurance.  Their Noxxons followers hesitated as well.  Kiva saw that the hold the Staff Bearers had on the horde was failing.

She directed her flames back at the Naaji, screaming as she channeled the immense power.  The one still holding its staff struggled to shield them both.  The Noxxons began looking around at each other, like they had just awoken from a nightmare.

Their backs relaxed from fully erect to a more natural slouch.  They began to throw down their arms and flee.  They ran from the battlefield.  It appeared that the Staff Bearers had lost control over their army.  Kiva's eyes followed the Noxxon army as they fled like cowards from a single Undaari.  Kiva turned back to the Naajis as the Noxxons fled, a smile creeping across her wild face.

"You will never harm another Undaari!"

They roared as their ruby scars and eyes grew brighter.  The Naaji with its staff managed to deflect the flames and charge.  The disarmed Staff Bearer picked up two Noxxon swords from the ground and began to fight.  It appeared they did not draw their strength from their staffs; they must just be conduits for their power.

They attacked with renewed frenzy, but Kiva was ready for them.  Her understanding and devotion to the Alackai had deepened beyond her wildest expectations.  She still felt strong as she charged back against the Naajis.  They were three powerful beings clashing under the setting sun.  The power they unleashed sent shock waves across the abandoned courtyard.

She could see rain begin to fall as nature tried to wash away the blood and destruction brought by the Noxxons.  She was thankful nature had a way of cleaning itself up after it was damaged.  The Alackai never allowed death and corruption to linger in Undaalan.  She would not allow these abominations to live any longer, either.

Kiva moved with terrifying speed.  She dodged around the first Staff Bearer's blades.  Kiva slashed at its inner thighs as she slid by.  As strong as she had become, she was surprised that the Staff Bearers were still able to fight.  They were injured all over, gushing inky blood across the courtyard and dangling chunks of flesh off their bodies, yet they moved as though they were fresh.  It was unnatural.

She needed to end the fight soon.  She could feel her energy beginning to fade.  It seemed she did still have limits.  She continued to hack and slash between the Naajis.  She used her flames to counter everything the Staff Bearers attempted.  She was entirely focused on the fight.

She was too focused to notice the Undaari Army marching up behind her with Skovi Shields at the front.  She also failed to see the doors of the keep open and the other five Shields step out into the rain, followed by Master Jerykka leaning on Intayr.

She had a singular focus; destroy the corruption in front of her.  Her breathing had become heavy.  She had broken a sweat as the Alackai's energy faded.  She kicked out at a Staff Bearer, opening her back for attack.  The second Naaji moved in to strike her with its staff.  She side stepped swiftly.  She spun about and hooked her blade around the spikes in its back.

Her blade was still imbued with the power of the Alackai.  She flung blue flames from her other hand into the back of the Staff Bearer at the base of the spikes.  She gave the cerulean flames everything she had.  The Staff Bearer screamed in pain as her flames ate away at its rocky skin.  She used the blade to cleave the stone from its skin, tearing out all five spikes from its back.

As the Naaji fell, its body fell apart, turning to ash.  Nothing solid hit the ground except the spikes she had taken.  She stood there in the rain, daring the other Staff Bearer to strike.  Blood was running down her legs from the wounds in her sides, her chest rising at an exaggerated pace.  She was almost out of energy.  The Staff Bearer moved to attack, seeing her vulnerability.  Kiva braced herself.

The Naaji failed to reach her.  Five Shields rushed from behind her to intercept the injured Staff Bearer, their blue walls raised high.  Kiva became aware of her surroundings as she looked around.  She saw Commander Khasan standing behind her with the Undaari Army.  Cheers erupted from all around her as the Undaari warriors celebrated her victory.  There were no other Noxxons around.

The other five Shields from the main hall charged forward, blue walls of their own encircling the Staff Bearer.  It was trapped by the ten Shields, unable to escape, too weak to penetrate its cage.  She noticed Master Jerykka and Intayr standing at the doors. Jerykka was leaning on Intayr, but back on her feet once again.

The fight was over.  The Undaari Army had made it to their rescue.  The remaining warriors of Entfall would get the chance to recover from the gruesome attack. She knelt on the ground there, trying to catch her breath, exhaustion overcoming her.

She could not believe she had done it. She had never realized how blessed she was with the Alackai. Jarreck had not been wrong about her. She was thankful for everything that had been sacrificed for her and was glad to pay it back.

She looked up as Jerykka approached her. Jerykka was wearing a huge smile on her face as she reached a hand down to help Kiva stand. Despite her injuries, Jerykka still had the strength to help her up. Kiva got lightheaded for a second and had to steady herself. The two powerful Undaari women leaned on each other and began to make their way into the fortress.

# Chapter 33
## Corruption

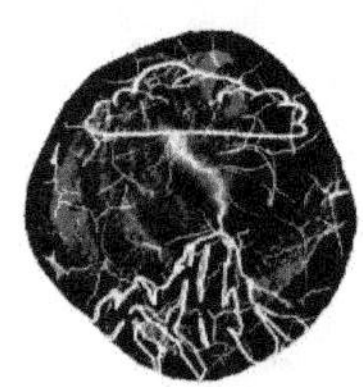

Jerykka could feel her strength slowly returning to her as she lay in the medical bay. Kiva had just left her side to help in the main hall while she recovered. Jerykka was getting antsy to return to her people. She did not like sitting back while her people fought this battle and died.

She did not understand why she was struggling so much with this recovery. She had been exhausted before. She was uninjured. But she was having difficulty sleeping, tossing and turning, while experiencing flashes of her past. She struggled to remain focused on the task at hand while her doubts washed over. Doubts she thought had been buried.

Her parents had been so proud of her when she was selected to join the Society. She had only been fifteen years old and the first member of her family to be Graced by the Alackai. Jerykka had not been sure about the decision, though. She had enjoyed her internships with her parents and did not want to leave her home. Something had felt off about the Society, but she joined anyway, just for her parents.

The training had not gone well. She had met a charming Undaari boy named Jarreck who had had no issues excelling in the Society, but she had struggled. It had not felt natural using the Society's teachings, just painful and uncomfortable.

She fell behind in her lessons and got into several arguments with her Master. Jarreck had been supportive, though. He had tried to tutor her, but she did not take to the Alackai so well. She had felt like such a failure next to Jarreck. She had been made to feel weak because she refused to inflict pain on herself to use the Alackai. It had just never felt right to her.

Somehow, she had still managed to make it to the end of her

training.  Master Gierdahl had brought them both to Entfall for a final training mission.  Down in the old Council Chambers, they had been going through their forms under the eye of the Entai.  Jarreck had conjured wondrous cerulean flames, fighting through the pain.  When it was her turn, she had failed.

She had stormed from the chambers, leaving behind a heartbroken Jarreck.  It had pained her deeply, seeing him so disappointed.  She had failed to become a Skovi.  She had failed her parents and everyone else in her life.  The images of Jarreck's face, in that moment, had haunted her throughout her dreams.

She woke again in a sweat, feelings of failure still present.  She needed to recover.  She needed to get to the Entai and hope that the Alackai had not forsaken her.  She knew she had taken extreme advantage of her gifts and feared the Alackai would not grant her much more, especially after her most recent failures.

It was a debilitating fear in the back of her mind.  Her doubts had grown after failing to save her people the last time she used it.  She did not deserve this gift.  She looked over to the bed next to her and could see Nazario was alert and recovering well.

She tried to push the negative thoughts from her head as she spoke to the human.  "How are you, my friend?  You gave Kiva quite the scare.  She seems quite taken with you."

Nazario let out a small laugh.  "I've been worse.  I'm almost recovered enough to get back on my feet.  Jaina and Brandon here have done well administering aid for me.  I'm thankful Kiva cared enough, and moved fast enough, to save me.  And glad to hear you call me friend again."

Jerykka nodded.  "Your medicines are quite powerful.  It would take our people much longer to recover from a wound as severe as yours.  I'm almost strong enough to go for a walk.  I must check in on my people."

Jerykka began trying to sit up.  The medics rushed up to her, warning her she was still not strong enough yet.  She shot daggers at the medics and attempted to stand anyway.  Her knees buckled and the medics caught her.

She needed to wait a little longer.  Jerykka laid back down, upset at herself for still not being ready.  She could feel her body healing, but for some reason, she just could not manage to get herself up.  She had depleted herself far worse than she had realized.

Nazario was the calming voice in the room.  "If you push yourself too soon, you'll set back your healing.  I've been pushed to the brink before.

I've learned the hard way that you have to be patient with yourself. It's difficult to sit back in war. But you'd only be doing a disservice to your people."

They sat in silence for a while. She was not sure what to say after that. She just felt disgusted with herself for failing. She no longer felt that she even deserved her position. For the first time in her life, she felt broken.

After a long, awkward, agonizing silence, Nazario spoke to Brandon. "What are you doing with a paper journal? Don't we have better ways to record everything?"

Jerykka had not noticed that the man was writing in a journal. She had lost focus on the world around her. Nazario's voice brought her back, though.

Jaina answered for Brandon, whose face and ears had turned bright pink. "It's a hobby of his. He finds passion and understanding in his drawings. It brings a whole new level of appreciation to what he's studying. It's also a way for him to keep his mind calm in a chaotic world. He really has excellent work in his journal. I've gotten to see some of it. He's recording all the people and places he's seen here."

Jerykka was curious. "All the people? Did he draw me?"

Brandon looked up, embarrassed. "I'm s-... sorry, I should have asked p-... permission first."

"May I see?"

Brandon looked at Jaina, his cheeks continuing to fill with blood.

Jaina continued to tease him a bit, "Aw. Is someone shy? I don't think your artwork is so terrible that she'll hurt you."

Jaina pulled the book from his grasp and stood up. She flipped through the pages of Brandon's journal until she found the correct one and walked it over to Jerykka. Jerykka saw herself in the book. She could feel the passion that was put into drawing her. In it, she saw the strength she had been missing for the last day. The strength she doubted she still had.

There was nothing but admiration for her people in the pages as she began to look through the book. She could not read the words written at the bottom, but she could easily discern what was drawn on each page. They did not have artwork like this in Undaalan. She was thankful for the passion and admiration of her people that Brandon had given to the pages of the journal.

She flipped back to the page with her likeness on it. She continued to review the picture with fondness. She felt that she was no longer that person. The throne had changed her. This whole war had defeated her. She just wanted to be her old self again.

"I'm not strong enough…" she whispered to herself.

Only Jaina had heard her, though she had not intended to even say it aloud. Her cheeks flushed when she realized her mistake. She avoided eye contact with Jaina, but Jaina still placed a hand on her arm.

Leaning in, Jaina whispered so that only she could hear, "Everything about you screams strength. You're overflowing with it, filling everybody around you. This keep would have fallen long ago, if not for the strength you filled it with. We all feel vulnerable at times. But not strong enough? You're unbreakable."

A smile crept across Jerykka's face. *Unbreakable.* The word had filled her confidence, along with a flood of other memories. Tears welled in her eyes as she remembered her strengths.

She had run from the Council Chambers up to the Entai's ramparts. She had hidden in one of the towers and refused to leave. Warden Leesom had come up to investigate the situation. When he had come across her, they spoke at length about her insecurities and disagreements with the Society. The man had been surprisingly comforting, taking her in as a warrior of Entfall. He had later told her that Entfall's walls glowed particularly bright around her as she cried in the tower.

He had explained to her that she had a special strength in her. One that most Skovi did not. That was why she had rejected the teachings of the Society. He had built her up with a new strength and confidence. He had taught her to be successful as she was, not how the Society said she had to be.

He had been so proud to name her his successor. She had felt invincible in that moment. Unbreakable. Her parents were even prouder about this than they had been about being chosen to join the Society. Even Jarreck had made it for the ceremony and had expressed his joy.

She finally remembered that her strength came from the inside; she needed to stop questioning herself. She needed to trust her instincts. Leesom had never doubted her strength and Jaina had just reminded her why. In fact, no one doubted her, except herself.

These humans certainly did not. Neither did her warriors. More importantly, Jarreck did not. Jaina had a way with words unlike anyone she had ever met. These humans did have something special in them. Jerykka pulled Jaina in closer, hugging her and giving her a kiss on the cheek as thanks.

She could feel the blood in her system circulate stronger as her cheeks were filled. She had been blaming herself for failing but remembered she was still there, ready to fight.  The burst in confidence gave her an energy boost.  She felt ready to get out of bed.  She handed the journal back to Jaina.

"Thank you, Brandon.  You've done a wonderful job capturing the beauty of our lands.  It's time for me to get back to things."

Jerykka stood up.  She was wobbly at first but steadied herself.  The medics tried to protest but she held up a hand to silence them.  She stood tall, ready to rejoin her warriors.  She knew from her talk with Kiva that their plight was getting desperate.  If they were to be overrun, she would be by their side when it happened.

As she slowly hobbled out of the medical bay, she could hear the humans speaking behind her.

Nazario said, "Jerykka is the strongest person I've ever met.  None of us would be here today if it weren't for her."

Brandon and Jaina replied in unison, "Yes, she is."

Nazario continued on, "I suppose I should be going with her.  I've healed enough to follow.  I need help getting this exosuit off before we get going though.  It's fried.  Shall we?"

When she arrived in the main hall, Jerykka could see the toll that the battle had taken on the Undaari.  There were only about two hundred left and most of them had collapsed on the floor, trying to get some rest.  The humans walked in behind her.  She could hear Jaina gasp at the sight of her warriors.

There were five Skovi using the Alackai to create a blue barrier at the doors, keeping it protected.  The upper portion of the doors had been melted, leaving cooled beads of metal all over the ground around the doors.  She could still hear sounds of battle outside and see bright red and blue flashes of light.

Jerykka spotted Intayr near the door, speaking with the Shields.  As Jerykka crossed the hall, the Undaari warriors began to perk up.  They saw her striding across the hall and found a new hope that they would survive.  She held her head high, even if she was not physically recovered.  Her internal strength radiated to her people, just like Jaina had told her it did.

When she reached Intayr, she immediately asked for a status update.  Intayr seemed surprised to see her but responded immediately.

"Master Jerykka, thank the Alackai!  The troops are trying to catch their breath.  The Shields here were able to join us just before we fell back to this position.  It wasn't enough though, Kiva jumped over the doors to give us more time. By the sounds of it, she's still giving them quite the fight. The Undaari Army should be here at any moment. She's saving our lives."

Jerykka nodded. She had known Kiva was stronger than she had ever realized and would buy them the time they needed. She was proud of Kiva. Her medic had been right. That gentle nudge had led to a great change. Jerykka leaned on Intayr, still struggling. The walk to the main hall had taken a lot out of her.

"I suppose it's time we save hers. Drop the defenses and open the doors. We're finishing this."

Intayr nodded. The Shields dropped their walls before he had even given the order. They each fell to a knee, chests heaving as they desperately tried to catch their breath. Two Undaari warriors rushed to open the half doors as the rest formed up quickly, prepared for one final confrontation.

When the doors opened, Jerykka could see Kiva locked in an incredibly fierce battle with the Staff Bearers. The abominations were struggling to fight back against her power; she appeared to be winning. Kiva was slinging cerulean flames and metal faster than she had ever witnessed. On the far side of her, the Undaari Army stood, just as mesmerized by the ferocious fight. There were no Noxxon warriors remaining in the courtyard. No Undaari moved as they witnessed the spectacle.

Jerykka watched in awe as Kiva used her swords and flames to rip apart one of the Staff Bearers. It turned to ash as it fell, as if it had only been held together by the corrupted spikes in its back. The other Staff Bearer prepared itself for a final attack. It was severely injured and did not possess a staff anymore, instead wielding two regular Noxxon swords.

The five Shields with the Undaari Army charged forward to protect Kiva. Jerykka watched as the five Shields in the main hall rushed forward to assist their companions. The Shields encased the Staff Bearer in their blue walls. She walked forward, leaning on Intayr. She was still recovering and pushing herself harder than she should, but she would not allow that to stop her any longer.

As she got nearer to Kiva, she let go of Intayr and completed the journey on her own, limping along slowly. Jerykka could not contain her excitement, smiling brightly. When she reached Kiva, Jerykka reached out a hand to help her up.

As she pulled Kiva up, she had a few things to say, "I'm so incredibly proud of you, Kiva. You've shown true strength of character and faith in the Alackai. I knew you had it in you. As did Jarreck. Thank you for so selflessly saving us. Now, let us walk."

Jarreck looked at the man, confused.

"Dad?" he asked, not sure he believed it.

Jace smiled at him. "I've been watching your journey for a long time. It's almost reached its conclusion. I'm so *very* proud of you."

"I don't understand. What is this? Is this another vision of the past?"

"No, Jarreck. This is happening right now. Inside the Alackai. There's so much we don't understand about her. She's been testing you. You're her chosen protector. There's been a corruption inside her, and she needs you. She had to make sure you were ready."

"Why would she choose me? How's this happening? Is it really you?"

"Walk with me, Jarreck."

Jace turned away from him and led the way into the forest. Jarreck stood frozen, confused by what was happening. This could not possibly be real. *Am I losing my mind? Is this some sort of trickery?* He watched as Jace stopped and turned back.

"Are you coming?"

Jarreck hesitated a moment more, glancing at the cabin, then followed his father. He decided he would take the opportunity to spend time with him one last time, even if it was just in his head. He hurried to catch up with him.

"Why am I here?"

Jace continued walking in silence. They were walking southwest from their cabin in the woods. The day had grown into evening. It was a beautiful, cloudless night as they strode through the Lenakai Forest. Jarreck could see the celeste glow in the forest brought by the Alackai. It was peaceful. A peace he found himself missing immensely.

Finally, Jace began to speak to him again. "I've been waiting for you to find me for so long. I had hoped you would do it while you were still young. I did not want you to join the Society. I've learned a lot in my old age. The Alackai is far more than we ever imagined. The Society has become so ignorant of her. Vreeham saw to it that we grew apart from her."

"I miss you, dad. I've been lost these past few days. The Alackai showed me what Vreeham did to you. I cannot believe I ever trusted him."

"It's not your fault, my son. I had begun to suspect he would come for me. I didn't know he had allied himself with the Noxxons, though."

"There's been so much happening. I have so many questions."

"Trust in the Alackai, Jarreck. She has Graced you for a reason. The Undaari weren't Graced with her power to join the Society or rule these lands. She saw the best of us in those that she Graced, though not all valued her gift.

"We were meant to be the protectors of others. The Third Society hid from the past and became ignorant of this. Only someone truly devoted to others, who truly trusted in her, can unlock the full potential of the Alackai within them. You're the best of us. The Alackai chose wisely."

"But father, we lost. Dralvic has returned from the dead and laid claim to the Black Scythe. He's too powerful for any of us to fight. I tried so hard, but he defeated me with ease. I don't understand what I'm supposed to do."

"Jarreck, listen to me. It's not over yet. There's still hope. Dralvic's plan to capture the Black Scythe came to light while I was still with the Society. He inhabited the body of another Skovi who grew to be a Councilor. He's been doing this for a very long time by acting from the shadows and growing ever stronger. He never revealed himself until that moment. He had trained Vreeham during that time."

"If you knew about him, what did you do? How did you stop him?"

"It wasn't me, Jarreck. I was but a guide for another. As you will be."

Jace continued leading the way through the forest. They approached another cabin in the woods and stopped at the wood line. He continued his story to his son.

"There has always been one bloodline with a special connection with the Alackai. The Skovi that had revolted against the First Society had this particularly strong connection with her. He worked with the Alackai to create a powerful weapon using his blood and a branch from one of her Entai. This weapon can only be used by one who shares his blood."

"The Lightning Bow."

Jarreck had heard of the weapon in his studies, but never known its origins or secrets.

"Precisely. As Master of the Ancient Text, I maintained the knowledge of this bloodline along with the ancient weapons. Dralvic accidentally revealed himself to me one day while asking about the Black Scythe. He had shown too much interest in stuff that he wasn't supposed to know about. I managed to separate myself from him and found the one person who could help."

Jace pointed out toward the cabin. "He lived here, in this cabin. I had built our cabin to be near him. Libran hadn't known of his family heritage at the time. I approached him and told him of my need for him. He didn't believe what I had to say. He'd never connected with the Alackai before I spoke with him."

"If he'd never connected with the Alackai, how could he be of help? Even with his heritage? Especially without training from the Society?"

"My son, haven't you been listening? The Society *doesn't* matter in the eyes of the Alackai. It's about what's inside your heart and your willingness to give of yourself to save others. Without question, this man abandoned everything he had built to go off on this mission with me. He doubted himself, but he was willing to do anything to protect his loved ones. He trusted in the Alackai."

Jarreck looked over at the man doing work about his house. He too had his wife with him. She was cooking a large meal for the two of them. Jarreck inspected the man. He was strong, but nothing special stood out about him.

As Jarreck continued to study the man, Jace continued speaking, "I brought him to an Entai. There, he connected with the Alackai for the first time. He saw the truth in what I'd told him. After this, we recovered the Lightning Bow and made our way to Dralvic. We had discovered that on his research missions, Dralvic had been going to Numitor Island."

"He was already working with the Noxxons that long ago? These past few days must have been decades in the making then. Every bit of this."

"Centuries, my son. We confronted him. Vreeham was with him. Vreeham was still young. He thought Dralvic's intentions were to study the Noxxons for a future battle. Dralvic had been slowly corrupting Vreeham, testing him to see if he would be a worthy ally. When confronted, Vreeham abandoned his master."

"If he abandoned him, why does he still work for him? I saw him in my vision. He was there when you died. Some of the Noxxons with him were branded. The same brand that Dralvic displays. Vreeham has been assisting Dralvic through everything."

"I cannot speak to how or why he rejoined Dralvic, as I didn't witness it, but I began suspecting him once he started gaining unprecedented influence within the Society. I only knew for sure that it had happened when he came after me with the Noxxons.

"Regardless, Libran and I confronted Dralvic on Numitor Island. I told Libran to use the Lightning Bow and end Dralvic. He hesitated a moment too long. Dralvic's spirit managed to escape the body before it was destroyed. We knew he'd gotten away but hoped this would still set Dralvic back significantly in his plans for conquest."

"Is Libran still alive? Where's the Lightning Bow now?"

"My son, Libran is here with me in the Alackai," Jace said as he pointed to the man in the clearing. "As far as the Lightning Bow goes, it's always been protected by the Alackai, safeguarded by the Entai where it was created."

Everything his father said finally clicked into place for Jarreck. His instincts had returned to him. He did not have every answer, but he had most of them. His father stared at the young man, Libran, for a few more moments, then turned back to the forest.

"Your mother would like to see you before you leave. I know she has missed you deeply. Let's return to her."

Jarreck continued to study the man in front of him before he realized there *was* something unique about him. It was his eyes. They were not normal Undaari eyes. They were purple.

# Chapter 34

## Champion

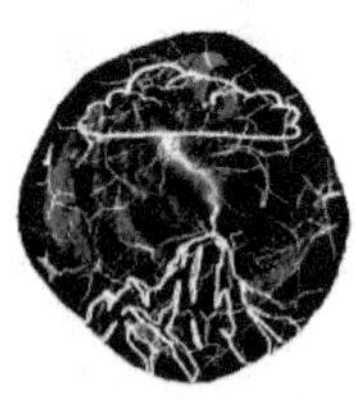 As he slowly opened his eyes, Lingdon realized he was no longer in the lake. The cave and the Heart of the Alackai were nowhere to be found, either. It took him a moment to orient himself. It was dark still, but he was outside. The sky was oddly purple above. As he looked around, he realized he was surrounded by trees. A forest. *I must be in the Lenakai Forest.* He had no idea how he had gotten there, but at least that monster was no longer threatening him.

As he took stock of his situation and tried to figure out how he had gotten there, he noticed an unusually beautiful tree standing in front of him. Its white bark was cracked and veined with glowing celeste light. It was a most wondrous sight to him. He moved toward its beauty, mesmerized.

It was pulling him toward it as though gravity had shifted and drew him closer. Lingdon's hand reached to touch the tree as if it acted of its own accord. Before his hand made contact, he stopped. He noticed another person watching him. *Where did he come from?*

Lingdon stared at the man, studying him. He was tall and strong but wore no armor or weapons. Over his casual clothing, he wore a bright cerulean hooded cape over his shoulders. Yet this man felt extremely dangerous.

As Lingdon studied him, the man began to walk forward, out of the tree line. Lingdon took a step back, debating if he should run. The man was clearly intent on reaching Lingdon. As he approached, the man's face became more visible in the glow of the tree's scars. He had an air of familiarity to him. Curiosity got the better of him, burying his desire to flee.

Lingdon noticed his eyes. They were purple. His father was the only other man he had ever known with purple eyes, but this man was not his father.  His confusion increased, knowing that purple eyes were extremely rare among the Undaari.

The man stopped in front of Lingdon and smiled.  He clearly knew who Lingdon was and was happy to see him.  This added to Lingdon's confusion.  The man studied Lingdon a moment longer then lowered his hood to give Lingdon a better view.

He placed a hand on Lingdon's shoulder and finally spoke.  "You've grown strong, my boy.  It's time for you to carry the weight of responsibility the Alackai has entrusted in you."

Lingdon still did not understand anything that was happening.  All his questions poured out, unchecked.

"Who are you?  Where am I?  How'd I get here?  What responsibility?  What's the Alackai?  Who *are* you?"

The man laughed boisterously before answering, "My young Lingdon, I've been watching you since birth.  My name is Unathi.  I was the Alackai's first champion against corruption.  She chose me to wield her power and revolt against the First Society.  I must admit, I still don't understand why she chose me of all people.  However, the Alackai is wise, and we must trust her, even if we don't understand her."

"It's an honor to meet you, Unathi, but I'm sorry.  I still don't know what you're talking about.  What's the First Society?  Who is the Alackai?  I heard Jarreck mention the name before, but he didn't have time to explain."

Unathi was noticeably disappointed.  "Have you learned nothing of the Alackai yet?  Or how to use your power?"

Lingdon felt guilty.  "I'm sorry, but not much.  My father showed me a few things without much explanation when I was a child, but he was murdered.  I was a slave for the past two years and only in the last few days began using my powers."

Unathi shook his head.  "So young.  You have nothing to be sorry about.  I just assumed with how strong you've already become that you had more training and knowledge.  I'm impressed by how far you've come with such little assistance.  The Alackai has chosen well again."

Unathi paused a moment.  He raised his hands to gesture around him.

"The Alackai is all around us.  She's a wise and powerful entity who gives life to our world.  She's what Graces you with your abilities.  Without her, the Undaari would never have become what they are today."

Lingdon's jaw dropped.  He had known the Undaari were sometimes gifted with magic, but he had never known the reason.

"That's wonderful to hear. I never knew that. How does that work? I got to see a cave that was lit up like this tree. Jarreck referred to it as the Heart. That's where I was before I came here. How did I even get here? I was held captive by a great monster inside the cave."

"You're no captive, Lingdon. That *monster* is the great protector of the Alackai. You are the champion of the Alackai. That creature answers to you, and *you* alone. It brought you to the lake so you could commune with the Alackai. Your body is still there, connected to the Alackai through the water."

Lingdon's eyes grew wider as every sentence from Unathi was more and more unbelievable. "I don't feel like I'm anywhere else. And that creature was definitely *not* doing what I wanted."

"No, it was doing what you *needed*. It's not just any creature. It's the embodiment of the Alackai itself. It's the Alkaios. It protects the Heart of the Alackai at all costs. The Alkaios is now yours to command. It will assist you in cutting out the corruption that has festered in the Alackai. It's not all powerful though, remember that."

"How do I control it? And why was I chosen for this responsibility?"

"Lingdon, how often must I tell you that the Alackai is wise and that you need to trust it. Ask not *why* you were chosen, only how you can be of service now that you have. The Alkaios is connected to the Alackai just as you are. It will understand your meaning."

"I don't think I can do this. I'm not ready. What am I even supposed to do?"

Unathi shook his head again. "This is *your* path to travel. I cannot tell you what to do. You were chosen. The Alackai trusts you, so you must trust yourself. I must be going now. I've taken all the time the Alackai has given me to speak to you."

Lingdon tried to protest and ask additional questions, but Unathi held up his hand to silence him. He smiled one last time before turning and walking off. He slowly faded into the distance. Lingdon stood there for what felt like hours, dumbfounded, not comprehending why any of this was happening. He did not want this responsibility. He did not want any of this. He just wished he could go back to his home and his old life before any of this.

Tears welled up in his eyes. His breathing quickened as he looked around the clearing. He was scared. He had never imagined there was anything special about him. Now he was being entrusted with the weight of the world. He sat down, not knowing where else he could go. He did not want to be Graced by the Alackai. He just wanted this to all be over. *Why did this happen to me?*

As he sat there crying, he lost track of time. He did not know how to leave this place. He was stuck. Without any of the answers that he felt he needed. *Why did the Alackai do this to me?*

Lingdon's ever growing list of questions caused him much anxiety. His heart raced as he struggled to control his breathing. All he ever wanted was his family. He could never have them back. He had made a new friend, but even he was gone now. Lingdon had no one. He would almost rather be a slave again. At least he had not been alone then.

It took several minutes of sobbing and self-pity before he realized there was another man standing by him. Lingdon was startled; he had not heard the man approach. This man was no stranger, though.

"Dad!"

Lingdon exclaimed before jumping up and embracing his father with a huge hug. The man smiled and wrapped his arms around his son, matching his intensity. Tears of joy poured down his father's face.

"Lingdon, I've missed you so much. I'm sorry I failed to protect you from the Yaxkin. I thought we would have more time before I had to lay these responsibilities on you. I'm sorry for failing at everything. I'm sorry you must now bear this burden because I failed. The Alackai has granted me a short time to speak with you, to give us both closure. She is wise and understands the importance behind our speaking."

"I've missed you so much, dad. It's been so hard without you. I don't understand how I'm supposed to do this."

"You're strong, my son. Stronger than I ever was. You have far more love in your heart for those around you, and you are selfless. Our family has always had a strong connection to the Alackai. It runs in our blood. The bloodline that started with Unathi. It's not a true bloodline as those tend to die out over millennia, but the Alackai has restored it multiple times with new families. Regardless of its purity, it has continued on inside of you."

"I'm related to Unathi? Is that how he knew so much about me?"

"In essence, yes, that's exactly how he knew so much. He spoke to me as well, when it was my time. A man named Jace found me. He knew of my heritage and showed me the Alackai.

"But I was scared. I hesitated when it was my time to protect her. You must not repeat my mistake. Dralvic only exists today because I failed decades ago.  Again, I'm so sorry you must bear my burden now."

Lingdon hugged his father again.  He could never blame his father for anything.  He was the best man Lingdon had ever known.

"Dad, I still don't understand.  What am I supposed to do?  I don't have control over my abilities.  I don't know what I'm doing.  How am I supposed to save the Alackai?  How do I defeat Dralvic?"

"After I failed, I trained with Jace for a time.  I wanted to assure myself that if Dralvic returned during my lifetime, I would be ready for him.  Then one day, when I was not so young anymore, the Yaxkin came and ended me in my sleep.  I'm thankful they spared you, but I still failed you.  I'm sorry you don't have more time to train before you must face your destiny.  The Alackai is out of time."

"I'm not ready.  Can you teach me more before I have to face Dralvic?"

"I cannot.  I have to leave.  My time here is up.  I had a guide who assisted me with my battle against corruption.  You need to get back to yours."

Libran placed his hands on Lingdon's shoulders and said one final farewell, "I'm proud of you son.  You're ready.  Do not hesitate as I did.  You cannot fail like me.  Go now, son.  Touch the Entai in front of you to return to the cave.  I love you."

Lingdon cried more.  "Don't leave me, dad."

It was too late.  His father faded away.  Lingdon did not feel ready.  He felt the Alackai had made a mistake.  *How am I supposed to defeat Dralvic after Jarreck had been beaten so easily?*  That was when he remembered Jarreck.  *Jarreck must be my guide!*

He took a few deep breaths to steady himself.  He did not have a choice.  He could not stay here.  He was thankful he had gotten to see his father one last time.  Lingdon wiped away the last of his tears.

He looked around the clearing to make sure no one else was coming.  *Why is this the place the Alackai had chosen for our meeting?*  Lingdon went answerless again.  He reached up to the tree that his father had called an Entai.  When his hand made contact, he felt a rush of energy.

Lingdon's real eyes snapped open.  He was back in the cave, still neck deep in water.  To his relief, the Alkaios was no longer behind him.  He slowly stood from the waters and made his way back to the shore.

He heard a groan behind him as he walked.  He turned and spotted someone lying on the ground on the far shore.  Whoever it was, they were injured.  He rushed to help the stranger.  How they had gotten like that was a question he left for later.

He reached the cloaked figure and turned him over. It was Jarreck. He was unconscious and thrashing in his sleep. His body convulsed as Lingdon tried to awaken the Skovi.

"Master Jarreck, please wake up!" he yelled to him, before turning his head and yelling for all to hear. "Help!"

A figure stepped into the opening of the cave. Someone had answered his pleas. He pulled Jarreck closer to his body, the man's head resting in his lap. He comforted his master, waiting for the figure to reach them and help.

The figure nonchalantly made its way toward him. Why were they moving so slowly? Jarreck was in serious danger. Lingdon struggled to sit still as he waited for help to arrive. His foot bounced faster the longer it took.

The figure was dressed in all black. The short person finally reached them. Lingdon couldn't make out the details of their features, but knew it was a man there to help them, despite his lack of height. The stranger knelt to examine Jarreck.

"How fortunate I arrived when I did. Jarreck is nearly dead already," the man said lowering his obsidian hood.

# Chapter 35

## Time

 King Cepheus sat on his throne while consulting with his advisors. The messengers were not returning from Entfall as expected, and he was worried this meant Entfall had been conquered. No one else would admit the possibility. There were many other theories being passed around by his advisors. The only thing that was consistent was they needed answers, and fast.

One of his advisors suggested they dispatch a King's Guard on the back of a zakeri. They could move much faster and avoid any obstacles that may be preventing messengers from returning. The King felt this was the wisest course of action and agreed to the plan. Too bad Vreeham's ropen was away carrying other messages. Still, this would be faster than sending yet another messenger on jentar.

The King called for the Commander of his King's Guard. He was never too far from the King. Commander Sanjiv appeared quickly, strolling through the hall with his white cape trailing behind him. He had once told the King that being a member of the King's Guard was a greater honor than being a Commander, which was why he continued to wear the white rather than the Commander's black.

After receiving the King's order, Sanjiv sent for one of his most trusted warriors and experienced zakeri riders. When Ferani made it into the chambers, Sanjiv explained the situation and gave him orders to fly quickly.

He had one more request before sending Ferani on his way. "Please don't get left behind by your zakeri again, Ferani."

Sanjiv had obviously said it as a friendly jab to lighten the mood. The King could see that Ferani still took it hard. Ferani had been forced to walk all the way back to Ambrecia on his own with nothing but his thoughts. He had only completed his journey the day before.

Ferani turned and swiftly exited, heading toward the stables. King Cepheus had good men working around him. The Noxxons would not have a real chance to harm the Undaari. They were far too disciplined and loyal. They were also the larger force and had the Alackai on their side.

Cepheus often coveted the power the Society wielded. He had taken special interest in Kiva when she had lost her father. He had been so proud of her when she was initiated into the Society, but often wished their places could have been switched.

He believed in the Alackai and her strength, how could any Undaari not? But he often wished he had been Graced with her strength. He had never wanted to be King but trusted and cared for his people. They had endorsed him, so he accepted the position.

Only a few minutes had passed when Ferani came charging back into the King's Court. This time, though, he did not come through the front doors. He had entered the King's Court from the ramp behind the King's throne that led up to the convocation deck. He must have landed the zakeri above and ran down as fast as he could. Ferani did not take the time for proper greetings or even catch his breath before speaking.

"My Lord... you must come... the Noxxons... they're coming..."

The King and all his advisors looked up in shock and confusion.

"What do you mean *they're coming*? They could not have defeated Entfall and made it here so quickly," the King demanded.

Ferani shook his head, gasping for air between his words. "No, my Lord... I don't believe these Noxxons came from there... There must be two thousand Noxxons marching up to our gates... They appear to have come from the east along the base of the Black Peaks... Please, my Lord... come with me... see for yourself..."

The King jumped out of the throne and rushed after Ferani. The other advisors and White Guard in the court chased after them. It only took seconds for the King to make it up the ramp. He was still a very fit man, only slightly slowed by his age and time on the throne. He strode over to the edge of the deck. He could hear screaming as he approached its edge. He looked out over his city and could see clouds of smoke and dust rising in the distance.

As he looked out over the city wall at the destruction heading for Ambrecia, he noticed his people were beginning to see the danger as well. There was chaos and panic spreading across the city. Many Undaari had never even seen a Noxxon warrior, let alone had their homes threatened by them. The King did not understand how this was possible, not with Entfall still guarding the Kingdom. Even if Entfall had been defeated, the Noxxons could not have reached Ambrecia so quickly.

Yet the Noxxon army would be upon them within the hour. He could see his citizens fleeing the forest and surrounding lands, trying to find safety within the city walls. He watched in horror as the scene unfolded around him. None of the Noxxon warriors gave chase. They continued to march in a crisp formation, unconcerned by the possibility of their escape.

The Noxxon archers, however, were not so kind. Many were raining arrows upon the Undaari civilians as they fled the horde. They attacked without prejudice, killing any Undaari they could. The women and children were not immune to the devastation. The King witnessed several young children struck through the back by the merciless Noxxon attack. A fury built within the King at the barbarism of the Noxxons.

Cepheus ordered the White Guard to gather all remaining troops within the city and prepare a defense of the walls. They had been caught completely unaware by the Noxxon forces approaching now. The Undaari were unprepared and vastly outnumbered. There were only a hundred warriors left manning the city after the army had been deployed to Entfall.

At the King's order, the gates into Ambrecia were closed and barred. The last of the surviving Undaari from the surrounding lands had made it inside. The Noxxon horde stopped marching in the fields east of Ambrecia, just outside arrow range. If the Undaari Army were nearby, the King knew they could swiftly defeat the invaders. His advisors could not have known of the threat, but he wished he had kept troops behind to secure the home front as well.

There were nearly a hundred dead Undaari men, women, and children scattered between Ambrecia and the Noxxon army. Thankfully, many more had made it inside the gates unharmed. The King turned to Ferani.

"I don't know how we can hope to repel this invasion, but I need you to fly as fast as you can. Get the army back from Entfall."

Ferani nodded and did as he was directed. Cepheus watched as he took flight on the feathery zakeri, giving the Noxxon army a wide berth for safety. Ferani could make it to Entfall in just hours if he pushed the zakeri to its limit. Now was not the time for caution. Every second mattered.

Cepheus turned to his advisors. He saw two Councilors of the Society had joined them as well, Gierdahl and Vreeham. He was thankful for their wisdom.  They were always able to examine every possibility of a situation.  They were going to need more immediate assistance securing the city.  He was hoping the Society could provide it.

"Are any of the Swords still within the walls?  We'll need their magic to fight against the Noxxons."

Councilor Gierdahl answered, "There are only three, my Lord.  The rest had been sent out to the various Undaari towns to ensure no panic was created during these times.  We were focused on maintaining civility during the threat.  We hadn't imagined the Noxxons would ever be on our doorstep."

Councilor Vreeham spoke as well, "I'm sorry, my Lord.  I have failed you.  I didn't believe there was any real threat.  I wanted to maintain the peace.  The Undaari needed reassurances they weren't in danger."

The King knew the High Councilor had not intended to leave them so vulnerable.  He could not have known the Noxxons would be able to march directly on Ambrecia.  The King looked back over the city walls to the Noxxon army.

He saw four Noxxons moving from the rear of the mass to the front. Three of them were the largest Noxxons the King had ever seen.  They were terrifyingly large, carrying massive staffs.  The fourth was cloaked and hooded but by far the shortest Noxxon he had ever seen.  It was more the stature of a Yaxkin.

As he watched them move forward past the Noxxon ranks, the King realized that the short Noxxon carried a scythe.  That was a truly unusual weapon to be carried by any warrior in the Three Kingdoms.  He was confused; there was clearly more to this than had originally been apparent.

Without looking at the Society's Councilors, the King gave orders, "Get those Swords to the walls.  No more Undaari will die here today.  We must protect our people at all costs."

Councilor Gierdahl stepped away to ensure the King's orders were followed.  Cepheus feared that even with the Swords, the Noxxon army would penetrate their walls without much resistance.  He continued to watch as the four Noxxons made their way to the front of their army.

The sun was setting to the rear of the Noxxons, making it difficult to see clearly.  The King realized that these four must be the leaders of the invasion force. He looked over at Commander Sanjiv. He was the only King's Guard not on the wall.

"Tell your men to use their bows. Strike those four Noxxons down, immediately. They're foolish to enter archer range. We'll make them pay before their attack can even begin."

The Commander of the White Guard pulled a golden horn off his waist and blew into it. The ensuing rhythm indicated commands to his warriors. Twenty white caped Undaari on the wall drew bows and unleashed arrows upon the Noxxon leadership. The four Noxxons moving forward did not hesitate or break pace.

Councilor Gierdahl returned as the arrows hung in the air. The other three Councilors had followed, no longer worrying about their identities being revealed. The King turned from the Councilors and watched as the Swords made their way to the ramparts. The arrows were closing in.

The foursome continued walking as though nothing had happened. They did not seem threatened by the attack. Just before the arrows struck them, one of the large Noxxons raised its staff and lazily deflected the arrows with crimson flames, leaving everyone on the convocation deck dumbfounded. The King could not comprehend what had happened.

Jaws still hanging, Cepheus and Gierdahl simultaneously whispered, "That's not possible."

Gierdahl looked toward Vreeham. "Kiva was right about the Noxxons. They've learned how to use the Alackai. I didn't want to believe it was possible. How can this be?"

Vreeham was not listening to Councilor Gierdahl. His face did not bear the look of shock as everyone else's did. He was smiling at the sight in front of him.

Gierdahl questioned him, "High Councilor?"

Jarreck was not ready to leave the quaint little cabin. He had been at peace for the first time in years. He felt like a kid again. He had missed his parents with all his heart. He was thankful they had gotten to enjoy a final meal together. His mother had cooked the same meal for him that he had enjoyed on their last night together. This time though, he got to enjoy the fruit pie. It was an unbelievable opportunity the Alackai had blessed them with.

His father stood from the table. "It's time to say goodbye, my son."

"Do I have to leave? Can't I just stay here with you forever?"

"No, Jarreck. The Alackai has shown us a rare kindness today. We were blessed with an opportunity to see each other again one last time, but our time together is at an end. You must return to the world."

"But dad, I'm not ready. I don't wish to go back to the death and chaos that has befallen Undaalan. Back to my failures."

"No one wishes to carry the burden of these times. We only wish to experience the enjoyable, but without the pain and suffering, that joy will sour. Without you, the pain and suffering will swallow all of Undaalan, and not just the Undaari, but the Yaxkin as well. It's not fair to be chosen to carry this burden, but it's never placed on those who are incapable."

Tears began to stream down Jarreck's face. His heart ached as he rose from the table. His father was right. All he wanted to do was hold his parents tight and never let go. But there was nothing else that could be done. He smiled at his mother.

"I love you so much, mom. I miss you every day."

His mother smiled back at him. "I'll always be with you, son. We both will. You've made us both so proud of what you've done for our people. The world is a much better place for having you in it."

Jace spoke next, "I'll walk you to the Entai. That's where you'll be able to return to the real world. You've done well. Better than I could've ever wished. You're a much stronger person than I ever was. Continue to trust in the Alackai. She has chosen you for a reason. You will not fail."

They reached the Entai. The sky was still purple, but much darker. Jarreck turned and hugged his father.

"Thank you, dad. I needed this more than you could ever know. You have gotten me back in the right mindset and given me hope. I'll make you proud."

"You've always made me proud, my son. I love you. Alackai's Grace guide you."

"And her Light protect you."

Jace smiled one last time. "It always does here."

Jarreck place his hand on the Entai. He felt its energy surge into him. He awoke with a start. It was dark in the clearing now. He turned back to the cabin, overgrown and abandoned again. That reprieve was just what he had needed.

Wait. There was a light inside the cabin now. Slowly, he made his way to the entrance. There were voices inside. No one else should be here. He drew his blade, calling upon the Alackai to support him.

He entered the cabin to find Councilor Gierdahl sitting at the dining room table. He was not alone. Gierdahl stood and gestured for

Jarreck to take the seat next to him.  No one spoke to him.  The silence was unnerving.  But it was nothing compared to the High Councilor sitting at the table with them.

# Chapter 36
## Challenges

Dralvic let out a chilling laugh. Lingdon felt it penetrate into his heart. His stomach sank as he realized no help had come. Quite the opposite in fact.

"No! Go away! Leave him alone!" he screamed as he leaned over Jarreck protectively.

"I'm not done with him yet," Dralvic threatened.

"What more could you possibly need with him?"

"Everything. He's mine until I'm done with him. And when I'm done, you won't recognize him anymore. Now move before I make you."

"No!" Lingdon screamed again, a storm raging inside.

He could feel her presence within him more readily than before. The Alackai had chosen him, and she would support him in his fight. Dralvic stepped back from him as the Alackai coursed through his body, tinging his skin with purple. To Lingdon's dismay, there was a smile on Dralvic's face as he stepped back.

"You want a fight, huh? I hope you're ready."

Lingdon pooled all his energy in his hands and thrust them forward. Purple energy erupted forth, shooting at Dralvic's head. With an athleticism unbecoming of a short, cloaked body, Dralvic spun away while using crimson flames to deflect the attack.

Again, Lingdon struck at Dralvic's new location. He could not let that evil man hurt Jarreck anymore. As Dralvic dodged again, Lingdon attacked again. The short man was fast, but Lingdon was going to catch him. Attack. Dodge. Attack. Dodge.

Hit. Lingdon's purple energy finally struck pay dirt. Dralvic was caught by surprise as the energy blew him back into the cavern's cold lake.

Lingdon stopped to watch the waters of the lake as the ripples settled. He had beaten Dralvic. Without the Lightning Bow.

But the hair on the back of Lingdon's neck still stood on edge. He could feel a dread inside him still. It could not be over. He looked around the cavern, waiting for Dralvic to attack.

That was when he noticed the damage he had caused around the Heart. There were smoking craters from his attacks. Statues were shattered along the cavern walls. The Heart itself had been knocked from its altar. He had nearly destroyed the Alackai's birthplace. What had he done? Even if he beat Dralvic, what was the cost?

Red lightning exploded from the surface of the lake. Water erupted like a geyser. Dralvic flew from the depths of the lake and landed on the shore, a sly smile across his face.

"Some champion you are. How like your father, a failure. Time to show you what it means to use the Alackai."

Red lightning shot from Dralvic's exposed hands. It ripped through Lingdon, throwing him back against the cavern wall. *Crack.* Something broke in his back. The Alackai rushed through his body, staving off the pain.

With a groan, he managed to stand. Dralvic let out a laugh. Lingdon threw more purple energy toward his enemy. It was far duller than his previous attacks, his energy being siphoned off. Dralvic smacked aside his attack with a glowing red hand.

"I'm impressed you still have fight in you, as pathetic as it is. You're stronger than your father was. He was wise to hide your existence. Had we known, we'd have ensured you were killed with him."

"You didn't kill my dad," Lingdon countered, throwing more pure magic at Dralvic. "The Yaxkin did. I was there. They enslaved me."

Another attack, but none of them were strong enough to hurt Dralvic. Dralvic walked forward nonchalantly, his cloak no longer dripping with lake water. The glowing ruby eyes slowly approaching in the low light shook Lingdon to his core.

"The Yaxkin were hired by Vreeham. With an ineptitude only he can find, he failed to end the family line. Another failure that I must now remedy."

Dralvic struck again. Lingdon drew his arms in, creating a wall of purple energy. It was barely enough to hold back the scarlet lightning. Dralvic struck again. Lingdon held the barricade. It was weakening. Another strike.

His shield shattered before him, and he collapsed. The lightning didn't connect, but he felt the pain regardless. His magic was broken. He had nothing left to fight with.

"Broken already? Pathetic. The Alackai was mistaken to choose you as her champion. You are nothing."

"You won't win. There are others who will fight."

"They will fight. And they will die. You get to watch as Jarreck dies next. Then you can die knowing you failed him as well."

"No..." Lingdon said weakly.

He started crawling toward Jarreck. He could not have failed. Jarreck stirred in front of him as he crawled. Dralvic watched him slowly close the gap. Before he reached his destination though, Dralvic stepped forward, cutting him off.

"Now, now. Don't think you can protect him. It's too late for that."

"I will never give up..." Lingdon said, continuing to crawl around him.

Dralvic didn't stop him, just walked alongside him. It was almost like having a friend walk by his side. A friend that could kill him any second.

"Why do you still struggle? You are broken. Beaten. Left without the Alackai to aid you anymore."

"I never had the Alackai before. I am more than just her."

Dralvic laughed. He nodded his satisfaction with the answer.

"You know. I must admit, I admire your fight. Perhaps I will show you mercy and end you first."

Lingdon ignored the threat. One arm moved forward and grabbed the ground. Then the next. Slowly, he moved forward. Until finally, mercifully, he reached Jarreck. He placed a hand on Jarreck's chest. He could still feel the rise and fall of his chest. He hadn't succumbed to his ailments yet.

"So, you wish to die together? So be it."

Dralvic drew a dagger from within his robes. How was he going to stop him now? Think. Breathe. Feel. He might be broken, but Jarreck was only hurt. He did not have much left, but maybe...

He gathered every last drop of the Alackai he still had within him. The ache in his back intensified. With extensive effort, he pushed the last of her energy out of his hand and into Jarreck's chest. He looked up at Dralvic.

With a scream of rage, Dralvic plunged the knife toward Jarreck. With the last of his strength, Lingdon shoved himself over Jarreck, the knife piercing his back. He felt himself scream but could not hear the sound.

Blackness consumed his vision. He felt his life drain away, leaving an empty body behind, shielding Jarreck.

Jarreck gingerly accepted the seat he was offered. *What is going on? Why are they here?* He glanced back and forth between the councilors, waiting for one of them to speak. He scanned the rest of the cabin while he awaited answers. Nothing else seemed out of place inside his childhood home.

"Jarreck. Your work has been exceedingly disappointing," Gierdahl said, taking the lead.

"You've jeopardized the integrity of the Society and risked the entire Undaari nation," added Vreeham.

"It's time we discuss your future with the order," finished Gierdahl.

"Disappointing? I have risked my life in the hopes of *saving* the Society and the Undaari people!" growled Jarreck, incredulously.

"Your insubordination has undermined the efforts of the Council to safeguard our future. Now you leave us open to the war Dralvic would bring upon us," Gierdahl said.

"As a result, you have been found guilty of treason to the Society and will be immediately expelled. You have one chance to appeal this decision," Vreeham said with a smile.

"You're the one in bed with the enemy! You're the one feeding Dralvic information and helping him attack our people!"

"No, I am saving our people. Cooperation has guaranteed the safety of our people. But your moronic actions have jeopardized everything," Vreeham corrected.

"Your only choice, if you wish to avoid exile, is to join Dralvic as well. This is your one chance at appeal. He will teach you more about the Alackai than any Skovi has ever known. We can grow so much with his help," Gierdahl offered, pleading with his eyes.

Gierdahl had been his oldest friend and mentor. What had caused him to switch sides? He was the wisest living man he knew. He could never fall for a simple trick. None of this made any sense to Jarreck.

"Now you must decide. Give up this one-man war against our savior, or be exiled from our nation, never to see the Lenakai Forest again," Vreeham stated.

"I can't join him. I can't believe you both turned your backs on our people.  They are doomed unless we can stop Dralvic.  He can't be trusted. He'll destroy us all."

"No, I won't," said a cold voice behind him.

Jarreck stood so violently his chair flew back and toppled over.  He turned to find Dralvic standing in the doorway of the cabin.  Without hesitation, Jarreck called upon the Alackai and lashed out with blue flames.

*Dralvic caught the flames.*  With a laugh, he stepped inside the cabin.  Dralvic held the fire in his hand then *breathed them in.  What was happening?  How was he doing that?*

"I will never betray the Undaari," said Jarreck defiantly, holding his head high.

All three men around him laughed.  The councilors at the table stood from their seats.  Stepping up next to him, each councilors place a hand on one of his shoulders.

"If we are forced to exile you, he will kill you.  And he won't be merciful with it.  Please, Jarreck, join him.  Do it for me.  You've always trusted me before.  Trust me now," Gierdahl pleaded.

Jarreck's shoulders slumped.  It seemed he had no choice.  He wouldn't survive this fight otherwise.  Maybe if he agreed, he could get close enough to Dralvic to assassinate him.  He might even pick up a thing or two along the way.

Slowly, he nodded, but he did not give up.  He stepped forward and saw the triumphant smile on Dralvic's face.  It pierced his heart.  He felt like he betrayed everyone on Undaalan.  He was a coward.

"Good, Jarreck.  You made the decision your father couldn't.  Now you don't have to be wasted.  Come, let's go save the Undaari," Vreeham said.

Those words stabbed like a dagger to the back.  His father had been so strong.  Jarreck was a disappointment and brought shame to his family. His head sank lower.

"Broken already?  I expected more," Dralvic said, his eyebrow cocked.

Jarreck drew his sigridir and lunged for Dralvic's throat.  Dralvic's eyes grew wide.  Red flames tore into Jarreck's side before he could connect. He tumbled to the ground but quickly recovered.

He popped up, conjuring cyan flames in his left hand while wielding his blade in the right.  He stepped toward Dralvic again but stopped.  Those flames had not come from him.  Dralvic had been caught unawares.  He turned to look at the councilors.  They both had crimson flames in their hands.

"That's not possible."

"Anything is possible with the Alackai if you follow Dralvic. We never have to die. Never have to lose our Grace. We can ascend beyond anything previously thought possible," Vreeham bragged.

That was it. He no longer had a choice. He attacked without regard to his own safety. Dralvic stepped back and watched as he targeted Vreeham. The High Councilor was the betrayer. He must die first if the Undaari were to survive.

The sigridir sliced through the air at Vreeham's head. The old man was slow and screamed, bringing scarlet flames to bear. Despite his enhanced Alackai abilities, Vreeham was too slow. The sigridir cut into Vreeham's skull.

The High Councilor fell to the ground, the sigridir still stuck. Gierdahl charged forward, throwing fire at Jarreck's back. His cape caught fire and he unclipped it while turning to attack. Dralvic was still standing back.

Jarreck turned and engaged Gierdahl. Red and blue flames clashed in the tiny cabin space. It had already been burnt out, there was nothing flammable remaining. Jarreck outmatched the old Skovi. He attacked, ducked, slipped to the side, and attacked again. Cerulean flames chewed into the Councilor. Gierdahl screamed and turned away.

Jarreck closed in, wrapping his arm around Gierdahl's ancient neck. He tightened it, cutting off his mentor's airway. Tears flowed from Jarreck's eyes as he crushed the old man's throat.

"I'm sorry, my friend."

He slowly lowered Gierdahl's body to the floor next to his blackened cape. Despite their new powers, their bodies were not ready for that sort of combat. His next challenge would be far more difficult. He turned to see Dralvic smiling.

"Have you gotten your revenge? Do you feel better now?"

"Better is not a word I would use to describe my feelings," he said, encasing his hands in blue flames. "Killing you might help though."

Jarreck charged. Dralvic called upon the Alackai, his corrupted version, causing his eyes to glow red. As Jarreck charged in, red lightning fired out. He'd seen this before and fell to his knees, sliding under the attack. With aqua flames still surrounding his hand, he popped up and swung at Dralvic. Dralvic flipped back, dodging the attack with a laugh.

"I'm impressed. You killed your mentor without a second thought. Why don't you join me, and I can show you how to be even more powerful?

Who knows, maybe you'll learn so much you can outgrow me. Then maybe you can kill me."

"Never. I already told you. I'll stop you from destroying the Undaari!"

"I'm here to save them, not destroy them."

"Save them from who? The Noxxons? *You* control them, remember?" Jarreck snarled.

"From themselves."

Jarreck swung again, unleashing a flurry of flaming blue punches. Dralvic ducked and dodged, using crimson flames of his own to shield himself as he moved. Jarreck pressed in closer, the Alackai coursing through him, becoming intoxicating. She was in control now.

The cerulean flames were coupled with cyan lightning. Dralvic broke a sweat defending himself. This was it. Jarreck's chance to defeat him. He struck wildly, breaking through Dralvic's defenses. Dralvic fell on his back, obsidian cloak singed.

"Enough," Dralvic yelled. "You've had your fun. I have too. Now, it's over."

The Black Scythe materialized in his hand. Dralvic returned to the offensive, swinging and twirling the Scythe around. Jarreck desperately deflected attack after attack before Dralvic connected with his shoulder. The butt of the Scythe knocked him backward. Dralvic leapt forward bringing the blade down at his chest. He stopped just before contact.

"Last chance, young Skovi. Join me."

"Kill me. I'll never betray my people."

"So be it," Dralvic said before driving the blade into Jarreck's chest.

Jarreck could feel his soul being ripped out. The Black Scythe drew him in, shrouding him in darkness. But he was not dead. This was worse.

# Chapter 37

## Master

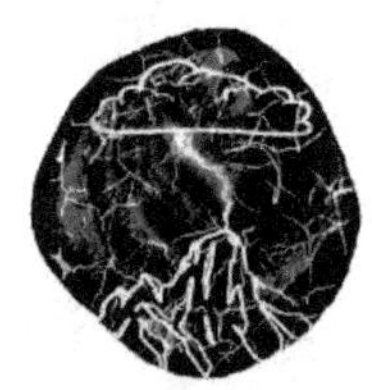

He heard a whisper in the distance.  A mere echo. *You have passed...*

His eyes snapped open.  Lingdon wasn't sure if this time was real or not.  He slowly scanned around the dark cavern.  Visibility was poor, but he was sure he did not see anyone else.  Anyone except the giant stone creature behind him.  There was a faint light outside the mouth of the cave. *Is it only just now morning?*  It felt like he had been within the Alackai for at least a day. *Maybe it's the next morning.*

The Alkaios lifted its head to look at Lingdon.  Despite the news about commanding the creature, he was still scared of it.  He had secretly hoped it had left the cave.  Lingdon cautiously stood in the water, not wanting to disturb the slumbering beast.  The Alkaios slowly stood as well.  He had the guardian's undivided attention.

He froze.  The creature was beyond intimidating.  Lingdon was barely any bigger than its fang.  After a few moments, Lingdon worked up the courage to move toward it.  The creature was standing up fully, filling the mouth of the cave. Lingdon reminded himself that if the creature wanted him dead, he would already be dead.

Lingdon inched forward, not daring to make any sudden movements. He felt his heart beating in his throat. The Alkaios watched his every move, purple eyes tracking him.  Lingdon's breathing was heavy.  As he neared the creature, he held out his hand, trying not to let it tremble.  He was still an arm's length away when the Alkaios reached its nose forward to touch Lingdon's hand.

The Alkaios' scars began to glow dimly around his hand.  He could feel warmth and energy emanating from the mighty beast.  Lingdon began to pat the creature affectionately. He could feel the bond that Unathi had said was there. Lingdon smiled with a newfound confidence. The Alkaios bent down, indicating to Lingdon that it could be ridden.

Lingdon climbed on board as though he were climbing a rock wall. He found a seat on the massive creature near the front pair of legs. It seemed to be the most natural place to ride. Once he felt secure, he spoke weakly, still unsure the creature would listen.

"I need to find Jarreck."

That was all the Alkaios needed. It turned its massive body around in the cave and sprinted toward the exit. It took one giant leap out of the mouth and spread its enormous, rocky wings. They climbed high into the air as it found its heading without further instruction.

Jarreck gasped as his eyes reopened.

*You have passed...*

*Was it real this time?* The night was fading away. Everything seemed back to normal. He was back in his childhood clearing. He could see the first light of dawn on the western horizon. He had been within the Alackai for a while. It had certainly felt much longer though.

The cabin behind him was still ruined. He saw the colorful zakeri circling around, watching his back. It noticed he had awoken and approached him. It nuzzled its large head under Jarreck's chin. He was not used to receiving such affection from a zakeri. They rarely bonded with anyone enough to be affectionate.

He rubbed the zakeri's head and thanked it for watching his back. It was a truly beautiful creature. He admired its majestic nature for a moment before turning back to the Entai. There was something different about it now. The fractures glowed bright in the last vestiges of darkness. As he studied it, he noticed an outline forming in the trunk. He watched as it took shape.

A door formed in the white bark. It swung open, revealing a hidden compartment inside. This Entai held the Lightning Bow within it. The Alackai had kept it hidden and protected here, awaiting her chosen protector to return and collect it. He reached into the opening and wrapped his hand around the tall longbow, withdrawing it from its resting place.

He could not believe he held it within his hands. This was the most powerful weapon ever created, scarred with the pure purple of the Alackai.

It was the same weapon that had been used millennia ago to overthrow the corrupt First Society.  He was in awe of the history of the bow in his hand. He studied it for another few moments.

The bow had been carved from a single branch of this Entai.  Its string was made of a golden fiber, similar to hair.  There was a bloodstain on its shaft where its creator had given his blood to unite himself with the Alackai.  The bow was cold to the touch, unlike nearly everything else imbued with the Alackai.  He suspected this was because he was not meant to wield its power, merely transport it to its true champion.

He turned to the pink striped zakeri, realizing he would still need to find Lingdon.  He had thought the creature guarding the Heart of the Alackai had eaten him, but his father had made it seem as though Lingdon were still alive.  Jarreck hoped he was.  He wondered where he would begin his search when the zakeri backed away from him.

Jarreck raised an eyebrow in confusion.  *Why is it acting that way?* As he stepped forward to try to wrangle it, it took flight.  After all its help, it abandoned him so close to the end.  Jarreck did not know how he would manage to find Lingdon in time to save his people without the zakeri.  He watched as it disappeared in the distance.  He realized it was heading toward Entfall.  Perhaps the Alackai needed it there more than with him.

Jarreck took stock of his situation as the sun rose in the sky.  He decided the logical starting point for his search would be back at the Scarred Mountain.  That was where he had last seen Lingdon, and that was where the guardian lived.  It was likely he would still be near there after everything that had happened.  The walk would take ages though.

Jarreck took his first steps of the trek through the clearing when he saw something flying toward him in the distance.  At first, he assumed it was the zakeri coming back, thankful it had decided to return.  Then he realized, whatever it was approached from a completely different direction. Something else was coming toward him.  He stopped to watch.

As it got closer, it dawned on him what it was.  His heart sank.  The Guardian of the Heart had come back for him.  It must be there to finish him off after he had luckily escaped.  Maybe the zakeri had fled knowing it was coming.  Jarreck sprinted for the trees, hoping to hide from this monstrous beast.  He had not even made it to the forest's edge when the creature swooped down into the clearing, landing next to the cabin.

Jarreck was about to dive for cover when he noticed there was a rider on the back of the creature.  He was very confused by the prospect of anyone being able to ride that thing.  His confusion increased when he realized that the rider was none other than Lingdon himself. As he watched Lingdon dismount the massive, stony creature in front of him, he realized it all made perfect sense.

Lingdon was the Alackai's champion. The creature was the guardian of her Heart. It would not be a stretch for the Alackai to Grace Lingdon with the ability to command the monster. As Lingdon approached him, Jarreck could tell there was a new strength and confidence to him. There was another change as well.

His irises were no longer speckled with purple; they were completely purple. This was the man who would save all of Undaalan from Dralvic, and Jarreck had to guide him down this path. Jarreck moved toward Lingdon with a big smile on his face.

"I'm glad to see you survived being eaten by this creature."

Lingdon smiled in return. "I'm glad I was able to find you. Rather, the Alkaios was able to find you. It'll help us on our quest."

"I'm glad it's on our side now. That creature was the only thing that seemed to cause Dralvic any sort of fear or hesitation."

"My father said the guardian isn't powerful enough to defeat Dralvic, not while he has his weapon."

"Maybe not, but this is," Jarreck said as he held up the Lightning Bow.

He reached out toward Lingdon with it, beckoning for him to take it. Lingdon hesitated then cautiously accepted it. As Lingdon's hand wrapped around the bow, the scars began to glow bright purple. It had been returned to its rightful owner.

Jarreck was in awe of the sight before him. Lingdon looked up at Jarreck, his eyes glowing purple as well. Lingdon's face turned to worry. The bow's glow began to fade, as did his eyes.

"I'm sorry, but I still don't know what I'm doing. What is this? My father said you could teach me."

Jarreck hesitated. "It's the Lightning Bow. It's your weapon against Dralvic. But I'm not sure we have much time to train, Lingdon. Ambrecia is in danger. And what do you mean your father told you? I thought he died years ago."

"My father *is* dead. But the Alackai showed him to me."

Jarreck understood. They had *both* been given this opportunity.

"I connected with her for the first time in the lake inside that cave. The Alkaios brought me there and pushed me into the water. I also met Unathi, the man who created the Lightning Bow and defeated the First

Society.  It was a surreal experience.

"My father said that he had learned from someone named Jace, but when it was time to strike, he hesitated too long and Dralvic was able to escape.  He said that I cannot hesitate and fail like he did and that you could teach me and be my guide."

Jarreck was at a loss.  *How am I supposed to train him in time? There's so little of it remaining.*  He looked at Lingdon.  He could see strength and desire in him.

Jarreck realized Lingdon at least had a little training and experience with the Alackai.  It would be suicide to send the boy against Dralvic without something more.  They only had time for a couple quick lessons, though.  He hoped it would be enough.

"Jace is my father.  I got to speak with him as you got to speak with yours.  How interesting that our families are so intertwined like this."

Lingdon's jaw dropped.

Jarreck continued, "You must trust the Alackai.  She will guide you in your struggle if you listen to her.  You are lucky.  You get to learn this at a young age.  I only recently discovered her true nature.  You have the power inside you to do everything the Alackai has asked of you.  You will be her champion and protect her as she has protected our people."

Jarreck led Lingdon through a few beginner's exercises.  He took to them naturally.  He was able to produce purple energy with ease.  Jarreck did not teach him the rigid movements of the Society, rather how to feel the ebb and flow of the Alackai's energy.

Lingdon's power was far purer than anything Jarreck could conjure.  Where Jarreck was only able to produce flames and at times lightning, Lingdon could produce beams of pure energy.  He could create thick walls to defend himself just as easily.

There was little for Jarreck to truly teach the boy.  It was a matter of instilling the confidence and knowledge he needed to use his abilities when the time came.  They only trained for a couple short hours before Jarreck realized they needed to start wrapping things up.

The Noxxons had been moving west along the Black Peaks.  He had not known their pace, but knew that at a normal pace, it could still be another day or two until they reached Ambrecia.  He looked at his new apprentice.  This boy was meant to be the best of them all.

"It's almost time that we go.  We didn't have much time to begin with.  Will your friend eat me if I try to join you on it?"

Lingdon laughed.  "I hope not.  It's already let you live once.  And it's meant to follow my command."

Jarreck was relieved; he did not want to have to find his own ride to Ambrecia.  He just had to make sure Lingdon was ready and his mind clear.

"Do you have any questions before we go?"

# Chapter 38
## Everlasting

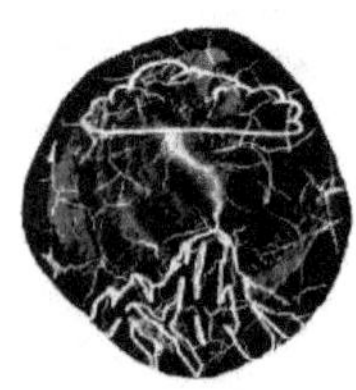

Kiva was still out of breath from her battle and could only smile back at Jerykka. They leaned on each other, both exhausted from the efforts they had given to save the Undaari. Jerykka led her through the main hall past the other Undaari and humans gathered around. They were all cheering for her. They were obviously happy to have survived and showed their appreciation for what she had done.

Kiva locked eyes with Nazario, who gave her a large, warm smile and raised his hand in wave. She wanted to stop and speak with him. She wanted to hug him and thank him for saving her. She just wanted to see him but knew that Jerykka needed her first.

As the two walked through the hall, Kiva expected them to turn and head toward the medical bay. Instead, Jerykka took her on a different path. It took a moment before Kiva realized where she was being led. They were going to the Entai. Again. Both of them needed the Grace of the Alackai to recover from the battle. This had not been the final battle of the war. Not with Dralvic still out there.

They slowly made their way to the chamber housing the Entai. They nearly collapsed at the base of the trunk, exhausted from the hike. Jerykka and Kiva smiled at each other again, then both reached out to touch the Entai. They whispered their thanks to the Alackai and took comfortable positions to meditate. The Entai's scars began to glow, and celeste tendrils came out of the ground to connect with both.

❧❧❧

Jaina and Brandon met Intayr at the doors of the great hall. He was still in shock over what he had witnessed. Commander Khasan of the Undaari Army had joined him. They were discussing what to do with their prisoner. Khasan looked up as they approached, examining the humans with curiosity, then reached an arm out and introduced himself.

"I'm Commander Khasan of the Undaari Army. It's a pleasure to finally meet you. The King spoke highly of you."

They each took his arm in turn and introduced themselves.

Jaina added, "We're all so thankful for your assistance. None of us would be alive if not for you."

Commander Khasan laughed. "We barely did anything to be honest. That woman did all the heavy lifting. I imagine at the rate she was going, that Skovi would have defeated the entire remaining Noxxon force."

Jaina nodded in agreement. "Kiva has demonstrated true selflessness and power with her actions. We all owe her as well. But if I might throw my opinion out there, I feel this abomination needs to be destroyed immediately. I've dedicated my life to diplomacy and finding peaceful resolutions to conflict, but that thing serves *no* purpose in life."

Intayr nodded his agreement, but the Commander argued, "We could question it for information and even study how it got its powers. It may prove useful to the Undaari."

Brandon countered, "I would t-... trust Jaina, she would never say anything like that if it weren't true. That thing will n-... never answer any questions you have. And the way it got its power was through dark, arcane magic. That's of n-... no use to the Undaari. I'm a man of knowledge and its pursuit, but I know that this thing needs to be d-... destroyed."

Khasan looked to Intayr. "Do you think we could get anything out of it? We might not ever get a chance like this again."

Intayr shook his head. "I trust their opinion. It's weak right now, but it'll heal. I don't want to be around when it does. These two have had more dealings with these things than I have. The King and Warden both trust their opinions as well. I believe Jerykka would destroy it if she were here."

Commander Khasan begrudgingly nodded. He gave the order for the Shields to end it. Jaina watched in horror as they pressed their blue barriers against the Staff Bearer, forcing it to the ground. It crumpled under their strength, and they still continued to press. They combined their strength and continued to collapse the energy barrier in on the Naaji. The Staff Bearer howled in pain.

Jaina averted her eyes as the Staff Bearer slowly began to crack and split apart. It was squashed underneath the shields against the stone ground of Entfall. The Shields reduced it to a bloody mass of skin, bones, and metal. It was a brutal, painful death, but not one anyone felt was unjust.

When the task was done, Jaina changed the subject. "There's still another battle to be had, I fear. Kiva told us there's another threat to the Undaari still. A man named Dralvic. He's the one who's behind the Noxxon attacks, but he hasn't shown himself in battle yet. And he has a new weapon that he's been trying to recover from an ancient artifact."

Commander Khasan was not happy. "I had hoped this war was over. I haven't received any new orders from Ambrecia. Our messenger should have returned by now. We don't have any zakeri here to relay orders more quickly."

Intayr replied, "That's unfortunate. We need to refortify Entfall and prepare for another attack. The Noxxons have to come through us if they want to attack our lands. If this Dralvic is still out there, we need to be ready for another fearsome attack."

Commander Khasan nodded in agreement. "We'll begin preparations for defense of the keep. There can't be many Noxxons left. We should be able to defend this location if we can refortify things."

Brandon shook his head. "No, it's t-... too simple. Why would he att-... attack here again? If he knew he'd have this w-... weapon and wanted to attack here, he would have waited and u-... used everything at once. If he has this weapon now, then I feel the attack here was just a d-... diversion."

Intayr disagreed. "A diversion from what? As long as Entfall stands, there's magic in the river that prevents anyone from crossing. The bridges to cross would be retracted if the Noxxons ever got close. There's no way for them to penetrate our lands."

Jaina spoke up. "But they already have. They retrieved the artifact from the Lenakai Forest. And we've seen they can now command the Alackai. What would stop them from using it to cross the river at another location?"

Intayr's eyes opened wide. Commander Khasan's face fell. Khasan turned and ran toward his troops. He began barking orders and his warriors immediately reacted, forming tight ranks.

Nazario had been near the war table when he heard the shouting.

He could not understand a lot of it, since he had removed his exosuit, translator included. He made his way to Brandon, Jaina, and Intayr. "What's happening? You all seem worried."

Brandon responded, "We b-... believe the attack here may have just been a diversion while Dralvic set a t-... trap elsewhere. Commander Khasan is preparing his troops to move out."

Nazario cursed under his breath. "I had been hoping this entire ordeal would be over, but you're right. That Dralvic guy is still out there, possessing Garren's body. We have to stop him and get Garren back. I can't imagine where else he'd strike other than the heart of the Undaari: Ambrecia. We have to help them."

Intayr raised an eyebrow as Nazario spoke. He whispered something to Jaina. Nazario could not understand what had been said. He looked to Jaina expectantly and she began to translate between Nazario and Intayr.

Having to wait for another person to translate would be a problem. Nazario rushed back into the hall with Jaina following. He tracked down Piers, who was catching up with Monkley on all the events that had been happening.

"Sergeant Piers, where's the *Inquisitor*? I need another suit. We have more work to do."

Piers looked back at Nazario uncomfortably. "It's north in the Lenakai Forest, but I can't bring it back. The damage from the Staff Bearers was worse than we thought, and I had very limited time to fix it before the Noxxons got to it. It blew several power conduits in the system during its escape, which took out more systems, including communications and weapons. It's even worse now. I can't bring the ship back, and even if I could, I don't know that I could safely land it in this courtyard by remote."

Nazario understood the dilemma. "It's okay Sergeant. We'll just have to stop by on our way up to Ambrecia... if there's time. Come with me. Both of you."

Jerykka and Kiva reentered the main hall from the back passages. They both looked strong and rejuvenated. Nazario suspected they had gone to the Entai to recharge. He wished he had the ability to do something like that. He was thankful to see both women back in action. He had grown fond of the Undaari people, Kiva in particular. Nazario had witnessed undeniable strength and determination in her, even if she could not see it herself.

Nazario turned and made his way to meet them with Jaina dutifully trailing. When he got close, he saw Kiva's face light up with a smile. She closed the distance with a spring in her step and embraced him in a bear hug. He was happy she was still around and enjoyed being held by her as he squeezed her back. It was odd being so much shorter than her. His arms were at her waist while his face rested at her chest. He did not mind. He could feel strength and comfort in the hug.

After their embrace ended, Jerykka placed a hand on his shoulder. "It's good to see you've recovered. Have we heard anything about Jarreck?"

Jaina continued to translate for him.

Nazario shook his head. "I'm sorry, Master Jerykka; there's been no word. But Intayr is just outside the doors with Brandon. We have more bad news. We fear Dralvic may be moving on Ambrecia."

Both Kiva and Jerykka looked at him with puzzlement on their faces.

Jerykka shook her head. "No, that's not possible. They would *have* to defeat Entfall to be able to cross the Entfall River because of..."

Jerykka trailed off. Nazario could see the realization in her eyes. The Noxxons had found a way to use the Alackai. They could have easily used it to cross the river unscathed. Jerykka yelled something under her breath. She quickly ran out the door to find Intayr.

Jaina looked guiltily at Nazario. "I didn't catch what she said. The translators weren't able to interpret it..."

Nazario narrowed his eyes at Jaina before the three of them followed Jerykka to the courtyard. Nazario could see Intayr busily talking with Brandon. Intayr looked up when they reached him.

"Master Jerykka, the Undaari Army is forming up. They're about to head for Ambrecia. We fear there may be an imminent Noxxon attack."

"I know, Intayr. Thank you for beginning preparation. I need this keep refortified. I want *your* efforts to focus on that. I'll work with Commander Khasan and the humans to get aid to Ambrecia."

Jerykka strode away from the main hall and toward the Undaari Army forming up in the courtyard. Nazario continued to follow, intent on helping wherever necessary, but struggled to keep up with her furious pace. Jaina could barely translate fast enough for him. He really needed a new suit.

Jerykka reached Commander Khasan, and they locked arms.

Commander Khasan spoke first, "I'm taking the army to Ambrecia. I haven't received word from them yet, but I fear that may never come. It's overdue at this point. We can't stay here to help."

"I understand, Commander. I'm not here to argue that. I simply wish for you to leave a contingent here to help assist with the repairs and to fortify Entfall in case we're wrong."

Commander Khasan hesitated for a moment.  "I can leave five hundred warriors to assist.  I fear that any more would have too big an impact on our force.  We *must* be going now.  We have to cross the river before nightfall."

Before the Commander could turn back to his soldiers, they spotted a zakeri coming in for a landing, its rider's white cape flapping in the wind.

"Ferani!" Jerykka exclaimed.  "What are you doing here?"

"The Noxxons.  They're at Ambrecia's walls.  We need the army there.  We don't have the warriors to defend the city or our people.  Please hurry."

The Commander needed no further convincing.  He quickly turned and pulled a gold horn from his belt.  He blew into it, issuing orders to the army to begin marching.  As promised, he left five hundred warriors behind to assist Entfall.

"This zakeri needs to rest before I return.  Are there any others here that I may take back?" Ferani asked.

Jerykka shook her head.  "No.  But come with me and we'll get it food and a short rest.  We'll need your help while you wait."

"I can't wait.  I must return to the King.  He's in grave danger."

"I'm aware of the situation, Ferani," Jerykka countered.  "But you won't do him any good if your zakeri dies in flight from being pushed back into service too quickly.  You can be of service here."

Ferani grumbled his protest but followed the Warden's orders.  He followed Jerykka back through the fortress, zakeri in tow.  When they reached the others, Jerykka informed Intayr he would have fresh assistance repairing the keep and sent him to organize the effort.  Jerykka also told the ten Shields that were still standing by that they were needed with the army and dispatched them to follow.

Jerykka looked to Kiva.  "You *have* to get to Ambrecia fast.  You will go with Ferani as soon as the zakeri has had time to rest.  Nazario, you need to go with her.  Is there any chance of using your ship to get there?"

Nazario shook his head.  He had already thought of that.  That would have made things easier.

"I'm sorry, but our ship is too badly damaged at the moment.  I'll send Piers to try and get her in the air again.  It'll take time, though."  He looked directly to Jaina and added, "Too bad the Senate blocked Bastion on the transporters.  Having a ship equipped with those would really help us about now.  Stupid budgets keeping us from getting all the equipment we need."

She shrugged before looking back at the Undaari.  Kiva was clearly worried they would not make it in time to save Ambrecia.

Nazario looked at her, concerned.  "Are you all right, Kiva?"

She shook her head.  "No.  Our people are in peril.  The King is like a father to me and he's in even greater danger.  I can't lose him.  I already lost my real father and Jarreck is still missing.  I have to get back and protect him."

Jerykka grabbed Kiva by the shoulders and looked her dead in the eyes.  "You *will* protect him.  Like you protected all these people.  We'll get you there in time."

Before anyone else could say another word, another zakeri appeared over the ramparts.  It landed quickly next to Kiva.

"Jarreck?" Kiva asked, but the zakeri had no rider.

Nazario watched as Kiva's body slumped.

She reached over to the zakeri and scratched its chin.  "Can you take me to Ambrecia?"

The zakeri lowered itself so that the Skovi could mount it.  Somehow, this feline looked fresh after its flight.  Kiva beckoned for Nazario to join her, but he shook his head.

"Take Jaina and Brandon with you, they'll help you protect the King.  I'll be right behind you with Ferani.  I need to take a detour on my way there and would only slow you down."

Kiva did not argue.  Ferani started to.  Nazario quickly cut him off.

"I'm sorry, Ferani.  But only you and Kiva can fly the zakeri.  Kiva can do more to protect the King.  We'll be right behind her."

Ferani was visibly fuming but did not argue.  Kiva reached a hand down toward Nazario.  He grabbed it with his own and smiled.

He planted a quick kiss on it before saying, "Try not to do anything too reckless.  I would like to spend more time with you after this is over."

Kiva blushed.  "I'll do my best."

Jaina looked awkward translating this for him.  Monkley rolled his eyes from Nazario's side.  She and Brandon mounted the zakeri behind Kiva and the three of them took flight.  They were on a direct course for Ambrecia.  Nazario had Piers take over translation duties for him.

"I need you two to join Ferani and I.  We'll stop at the *Inquisitor* then head for Ambrecia as well.  This war is about to end, one way or another."

Jerykka echoed, "One way or another. I'll catch up to the Undaari Army and march to Ambrecia with them. Intayr will oversee Entfall while I'm gone. Let's end this."

There was nothing left to say. Ferani, Nazario, Piers, and Monkley made their way over to where the zakeri was being housed inside the main hall. The stables had been destroyed in the attack, so they had left it resting inside. It looked up at their arrival, ready to fly again.

Ferani led them back out into the courtyard where they mounted the majestic zakeri. They took flight, making the short trip north to Eilenar. The Undaari Army would be arriving there soon. The *Inquisitor* had landed in a field to the west of town. The sun set on their right as they rode.

There was a large group of Undaari inspecting the ship, unsure of what it was or where it had come from. When they landed the zakeri next to it, Ferani immediately made his way to the spectators and asked them to stay clear. Nazario quickly equipped himself with a spare Reliant Exosuit over his charred maroon uniform.

"Too bad we don't have any Valiant Exosuits. Could really do with the full armor and dual Valor cannons."

"Couldn't we all," Piers agreed.

"Or some Grav Boots. Then I could fly myself to Ambrecia."

"Wouldn't that be something," Monkley laughed as Nazario finished equipping himself.

Nazario wondered if the Grav Boots could keep up with a zakeri. Technically, anti-gravity boots, but still, they allowed a person to fly. A privately owned set might be on the *Jericho*. Maybe he could test that out in the future. He gave Piers additional orders.

"I need you to stay with the ship. Get her flying again."

"Yes, sir."

Nazario's face became very solemn. "Sergeant Piers, listen to me. The Noxxons *cannot* win this. Get her flying and get her talking. I need you in low orbit monitoring the battle. If the Noxxons win, if they kill all the Undaari in Ambrecia, get the fleet to end them. They must not be allowed to destroy the rest of the Undaari. That's the biggest priority."

Sergeant Piers replied, "I understand, sir. It won't come to that, though. I've seen these Undaari fight. They'll win this."

"I sure hope you're right, Sergeant. We need them. I would hate to lose them after everything."

Nazario exited the ship. He mounted the zakeri behind Ferani with

Monkley in the rear.  They took flight again, heading northwest toward Ambrecia.  The sun had dipped below the eastern horizon.  Nazario hoped they would make it before daybreak.

# Chapter 39
## Preparation

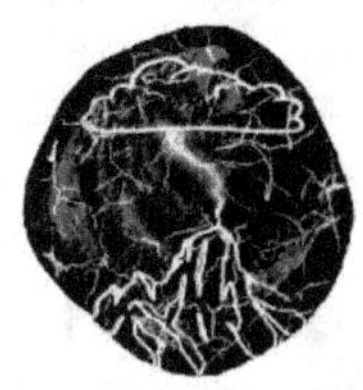 Jerykka was confident that Intayr could manage the keep while she was away, but she still had to remind herself. Entfall might be her charge, but she had a more important role to fill. Intayr would direct the seven hundred Undaari now at Entfall on their various tasks: disposing of the Noxxons, preparing the Undaari for funeral, and repairing the walls with what materials were currently available. She did not need to worry about Entfall's safety or productivity while she was gone.

It was time for her to get going. She would intercept the Undaari Army in Eilenar. Taking the secret escape tunnels, she could move much faster than the army. She would likely even beat them there.

As she made her way into the keep, she thought about everything that had happened. It had been a terrible few days. She had nearly lost everything. She missed Jarreck more than ever and wished he could have just stayed by her side.

She hoped she would see him again before this was over. She would need his strength. He always brought her comfort when they were together. But they still had not received word about his life since their failure on the mountain.

It was hitting her hard as she entered the dusty old tunnels below the main hall. They were one of the secrets of Entfall that only she knew about. Sealed from the inside by magic, they could not be opened from the outside under any circumstances; not even by her. All tunnels in Entfall's systems were like this as they were only for escape. All save the one the Shields had used, as its purpose had been to allow the Second Society safe passage into the keep while it was under siege.

The tunnel she took came out a distance to the north of the lake that the keep watched over. It was hidden by large rocks and unmarked. No one would accidentally find it, and had she not exited from the tunnel, she was not sure she could even find it. Not that she could open it from the outside anyway.

As she exited, she oriented herself to her surroundings. It had been nearly pitch-black in the tunnel. Her eyes had compensated for the darkness using the Alackai, but they still needed a few moments to adjust to the light outside. Though the sun was fading behind the horizon, it was still much brighter out here.

Jerykka needed to get to Eilenar soon. The army would be nearly there by now with their head start. She made her way through the thick forest. She had missed the smell of the woods. There were so many fresh scents from the foliage. She could see twenty different flowers on her stroll. Jerykka even saw some of the large, bell-like sakari flowers that produced their oil.

The Undaari loved the forest, yet she had been trapped inside the stone walls of Entfall for several days. Though she loved her home in Entfall, she was thankful to escape its confines. The Warden just wished it were under better circumstances.

She felt at peace in the forest and appreciated this brief respite, free from death and destruction. She almost wished she could stay here and forget about the chaos of the world around her. However, she knew it would never be her place to live in the forest again. It was a nice thought, though.

She reached the town of Eilenar shortly after. The Undaari Army had not crossed the river yet, so Jerykka made her way to the bridge. It would be retracted at any moment for the night. The darkness made it difficult to monitor oncoming traffic, so it was withdrawn every night at sundown. During the daytime, the Undaari protecting the bridge could see for a long distance. At the first sight of any Noxxons, the gate would automatically be withdrawn.

When she reached the bridge, she saw four gracas were already strapped to the bridge and ready to retract it on the massive roller system. She went to the guards to warn them that the Undaari Army would be returning soon. Jerykka did not want them to retract the bridge before the army could cross.

They did not wait long before they saw the warriors approaching along the river. She was glad for their haste. Jerykka did not wish to waste time in Eilenar that could be used closing the distance with Ambrecia.

The sun had completely disappeared by time the Undaari Army had made it across the bridge. The gracas effortlessly retracted the advanced feat of Undaari engineering. Jerykka found Khasan at the head of the Undaari force surrounded by the ten Skovi Shields. Commander Khasan had a confused look on his face.

"What took you so long?" Jerykka jabbed.

Khasan smiled through his confusion. "Jerykka? How'd you beat us?"

"I have my ways, Commander. More importantly, we need to get to Ambrecia as quickly as possible. I've decided to join you. We could do with every advantage and able-bodied warrior we can get."

"I agree. But it'll still be a two-day march to get to Ambrecia."

"We could cut that down if we don't stop for rest. Did you not bring any jentar with you?"

The Commander's face filled with curiosity. "We only brought two hundred. Our cavalry would be ineffective at Entfall, so we left those few here in the stables. We can't get our entire army there on their backs though."

"No, but we could get aid to Ambrecia faster if we took the jentar now and rode through the night."

Khasan pondered the idea. "Two hundred Undaari would not be able to defeat the Noxxon forces attacking the walls. Not if they have more of those Staff Bearers. But they might be able to buy more time for the rest of our warriors to reach the battle. We'd face heavy casualties. It's suicidal."

Jerykka nodded. "I realize that. It's your army and your call, but I'll be joining you. As will these ten Shields. That may tip the battle in our favor. With or without you, I'm taking a jentar tonight and pushing through."

"I'll ride with you as well. Let me gather volunteers."

It only took a few minutes to gather up all the necessary volunteers. Commander Khasan had several lower unit Captains at his disposal. He chose Captain Kouji to lead the army in his absence. Though it would be dangerous, Khasan ordered them to push through without breaking for the evening.

Jerykka, Khasan, the ten Shields, and nearly two hundred Undaari warriors moved to the stables and mounted up. Jerykka and Khasan took the lead with the Shields directly behind them and the other warriors bringing up the rear. Before they began their ride, Commander Khasan gave a word of warning.

"We're going to push these jentar to their limits. There's no time for caution tonight. We ride directly into battle against a larger Noxxon force that threatens our homes and our people. Alackai's Grace guide us all!"

He blasted his horn again and as one, the Undaari cavalry began their long charge to Ambrecia on their shaggy white jentars. Jerykka hoped they would not be too late.

"How long have you been using the Alackai?"

"Many decades. Far longer than I'd care to admit," Jarreck answered as they finished preparations.

"Then how am I expected to be more powerful than you? Cause I have to be. I saw what Dralvic did to you."

"It's not about training. Not anymore. I thought it was, but really, the Alackai's strength comes from who you are inside. You are something special. You have a pure heart in ways I never did. That's how."

Lingdon looked at the ground before he whispered, "I felt the knife penetrate me. Dralvic defeated me like I was nothing."

"When? You never fought him."

"I did in the Alackai. It felt like some sort of test."

A shiver ran down Jarreck's spine. He recalled a very similar feeling with the Black Scythe. Being trapped inside its blade, his soul feeding Dralvic. A fate he did not intent to repeat.

"I was tested as well. The Alackai wasn't testing your skills. She tested your strength of heart. Whatever your test was, know that you're here. You passed. That alone should be assurance enough for you."

The sun had just passed its peak in the sky as Jarreck and Lingdon wrapped things up. The training had gone well. Jarreck wished he had more time to train him. This was a lot of responsibility to place on a boy just fifteen years old. A boy who had only just gained control of the Alackai days before. The plan was a long shot at best, but it was their only hope.

Only Lingdon had the ability to strike down Dralvic for good. The Alkaios, Kiva, Jerykka, the humans, and himself were only pawns in the grand scheme of this battle. They could assist and distract, but they were not the ones who had to bear this weight.

As they packed up their gear, Jarreck looked at Lingdon fondly. He was a good kid and a fast learner. He was unusually blessed by the Alackai. Jarreck could not help but see the boy as a son he would never have. He felt guilty that the boy was not afforded more time to learn. He was far from being fully trained.

He was nervous about having to send Lingdon into battle. If the boy failed or even hesitated, they would lose. Jarreck was a seasoned Skovi and was not sure that even he could handle that amount of pressure, let alone Lingdon. But there was determination in his eyes. The Alackai was right to give him the chance to speak to his father and Unathi.

"Lingdon, our time for training is up. There's no more I can teach you before this fight. You've done exceedingly well and surpassed all my expectations for such a short lesson. I wish we could've had more time to prepare, but we're at our limit."

"Do you think I'm ready? I feel like I have so much left to learn and practice."

"You do. But you're as ready as I can make you with such constraints, Lingdon. I'm not going to lie, no matter your level of training and experience, I wouldn't wish this task upon you. It's not fair that you're being asked to complete to do this, but as my father reminded me, the Alackai is wise and would not ask us to do more than we're capable of. She trusts you. So do I."

"I still don't fully understand the Alackai."

"And you never will. I've been a Skovi my entire life. I have communed with the Alackai through the Entai countless times. I'm still learning more and more about her each day. She never communicates with us directly, but she influences our intuition and lends us strength. She's our deity and protector. She gives life to our people and lands.

"Beyond this, I don't know much else. No one has ever seen her true form or spoken directly to her. We don't know where she came from or when she was born. We don't even know what she wants in return for the gifts she has granted. She seems to give of herself freely and we must be thankful and trust in her divinity."

Lingdon smiled and relaxed his shoulders, "This is the first time that I feel some sort of understanding of her. What you said makes so much sense to me. Everything Unathi and my father had said felt so rushed. So incomplete. Thank you for giving me that."

Lingdon glanced around the clearing, and his eyes settled on the giant Alkaios. "One last question. Do you have any idea how I'm supposed to use the Lightning Bow? It's so massive and doesn't seem to have arrows."

"That's a great question. I assumed you'd been given the instructions during your time in the Alackai. I surely was not since I could never wield this weapon.  I would imagine that since it's powered by the Alackai, it does not need arrows.  I'm guessing you just draw the bow back, aim at your target, and release.  Might as well give it a try before we go, so you know for sure."

Lingdon retrieved the bow from next to the resting Alkaios.  He had left it there for safekeeping.  Jarreck followed him so he could watch.  Lingdon drew the string back easily, as though there were no tension behind it.  The scars in the wood began to glow purple, shining on his face as he pulled back.  Lingdon quickly took aim with glowing eyes, as well as he could without an arrow, and released the string.

The instant Lingdon released the drawstring, lightning formed within the bow as an arrow.  The string shot forward and launched a massive bolt of purple lightning in front of Lingdon.

Jarreck watched in horror as the purple lightning bolt traveled nearly instantaneously to its target, striking the cabin in the clearing.  The resulting explosion was fierce, forcing Jarreck to shield himself.  When the dust settled, the cabin had been completely leveled.  All that remained was a smoking crater and debris.

Jarreck's jaw dropped in shock.  Not from the power displayed, but from the surprising loss.  That cabin had stood for decades, since before he had been born.  His heart sank at the loss.  *Why did Lingdon have do that to me after everything?*

Lingdon stood still, staring at the destruction he had created in that instance.  He looked back to Jarreck.  Jarreck was still staring at the cabin, unmoving.

Lingdon raised an eyebrow and asked, "Master Jarreck, what's wrong?  It worked!"

"It would seem I forgot to tell you that I grew up in that cabin.  My parents died in that cabin.  It has stood there, unchanged since I was a child."

Horror now reflected in Lingdon's purple eyes.

"I'm so sorry.  I had no idea.  Please forgive me," he said desperately.

Jarreck shook his head.  He took several moments to calm his heart.

"No, it's fine.  I've avoided this place and let it control my fears for years.  It's time to let go of my past and move forward.  We can't let our past weigh us down."

Jarreck shed a single tear for his past.  He had needed that weight off his shoulders for a long time but never had the strength to do it himself.

It was time to live in the present.  It needed him much more than the past.

"It's time for us to leave.  The afternoon grows late.  We must reach Ambrecia as quickly as possible.  Once we land, you cannot hesitate.  As soon as you see Dralvic, you must use the Lightning Bow and strike him down."

Lingdon nodded.  "I'll do my best.  I won't let you down..." he said, then looked at the Entai and added, "nor my father."

Lingdon slung the bow across his back and clambered up the great creature.  He patted the beast on its back before reaching down to assist Jarreck up.

Once Jarreck was on board, Lingdon asked, "Are you ready?  The Alkaios is quite intense to ride upon.  Makes a zakeri look like a sigrune."

Jarreck nodded his response.

Lingdon spoke to the Alkaios.  "We need to get to Ambrecia, as fast as you can.  It's time to fight."

The Alkaios stood up fully and let out an ear-shattering roar.  Jarreck had to cover his ears.  It spat purple lightning up into the sky.  Jarreck's jaw dropped as he witnessed the power.  The fractures across its body lit up brightly in purple.  It leapt into the air with great force, nearly dislodging Lingdon and Jarreck.  They zoomed through the air at a frightening pace.

# Chapter 40

## Betrayal

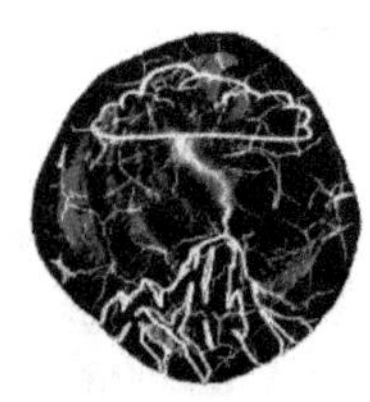

Councilor Gierdahl was unable to inquire further before the short Noxxon at the city wall began to speak. It lowered its onyx hood to reveal a human face. Everyone atop the convocation deck audibly gasped. It appeared the humans had betrayed them. Gierdahl did not understand how they could have accomplished this.

The man started to speak, and though he appeared to be speaking normally, his voice could be heard throughout the city without difficulty. The ruby fractures on his scythe glowed brightly as he spoke. It was an ominous picture, like Death itself had come to their doorstep.

"Fear not, my Undaari brethren. I have not come to destroy you. In fact, I've come to save you... from yourselves. Those who lead you now have grown weak. Their ignorance has put your lives in danger. They have left you vulnerable with their inability to lead.

"I am here to offer myself in their place. Your army is gone, off losing a battle elsewhere. Your precious Society of the Scar is scattered across the Lenakai Forest. Your King and his Commanders have *failed* to even protect their borders. The Alackai has abandoned your people and chosen to Grace the Noxxons instead.

"If you choose to forsake your *failed* leadership and endorse me as your King, the transition will be peaceful. I will lead your people into a new age of magic and prosperity. You shall *never* have to worry about the fragile peace or outside threats from the Noxxons, Yaxkin, or even these *humans*.

"I am a generous ruler. I shall give you until daybreak to choose the peace and power I have offered you."

The human at the head of the Noxxons turned and led his giant followers back to their army.  The Noxxons did not break ranks as their war drums began to beat.  A shiver ran down Gierdahl's spine.

King Cepheus was mortified by the words spoken.  His normally energetic composure fell to drab.  He turned to his advisors, face stricken.  Their faces matched his own.

"Have the humans betrayed us?  How did they join and amass such a large Noxxon force so fast?"

High Councilor Vreeham spoke quickly, "It would seem as though the humans we met were merely a distraction to lower our guard.  They've tricked us and spied on us, allowing the Noxxons to breach our lands.  They've tried to destroy us from within, but the Undaari are stronger than that.  We won't fall to their treachery."

Councilor Gierdahl seemed unconvinced.  "I trust Kiva and Jarreck.  Kiva spoke highly of these humans and what they've been willing to do to help stop the Noxxon threat.  I wouldn't be so quick to mistrust them.  This could be a trick of the Noxxons to sow discontent and mistrust within our people."

Vreeham countered, "It's painfully obvious that the humans have been working with the Noxxons all along.  Neither Jarreck nor Kiva have proven themselves to be reliable.  They've probably been assisting the Noxxons as well.  Probably helped them sneak up on us.  It's time to see the truth.  The humans have chosen their side in this war.  They will *all* be handled with swift justice for their crimes against the Undaari.

"They've created the opportunity for the Noxxons to cross into our borders and reach our capital without challenge.  Perhaps the human man was right, we've been ignorant.  Kiva certainly seemed to think so as well... if I recall correctly.  She spoke just like this human did."

Councilor Gierdahl looked defeated.  "I'm not sure what we can do at this point.  We must fight and hold out for our army.  We must trust in Ferani to bring back aid and for Jarreck and Kiva to return.  We won't have any real answers until then.  I refuse to assume such transgressions."

"We should consider the human's words.  We can't win while our army is gone.  We must buy time for them to return," Vreeham suggested.

"Give up?  That's not our way, Vreeham," Gierdahl said with disgust.

The King was no longer paying attention to the Councilors arguing.

They did nothing but bicker anymore. They'd been such a distraction lately. He could no longer stand their words.

He stood above his city, watching his people panic and attempt to barricade themselves within their homes. He could see parents comforting their children; horrified parents forced to lie to their kids in reassurance that everything would be just fine.

He wept as everything came to a grinding halt in the city he loved so much. *My inaction has failed these people. I'm to blame for all of this.*

As he watched his people prepare for the worst, one thing stood out to him. Not a single Undaari man, woman, or child stood in the central courtyard below him. Not a single Undaari questioned his leadership. Not a single Undaari asked for them to surrender to their invaders. Except for Vreeham, at least. An immense sense of pride washed over the King.

His people still had faith in him. They knew this offer was hollow. They would choose to fight until their last breath rather than face rule under the Noxxons. He turned back to his advisors.

"We will *fight*. No one shall be subjugated to Noxxon rule. Our people will live, or die, free. We will stand strong against the Noxxons with every ounce of strength we have. We will survive until our army arrives and rids the world of these Noxxons."

His advisors cheered and pumped their fists. He felt a new confidence in his leadership and their people. It would be a hard-fought battle, but perhaps they could survive long enough to win this. Night fell over them.

Councilor Gierdahl joined the King at the edge of the convocation deck. The rest of the advisors and Councilors departed for one last night of peace. The city was still. Many families had put out their lights for the night already.

The King continued to look out over the city with Gierdahl at his side. It was the darkest he had ever seen Ambrecia. The darkness had fully set in. The twin blue moons traversed the sky near the eastern horizon. The stars above him could be seen shining brightly. It was a beautiful last night of peace.

*If I can just ignore the sounds of the drums.*

Councilor Gierdahl broke the silence between them. "My King, you've always stood strong for our people. They've always loved you. You won't fail us now. But I fear there's more to this than we're seeing. I hope that all the details can be brought to light before any harsh actions have to be taken."

The King looked at him.

"You know, I've always valued your opinion, as much as your High Councilor's to be honest. I thank you for your kind words. But there's only one person that I know, without a shadow of doubt, that I can trust completely. My dear Kiva has always proven herself. When we see her again, I know she will guide us to the truth of the matter."

"She's always proven herself capable, but the Council doubts her intentions. She's proven to be too loyal to her former master, rather than the wishes of the Council. She's too much of a wild card in their opinion, rather than a loyal Skovi to the Society and your cape," Gierdahl responded.

The King laughed at the statement. "She's always been wild and free. Like the jentar of old. But that's my point; she's independent and thinks for herself. She's faithful, but not blindly.

"When I lost my wife and child, she lost her father. We found comfort in each other to fill those missing places in our hearts. I could *not* have asked for a more capable daughter. I'm glad she gives the Council such trouble. They need a little bit of that to shake things up."

Councilor Gierdahl nodded. "The Council grows tired of her trouble, though. But she was right about the Noxxons. As was Jarreck. Perhaps we should've heeded their warnings. She may have been right about our ignorance, but I disagree with Vreeham's accusations. Still, I would question her decision making at times. If she had followed our orders, she would be here now to assist us."

"The Alackai does not follow the Society's orders, Councilor. If her gut led her elsewhere, we should trust it was even more important than here. She'll be exactly where she's needed most."

"I hope you're right, my King. We'll need every bit of strength and assistance we can muster."

The King smiled. "The Alackai has never abandoned our people. She won't now." The King paused for a minute before continuing, "You know, I had been considering endorsing Kiva as my replacement. I haven't had the opportunity to speak with her, yet. But my time as King is nearing its end. I'm getting old and beginning to slow."

Councilor Gierdahl was taken aback.

He protested the statement. "Members of the Society can't be ruler of the Undaari, though. She can't be Queen."

"We shall see what the future holds. Nothing's been decided."

ᐁᐁᐁ

It was well into the evening when Kiva finally saw the lights of Ambrecia in the distance. The city was dimmer than she had ever seen it, but at least it was not on fire. She was thankful it had not been destroyed by the Noxxons yet. As she neared, she could see that the Noxxons had indeed reached Ambrecia but had not started their assault.

She could see their firelight as they stood in formation. As she grew closer, she heard their war drums beating in unison. She recognized this tactic from Entfall. They would attack first thing in the morning, once the Undaari were exhausted from a restless night. She felt Jaina's grip on her tighten as she recognized the situation as well.

Kiva did not think the Noxxons would be able to see or attack her from this height, but she swung the zakeri wide around them to be safe. She brought the zakeri down over the walls and saw how minimal the manning was. There were barely any warriors left to defend the city. This battle would not last long.

She could see the King on the convocation deck with the Commander of his King's Guard. She brought the zakeri in for a landing on its edge. The trio quickly jumped off the zakeri and rushed to the King's side. They all paused a few paces from the King and bowed in his presence.

"Come now, Kiva, this is no time for formalities," the King said with a wide smile.

He reached down and pulled her up and brought her in tight for a hug.

"We have much to discuss. My advisors have left to try and get some rest before the battle begins. I know I will not sleep tonight."

"Yes, my Lord. The Undaari Army is moving as fast as it can. We only just defeated the Noxxons at Entfall. The battle was far too close for comfort. It'll still be another day and a half before the army reaches us though. I'm not sure we'll be able to hold out that long. Not with what few Undaari I saw defending the walls."

"Our people will fight with their last breath. If we do not have the strength to survive until the Undaari Army arrives, then at least we die free from Noxxon rule."

King Cepheus turned to confront the humans accompanying Kiva. He drew his sigridir and his White Guard Commander mimicked his actions.

"Now... It was my understanding that we had an alliance with you. It's been advised that we execute all humans on sight after your betrayal. But I trust Kiva, and she appears to trust you. Can you give me one good reason why we should not detain you right now?"

All three of the newcomers jumped back.

Unsurprisingly, Jaina was the one who replied, "I'm sorry, my Lord, but I don't understand. We've been fighting side by side with your people against the Noxxons since we arrived. We've fought even when I had hoped for peace. We've been trying to demonstrate our commitment to the Undaari and this alliance."

The King continued to question her, "Then why was there a human leading the Noxxon army, demanding to be named ruler of our people?"

Both Jaina and Brandon raised their eyebrows at the accusation.

Kiva stepped forward and offered, "I actually have the answer to that. We ran into this human on the Scarred Mountain when we tried to ambush the Noxxons. His name was Garren. Only now, his body has been inhabited by Dralvic. I don't understand how he's survived, but he's back."

The King's face dropped. That was a name that most Undaari recognized. Both he and Sanjiv lowered their blades.

"So that wasn't really a human?" the King asked.

"No. Garren died, but his body was repaired and inhabited by Dralvic. He had other Noxxons with him as well that he corrupted with the Alackai. They're abominations with devastating power called Naaji. We managed to kill all the ones at Entfall, but not without great personal sacrifice. Had the Alackai not strengthened us to fight them, Entfall would have been defeated," Kiva explained further.

"Are these Noxxons much larger than their brethren and carrying staffs?" inquired the King.

Kiva's heart sank. "Are there more here? We only barely survived the others, and we had all of Entfall fighting."

"There were three of them standing next to Dralvic. One of them used the Alackai to shield them from an archer volley."

The King was full of nothing but bad news this evening.

He shook his head in frustration. "You warned us that they had figured out how to use the Alackai. You and Jarreck. We should have listened. Where is Jarreck anyway?"

Kiva had to look away to answer, "Lost."

"Oh no. I had been counting on him. I'm sorry."

Kiva was about to respond when she saw another zakeri fly over the wall of the city. Ferani landed his zakeri next to hers and disembarked with Nazario and Monkley. Nazario approached the King, wearing his fresh new exosuit, and bowed.

"King Cepheus, we're here to assist you. I realize it's not much, but we stand by your side, ready to provide any help we can."

"We'll accept any help you can give us. Ferani, please take the zakeri to the stables then assist in the defense of the wall."

"Yes, my King," Ferani said as he bowed. He quickly mounted his zakeri and whistled to the other. When he took to the air, the second zakeri followed.

"Now let us prepare for this battle. Rest if you can. Dralvic said the attack would start at sunrise and the night is already getting old," the King stated.

During the final few remaining hours, Nazario and the other humans finished preparing their equipment. Weapons were cleaned and calibrated, sensors were tested, and sights were adjusted. Everything was function checked twice over. They also developed their plan of attack. There was not much left to do. The Undaari had too few warriors and defensive positions here in Ambrecia.

Jaina, Brandon, and Monkley would remain on the convocation deck with the King and Commander Sanjiv. They would take up sniping positions as they had during their failed ambush of the Noxxons. Kiva and Nazario would make their way down to the wall when the battle began. They would try to assist the Undaari and keep the Naajis from completely overwhelming their defenses. They only needed to buy time, not win the war.

The first tinges of pink and orange light began to glow on the western horizon behind the city. The Noxxon war drums immediately doubled their pace. The battle was imminent. Kiva and Nazario looked at each other then stood from their place on the convocation deck. They departed silently, leaving Jaina, Monkley, and Brandon with the King and his Commander.

The King watched them leave, "Alackai's Grace guide you."

"And her Light protect you," Kiva replied.

The King was sorry to see her go. He wondered when the right time would be to speak to her. It was not now, on the cusp of battle. She needed a clear mind now, but perhaps after. He looked around the convocation deck. He preferred the current emptiness of it, tired of dealing with the bureaucracy. He considered sending his advisors and the Council to the wall to help defend the city, but they were old. They might interfere with the other warriors.

King Cepheus stood from his seat and moved to the edge of the deck to get a better view of the impending battle.  He watched as Dralvic moved to the front of the horde again, this time unescorted.  He approached the wall again and looked around.  It was obvious that no one had decided to surrender.

Dralvic made a single comment.  "Pity."

He raised the Black Scythe and swung it in an arc through the air at the city walls.  A massive wave of crimson energy burst forth and smashed into the gate.  It collided with enormous force and shattered everything.  The gate was blown away and the wall surrounding it crumbled under the power.  Dralvic left a gaping hole in the only defense the city had.  He turned around to the Noxxons behind him.

"Tear it down."

# Chapter 41

## Speed

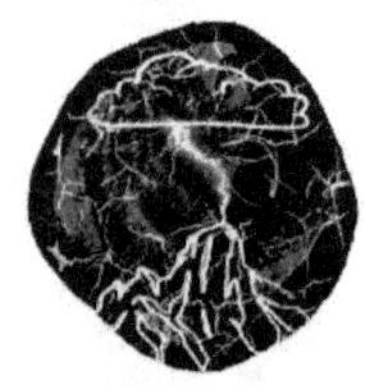

Jerykka raced on her horned jentar through the Lenakai Forest. She was nearing its edge but could see that the sun had already risen on the horizon. The Noxxons could have already defeated Ambrecia by now. She urged her shaggy jentar faster, knowing she was risking its life at this pace. She was breaking away from Commander Khasan and the Skovi Shields. The rest of the cavalry could not even be seen through the thick forest.

She broke through the tree line, charging at breakneck speeds. She was close. Her blood was pumping. She needed to go faster. Her entire focus was on reaching Ambrecia before it fell. She was almost there. She had one final, long hill to climb before Ambrecia would come into sight.

Her jentar labored heavily underneath her as its long hair flapped with each hoofbeat. Her eyes glowed with the Alackai as she channeled its energy into the jentar to sustain its pace. She felt bad for pushing this innocent animal so intensely, but she would be even more sorry if she did not make it in time.

As she crested the final rise to the city, she saw that the battle was already raging and Ambrecia was losing quickly. The Noxxons had already made it into the city. She brought her legs on top of the jentar, squatting down, ready to jump into action when she reached the fight. She called the Alackai up in her hands. She would strike hard and fast, attempting to draw the fight away from the city.

She crossed the final field. She noticed that, at the rear, three Staff Bearers and their leader stood watching. They had not even entered the battle yet and had almost won already. She would attempt to strike down Dralvic immediately, hoping to catch him by surprise. She leapt high into the air, her jentar veering off to avoid the Noxxons. She came down directly at Dralvic, cerulean flames erupting from her hands.

The flames had barely left her hands when a Naaji turned and swung his staff upward. It threw crimson flames into her side and knocked her sideways. The flames ate into her side leaving her skin scorched, her armor and burgundy cape doing little to protect her. She crashed into the ground hard, tumbling to a halt. Jerykka rebounded quickly. She shot back up, pat out the smoldering cape, and charged back in.

Dralvic did not even acknowledge her presence. Without looking, he simply raised his hand in a short wave to his Staff Bearers.

"Have your fun," he told them. "It's time I end this."

Dralvic nonchalantly walked toward the city then paused. He turned around to see Commander Khasan and the ten Shields charging into battle. He smiled and swung the Black Scythe sideways through the air. Another arc of crimson energy shot forward.

Khasan was quick, diving off the side of his mount, allowing the blast to shoot over the jentar where his chest had been. Some of the Shields were quick, but not all of them were expecting an attack of this ferocity. Six of the Shields drew up their blue walls. These were instantly shattered by the power of the Black Scythe, killing their conjurers. The other four managed to dodge the blast and avoid injury, same as Khasan.

All eleven jentar were now riderless and immediately fled the battle scene. Commander Khasan and the remaining four Shields bounced up and drew their weapons, prepared for a fight. Dralvic laughed.

"You're not worth my time," he said, turning away and heading to war.

The Naajis shifted together, covering his back as he departed. Dralvic walked leisurely toward Ambrecia, monitoring the Noxxon horde. Some had broken through the fighters at the wall, but the Undaari were putting up a respectable fight. They held the majority of the Noxxons back at the broken gates, taking advantage of the choke point.

Jerykka was back up and fighting against a single Staff Bearer. This one had directed its attention to her while the other two focused on the four remaining Shields along with the Undaari Commander. Jerykka threw fire at the Naaji and locked herself into a heated battle. The Shields created their blue barriers and engaged the other two Staff Bearers. Commander Khasan did not stay in the fight long, instead turning to join his charging cavalry.

🌀🌀🌀

The rest of the Undaari cavalry crested the hill, jentar laboring from the intense ride, and charged the rear of the Noxxon army. They gave a wide berth to the Naajis and their battle. Commander Khasan ran to intercept them, jumping onto a jentar with one of his soldiers to charge the rest of the Noxxons.

Dralvic turned as the stampede closed in on him. He took a wide, low swing with his Scythe. Khasan watched in horror as a large ball of vermilion energy emerged from the blade and lobbed into the air. It crashed down into the front ranks of the Undaari cavalry with explosive force. Twenty riders with their jentar were blasted into oblivion. Many of the surrounding jentar were knocked sideways and even more reared up in fear, dislodging their riders.

The cavalry lost all their organization and had to gather themselves before they could complete their charge. Khasan scrambled to get his warriors back into formation. Many Noxxons turned at the sound of the explosion. Seeing the cavalry, they screamed and charged in a frenzy, never missing an opportunity to spill Undaari blood.

A few hundred Noxxons maintained the assault on the city. The arrival of the cavalry had distracted most of the Noxxon horde. The Noxxons were nearly through, many of their warriors had been able to climb up the wall and battle the Undaari up close, quickly slaying their enemies.

The battle spread from the city walls across the entire open field leading to the city. Blood was spilled everywhere as the battle raged on. While the Staff Bearers clashed against their opponents, the Undaari cavalry fought the Noxxon warriors, outnumbered ten-to-one.

Jerykka felt unusually calm during her fight with the Naaji. She moved quickly as she dodged around the Staff Bearer's attacks. She drove in for an attack, trying to injure the Staff Bearer at the knee to slow it down. Her fist was encased in cyan flames as she landed a powerful blow. She heard the Staff Bearer's knee pop as it shrieked in pain.

It reeled back, then its shriek turned to a roar as its eyes brightened. It charged back at Jerykka with frightening speed, seemingly unfazed by its injury. She was faster, able to sidestep its attack and send blue flames into its thick charcoal skin. That blast sent the Staff Bearer tumbling sideways. It rolled once then landed back on its feet.

Before she reengaged her foe, Jerykka took a glance at the Shields fighting the other two Naajis.  Though the Shields outnumbered the Staff Bearers, they were outmatched in every other way.  They struggled to even maintain their defenses against the superior adversaries as they desperately slashed with blades.  The Staff Bearers appeared to be toying with the Shields.

She turned back as her target began to charge again.  She encased herself in the cyan flames of the Alackai and charged directly at the Naaji.  It swung its staff at her head as they closed in on each other.  She crouched underneath the wild attack and leapt up at the Staff Bearer, crashing into its stomach with her shoulder and driving its breath from its lungs.

The giant Noxxon flew backward and landed on its spike filled back.  It rebounded like the attack was nothing.  It began to spew crimson flames across the battlefield, slowing Jerykka's movements and limiting her avenues of approach.  Jerykka circled the Naaji across the battlefield, eyeing her Naaji foe, while assessing her options.

She looked back at the Shields battling behind her.  There were only three left standing.  She watched as one of the Staff Bearers shattered another Shield's barrier and crushed him under its power.  She knew that the final two Shields would only last a few more minutes.  She needed to end this battle with her single opponent before the other two moved in on her as well.

Jerykka completely turned her back to the Naaji, hoping to draw it out from its flaming maze.  The Staff Bearer charged at her.  She could feel its feet pounding on the ground as it reached her in seconds.  Jerykka was ready for it though.  She waited until it was right on top of her before she dropped to the ground, dodging its attack, then drove her blade up into the Naaji as it passed over her.

She was able to penetrate its thick, rocky skin and slash deep into its body from abdomen to groin.  It fell over as inky blood gushed out of it. It rolled to its back to try to stand up, but its core muscles were too damaged. Its insides began to ooze out of its stomach.

Jerykka took advantage of the wound to end it.  She drew the Alackai into her fist and plunged it straight into the hole in its stomach.  She ignited the Naaji with cerulean flames from the inside, incinerating it.

Jerykka was tired from the battle.  She looked up as the Naaji faded to ash and witnessed the other two Staff Bearers finish the remaining two Shields.  They turned on her as they saw her defeat their third.  Afternoon had fully set in.  The two Staff Bearers charged in rage.  Jerykka prepared herself for their combined attack.

Kiva and Nazario stood alone against the Noxxon horde. By time they had reached the gaping hole where the gate once stood, many Noxxons had already poured through. They would not be able to catch those that had gotten in, but they could still slow the remainder. There had been three Swords protecting the walls, but one of them was caught in Dralvic's attack. The other two were separated and supported the remaining Undaari warriors on their sections of the wall.

Noxxon archers were countering the Undaari on the ramparts. More Noxxons scaled the crumbling wall to attack their enemies. The Swords augmented their weapons with the fire of the Alackai. The Undaari warriors used their bows until the Noxxons closed in on them, then switched to sigridirs. Each Undaari warrior moved quickly and precisely, killing several Noxxons before being overwhelmed. The Undaari numbers dwindled rapidly under the sheer size of the Noxxon army.

Kiva could see how quickly the battle was turning against them. She and Nazario fought hard to keep the horde from completely overrunning Ambrecia, but there were too many for them to stop alone. Kiva threw blue flames all across the gap in the wall to stall the advance of the Noxxons. They fought each Noxxon as they broke through in close quarters combat. Kiva did not even notice that in the chaos, most of the Noxxons had broken off to fight the Undaari cavalry.

Nazario's suit was fresh and fully powered, but it was losing energy quickly. She watched as his energy weapon became less effective. His arm cannon had been blasting Noxxons constantly. He had his long, serrated knife in his off hand.

Kiva still felt strong, but she could see sweat dripping down her partner's brow as his chest rose and fell rapidly. He slashed and blasted Noxxons as quickly as Kiva in the beginning, leaving a pile of dead Noxxons encircling him, but he did not have the Alackai to sustain him.

She was surrounded by even more bodies. Kiva was determined to stop the entire horde herself. There were cerulean flames burning across their arena. Her sword was bathed in Noxxon blood.

Though she had been injured several times, her wounds were barely perceptible with the Alackai coursing through her veins. The flames choking the city entrance were dying. She was glad to not be alone but knew that Nazario would not be able to fight much longer. He was an impressive warrior but did not have the Alackai's Grace.

As she fought, she saw a swarm of Noxxons take down Nazario. She screamed, firing a stream of cerulean flames into the mass on top of him. She launched the Noxxons off Nazario so he could recover. When she turned back to the Noxxon swarm, she noticed her cyan flames blocking their path had been completely extinguished. She was confused for a moment, then noticed a new adversary had entered the battle.

Dralvic was standing in the gateway to the city. He sniffed deeply, eyeing the remains of his conquest. He watched as his Noxxons overwhelmed the remaining Undaari on the walls of the city. His eyes fell on Kiva and Nazario standing in front of him. Dralvic let a big smile creep across his face. The few hundred Noxxons surrounding him had stopped to watch him.

"I'm impressed you both still stand to fight me. I would've thought you dead after our last skirmish. I admire your strength and tenacity. I value these traits.

"As a courtesy, though I already know you're too prideful to accept, I would offer you an opportunity to lay down your arms and join me. You can lead my armies as we establish a lasting peace across Undaalan."

Those Noxxons not engaged with the remaining Undaari cavalry now crowded in behind Dralvic. No more warriors fought from Ambrecia's wall.

"Garren, please. Don't do this. I know you're in there, you have to fight him. Come back to us," Nazario pleaded with Dralvic.

Dralvic hesitated a moment before laughing. "Do you really think you can save this weak human? He's gone. Now join me or you'll be next."

Neither Kiva nor Nazario bothered to answer. They simply attacked simultaneously. Nazario fired his Valor arm cannon and Kiva sent streams of blue flames at Dralvic. Dralvic spun his Scythe around in a flash, deflecting the attack without effort.

"Shame," Dralvic said sarcastically.

He swung the Black Scythe in a downward motion, pointing it directly at the pair in front of him. Kiva had Alackai enhanced movements and was able to dodge the crimson blast.

Nazario was not so gifted. He tried to dive away from the attack, but it was too quick, leaving him no chance to escape. The energy crashed into his side, sending him spinning down the white cobblestone roadway.

Kiva screamed a profanity. Nazario lay there motionless. She ran to his side. The entire left side of the suit had melted to him. Half his maroon uniform had burned away. The light had gone out on his chest. His breathing was labored, and his body was badly burned. He was barely even capable of opening an eye.

Kiva tried to save him with the Alackai, surging its energy into him again. She only managed to get his attention for a moment.

Nazario weakly said, "I'm sorry I failed you. It would've been nice to spend some time with you. Kick his ass."

Then he was gone. Kiva screamed. Every muscle in her body tensed as her voice pierced the air. It drowned out even the Noxxon drums. Flames around the arena grew in size as the Alackai flowed through her body. Her heart began to slow as the Alackai filled her being. Dralvic watched her with an air of curiosity as she mourned. The Noxxons behind him began to charge into the city.

"This is very interesting. You've grown fond of this human. A weak creature from another world. Pathetic."

Kiva's last tear fell from her face. She stood up, the Alackai racing through her as her body relaxed and her heart calmed. Her glowing eyes locked on Dralvic. Her hands were encased in flames as she charged Dralvic viciously, unleashing cyan lightning in her anger.

She clashed against him. Dralvic let out a nearly imperceptible gasp as he was pushed back by her ferocity. She hacked at him. Kiva threw cyan lightning at him. Attack after attack. Dralvic was falling back. He barely deflected one attack. Was struck by the next. Deflected another. He was struck multiple times, but nothing fazed him. Kiva's attacks only managed to leave minor cuts and burns to his extremities.

Then Dralvic began to battle back. He spun the Scythe around quickly, countering with its power. Kiva was fast, dodging his attacks. She spread destruction around with the Alackai. The Noxxons surrounding their arena were burned on the spot. She twisted her flames everywhere, striking down the Noxxons assaulting her city, while keeping Dralvic at bay.

Other Noxxons fled the arena and began demolishing the buildings of the city, spreading fire across the roof tops. They broke out across town and began to slaughter every Undaari citizen they could find. The city was filled with smoke and the screams of the massacred. Kiva fought hard and tried to spread her flames around to slow the Noxxons while fighting Dralvic. Many escaped her destructive powers, but she could not give chase.

Dralvic attacked with new energy, his Scythe glowing red. Kiva was still trying to win the entire war single-handedly. Dralvic landed a powerful blow to Kiva's side. She had been too distracted to dodge the attack.

She barely drew up a shield in time.  Dralvic sent her flying high into the air.  Kiva encased herself in the Alackai's flames before crashing down through the roof of an undamaged home.  She landed on a bed, startling the family cowering inside.

Monkley, Brandon, and Jaina fired at Dralvic with their Peacemaker energy rifles.  Without Kiva or Nazario in the line of fire, they could focus on him.  Dralvic simply spun his Scythe around quickly creating a shield in front of himself.  With his offhand, he created crimson flames and launched them in a wide arc around his shield, which engulfed the front of the convocation deck.  They just managed to dodge the flames, but Jaina knew they would not be able to risk further attacks.

Jaina watched in horror as Dralvic made his way toward the palace, his Noxxon army swarming passed him.  Monkley had questioned if he could kill Garren, but after seeing Nazario die, he committed to stopping him.  Jaina had told him saving the Undaari was more important than trying to save Garren.  He had not spoken since, his jaw clenched in anger.

Jaina was not happy with the choice either but saw the desperation of the situation.  The Undaari cavalry had been overwhelmed, their bodies were scattered across the field in front of the city.  There was little resistance to the Noxxon horde.  Even with severely reduced numbers, eight hundred Noxxons could do serious damage against a town without any remaining defenses.

Commander Sanjiv had tried to convince the King to escape through the city, but the King had refused.  His advisors had fled, but the Society's Councilors stayed behind with the King.

Cepheus had decided to face this threat head on alongside his people. Sanjiv was the last of the White Guard in the city and stood with the humans to defend the King and the Councilors.  They barred the access up to the deck, though this would do little to slow down their threat.

Jaina watched the King as he looked out over his dying city, weeping for his people.  The city was burning; the Undaari were being slaughtered.  Their warriors had fought hard throughout the day.  The sun was setting on the horizon, as it was on the Undaari.

The Noxxons flooded over the city as Dralvic burst through their weak barricade.  Commander Sanjiv stood in front of his King, ready to die to protect him.  Jaina could hear the screams of the Undaari below them.

Out of the corner of her eye, she saw streaks of turquoise in the air; the zakeri in the stables had escape and taken to the air, evacuating the city. Her eyes darted all around as she searched for an escape. Adrenaline was coursing through her body.

One of the zakeri landed on the convocation deck by Sanjiv and King Cepheus.

Sanjiv looked at the creature and yelled to the King, "Leave! Take the zakeri and save yourself, my Lord."

"I will not abandon the city while my people are slaughtered!"

The zakeri circled protectively around the King before it saw Dralvic. It jumped and playfully stepped toward the man before it paused. It cautiously stepped towards him, then took a step back. It growled as it seemed to realize Dralvic was no longer Garren.

Dralvic laughed. "Pathetic creature."

He swung the Scythe at the zakeri. It leapt into the air a split second before crimson flames struck the ground where it had been. The zakeri fled the scene like the others had.

"You should have left while you had the chance, *my King.*"

Dralvic slowly approached Cepheus, a wide smile across his face. He opened his mouth to speak but shut it as Kiva vaulted up the stairs and leapt over him, landing on the convocation deck between Dralvic and the King. She flung fire at Dralvic before she started moving again, trying to draw him away from the King.

Dralvic let out a howl of rage, striking at her with the Black Scythe. His attack missed as Kiva ducked and sent the red flames flying at the Councilors. The High Councilor conjured a vermilion wall of energy to defend himself and consequently, all the Councilors around him. Dralvic and Kiva were locked in battle. Everyone else turned to stare at what the High Councilor had done.

Jaina spoke accusingly, "I thought the Councilors lost their ability to use the Alackai prior to ascending to that rank."

Councilor Gierdahl focused in on the accusation, trying to pick up his jaw. "They do. High Councilor, what have you done?"

The High Councilor responded angrily, "I've saved myself from the weakness of the Society. Dralvic taught me how to be strong. He showed me that immortality was attainable through the Alackai, not through the teachings of the Society. He gave me strength and rewarded me for my actions.

"After I watched him die decades ago, he came back to me, a

shadow of himself, but still alive.  I knew then that he'd be my savior.  He allowed me to retain the Alackai long after I was supposed to lose it."

Councilor Gierdahl's face bore his horror.  "How could you betray everything we stood for?"

King Cepheus drew his gold sigridir.  Monkley and Jaina turned their Peacemakers on the High Councilor, ready to attack.  Sanjiv moved toward the High Councilor, blade drawn.  Dralvic and Kiva were still focused on the other, neither paying attention to the events unfolding on the deck.  Their fight was devastating the white convocation deck and palace walls.

Jaina could hear the ferocity of their battle, but it felt as though time had frozen in their small spot on the deck.  The Councilors were eyeing Vreeham questioningly.  No one dared make the first move.  Brandon grew pale and muttered something unintelligible.  Jaina looked at him, confused.

"Dragon..." he murmured again.

"What are you talking about?" Jaina questioned, lowering her rifle just a degree as she looked at him.

Brandon pointed over the city walls.

"DRAGON!" he screamed.

Everyone turned to look.  There was a gigantic, winged beast soaring toward the city.  Jaina could hear its roar pierce the sky.  She watched it spit lightning across the battlefield outside the city.  Her face turned cold as the blood drained from it.  She watched in terror as it approached the city and the palace.  *What other weapons does Dralvic have?*

# Chapter 42

## Fight

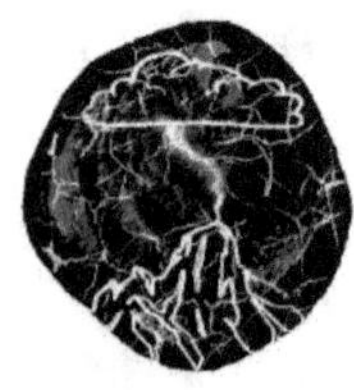 The Alkaios raced through the sky with Lingdon and Jarreck holding on for dear life as the wind buffeted them, threatening to unseat them. Jarreck could tell they were making great time as the sun set to their right. They might even make it before the sun had passed over the horizon. He could not believe the elegance and speed of such a massive creature. Or that a creature seemingly made of rock could fly.

As they passed over the treetops of the Lenakai Forest, he could see smoke in the distance. Jarreck's stomach sank as he realized the battle had already commenced. The Noxxons had marched to Ambrecia faster than he had anticipated. They must have destroyed Entrea even earlier than he had thought.

They broke past the edge of the tree line and over the open fields leading toward the city. Jarreck saw hundreds of Noxxon and Undaari bodies scattered over the field. There were still three bodies moving on the plains. Jarreck recognized Jerykka's burgundy cape immediately, locked in a deadly battle against two Naajis. He had a more important destination but pointed out the fight to Lingdon.

Without slowing, the guardian banked and redirected toward the fight. As it passed over, it let out a terrifying scream and shot purple lightning from its mouth. The lightning struck the Naajis, frying one to a crisp, and injuring the other. Jarreck smiled, knowing that the odds had swung heavily in Jerykka's favor.

They continued their path toward the city. Jarreck could see Noxxons flooding the streets. *We're too late.* The Alkaios spit lightning into the crowds of Noxxons as they approached the palace. Jarreck saw crimson and cerulean flames dancing on the convocation deck and pointed them out to Lingdon. The guardian landed on the palace, wrapping around the building's exterior high above the convocation deck. It allowed the two Undaari riders to drop to the convocation deck and join the battle against Dralvic.

As they hung in the air above the battle, the Alkaios shot purple lightning past them at Dralvic. Dralvic brought the Black Scythe up to shield himself. Kiva shot cyan lightning of her own at the ancient Skovi. Jarreck landed smoothly, bringing his own power to bear.

Dralvic was holding back the power of the Alkaios' purple lightning, Kiva's cyan lightning, and Jarreck's cerulean flames, though barely. Their combined attack was powerful, forcing Dralvic to give up ground as he slowly stepped back under the onslaught, on the cusp of a swift defeat.

Lingdon did not land so nimbly. He stumbled and took a few moments before he could draw the Lightning Bow from his back. Dralvic planted his feet. He deflected the attacks away from himself. The Alackai's energy crashed into the palace wall just below the Alkaios' perch, leaving a large crater. The palace destabilized above the deck, forcing the Alkaios to take flight, as debris crashed down. Dralvic's eyes locked on Lingdon holding the Lightning Bow.

"No! You're supposed to be dead!"

He swung the Black Scythe at Lingdon without hesitation. Lingdon was able to draw the Alackai into a purple shield in front of himself. The sheer force of the Black Scythe still knocked him sliding across the deck. The Lightning Bow skittered away from Lingdon and fell off the deck into the courtyard below. Jarreck and Kiva reengaged Dralvic.

Dralvic taunted Jarreck, "What took you so long to get here? I was beginning to think you ran away from this fight, like your *father* tried to."
It was just a taunt, but it still filled Jarreck with rage. He looked at Kiva before making his next strike. He had a lot of experience fighting with her at his side. They were fluid, each feeding off the other in battle. Their coordination allowed them to strike with speed and precision, without interfering with the other. Now their powers had grown, creating an even more lethal force. It made it difficult for their enemy to focus on a single target.

⁂⁂⁂

Lingdon barely moved. Jaina looked at him, surprised by his purple shield. High Councilor Vreeham turned on him, calling upon his own Alackai to strike him down. Red flames erupted from the High Councilor's hands. Jaina jumped in front of Lingdon. She was not sure why he was there but understood there was something special about him after Dralvic's attack.

She raised both her arms in an x before her, bracing herself for the attack. Crimson flames struck a blue shield in front of her. Everyone on the convocation deck stopped and stared at it. She realized that the shield had been conjured by herself. No one was more stunned than Jaina.

Dralvic spat in anger, "What sort of *trickery* is this? Humans *cannot* possibly use the Alackai. They're not even from this world."

Jaina looked at Dralvic for a moment. *This isn't a trick.* Jarreck pressed his attack. Kiva joined in. Jaina looked at her hands for a moment and noticed an aqua hue to her skin. She could feel the energy coursing through her body. Adrenaline had been nothing compared to this. She looked up at Vreeham. He still stood there, unmoving.

Kiva had to ignore what happened with Jaina. All her concentration must be on Dralvic. She could not afford to make a mistake. She could not even acknowledge that her Master was still alive. Dralvic was more than a match for the two Shades. He was even smiling at the challenge but had yet to break a sweat. He was not even breathing heavy like she was beginning to. The arcane arts granted such unlimited energy.

Behind her, the Alkaios was spewing lightning at the Noxxons in the city. It even swooped down occasionally and snatched up several of them in its mighty maw. Dralvic shot a dirty glance at the creature as it flew behind him.

He shot crimson energy from the Scythe at the Alkaios. He struck it in its side, causing it to howl in pain and anger. Purple blood spilt from the wound in its rocky skin. It took flight high above the city, escaping the danger. Kiva attacked with her lightning before Dralvic turned his focus back to the fight. Jarreck swept cerulean flames around him.

Dralvic was struck by the lightning but deflected the flames. His obsidian robes were singed all over with holes worn in them. He swung his Scythe back at Kiva. She sidestepped and flung more lightning at him. Jarreck closed in on Dralvic as Kiva's lightning found its mark. He swung his sigridir at Dralvic's Scythe.  Dralvic twisted the Black Scythe around and hooked it around Jarreck.

Jarreck shielded himself, but Dralvic still threw him into the palace wall.  Kiva landed another bolt of lightning into Dralvic's back.  He screamed and turned back to her, swinging his blade furiously.  Flash after flash of crimson energy sliced at Kiva.  She could barely deflect the attacks.  Blasts crashed into the deck all around her.

Lingdon finally recovered from the attack and stood up.  He charged in next to Kiva, drawing upon the Alackai to join the fight.  He moved to engage Dralvic, hurling purple energy at him.  Dralvic began laughing at Lingdon, focusing on him instead.  Kiva rushed to Jarreck's side as he still lay on the ground.  He stirred and hopped back up.

High Councilor Vreeham launched an attack against the rest of the fellowship.  He used the Alackai to shove the other Councilors away from him.  In their frail old age, they were knocked unconscious as they hit the ground.  Vreeham's cover had been revealed.  He fought against the others to prevent his capture.

Jaina was not sure what she was doing.  Now that she had discovered the Alackai within her, she let it control her movements.  She conjured blue flames to strike at their aggressor.  Monkley and Brandon both fired their energy rifles at the High Councilor.  Sanjiv and King Cepheus encircled the old man, sigridirs in hand.  Sanjiv demanded Vreeham's surrender.

The High Councilor, however, seemed powerful with the arcane arts.  He fought back ferociously against the superior numbers.  His flames shielded him from attack.  He struck at the group surrounding him.

Jaina used the Alackai to shield them.  There was little other protection for them.  She struggled to keep the aging man at bay with her unfamiliar power.  Vreeham cackled as he spread crimson flames around. *He's just as powerful at the Staff Bearers are.*

Monkley and Brandon depleted their rifles quickly.  Vreeham absorbed everything they had shot at him with the Alackai.  Jaina continued striking at him, untrained.  Monkley pulled his own blade and leapt in close to attack.  Brandon stood back, helpless.  Jaina conjured more cyan flames and attacked.  The High Councilor laughed as he deflected her attack.

"Weak.  The Alackai was mistaken to Grace you.  You humans are worthless beings."

As he taunted, Jaina and Monkley both struck.  They maintained the High Councilor's attention.  Commander Sanjiv slipped behind the old man and slid the blade around his throat from behind.  He again demanded Vreeham's surrender.

Jaina thought they had him beaten, but the High Councilor leapt backward against the White Guard.  He slammed the back of his head into Sanjiv's face.  As Sanjiv fell backwards, Vreeham's crimson flames engulfed the White Guard and threw him from the convocation deck.  Monkley and Cepheus jumped in, swinging their blades while Vreeham had his back to them.

Jarreck, Kiva, and Lingdon fought together as one against Dralvic. Jarreck and Kiva struck Dralvic with fire and lightning simultaneously, but he spun the Black Scythe around, absorbing the magic with his dark weapon. Dralvic focused more intently on Lingdon while twirling the Scythe around, a smirk across his human face.  Lingdon was the only threat to his reign.

Purple energy erupted from Lingdon's hands, but Dralvic dodged it; Lingdon was sloppy.  His wild attacks narrowly missed his own companions behind Dralvic.  They dodged and attacked again.  Kiva and Jarreck fought with a practiced precision as they combined their magical onslaught, but try as they might, their power was no match to Lingdon's raw magical prowess.  Dralvic deflected their next attack, sending the blue lightning and flames careening at Lingdon.

Lingdon barely dodged the attack.  Dralvic fired more crimson flames at Lingdon, who narrowly managed to shield himself.  Jarreck jumped in again, trying to separate the weapon from the user.  Kiva flung more lightning at Dralvic's head. Dralvic rolled to the side, dodging both. He had broken a sweat.

It was a never-ending battle.  Dralvic switched his focus.

He bore down on Jarreck while issuing taunts to throw him off. "Come now, old man.  Are you beginning to tire?  The Society has left you weak.  I'm a thousand years old and still stronger than you could ever imagine."

Jarreck countered with a taunt of his own.  "And this fifteen-year-old boy already has more power in him than either of us.  It's terrible that it took you thousands of years to reach this level and him just a matter of days."

Dralvic scowled at Jarreck, charging in to attack. "He's only alive because Vreeham failed yet again. At least his father is no longer around. Pathetic man."

Lingdon and Kiva took advantage of the distraction and sent their attacks directly into Dralvic's back. Jarreck could hear Lingdon yell as he attacked wildly. Dralvic's laugh turned to a scream as the attacks ate into his back, but he stayed focused on Jarreck. He slashed the Black Scythe through the air, vermilion energy blasting at his foe.

Jarreck managed to duck under the attack and continue battling back. He was beginning to tire, his breathing growing heavy. The Alackai would not sustain him much longer. Dralvic appeared to have limitless energy. *If we don't end this soon, Dralvic will simply outlast us.*

"We must end this!" Jarreck screamed to his companions.

They began to fight with a desperate fury. All three struck in unison. Dralvic spun his weapon, absorbing all three attacks. Horns sounded in the distance. Dralvic turned his back to them to stare out over the city. Jarreck leapt in, swinging his sigridir at Dralvic's neck.

"Yes, we must," Dralvic said softly.

Dralvic swung around swiftly. The Black Scythe skewered Jarreck through his side before he reached Dralvic, rocketing him backwards. Jarreck skittered across the deck, coming to a stop in a pile.

The Undaari Army had arrived as the sun disappeared behind the horizon. Kiva had not expected them until the next day. They had made unexpectedly good time. The army charged the Noxxons in Ambrecia. The Noxxons would not be able to withstand the attack. Kiva turned back from the sight to see Dralvic strike Jarreck.

"No!" she screamed.

Dralvic created a massive wall of crimson flames between himself and his adversaries. He turned away from his foes, toward the other battle on the deck. Kiva followed his eyes to the King.

Cepheus was swinging his blade at Vreeham. He was fighting as though he were still a young warrior. He was side-by-side with Monkley. Jaina was defending them with the Alackai as they tried to kill the traitor.

Kiva froze, unsure if she could pass through the crimson wall. She watched as Dralvic closed in on the others. Monkley turned, seeming to sense the danger approaching.

"Garren... please..." Monkley pleaded with his best friend.

Kiva watched as Dralvic paused, recognition seeming to flash across his face. *Maybe Garren really is still in there.* Then it was gone, Dralvic swing his Scythe towards the group of fighters. They all dodged, but the King dove the wrong way, leaving him separated. Dralvic closed the gap, no one could interfere.

Dralvic swung his Scythe directly at the King. His crimson flames blasted toward the King. Kiva reacted faster, shielding herself in cerulean flames and charging through the crimson wall, desperate to protect her adoptive father.

She could not reach him in time, so she raised a blue wall of energy in front of him. The Black Scythe was far too powerful, however, shattering her defenses and striking the King.

Cepheus was lifted off the ground and sent tumbling through the air, crashing into the remains of the palace wall behind him. His spine broke on impact with a loud crack.

Kiva rushed to his side. He was still alive and breathing, but barely. She knelt down next to her father, begging the Alackai to save him. He reached a hand up and placed it on her cheek.

He weakly whispered, "My Kiva..." before passing away in her arms.

Lingdon struck at Dralvic, who was laughing again. Dralvic bore down on Lingdon, unleashing a flurry of attacks. It was just the two of them fighting.

Lingdon fell back under the pressure. He used his purple energy to deflect attack after attack. He desperately tried to strike out at Dralvic. Dralvic was no longer toying around. Lingdon fell backwards, landing on his butt. Dralvic swung his Scythe at him.

Cyan lightning seared into Dralvic's back, throwing him forward. Kiva was crackling with electricity as she charged back into the battle. She had now lost two men she loved on this day. Jarreck was down as well, in danger of being the third. She would not lose anyone else.

Lingdon looked across the deck at everything happening. The High Councilor had resumed his attack, slowly breaking down Jaina's defenses. She struggled to protect herself and the others from Vreeham's might. He was closing in on his prey, streaming crimson flames at her. They were falling back under his power. They vainly tried to swing their blades at Vreeham from around the barrier.

Kiva was still closing on Dralvic and had his full attention. Throwing lightning at him. She seemed the biggest current threat to his victory. Lingdon had barely been able to defend himself. Dralvic was slicing back at Kiva, forcing her to give ground right up to the edge of the deck.

The Undaari Army below had entered the city and were beginning to root out the Noxxon invaders. More screams erupted from below them. Metal clanged throughout as Undaari and Noxxons fought.

Jaina could no longer hold her shield. She had never been trained with the Alackai's use. Vreeham collapsed her defense with explosive power, throwing Jaina and Monkley back. Brandon was curled up in a ball on the ground, shaking and covering his ears. The High Councilor had his hands encased in crimson flames, stepping forward to end the humans. Monkley pushed Jaina behind himself, shielding her with his body.

Lingdon's heart raced. Time felt as though it were moving slow. His eyes bouncing everywhere, between each battle. *How can we possibly win this?*

Suddenly, Jerykka came vaulting up the wall, eyes glowing cyan as the Alackai coursed through her body. Lingdon could see the blue hue in her skin. She looked fresh, and even more, she had the Lightning Bow on her back as she landed next to Jarreck. She knelt next to him before throwing the bow to Lingdon. Jerykka placed a hand over Jarreck's wound as Lingdon caught the Lightning Bow.

*Where had she gotten this?* Lingdon stared at the bow in his hand. He had thought the battle was over because he had lost it. Jerykka turned from Jarreck and shot her cerulean flames at Vreeham. The flames ate into the side of the High Councilor and forced his attack to fly wide. Vreeham screamed as he went tumbling sideways.

Lingdon did not hesitate. His instincts kicked in, remembering what he was meant to do. He drew the bowstring back. Purple scars along the bow's shaft began to glow. His eyes were bright purple in the new night's darkness. The purple glow emanated out, filling the convocation deck, drawing Dralvic's attention. Kiva was on her back as Dralvic had been preparing to land his final attack with the Black Scythe.

"That's not possible..." he hissed.

Kiva rolled away as Lingdon released the drawstring. Purple lightning formed into an arrow. In an instant, it erupted forward, striking

Dralvic in the center of Garren's body. The force of the ensuing explosion was enormous. Everyone on the deck was thrown back as parts of the deck broke apart and fell to the courtyard below. Dralvic was instantly vaporized.

The Black Scythe flew back and crashed into the wall of the palace, shattered. The fractures in it extinguished. The High Councilor screamed in fear. He was alone in the fight. Jerykka watched as he struggled to stand after his injury. He ran for the Black Scythe. Jerykka stormed after him with Kiva trailing. Jaina moved to Brandon, trying to comfort him. Monkley pulled out his first aid kit and ran to Jarreck's side.

Vreeham gave a desperate fight. He flung spurts of crimson flames at his pursuers. Jerykka easily deflected the weak attack. He reached for the Black Scythe and tried to use it to save himself. When he picked it up, the blade was no longer attached.

Before he could continue to fight, Jerykka charged in. Her fists were glowing with the Alackai. She ran at the old man and jumped into the air. She came down on Vreeham, driving her fist into the side of his skull. The Alackai blasted into his head and shattered his skull. His limp body fell to the ground.

She turned and looked for Jarreck. She saw Monkley attending to him. She rushed to his side. His breathing was ragged. His eyes cracked open as she touched him, and he smiled at her. She was incredibly thankful that he had survived. She rushed forward in a strong embrace, kissing him passionately.

"Thank the Alackai you've survived this chaos."

# Chapter 43
## Resilience

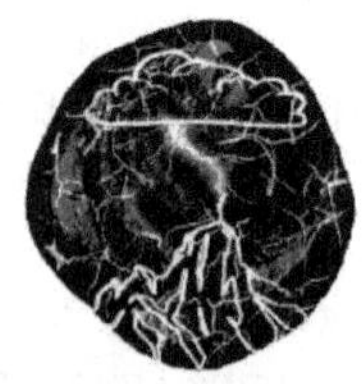

Jerykka realized she could still hear fighting from the city below. She ran to the damaged edge of the convocation deck. She watched as the Undaari Army engaged the remaining Noxxons in the city. The Noxxons were acting confused, looking around at their surroundings, no longer attacking the Undaari or even wielding their weapons. Dralvic's control over them must have broken. The Noxxons cowered away from the Undaari.

Jerykka looked at her companions. There was no King anymore. The Commander of the White Guard was gone. The High Councilor was defeated. She had not seen Commander Khasan since she had engaged the Staff Bearers. She was the last of the Undaari leadership.

Her eyes settled on Jaina, who nodded. Words resounded in the back of Jerykka's mind: *Peace is always worth the risk.*

She called out over the city, using the courtyard's acoustics.

"Undaari warriors. Stand down. This may be difficult but give the last Noxxons a chance to surrender. Should they choose to do so, they shall be granted safe passage home."

Yells of anger arose from the Undaari below. They were upset with the prospect of allowing these murderers to go free.

"These Noxxons were under the control of an evil being. If we hope to ever foster a lasting peace with the Noxxons, let us take this first step. We must grant mercy and forgiveness, otherwise this never-ending war will consume us all."

The warriors below still grumbled but followed her orders. So did the Noxxons. Not a single Noxxon warrior tried to fight; they all surrendered, throwing down their weapons. The war was over. There were less than five hundred Noxxons surviving the war out of the seven thousand that had entered it. They had lost even greater numbers than the Undaari.

Jerykka looked again at the others. Jarreck and Kiva had been working to revive the remaining Councilors. Lingdon was helping the humans up. Jaina was smiling at her. She watched as Monkley started speaking, seemingly to no one. She could see that the city had suffered great losses, but only about a quarter of it burned. It would recover.

While everyone was picking up the pieces of the battle, the Noxxons were being escorted from the city. The citizens began to gather in the central courtyard below the convocation deck, looking for answers. Jerykka would do her best to provide them.

"The Undaari have shown their strength and resilience in the toughest days our people have *ever* seen. They've proven why the Alackai has continued to Grace our people and lands. It's unfortunate that these times came to be, but our people never gave up hope.

"The Alackai never abandoned us and sent her greatest champions to fight for us. We have much to rebuild, but we'll rebuild stronger than ever. We've made new discoveries about our history and ourselves, as well as forged new alliances for the future.

"It's a sad and dark day in history. A day that also marked the end of King Cepheus' reign. We'll mourn his loss, but we'll move forward, as he would have wanted. We'll choose a new leader. Someone who would've made the King proud. The King's time was cut short, and he was unable to endorse his successor. We'll have to work together to find a new beacon for the Undaari people."

The Councilors had recovered from the attack behind her. Councilor Gierdahl moved forward to join Jerykka at the edge of the deck. He placed a hand on her shoulder before he spoke to the Undaari.

"Actually, my friend, that's not entirely true. In confidence, the King told me who he'd intended to endorse. Someone who is a true savior of the Undaari people. Someone who has given of themselves, without asking for anything in return. Someone who has shown wisdom and strength beyond comparison. Someone..." the Councilor paused for a moment to look behind him at those gathered around. He continued with a smile, "Who was like a daughter to him. Ambrosi'Kiva."

Cheers erupted from the Undaari gathered below. Jerykka smiled as the people below affirmed their new Queen without hesitation. The depth of Kiva's relationship with the King was common knowledge. Many must have seen her stand against the Noxxon horde as it penetrated

Ambrecia's wall. Councilor Gierdahl gestured for Kiva to step forward.

"The Council of the Society of the Scar would *gladly* allow her to step away from her oath to serve this higher function for the good of all Undaari."

More cheers erupted. He looked directly at Kiva, as did Jerykka. Kiva was frozen. Jerykka was pretty sure this was the first time she had ever seen Kiva show fear. Kiva's cheeks flushed as they all looked at her. Gierdahl gestured Kiva forward and she obliged. He looked her in the eyes and spoke softly to only her.

"He would be so proud of everything you've done for the Undaari, Kiva. You've proven yourself beyond any doubts. The Society has all but fallen, and from the looks of things, needs some serious guidance moving forward. I would suggest bringing it even more into the light. The Council no longer needs to be a secret. Nothing should be. Perhaps it's time to unshackle the Society from the fear that binds it. We're yours to restructure as you see fit, my Queen."

He bowed low for Kiva. Everyone on the convocation deck followed suit, Undaari and human alike. The entire city fell to their knees in fealty. No one disagreed with the endorsement.

Jarreck entered the Society's Archives. He was fully recovered from his injuries thanks to the human medications. He did not think he would have survived without them. The Undaari did not have such effective healing compounds. He sat down at the desk in the corner and opened the tome he had been working on. The events of the past several days needed to be chronicled. He was finishing the records from the war:

*The Undaari people were motivated to clean up the devastation. They intended to wash away any signs of the destruction that Dralvic had wrought. They were ready to move on and live their lives in peace. The people held a massive funeral service for all the Undaari lives lost. This included Ferani, who was slain on the rampart walls, and Commander Khasan who fell in the middle of a ring of Noxxons. The Undaari Army burned the bodies of the Noxxon warriors who had carried out Dralvic's orders.*

*It took a few days after Dralvic was defeated for the humans to coordinate assistance for the Undaari. This was done in* trade for the human scientists to get to study the Alackai and some of the building materials made with the fractured black stone. A treaty was struck between the two people to ensure lasting peace and cooperation.

The humans were in awe of the Undaari people and marveled at their architecture. The Undaari were even more enamored by the humans, reveling in their technology. Many evenings were spent getting to know each other and learning each other's languages without the use of translators. The people of both species celebrated their differences and the new alliance.

Ambrecia, Entrea, and Entfall all had significant work to be done. The humans were able to use some of their technology for the heavy lifting as stone walls and structures were rebuilt, just as tall and strong as they had been previously.

The Undaari people enjoyed their new company. They felt it refreshing to have such a civilized race in their lands. The Noxxons and Yaxkin rarely brought anything but trouble. The human assistants were offered land and homes in the wake of the cleanup project. A few gladly accepted.

Kiva had been hard at work with Jarreck and Jerykka in Entfall assisting with the repair of the outer wall. Because of the building material, they needed the hands of those who were Graced with the power of the Alackai to repair it. She also tried to take her mind off the upcoming coronation. She had requested that it be delayed until all of Undaalan had been repaired.

The Noxxons were quiet as they hid in their homes, trying to recover from the war. A few Undaari had been dispatched to attempt a negotiation for peace and cooperation for the future. These emissaries had not yet returned as the Undaari neared the completion of their repairs. Kiva was growing worried that Jerykka had made a mistake in granting them mercy but decided to wait longer before deciding further action. Jerykka was not one to make mistakes in judgement.

Jerykka had returned to her station as the Warden of Entfall, though she continued to doubt her worthiness as the Shield of the Undaari. Her people within Entfall still trusted her completely and felt that without her, the Undaari people would have been eradicated. She struggled to believe that, after how close they had come to annihilation. Regardless, she led the repairs of Entfall and worked to rebuild its protections.

The remaining White Guard in Entfall were sent to Ambrecia to begin training new members, chosen from the Undaari Army. Despite Kiva's protests, the White Guard was still a tradition that would be carried on during her reign, though Jerykka would not have to suffer their presence in Entfall any longer.

The Society of the Scar had been reduced to barely more than ash. There were four Councilors still alive. Seven Swords survived the attack as they had been elsewhere in the kingdom. All ten Shields had been killed defending Ambrecia. Kiva had left the order, leaving four Shades. Other than Jarreck, none of those were accounted for. They had been on missions outside the kingdom and could easily have been killed by the Noxxons.

Under Queen Kiva's order, the Society was brought completely into the light and would serve in the public's eye. They would work side by side with the Undaari people to rebuild their order and help the people grow. The idea was to use the Society to bring the people closer to the Alackai, as originally intended, rather than be the sole bearers of her Grace.

Jarreck had worked hard with the Council of the Society to establish new rules and procedures. He taught them much of what he had learned from the Alackai. He ensured that the Society grew from these experiences and became the beacon of light it was meant to be.

Lingdon had chosen to become a Skovi. There was room among the Shades now that Kiva had vacated her position. He asked Jarreck to continue his training from where they had left off. Jarreck reluctantly agreed. Jarreck had been ready to follow other pursuits outside the Society, but felt that in this case, Lingdon's needs were greater than his own.

Jarreck sent the boy on a quest of his own before he would begin his training. Lingdon flew the Alkaios back to the Entai where he had recovered the Lightning Bow and return it. It was no longer needed as the Alackai's champion had met his destiny. After that, he brought the Alkaios home to rest and recover. It was time the guardian went back to its duty.

Lingdon happily completed his tasks. He was able to commune with the Alackai again through the lake in the Heart. He had been able to tell his father that he had made him proud.

*The Undaari would grow from this experience.  They had been on the brink of annihilation, but alongside the humans, there would be a new period of prosperity across Undaalan.*

Jarreck looked over his work.  He was satisfied with the records.  There was still a lot of work to be done, but this officially marked the end of the war story.  He left out any knowledge of the arcane arts.  He wished to continue his father's position from outside of the Society.  He was ready to be done with the Society but had one last task to complete.

Kiva took a deep, steadying breath as she stood in the Queen's Court, alone, save for a few new White Guard warriors.  The Undaari people, along with some of their new human friends, were gathered in the courtyard below the palace.  The crowd that had gathered overwhelmed the space and spilled into the surrounding streets and neighborhood.

There were many people gathered upon the convocation deck.  The four remaining Society Councilors, with Gierdahl having been named the new High Councilor, were in attendance.  King Cepheus' advisors now sat as Queen Kiva's advisors, but she had not yet had time to review their usefulness.

Jerykka's number two, Intayr, had been selected as the new Commander of the White Guard.  He was the first Commander of the White Guard not to be promoted from within.  As the entirety of the remaining White Guard came from Entfall, they all knew his worth and had promptly agreed to the selection.  Captain Kouji, who had led the Undaari Army into the final battle, was promoted to Commander of the Undaari Army.  Both dutifully stood by the Queen's side.

Jarreck and Jerykka sat together at the front of the deck facing out into the crowd, a place of honor.  Lingdon sat next to them, now wearing the traditional cape and clasp of the Society.  Opposite these three Undaari, across the deck, sat the four remaining human heroes: Jaina, Brandon, Piers, and Monkley.  They wore elegant, formal outfits to celebrate the joyous occasion.

Kiva walked down the central aisle of the convocation deck.  Cheers began to build as she approached the front.  She knelt near the edge of the convocation deck before her people to signify that she was their servant and never the other way around.  As Commander of the King's

Guard, Intayr was responsible for draping the gold cape over Kiva's shoulders.

He then invited her to rise as Queen of the Undaari. She stood tall and proud of her people. She would always admire the strength of the Undaari after this war.

Kouji bowed before Kiva and presented the gold sigridir to her. She hesitantly accepted the honor of carrying this blade, still not entirely sure she had earned the role. She gained possession of the sigridir and pointed it high into the air. Every Undaari and human bowed before her.

Kiva spoke to her people, "You will never know the honor you bring me. I'm so proud of all the Undaari for their strength and resilience. I greatly miss King Cepheus and the leadership he gave to the people. I pray to the Alackai for enough wisdom to lead nearly as well as he did."

She bowed one last time to her people before turning and walking back down the deck. It was official. Kiva was the new Queen of the Undaari. She would be their first leader Graced by the Alackai in centuries. She would do her best to serve the people and help them build peace and alliances with the other people across the Three Kingdoms.

She would start by finally holding the funeral for King Cepheus. She had not been prepared to say goodbye, but Kiva knew it was time to do so. The Undaari people would celebrate one of their greatest Kings in style.

# Chapter 44
## Arrival

Back on the *Jericho*, Commander Braylon worked with the Public Affairs team. Together, they sifted through video footage and reports from the ground team. Everything was recorded and documented from Undaaleria and downloaded into the ship's records. They put together episodical updates regarding the efforts of Nazario and his team for the people still stuck on board the massive ship.

After the final battle had been fought in Ambrecia, the remains of the ground team were able to take the time to upload all the video they had gathered to the *Inquisitor* and send it back to the *Jericho*. The people on board had been struggling to understand what was taking so long to gather the energy source on the planet. They were anxious to complete their journey to their new home. Their patience had already been pushed to the limit.

Braylon believed in transparency and trusted in his people to make educated decisions. He was able to demonstrate all the events that had led them to where they were. Over the three weeks after Dralvic was defeated, Braylon and Public Affairs aired ten episodes of their documentary. Those who were not able to go to the planet to assist in the recovery, were able to sit back and admire the adventures of the late Major Nazario, and his team, as they worked alongside the Undaari.

The results were phenomenal. To celebrate their success, the humans prepared gifts for their new friends. The Undaari population was only about fifty thousand people in Ambrecia, but the humans wanted to shower them with their thanks.

There was excitement and life among the survivors for the first time since they were preparing to depart Earth. Braylon was joyful and proud of them for being such hearty people. General Titus had admitted his errors and stood behind him. Braylon never mentioned the mutiny again.

It had taken three weeks of study, but Brandon and the engineering team finally determined a viable capture method for the Alackai's energy. The *Jericho* had limited ability to store energy, but it had just enough battery capacity to limp the rest of the way to Undaaleria. Brandon would just need one big favor from the Undaari to make it happen.

The team returned to the *Jericho* aboard the *Inquisitor,* which newly promoted Major Monkley now commanded. Jaina and Piers also accompanied him, and they were all excited to return to their home. Though they loved Undaalan, they were ready for a chance to relax. They were joined by several Undaari friends: Kiva, Jarreck, Lingdon, and Jerykka.

It would take a day to adapt the *Jericho's* systems to accept the new energy source. During that time, Jaina and Monkley led the Undaari on a tour of their ship. The tour would start with the Command Deck and meeting Commander Braylon.

After they were introduced, Commander Braylon began to speak to their visitors, "I truly must apologize for the events on the planet, not just what happened with the Noxxons, but our role in attacking... I believe the name was Entfall."

Jerykka smiled and nodded. "You are correct. That's my home. Jaina and Brandon explained the desperate position your people were in. They're the only reason we have not terminated our friendship. This mistake has been forgotten."

Nevertheless, Commander Braylon insisted, "I thank you for that. And I truly thank you even more for saving Entfall and preventing our mistake from drastically impacting our future relations. You not only saved your people, but ours as well."

They continued their tour, leaving the Commander behind. They showed the Undaari the science labs where they were able to see virtual holograms of Earth before its destruction. This included many animals and miraculous vistas. They spent a lot of time here as Jaina showed them some similarities with a lot of the animal life on Undaalan. Now the Undaari got to see much of Earth's wildlife in return, some of which the humans intended to bring to Undaaleria.

They got to see the engineering bay and even the massive engines. They were shown everything, but the city was kept for last. Jaina felt that it was the best view on the ship, especially with the view of the stars through the massive viewports.

They walked the Undaari dignitaries through the streets of the Haven. The Undaari were awestruck by the size of the buildings and the breathtaking views all around them. Humans lined the streets and stood on their balconies to get a view of their newest heroes. They had all watched the documentary and every person in the group, humans and Undaari, had become icons to them.

The Undaari were escorted to quarters in the central building where they could stay the evening. The retrofit would be done by morning, and they would regroup then. The Undaari found their apartments to be luxurious. They were impressed by all the technology now at their fingertips. The beds were a little short for them though.

Monkley left the group to return to his quarters. Jaina wanted to hang out with her friends a little longer. Before long, they were joined by Brandon. He had put the engineering team to the task and trusted they would complete everything without him. He wanted to introduce his friends to something he held dear. He held up his computer for all to see.

"I wanted to show all of you, J-... Jaina included, something that I have loved with a passion since my youth. These are three old fantasy movies from centuries ago. I will show you the first t-... tonight and should you enjoy them, we will have other movie nights in the future. Very few humans even watch these anymore as the stories have died out."

He played the first movie and made popcorn for them all. As they watched the movie, the Undaari were fascinated by the people in them, and how similar they looked to themselves and the Noxxons. They could not believe that the movie was not real footage.

It was hard for the Undaari to separate the fantasy from reality, but they enjoyed the movie immensely. Even Jaina, who had never been interested in the genre before, had newfound adoration for it. She curled up to Brandon as they watched, laying her head on his chest.

Brandon awoke early the next morning and made his way to the ship's power plant. He had slept in his quarters that night, enjoying a fresh shower and the cleanliness of his sheets for the first time in a month. The engineering team had completed their work during the night as expected.

He double checked everything to ensure it was ready and would work the first time. At full charge, it would take the ship two short jumps to reach Undaaleria. If this worked correctly, they would be in orbit above their new home by that evening.

He was going over the calculations and checking the makeshift device a third time when Jaina led their fellowship into the area. He showed everyone the modifications and explained that they had created a target to be struck with the Alackai's energy that would transfer the energy into the anti-matter reactor, bypassing the anti-matter storage system. They could not simply fire the energy directly into the chamber, because naturally, nothing was that easy.

He looked at Lingdon and Jarreck. "Thank you again for agreeing to br-... bring the Lightning Bow here. It will generate power much quicker than anything else you could bring. It will make this g-... go much faster and more efficiently."

Lingdon shook his head. "It wasn't my decision, but the Alackai's. She granted me permission to retrieve the bow again after I'd already returned it to her. She seems to like you humans."

Jarreck added, "I suppose we were right to trust you. The Alackai has shown that you're worthy."

Brandon was thankful. He was still in awe of her. He had been in even more awe when she had chosen to Grace Jaina. They had been so busy that he still had not had time to discuss this with her. That would be next on his agenda. Once they had gotten the *Jericho* to Undaaleria.

"All right Lingdon, all you have to do is aim the b-... bow at this target and fire. I will monitor the energy levels on this tablet here and once we have reached capacity, we will make our first jump with the TREX Drive. We will d-... do it all a second time and that jump will bring us home."

Lingdon nodded his relative understanding of the task. He pulled the bow off his back, took a deep breath, aimed, and fired.

The *Jericho* finally reached its destination. The people were gathered in the city looking out at their new home through the giant viewports. It was the most beautiful sight any of them had seen in months. It was a blue world just like Earth had been, though smaller and with less landmass. It was already perfectly terraformed for them, so they did not have to wait the year for the ship to make it safe. They only needed to begin setting up their new city.

Overhead, on the visual intercom system, Commander Braylon gave the order for everyone to return to their quarters and seal their balconies. No one could remain in the city if they were not sealed in their apartments. It was nearly time to land the city on the planet.

Once the Haven had been cleared, Braylon initiated the countdown. From the Command Deck, they locked every opening on the buildings. He was accompanied by their Undaari visitors and the remains of the *Inquisitor* landing party. They would fly back down to the planet after the city had been dropped.

There was plenty of room on an unoccupied continent to house the city without any deforestation. The Undaari had insisted that the humans adapt to their more conservational ways. The humans were happy to oblige as plant life had been nearly extinct on Earth.

Warning buzzers went off in the city as the lower viewport windows began to retract on each other. Once the viewport was completely retracted, the buildings began to jettison, one at a time, starting with the central spire and working outwards from there. The *Jericho* was in geosynchronous orbit with their landing zone, so it would be a straight shot down to the ground from the ship.

It was an incredible sight to behold. It would take approximately an hour for each Haven-Class dropship to fully settle on the planet. As they fell, deceleration thrusters fired to control the entry. These buildings were not hardened enough to handle an uncontrolled descent.

Once they neared the surfaced of the planet, drilling engines fired as well. These dug a perfect hole into the ground for the buildings to slide into. Each buried about a third the length of the building into their new foundations. The buried portion expanded slightly to create a tight, stabilizing fit.

In a matter of about two hours, every building had dropped from the *Jericho* and seated itself into the surface. The humans established a city on a new home world in that short time. Balconies began to open as the ships settled into place. Doors opened to allow the people out to explore.

It was a paradise by anyone's expectations. Other ships began landing around the city as more people were shuttled down and city services were established. The science labs had sections to be jettisoned as well to establish research and finalize the new colony.

The *Inquisitor* had brought its passengers back to Ambrecia after a flyby over the new city.  The Undaari were thankful for the opportunity to meet and see their new friends and the ship from which they hailed.  They felt more confident in their new relationship.

Jerykka returned to Entfall with Jarreck and Lingdon joining her. Kiva took her seat on the throne in Ambrecia.  The four humans were offered homes on Undaalan.  Monkley and Piers politely declined the offer, though they truly wished they could have accepted.

Jaina and Brandon acquiesced, choosing to build a cabin with separate rooms, in the traditional style of the Undaari, near Entfall on the lake's edge.  From there, Jaina would be able to study her connection to the Alackai and learn more of their culture.  She would also be able to serve more closely as Ambassador to the Undaari.  Brandon would be able to continue his scientific research.

His small team had chosen to take up residence nearby as well. One group would live among the Undaari in Eilenar.  Another group of engineers would move into Entrea, working alongside the Undaari, as they recovered from the Noxxons and began to work the quarries again.

Everyone from the *Jericho* was given time to settle in on their new planet. After three days, they gathered around the central spire to have their first meeting on the new world.  Governor Anderson led the town hall. Everyone had known their mission and roles in the new society prior to departing Earth.  What they did not know, was the name of their new home.

The planet was already named Undaaleria, and they would respect their neighbors.  This continent was undiscovered and nameless, as was their new city.  They would vote on new names this day.  Many names had been submitted over the past three days.  Before the names were voted on, Governor Anderson recounted their progress and plans moving forward.

The *Jericho* would remain in orbit as an orbital station and defense platform for their new home.  Commander Braylon would retain control over the ship.  It would be the primary home of the peacekeepers, though many would be located on the planet, within the city, to help establish and maintain law and peace.  Braylon would have no control over the lives of those on the planet.  A civilian would always be in charge there.

The science labs in the city had been busy cataloging the plant and animal life in their new home. They began to research what animal life might be able to be revived from Earth to fit into the new ecosystem. As there was minimal animal life here, they were able to bring life back to many animals from Earth.

They had cellular cultures as well as fertilized embryos that could be grown and cloned to create life. Many herd animals were brought back: deer, horses, giraffes, bison, elk, and elephants. Along with a few carnivores to maintain the circle of life: wolves, bears, tigers, and lions.

The seas were explored as well. They found massive underwater animal life. The whale-like creatures on this planet dwarfed those on Earth. There were a few predators of the deep as well. The submersibles were able to avoid their jaws.

Throughout the city, many people began to adopt the ways of the Undaari, incorporating local and Earth plant life into their homes and the sides of the buildings. They would help their city to become one with the land, as the Undaari were. They would always maintain a strong relationship with the Undaari people, sharing culture and technology, while maintaining friendship and peace.

At the end of the town hall meeting, the votes were cast. The continent they settled their new nation on was to be named Undaadfinitas. They chose this name to combine the name of their allies with the Latin word for alliance and relationship. The city would be the nation's new capital, bearing the name of their legendary savior: Nazario City.

# Epilogue

Six months had passed since Nazario City was founded. Many technologies had been shared with the Undaari, including communications to help relay information between their towns faster. These same devices could reach the human colony as well.

Queen Kiva had recently used this system to invite several important humans to a ceremony they were having. They were honoring the fallen of the Noxxon war. As several humans had sacrificed themselves to save the Undaari, they would be honored as well. Key leadership among the humans, as well as the surviving heroes, had been invited.

In the central courtyard of Ambrecia, they gathered. It was a formal occasion with elegant decorations across the entire city. Many pink and purple flowers blossomed across the city for the first time this season. It was a wondrous sight to behold.

Brandon and Jaina stood together at the front of the crowd. They were joined by Monkley and Piers. A short distance away, Commander Braylon, his husband Taylor, and General Titus escorted Governor Anderson. They had brought a few friends along who had played major roles in establishing the new world.

Up on the convocation deck, Kiva was flanked by her closest friends: Jerykka, Jarreck, and Lingdon. She approached the edge of the deck and the cheers from the crowds below began to roar. She raised her hands into the air to ask for quiet.

"My people. We are gathered here today to celebrate the lives and sacrifices of those who gave everything for us. Thousands of Undaari died during this war. I wish we could take time to honor every single life lost, but today, we can certainly honor those whose efforts swung the battle in our favor."

She gave an elegant speech remembering all those who had sacrificed and led the Noxxons to defeat. As she concluded, she signaled to a member of the White Guard to unveil a new sculpture that had been commissioned.

It was displayed in the center of the courtyard. The sculpture depicted the life-like forms of King Cepheus, Commander Khasan, and Major James Nazario. The base was massive, with the names of every life lost, Undaari and human, engraved across it. It was carved from the same pristine, white, marble-like rock as the city, surrounded by brightly colored gardens.

"Now as I hear it," Kiva continued, "the humans have their own special ceremony for the fallen. They call it a Remembrance. Please bow your heads in respect for their fallen."

The crowd did as the Queen requested. Commander Braylon stepped forward, near the new sculpture. He could feel his heart race as he prepared to speak to the Undaari for the first time. Moments later, a loud whoosh filled their ears. Falling through the sky was a large metal casket. Tiny engines fired last second, allowing it to land softly between Braylon and the sculpture.

"Today, we commit Major Nazario's body to memory. As his casket descended from the Heavens, heat and pressure turned his body to diamond."

He opened the casket door as it stood vertically to reveal a diamond. From a small side compartment, he withdrew a folded UPC flag. He placed the diamond on the flag then scanned it with a small handheld computer.

"His likeness and many memories have been etched into this diamond. They shall live on in eternity as he deserves. The UPC flag supports his memory as he supported the UPC. The Undaari have been kind enough to erect Nazario a final resting place."

He picked up the diamond and stepped up to the statue. Reaching up, he placed the diamond in a small recess on Nazario's chest. There, the diamond would remain. He turned about and stepped to Monkley. He handed off the UPC flag with a crisp salute.

"Peace never dies," he declared.

"With keepers in the skies," replied the humans in attendance.

As the gathering closed, everyone in attendance dispersed to celebrate the lives of the fallen across the city. Many would go to taverns or smoke houses to enjoy each other's company. The human guests were invited along as well.  Most had yet to experience the Undaari culture's celebrations.  They could smoke inushka and drink raza with the Undaari.

Braylon studied the intoxicants, unsure if his people should take them.  Being a peacekeeper required a clear head.  Titus seemed to have little concern as he took a shot of the raza.  Raza was a drink similar to alcohol.  It gave the people a buzz, but avoided many of the side effects, including loss of inhibitions and mental function.

Taylor eyed the Inushka.  It was a plant that the Undaari smoked on celebratory occasions.  It gave their people a small high coupled with intense emotional euphoria.  It enhanced their senses and allowed them to experience the world more deeply.

Braylon smiled.  "When in Rome."

Braylon decided it was worth making an exception for this.  He cheers with Titus and the two took a shot.  Taylor took the Inushka pipe and inhaled deeply.

Once he released the smoke, he said, "Meeting these people was my father's dream.  I wish he could have been here to celebrate with us."

"Your father fought well in the Rebellions.  It would have been good to have here with us.  I'm sorry," said Titus.

"I'm sure he's still happy knowing you got to live out his dream still," added Braylon.  "Him and Garren.  Maybe they're together now with Jason."

Brandon and Jaina both shed tears of joy and sadness for their fallen friends. Nazario, Garren, James, and Reigns had all been great friends and people.  Brandon held Jaina's hand in comfort.  Jaina wanted to spend the time with their friends and so did he.

Before they moved away, Brandon noticed Queen Kiva exiting the palace.  He started to wave, but saw she was heading toward the new sculpture rather than him.  He watched silently as she unfolded a blue cape and draped it over the shoulders of Nazario.  A blue cape she no longer had a use for.

He heard her speak with a tear glistening in her eye, "Alackai's Grace guide you."

She turned and reentered the palace, barely giving him and Jaina more than a half-hearted smile.  He stared after her before remembering that was where he wanted to go as well.  He led Jaina into the palace and up to the convocation deck.  The White Guard knew the two humans had been granted unrestricted access to the palace and the Queen.  When they reached the deck, they noticed that only the four Undaari they sought were there: Kiva, Lingdon, Jarreck, and Jerykka.

They embraced each other in greeting.  Brandon struggled to make eye contact with the others.  He missed them but had been avoiding meeting with them again.

Jarreck seemed to notice his discomfort and asked, "What troubles you, my friend?"

"It's nothing."

"Nonsense," Monkley said, also joining them.  "I've spent far too much time around you to know how much you like to talk."

"It's just..." he struggled to find the words.  "We just celebrated the lives of all the heroes, and they'd fought so hard for this world, but Kiva still honored me all those months ago and I did nothing of the sort.  I collapsed during the showdown with Dralvic.  I'm no hero."

"Of course you are," Kiva said.  "You're an integral part of everything."

"Not every hero must be a warrior," Jarreck offered.

"Yeah, Brandon.  Without you, we'd have been lost.  Your insights were invaluable and brought our people together.  Not to mention, your genius got the *Jericho* here safely," Monkley added with a smile and pat on the back.

With a sigh of relief, Brandon finally relaxed his shoulders and allowed himself to get caught up with everyone's news, no longer requiring translators to talk.  Brandon and Jaina explained they were now dating and shared a bedroom in their cabin near Entfall.  Kiva was adjusting to life as a leader, but still insisted on being directly involved with her people and lands.  Lingdon had completed his training as a Skovi Shade in record time and now led the training of the others.

Jarreck had left the Society but separately retained the role of Master of the Ancient Text.  Jerykka remained Warden of Entfall with one change: she had convinced Jarreck to join her.  They had recently discovered that Jerykka was pregnant, and they had been waiting for this event to reveal the news.

Jerykka told them, "We believe it to be a girl.  We will name her Jazara, after Jarreck's mother."

As they celebrated each other's accomplishments over the past six months, Brandon had one more thing he wanted to celebrate.  As his friends laughed and enjoyed one last evening together, Brandon knelt before Jaina.

"J-... Jaina, you have b-... become the light of my life.  You have st-... strengthened and empowered me to b-... become my best self."

Brandon had to pause a second to catch his breath.  He was beginning to sweat.

"You have supported even my wildest p-... passions.  So here, in front of all our closest friends, I wanted to ask you: Will you m-... marry me?"

Their friends all cheered loudly as Jaina kissed Brandon in acceptance of the proposal.  Brandon had arranged to create a small black stone ring from some of Entfall's debris.  Beautifully crafted by the Undaari artisans, it was fractured in cyan and warm to the touch.

Once the cheers had settled down, Brandon brought up some other news that he had been wanted to share.  "As you kn-... know, our scientists have been doing research into the di-... diversity of the life on this planet.  This has included cataloging genetic variances in the blood of all living creatures.  They made an interesting di-... discovery."

He paused a moment, unsure if the Undaari understood the scientific jargon.  "It would appear the Noxxons were created.  They didn't naturally evolve on this pl-... planet as the Undaari and Yaxkin did.  The genes of a small mountain creature that you call a nola were manipulated to c-... create the Noxxons.  That is why they differ so much from the other races.  They don't b-... belong here."

The Undaari around them were shocked.  They were very confused on how this was possible.  Though perplexed, Jarreck was the first to speak on it.

"That actually makes sense.  They arose seemingly out of thin air while the First Society was experimenting with the arcane arts.  I would not at all be surprised if the Society created them by accident and unleashed our greatest enemy upon us."

Kiva was worried.  "That means that the First Society created our own doom.  Just another reason that the Society was always feared."

"But you created peace with a race that was only interested in slaughtering our people.  Who knows what the future holds, but this information may give us a means to work alongside with them more effectively.  Thank you for giving us this knowledge," Jerykka pointed out while Jarreck nodded.

Kiva smiled, pointing at Jerykka.  "I'm pretty sure it was *you* who brought the peace.  I just followed your plans."

Brandon now looked directly at Jarreck.  "I was hoping I m-... might ask a favor of you. It's a massive favor that I know will be difficult to grant, but I wanted to ask anyway. I thought this good news and celebratory oc-… occasion might help. Is there any chance that we can study the Heart? We won't t-… touch it or harm it. It's incredible and would give us so much more knowledge than we c-… could ever imagine."

"There's no way. It's forbidden. You know this."

Jerykka placed a hand on Jarreck's thigh as they sat together. "My love, you know these people are trustworthy. You know what they face. You no longer owe the Society any loyalty. Take Lingdon and escort them. You don't have to allow anyone else, just you four. I think it would be a good idea. They've done so much for us."

A week later, Brandon, Jaina, Jarreck, and Lingdon hiked up the Scarred Mountain. They carried several noninvasive pieces of equipment to study the Heart of the Alackai. Brandon had heard of its importance from the reports but had not witnessed it himself; no human had.

When they reached the cave, they asked Lingdon to lead the way in case the Alkaios was still awake. It had returned to its slumber in the lake, its back rising out of the water again like a small island. They walked around to the Heart and began setting up their equipment. As they were setting things up, Brandon examined the sphere.

"This thing appears to be a p-… perfect sphere. It's too flawless to have been naturally made."

Brandon began to run scanners all over the Heart. It was impressive. The energy readings were far higher than any other place on the planet, but the signature had been somewhat masked by the mountain. After Brandon finished his planned scans, he began to review the information.

He struggled to believe what the scans had revealed. The sphere was mathematically perfect. There was not a single flaw in its surface. It was also made from a metallic rock, different than anything currently documented on the planet. It was unique and far stronger than most metals.

The deeper scans revealed even more astonishing news.

"I don't believe this," Brandon said. "There's some sort of chamber in the center. It contains several nucleic acids, ones that are used to build life. The Heart must have been sent to this planet from somewhere else. It brought the building blocks of life and seeded them on this planet, allowing life to evolve naturally."

Jaina tried to clarify. "As in another alien species sent this here to seed this planet? Like to terraform it?"

Brandon nodded. "I believe so. I d-... don't think the energy source was an intended product of the seed either. I think it got p-... picked up along the way and united with the protein markers. It allowed the life that evolved here to be one with this highly p-... powerful element. This really is the Heart of the Alackai. It created her and gave her life, then she cr-... created life across the planet."

Jaina was even more curious now. "Where did it come from?"

"That's another mystery. Based on orbital information of this p-... planet and dating of the Heart, I can compile an educated guess as to the trajectory it came from. It would be helpful if we discovered more on other planets. Unfortunately, without more d-... data, it would still be a massive area of space."

Lingdon asked the most important question of all, "But who created this seed?"

*The following is an excerpt from the journal of Doctor Brandon Jimenez:*

Ambrecia

Zaheri

Shavi Meditation

Master Scrybba

Alhaias

Staff Bearer, Naaji

Heart of
the Alachai

www.ingramcontent.com/pod-product-compliance
Lightning Source LLC
Chambersburg PA
CBHW060307100726

47907CB00002B/313